The Vampire Painter

Angela Flatt

http://animatiatrain.com

"The Vampire Painter" Written by Angela Flatt
Edited by Rachel Robson
Audiobook Narration by Ryann Rambo
Book Cover Illustration and Design by Angela Flatt

Cover Design Elements from Canva:
"Empty Painting Frame with Golden Engraved Wooden Borders" by SivStockMedia
"Crack Wall Fire Background" by R_Tee on
"Royal Wallpaper Damask Pattern" by Maryna Stryzhak

Library of Congress Cataloging-in-Publication Data

Name: Flatt, Angela, author
Title: The Vampire Painter/Angela Flatt
Description: Sacramento: California, 2025
Identifiers: LCCN 2025914272 (print) | ISBN 979-8-9923256-4-5 (paperback) | ISBN 979-8-9923256-5-2 (hardcover) | ISBN 979-8-9923256-6-9 (ebook) | ISBN 979-8-9923256-7-6 (audiobook)

Table of Contents

For Michael.

Everything I do now is for you.

Prologue

Sarracenia

She smiled.

Her lips curled up in the smallest of measurement - the first movement she had performed in hours, done so slowly that another minute had passed before she had completed the action. The fire crackled from behind her as its shadows danced along her features.

The painter had yet to look back up at her, so focused he was on whatever detail he had deemed worthy of extra time. The brush scraped up and down the canvas so rhythmically, she could hear how it lined up with his heartbeat.

Brush. Thump.

Brush. Thump.

Brush. Thump.

As if it were not just his arms and hands crafting the portrait, but rather that his veins themselves were protruding out, bleeding his very essence across what had once been a blank board.

For his sake, she hoped this was the case.

At last, he peered up, and the rhythmic stroke of his brush paused, for only a single breath's length, but just long enough to have gained her recognition and approval.

He was observant. Good. He wouldn't be worth half his skill otherwise. She didn't care about prestige. Or the money she had spent on this painter.

The fire popped and snapped behind her once more, which tempted her to turn around fully and gaze upon the barren space just above the fireplace.

She managed to resist, but she had inspected that empty spot so many times that she could recreate it perfectly in her mind. Every chip of paint, every termite-gnawed hole, every speck of dust left behind.

She thought about the picture frame, set at its side, just out of the flames' reach. The one that had never been hung up. Even after she had spent so long deciding over its design. So many choices, but it had to be perfect.

There had been ones with oriental and intricate details. Cherubs trumpeting along each corner, their wings and shrouds flying past the limits of the frame. Vines woven around, flowers budding from their sprouts as the golden plants seemingly grew around the frame. These were easily the most lavish, and best crafted, but they would have outshined the beauty of the painting.

Briefly she had contemplated a simple one for just that very reason. These were even more difficult to decide upon; they were all so crude, and without the ornate details, how could one possibly determine a poorly made frame one from one which was well-made?

At last, she had picked one in between. The gold it was forged from gave it luxury, as did the braids it had been woven into. Yet the design stopped at the braids, so as to please the eye just enough before the gaze moved on to the portrait.

Now it sat in the corner, home to resident dust mites.

Its abandonment was no fault of hers, to be sure. She could hardly be blamed for the incompetence of these artists, all of whom had come to her so highly recommended. It consistently astounded her. The lack of taste amongst her town's noblemen consistently astounded her. But she had little choice.

Just as she knew every inch and crevice of the space above the fireplace, she was familiar with each feature of her face held. She knew the exact length of the curves between her cheeks to and chin. She knew the volume of her lips as she licked and bit them. She knew how round and large her eyes were in her skull.

2

She had no doubt that, if blessed with even a drop of artistic blood, she would be able to recreate what she so desperately longed for.

It was also true that, despite never having seen her actual own face, if she were to spot a doppelganger in the streets, she would recognize herself immediately. She knew because this had happened before.

Throughout her childhood, she was told so often about her resemblance to her mother. She could agree to some extent — after all, it was apparent they had the same hair, same shade of skin, same shape in body. As for her face, she would just have to take everyone else's word for it.

When she thought of her mother now, she thought of the way this woman used to stare at her. For hours at a time, no matter what she was doing. As a young child playing around the castle, this hadn't struck her as particularly odd, and in fact became routine. Yet as she grew, she found less interest in games, and more fondness for reading and other rather inactive ways to pass the time, she found her mother still staring.

Sometimes, she wouldn't even realize her mother was in the same room until she looked up. If her mother disapproved of the way she gasped upon noticing her presence, she never made it known.

She would remain, often standing at the door, in total stillness. And then her lips would curl up.

She never asked the reason for her mother's staring; certain she would never get one. However, as she grew, she began to have her suspicions. After all, her mother was in the same position of never having seen her own face, and when others told her how similar they appeared, it must have made her curious. How strange it would have been – to finally have an idea of what you looked like in childhood, only to see your younger self sitting before you, playing or reading.

Her mother must have wondered if her cheeks had ever been quite so puffy, or her lips quite so small. Even she couldn't imagine her mother as a child, helpless and frail. But it wasn't difficult for her to understand the logic behind staring at someone, wondering to what extent the resemblance truly carried over. She knew, because she had done the same to her mother.

Not while she was alive, oh God – she would never have been able to stare directly at her mother the way she had done to her.

As is tradition, an artist had been commissioned to paint her mother's portrait. She still remembered that man, how he had come so highly recommended, had been the painter of kings and saints. She had half expected a god to enter their house. Instead, in came in a fragile-looking old man, with large spectacles on his eyes and a slight twitch in his wrist.

The painting process had taken days, almost weeks, but her mother sat still, without a single complaint. She had years of practice, after all.

Once completed, the artist walked over with the canvas, and this had not been an easy task for it was rather large. Her mother had taken lifted it with ease, and once it was in her hands, her eyes traveled up and down, inspecting every inch, every detail.

She remembered this moment clearly. How all those nights of waiting for her mother's portrait to be finished had seemed miniscule in comparison to the time it took her to investigate the results. She thought she would burst from the anxiety.

Then, at long last, her mother sighed. Deep, full, down from the bottom of her ankles to the top of her head. The sound of someone who finally received the answer they had been looking their entire life for.

Her mother's lips curled up.

The portrait was hung on the walls immediately. This would be the version of her mother which she would spend years, even after her departure from this world, staring at. As she grew older, taller, and fuller, she wondered just how much she resembled the woman looking down at her. If her eyes carried the same coldness of black ice. If her lips were just as invitingly red.

Now, she was here. The full-grown daughter and heiress of the estate. And she wanted to feel give such the sigh of such contentment that her mother had so long ago.

Her mother's portrait to this day hung along the mansion's walls. She had gone back and forth on leaving it up or taking it down. On the one hand, she longed to gaze upon the face she had come to think of as her own. On the other, the persistent reminder of what she didn't have pierced far deeper into her soul than her mother's gaze ever had.

So, she had become resolute that her mother's portrait would remain intact until the day came that she was at last equipped to replace it.

Then the artist placed down his brush, putting an end to the rhythmic sound of it which had reverberated around the room. She took a short breath, enough to raise her chest but not enough to make a sound.

Perhaps that time had finally come.

He lifted up the canvas, as delicate as a groom carrying his bride, so as not to disturb the drying process. In truth, it would have been easier for her to rise from the chair she sat in and walk over to inspect the painting. But he knew better than to ask that of her.

Once he had ventured as close to her as he dared, the artist spun around to reveal his work.

She recognized the room he had painted. She recognized the dress his subject wore. Recognized the way her hair had been pinned up, the jewelry around her neck and wrists. Her eyes fell upon the subject's face, and...

She sighed.

Now at last, she stood, hands folded firmly at her lap as she strode in closer. She held them out, and the artist gave her a strange expression. He didn't seem to understand what she was requesting of him. Her lips only curled up higher, and after a few moments more hesitation, he relinquished the painting to her hands.

She turned and carried the portrait over to the fireplace where the abandoned frame lay waiting. She lifted up the canvas and threw it directly into the flames.

The crackling sound it produced almost eclipsed the noise which had escaped from the artist's mouth. But she had still heard it.

She turned to face him, and still he made that noise — strangled and confused, as if he had forgotten how to form proper words. What a fool.

Those were the last sounds he ever made before she reached out and slashed his throat with her bare hands.

Then it was just her and the fireplace. The flames continued to eat up the waste of paint and paper. Why was it so difficult to find just one artist who could capture her in totality?

Her mother had been so pleased with her portrait because it looked exactly like her in all ways. Blobs of oil somehow became the shine her eyes gained whenever the rest of her face refused to show strong emotions. When she stared at that portrait, what stared back at her was no painting. It was her mother.

Her calculating, frightening, beautiful mother, even after all this time, even after death, still looked down upon her.

She thought about the insipid work she had seen tonight as she stepped away from the blood pooling at her feet. Was that really how others saw her? As this bland, dull, lifeless husk of a woman? Was she really so plain? Had everyone lied to her this entire time about the resemblance to her mother?

If she were capable of tears, she was certain she would shed them at this point. But there was no point in standing around, wasting time being frustrated.

She called to have the body removed from the room, and for the blood to be picked up and cleaned. She would eat later.

Now, she had another letter to go and write.

Chapter 1

Venus

V enus. Her name was Venus.

She said it in her head over and over. Whispered it to herself, allowing it to roll off her tongue with familiarity.

Venus. Venus. Venus.

When people called her by that name, she would answer to it as naturally as breathing.

Venus. Venus. Venus.

The roads became rocky beneath her feet, and she couldn't decide if this was easier to ride on than in the grass. On the one hand, her horse didn't have to deal with mud or weeds. On the other, the rocks varied in sizes, which caused the animal to stumble.

Yet she had to be mindful about the impact the environment would have on her outfit. She had thought long and hard about the sort of outfit she should be wearing when she presented herself to the countess. There was no way she would be able to bring more than one, knowing that she would be traveling with her painting supplies.

A lady of such high stature would have certain expectations of those entering her house. It wouldn't do for her to show up in a fancy gown that was muddied and ripped from the journey, but it also wouldn't do if she showed up underdressed. Then again, even the wealthy understood how messy creating art could be.

So, she settled on something practical. A blouse and skirt, which were made of sturdy materials. Above that, she wore her apron, and her hair neatly tied back. Hopefully, she looked the part of a painter.

She held on tightly to her supplies. She had to leave behind her oils and pigments — she could easily make more, though — as well as her jars. However, she had kept her canvas and brushes. Those were not as easy to come across.

Her glasses sank deeper into the pocket of her apron, next to the remaining coins she still possessed. She counted the coins in her head to determine if she had enough for a night in an inn. While there would be benefits to arriving at the countess' mansion early, Venus did not want to show up looking as though she had just spent the last few weeks on horseback.

At that moment, her stomach grumbled, and she let out a pathetic whimper. A night at an inn meant no more money for dinner, and what good would rest do if she had no food to restore her energy? Another sound began to tickle her ears. At first, she thought it was her stomach complaining in protest, but as the noise went on, she realized it was coming from a distance. She looked over to see a babbling brook.

She smiled, hardly believing her luck. She knew that where there was water, there would be insects. Venus directed her horse over to it. Soon enough, flies were darting across her eyes, unsatisfied with the brook, wanting instead to taste the salt in her sweat.

She paid them no mind as she stepped down from her horse and tied it to a tree. As the animal drank from the brook, she removed her glasses from her pocket. The coins she kept tucked inside her apron, trusting her luck with the water more than her luck with potential thieves. The glasses, however, held value solely to her.

Only after this was safely tucked away did she bend down to the water and cup herself a handful to drink. It cooled down her throat and nestled gently into her stomach. She had slurped it down so quickly that it dribbled from her lips to her chin.

Once her thirst was quenched, Venus got to digging around in the mud, being mindful to keep her apron in front of her skirts. The coins inside the pocket pressed against her knees, making her grit her teeth. But she battled on until her fingers came across something writhing and squirming in the earth.

She pulled up to reveal an impressively large grub.

She sat the creature in her lap as she tore away a single strand of thread from her apron. This she tied around the grub before tossing it straight into the water.

Then, she waited.

As she sat there, her mind began to wander. She wondered what kind of person the countess would be. The rumors told only of her strict rulings as a landlady, and how everyone in town had to pay rent to her. Despite this, hardly anyone had actually seen the countess. Apparently, she rarely left her house.

These rumors had come from people who lived in nearby lands — farmers, gardeners, or fellow noblemen who had nothing better to do than gossip. She had never heard about the countess through the artists who had painted her. Only that there were many, and yet still more were demanded.

Venus asked herself, not for the first time, just what exactly it was about her skills which she felt would please this insatiable woman. In truth, she was very skilled, her long list of clients should be a testament to it. Not that she would be able to share this list in full.

But was she more skilled than the many other artists who had come forth and presented their best efforts?

Then, she thought about the unthinkable. What would happen should she fail?

Would she return with a reputation so ruined, she could never paint again? Venus chortled, knowing full well her reputation was sullied to begin with. Well, whatever should happen, she had accepted the invitation, and she would see it through. If this were to be the last painting she ever produced, then she would make it her masterpiece.

The string around her waist began to tug. She sat upright, focusing her attention on pulling it back in, but not too quickly so as to scare off her catch. Inch by inch, she made her way closer to the brook, all the while pulling at the string, until she was close enough to swoop down and claim her prize. The fish wriggled and thrashed within her grasp. The grub was partway stuffed down its throat.

She took hold of the body with her free hand. This did little to ease the fish's thrashing. Once she had a firm grip, she twisted its head, killing it instantly. The fish went limp in her palms. Venus laid it on a rock to dry out as she fetched firewood. She kept a close eye on her claim, peering throughout the grass and bushes to ensure no predators became emboldened enough to try and take it for themselves.

Once the wood was gathered and flames were created, she went back to her fish. She sliced it, pulled out its bones and innards, then skewered it onto a stick for cooking. Without any kind of seasoning, the meal was bland. But her stomach wasn't opposed to finally having something to digest. Besides, she took pride in being self-sufficient and her ability to provide for herself. That pride was what made her food so delicious to her.

'*You have always been able to provide for yourself,*' Venus reassured herself. '*That's what got you all the way out here in the first place. If the countess likes your painting, then all of this was worth it. And if not, then it was still worth it, for the journey will prepare you for the next one.*'

She smirked. She had been so preoccupied by the automatic notion that she would fail, she hadn't actually considered what her success would mean. Venus looked down at the remains of her dinner and realized that success meant she would no longer have to do this.

She killed her fire and crushed the bones before burying them. She went back to the brook and washed her hands before taking off. The sun was beginning to set, and she wanted to make it to the town by nightfall. She rode alongside the brook; in case she needed another drink. As she walked further down the path, she spotted a tree growing its roots into the waters. Upon closer inspection, she realized it was a peach tree.

She reached up and plucked at the fruit, placing it into her apron. Breakfast for tomorrow. She picked a second one, dinner for her horse. Then, she picked another and took a bite. Desert for her.

...

Securing a room at an inn had gone smoothly enough. The doorman took her horse around the back. She sat down on her bed, grateful for the break, however, she didn't sit there for long. Despite her small washing, she still felt a mess. On her way to the inn, she had spotted a well nearby. She could bring a bucketful up and rinse out her feet, at least.

She went to the front to ask the innkeepers if they kept any pails, when a noise outside caught everyone's attention. There were horses and men shouting as a large group of people were walking in the streets. No, not just walking — they were being escorted. It wasn't hard to guess why. Anyone would be able to recognize the brightly colored clothing and golden adornments.

As the guardsmen continued to march the group of Romani people down the streets, several on-lookers began to peer out of their windows and doorways. Venus could hear the cheering. A moment later, she realized she was standing outside herself, her body having moved on its own.

One guardsman stopped and inspected her. His brows furrowed, and his eyes went up and down. He stared as if she were the first woman he had ever seen in his life, and he didn't know what to make of her. She knew this look, and she also knew that no good came from pointing it out.

Instead, she directed her attention back to the Romani at hand. There, at the edge of the crowd, was a girl who looked about twelve years old. Her feet dragged against the harsh pavement.

Venus thought about how her own feet and arms were tired from travel. Except she had been moving on a horse, and of her own accord. No men had walked her down the streets. She could only imagine how difficult this must all be on a child. How hungry she must be.

She was tempted to approach the girl and ask her what had happened, but she was able to put the pieces together herself. Most likely, they were traveling together due to the changing seasons. There was a high chance that they were planning on setting up camp nearby. And Gadje never cared to see too many Romani gathered in one place for too long.

She felt around in her apron pocket for what she knew wasn't there – the remainder of her coins had gone to the inn. But she felt the peach she had intended on saving for breakfast the following morning. She stepped forward, moving with the crowd, pulling up her skirts and running until she caught up with the girl.

She paused for just a moment to look up at Venus, but that was all it took for everyone to stop moving and watch. The guardsman who had been staring at her called out, ordering for her to step aside and move along. Venus paid him no mind, as she reached into her apron and produced the fruit. She held it out to the girl, who made no movement, except enlarging her eyes.

Venus held it up a bit higher, and gave a small nod. People around them were beginning to murmur.

At last, the girl's hand flashed upward and snatched away the peach. Venus had half expected her to store it away for a more convenient time, but the girl bit eagerly into the fruit. She rotated it around her lips, consuming every last inch of its flesh as if she were afraid that if she didn't make it disappear as quickly as possible, it would be taken away.

She was probably right on that front.

Venus shuddered when she felt the touch of a hand gripping onto her shoulder. She looked up to see the guardsman who had been staring at her, now so close she could see the red in his eyes.

"Madam," he stated, his voice low. "You need to move along. Get off the streets."

His calm demeanor didn't match his face. She was familiar with this type of man. His tone may be passive, but the red in his eyes shone. Like a snake hunkering down, lying in wait for the mouse to run. He was speaking softly so his colleagues would hear how unprovoked he was. But as they stood there, his hand still on her shoulder, she knew deep in her bones that he wanted her to cause a scene. To give him a reason for the red in his eyes.

She did not reach up to swat away his hand, but rather, Venus stepped back so abruptly that her shoulder was twisted out of his grip. His eyes went wide at the motion. He looked back and forth between his hand and her, as if trying to decide who was to be blamed – her for breaking free, or him for letting her.

Venus hurried off before he could make the decision. As she walked away, she couldn't resist the urge to turn and take one last look at the little girl, who must have sensed that she was being watched, for she returned the gesture and gave a final look back at Venus.

Under her breath, Venus whispered: "keep them safe."

Chapter 2

Venus

The following morning, she stood in front of the house. No, that wasn't the right word to describe this place. A house was something modest, something simple, where an unremarkable family lived during their ordinary lives. She could only imagine what these walls had seen, as they loomed up in towers, with rooftops so pointed they could pierce the sky.

She couldn't determine if this place had been intentionally painted black or if the color had faded away over time. Parts of it didn't match one another. Certain rooms must have been additions, but just how many she couldn't say precisely. She counted at least three different styles, all stitched together as into some horrifying quilt of a building.

The idea of a group of people being able to plan and then deconstruct to rebuild any portion of this place seemed ludicrous. She could sooner believe that the house had grown new limbs, albeit mismatched ones. Speaking of growth, another detail which unsettled her once she had noticed it, was the fact that none of the windows were visible.

Her eyes peered over the building once more, twice more, trying to find evidence to the contrary. But no, — it didn't matter where she looked, every single window was completely covered by large, hideous plants.

There was an unknown element to this place beyond its surface. It made her think back to that guardsman who wanted her to cause trouble, simply so he could stop it. She thought again of a snake, curled up and waiting for its prey. This place... there was something sentient about it. The lack of visible windows served as eyes shut tight in slumber, lying in wait for just the right moment.

Venus let out a shaky breath. This was the home of her countess? She checked the address on the invitation she had once more. There was no mistake. This was her destination. Still, she stood outside the gate. She knew how long the painting process would take, andtake and thought that her horse would be more comfortable at a nearby farm. She would have to negotiate pretty heavily if she wanted to leave so soon already. She hadn't come all this way just to turn back now. Whatever awaited her behind those doors was up to fate. She approached the iron gates, unsure how she was meant to get past them. She laid a hand down, searching for some form of latch beneath the never-ceasing growth of plants.

There was a loud clamor, startling her to so that she jolted back. She thought for certain an alarm had been triggered. Every instinct in her body warned her to run, but she held firm, assuring herself that she would only have to convince whoever was coming of her purpose here.

No one came.

Instead, the gates began to roll open. Venus twisted her gaze back and forth, desperately searching for who or what was causing the gates to open, but her eyes fell upon nothing. Her blood chilled, and she froze in place as the iron completed its autonomous dance, mouth wide open for its feast.

'No', she thought.

She would take this beast head on. She was a fighter. She was a survivor. The snake did not capture all the mice in the field.

She took a step forward. And then another. And another. Until at last she had passed the threshold. Half of her expected... something to happen. In her mind's eye, she could see the house becoming fully alive, gates curling in on her, pulling her down into the ground and swallowing her whole, leaving her soul to be trapped inside her rotting corpse for eternity.

Even the more practical half was anticipating a reprimand of some sorts. A guard, butler, anyone, to come out and inform her that these premises were restricted. Yet if that was the case, then why open the gates?

She told herself to quit stalling, the countess was clearly expecting her and now she was making a noblewoman wait. From her experience, Venus knew they were not the patient sort.

She peered around the space between the gate and the mansion. It must have once been a grand garden. She could see traces of statues and foundations beneath mountains of vegetation and weeds, the same ones which had engulfed the gates.

Venus found herself feeling sorry for the statues, which remained unloved beneath their botanical bonds. She had never been one for sculpture, but she had studied them. The toil and pain one suffered to bring stone to life, just for it to be tossed aside as an inconvenience.

Venus couldn't help but notice that the plants surrounding the windows were different from the ones in the garden. They weren't random weeds, strewn about in a sporadic fashion. They had a distinct shape, although she couldn't determine what precisely they were.

The doors were before her then, and she went to knock upon them, but just like the iron gates, they creaked open with no apparent controller. She hesitated less then, however, and stepped inside.

If the exterior of this place hadn't convinced her that it was a house, the interior was even less convincing. The windows, which had been concealed from outside, were revealed completely from the other end; there were no rooms for them to reside in. This place seemed to be nothing but one great, giant room.

There was a staircase right at the center. It was enormous, reaching almost almost both ends of the walls. The carpet covering it was stained red, the singular contrast to the stone floors and black walls. Bold, even in the room's poor lighting. She took her glasses out and placed them on, hoping they would allow her to see details with at least some slight clarity.

The place was so empty that the tiniest of steps Venus took resounded in echoes and caused dust to swirl up around her. It was so cold. Outside, it was late spring, soon to be summer — how was it so chilled in here?

Then again, she supposed the lack of heat was meant to cover up the smell. It never quite escaped her nostrils, even when she assured herself that eventually she would get used to it and stop noticing. Just as she thought that moment had come, there it was again. Teasing, constant. A mixture of different types of rot.

Without hearing a sound, Venus was suddenly aware that another had entered vast room. Her eyes followed up the staircase until they reached the top. There she stood.

The Countess Luchia de Sarracenia.

The first detail Venus took in of her new patroness was her skin. Despite how dim the room had been, the countess was so pale she almost seemed to glow, as if all the color had been drained from her body, and nestled at her red, red lips.

It wasn't just the color, however. Even at this distance, Venus could not see the normal signs of aging skin. No wrinkles, no skin marks, not even pores. The countess' flesh was as smooth and undisturbed as an infant's, as if her skin was marble that molded to her every movement.

And her eyes. Venus had seen black eyes before, many times. But there had been a warmth to those, like coals before the fire. These eyes reminded her of black ice. The countess had her gaze fixed on Venus, and those eyes held her firmly in place.

"Are you it, then?" She demanded.

Her voice rang around the emptiness, so that her words were repeated back in multitude. She was everywhere.

Venus' spine shivered down to her core. It took another moment before her lips began to work again in a manner which allowed her to answer.

"Y-yes..."

She hated herself for the way she sounded. She had wanted to enter bold, confident. *'I am the painter of noblemen, and I am here at your request to capture your soul on canvas!'*

Instead she was acting like a child being scolded. So many artists had come prior attempting to please this particular countess, and all had failed. If she was clearly unimpressed already, then what could Venus possibly do to earn her favor?

The countess didn't reply to Venus' statement but instead moved those black ice eyes up and down, inspecting her. Just like the red-eyed police guardsman had. She felt far more afraid with this inspection, however.

She stood there and waited for it to be done, to be told what to do. For the questions which were soon to follow — where was her carriage parked, where were her assistants, attendants, whatever else traveling artists needed on the road? Why were her clothes so shabby? Why did she carry all her equipment in her arms? Just what exactly was she?

"Come along."

This sentence was not said with patience. In fact, by the time Venus turned up her head to look, the countess had already begun to walk away.

She scrambled, nearly dropping her canvas as she gracelessly ran to and up the stairs to follow. There was a rise in her stomach, a mixture of fear and excitement.

She was given a chance. Despite everything, odds against her, she was given a chance.

Atop the staircase was a hallway. Venus was surprised to see doors along its walls. So this was intended to be a house, then. However, the switch from windows to doors meant that the space went from dim lighting to none. She kept up her pace, eyes focused on the countess ahead, who despite her slower walking methods appeared to be moving down the corridor rather quickly. It must have been a trick of the shadows.

At the very end of the hallway lay an open door, inside was a room lit up by a fire. Venus was surprised she could see it from the other side, but with it being the only light source, it was difficult to miss. They walked on, and yet it never seemed to come any closer. In her youth, Venus had spent many nights chasing the moon, thinking if she simply ran hard enough for long enough, that eventually she would reach it. Obviously, it had remained in place, taunting her from that endless sky. Now, so did this open door, with its flames just beyond.

She adjusted her glasses, which did little to make things brighter, but did bring into focus some details she had missed whilest her eyes had adjusted to the dark. There was a sizable space in between the doors, all of which had a distinct pattern of dust residing in the middle. Or rather, lack of dust.

These patterns came in many sizes and shapes, including ovals and rectangles. She wondered if this was a type of fashionable paint job on the part of the interior designer — because it was much too distinct to be laziness — but as they reached their destination, Venus got her answer. At the very last door right next to the room with the fireplace, hung a portrait. The dust patterns along the rest of the walls must have been portraits removed.

That wasn't what intrigued her about this piece of art, however. From the way the artist had captured the pale flesh and black ice eyes, she had concluded that this was a depiction of her countess. But if that were the case, then why was she here? Why had there been so many rumors of her insatiable nature towards artists if, in fact, she already had her portrait?

Then Venus took closer inspection. She could see how much more prominent the cheekbones and chin were in this painting. The lips were

17

slightly thinner, and the hair a touch thicker. She looked down at the name placard, then ran her fingers over the imprinted words.

Countess Bianca de Sarracenia. Died 1532.

She felt a sudden ache within her chest, and placed a hand to it. The woman in the portrait shared the same, dismissive look as her daughter, staring down at Venus as an inconvenient pest, rather than an invited guest.

Strange how it did not give a full age with her birth. Perhaps she had married into the estate, and it was never given? Highly unlikely but Venus could hardly fathom any other explanation.

Behind her, the current countess cleared her throat. This broke the spell on Venus and transported her back into the hallways. For the first time since arriving, she was grateful for the dim light, as it hid her reddening cheeks.

Yet as she went to follow the countess, the tilting of her head in Venus' direction made her believe that this noblewoman knew exactly what the dark concealed.

Inside the room there was indeed a fireplace. Large and looming, stretching out almost to the walls just as the staircase had. Its mouth opened upward, creating the illusion of the entire wall being on fire. That was, except for the blank, rectangular space right above it.

It was by far the warmest room Venus had been in thus far. At first, this was welcomed, as the cold atmosphere otherwise had chilled her arms and fingers, which wasn't helped by her holding onto her painting materials.

The noblewoman was sitting in a chair of red velvet which sat in the middle of the room. Before Venus, stood an easel. She approached this and set up her canvas, grateful to at last be able to place it down. Then, she began to take out her brushes, charcoal and paints.

Deep from within her apron, she pulled out her scraps of parchment. She walked over to the countess, paper and charcoal in hand, and perched down beside her. Her irises followed Venus, but beyond that, she made no moves.

Venus held up her thumb, measuring out the proportions of the countess with her hand. From there, her view of the noblewoman shifted. No longer was she the intimidating patroness who saw Venus as a pest in her domain, but rather she became an amalgamation of shapes, lines and colors which Venus would have to copy and recreate onto paper.

It was a mixture of math and alchemy. The calculations between the features of the face, the head, the neck and torso. A breakdown of a person, similar to how an architect plans out the structure of a building while considering the size and space, these were the calculations she had to memorize before she began to paint.

She got up and walked around the countess, studying her whole profile. She drew the nose repeatedly until she understood the curve of its bridge in relation to the nostrils. She sketched the lips at multiple angles so she could learn how the upper lip curled over the lower one.

But the eyes. Venus struggled with the eyes.

It was always intimidating to look a superior head on, even as indirectly as required for painting. However, Venus had never seen a more piercing stare from a pair of authoritative eyes before. Not even from the police guardsman.

At last, she had adequate study materials to begin. Now, came the magical part. The process of capturing the soul onto paper, using nothing but sketches and paint. Such details were lost on the average person, but to Venus, and the painters of the world, they lay before them like a map.

She wasn't too sure where exactly it was she went when creating art. There was some place between here and another realm where dreams existed. No one around her had ever understood this sentiment, at least not growing up. They told her this was all just in her head.

At any rate, her insecurities melted down as her mind began to focus more. Muscles took over where the brain had been too nervous.

Finally, her charcoal reached the canvas and took its first stroke. She started with the head, simplifying its shape to a basic oval, before moving on and roughing out the neck and shoulders. She drew in two more ovals to represent the countess' hands on her lap, and that was where the painting would end.

Venus stared at her crude outlines. Art never looked like much at this stage, but it was important to get the composition down first before diving into the finer details. She knew that eventually, this batch of scribbles was going to be something spectacular.

She continued on, sketching out the proportions of the countess' dress, then her hair, and finally her jewelry. Once she had the basic outlines completed, it was time to move onto her face. This was the trickiest part. In her experience, patrons could forgive irregularities to their hands or clothes, but they couldn't forgive the slightest miscalculation towards their face.

Venus wiped more sweat from her forehead. She had been so lost in her work that she hadn't noticed how uncomfortable she had become in this warm room. The heat and sweat created a fog on her glasses, so she took them off.

She returned to her canvas and made another glance towards the countess. She paused, however. In all this time, the countess had not moved. It was natural for clients, no matter how hard they tried, to shift at least a little in their poses. When working throughout the day, Venus would hardly notice if their arms lowered, or their shoulders tensed. But this countess had been the stillest model she had ever worked on. Even when she had followed Venus' actions with her eyes, the rest of her had been perfectly motionless.

Yet now, as Venus continued to study her, she couldn't help but notice a small change. The countess was smiling.

It was not a kind smile. It reminded Venus more of the smile she got from wealthy individuals who saw her trucking her skirts through the mud or walking instead of riding a carriage. Yet, there was also something more childish in the way this countess held her grin. She kept a secret locked in those lips. This thought unnerved Venus, but there was little point in dwelling on it. It was hardly the first time a noble person had flaunted their position of power over her.

She took her charcoal and sketched in little lines at the lips, now giving the countess two sets of mouths. The paint would cover it eventually, but the image was still unnerving.

Next, she had to set up the undercoat. This would give a more natural looking hue to the colors. Venus attempted to look back over at the countess in the most covert manner she could accomplish, thinking to herself that this noblewoman's complexion resembled white chalk more than human skin. An undertone of reds and browns would be too dark, but it was the only way she knew how and didn't think now was the best time for experimenting.

Besides, it had been hours at this point. Or at least, she felt it had been hours. There was no clock. Surely, the church bells would signal the passage of time, but she heard nothing. However, her own internal clock continued to tick. All at once, Venus realized how hungry she was.

She placed down her paintbrush. Completing the sketch and undertone painting was more than enough for one day. The countess more than likely had other duties to attend to, as well. She sat there and waited for the countess' permission to be dismissed. The noblewoman did not move from her position. Venus began to wonder if she had realized that the painting had ceased. Would stating as much be impertinent?

The more they stared at one another, the more the countess' features began to blur. Just by continuing to look at her, the details of her form and face became mixed together as blobs of color and shapes. Venus rubbed at her eyes.

"Would…" she risked. "Would the Countess de Sarracenia care for a break?"

It was better to ask about her the countess' own needs than let on how fatigued Venus herself had become.

"You may take one if you need." Her response was so quick and so thunderous that it shocked Venus.

Then she took a moment to digest what the countess had said to her. She may take a break if *she* needed one. Would it be a sign of weakness if she did? Especially since the countess apparently had much higher stamina. Although, she was merely sitting there while Venus exercised her mind and body.

The countess surely must have been aware that a painting such as this takes time, considering how many artists she had gone through. Perhaps that was why she was able to sit for so long. All the same, was she prepared to stay this way the entire day? Into the night?

Venus shook her head and made it a point to worry about the future as it happened. Right now, she was hungry, and she decided she would rather show weakness now by resting for a moment, over handing off a poorly produced portrait.

Yet as she got up, she paused. She hadn't eaten any breakfast since she had given away her peach to that Romani girl. She hadn't seen anyone besides the countess within these walls and given the lack of maintenance around the front and inside, she doubted that there were any servants around.

This brought up many different questions, but presently, Venus was

21

questioning just how freely she would be permitted to walk around. Certainly, the countess wouldn't allow her to wander in search of her kitchen and eat her food unsupervised?

"I have a greenhouse around back," the countess said, as if reading her thoughts. "Inside are many fruits and vegetables. Eat your fill there."

Venus didn't say a word, but nodded and curtsied, then bolted out of the door.

Chapter 3

Venus

When the countess said she had a greenhouse, Venus had no idea what sort of vision she should anticipate. On the one hand, she was a wealthy noblewoman, so it would make sense for it to be lavish. On the other, given the state of the rest of her home, plants included, she had half expected it to be filled with ancient, rotted vegetation.

In the end, she felt that the countess had undersold it.

The entryway was littered with tall trees, ripe with fruits. Peaches, apples, pears... many more which she could not name. At her feet were strong, healthy roots of carrots and squash. In the middle of the room were tables which held herbs and spices, some of which Venus hadn't seen since childhood. Tears pricked at her eyes at the sight of them. Oh, the flavorful feast she could create!

Then, she peered towards the back of the greenhouse. There was another set of tables, housing plants which she didn't recognize. Greenhouses were often used to hold exotic plants from around the world, it shouldn't surprise her that the countess was a collector.

However, these plants seemed to have... mouths and *teeth*. They excreted a strange type of moisture around their bodies. Their coloring was bright, rich reds. In the human world, society has been conditioned to see bright colors as a luxury. It took high amounts of pigment to recreate it. Yet in nature, it was a gamble if bright colors meant to one should run away or come closer.

The shades of red on these exotic plants reminded Venus of the red on the countess' lips. Perhaps these plants were harvested for beauty reasons.

She couldn't stop herself from looking at them, or thinking about that pair of red, red lips...

She shook her head, breaking the spell. She could wonder about the exotics later. For now, she had to pick what would give her the most energy and get back to her work.

...

This was to be their routine for some time.

Venus needed to return to the greenhouse here and there, but she tried to bring up enough to sustain herself throughout the day. She slept next to her canvas, on the hard, marble floor. She never knew for how long, without a clock or windows. Somehow, it was always daytime when she went out to the greenhouse.

Either way, it left her muscles sore. One time, she got a cramp in her forearm so overwhelming that she dropped her brush to the ground. She had to massage it down before she was able to continue, although her arm remained in pain until she slept it off.

All the while, the countess stayed in her seat, never moving. Venus had yet to even see her blink. She had a feeling that the countess might be moving around while she slept — an idea which both comforted and frightened her — but how was she able to go back to the exact same position each morning?

Surely, she must move at some point, however. She must rest. She must eat.

They spoke not a word to each other. Now that Venus had permission to run out to the greenhouse, there was really no further need for pleasantries. She preferred it that way. The less she knew about the countess, the more objective her painting would be. No emotions to distort it, just pure, mathematical facts.

This method made her far more productive. Without the usual number of breaks, she was painting far faster than she ever had before. That said, she had no intention of ever repeating this process. The ache her muscles endured was never ending. The dim light in the room blurred her vision, so every time she stepped outside, she thought she might go blind. And the heat. That relentless heat which drove off any small amounts of moisture she managed to retain.

The greenhouse had become her only sanctuary. The blossoming of the fruits and vegetables were her only sign that life and time were moving forward with the rest of the world. However, the promise of the greenhouse was also her greatest heartbreak. She knew that her time there could only last so long, and that she would once again have to return.

Each day when she woke up in this room, next to that canvas, and peered over at that smiling countess... she thought that she would go mad.

'I just need to finish...' she thought. *'Once I have finished, I can go. Succeed or fail, I can leave.'*

She chose to focus in on her work. With every brushstroke, she was determined to make this piece worth it. Her time here would not be in vain. It was the only thing she could do to keep pressing forward.

Then, one day, when she was returning from her lunch of beets and apples, she heard a noise. It was unfamiliar at first, and it took her a moment to figure out what it was.

Crying.

There was no question as to who it was, considering the circumstances, but the idea of the countess being capable of weeping seemed unfathomable. Perhaps, she too, was becoming tired of these conditions. Conditions which she herself had put in place.

Venus walked up to the door slowly, walking only on the tips of her feet so as to make as little sound as possible. She leaned her ear in closer to the opening.

"Oh, mother..." she at last recognized the voice as the countess' and could no longer deny what she had originally deemed impossible. "Oh, mother..."

A new ache nestled down inside of Venus. It wasn't a sharp pain like what she felt in her stomach, nor a dull soreness like her muscles got, but somewhere in between. It was a pang in her heart.

She wasn't quite sure why she was reacting this way. She supposed it was only human to hear someone crying and feel a sense of pity towards their plight. But this was more than that. It was as if someone had twisted at her own heart strings.

She peered over at the portrait which hung directly outside of the fireplace room. She stared back at the eyes of black ice which had belonged to the countess' mother. She wondered what their relationship must have been like, and what the reason was for the countess' tears now.

Then for the first time in a long time, Venus thought about her own mother. Memories flooded back of her life prior to becoming a painter, of small but warm meals, of feeling a sense of belonging, but also dreaming of something more.

Her mother's face was clear in her mind. The way her eyes crinkled when she smiled or frowned; the exact tones of her laugh, or how she would throw her head back just a little whenever she let one out; how her hands had a softness to them despite the calluses.

How they had not left on good terms. Or any terms, really.

Venus knew she would never see her mother again. A part of her thought she had found peace in this knowledge, but hearing the countess' weeping out, whatever the reason, for her own mother... it tore at Venus from deep within. She had forgotten how human they both were.

The heartache soon subsided and was replaced with determination. Not a hot fire, a burning passion to finish in glory, but a collection of calm, resolute thoughts.

She would complete this portrait.

She waited until the sobbing ceased before entering the room. The countess was once again in the pose Venus had become so familiar with. The fact that she could switch so quickly unsettled the artist. She ignored it as she inspected her work.

The composition was complete, now it was a matter of smaller, refined details. She stared at her painting, really looking at it for the first time in an eternity. How the shadows and highlights had lent themselves to creating the illusion of depth and dimension. How the countess seemed to glow in this dim lighting, as if she were the light source rather than the flames behind her.

How red her lips were, so bright that Venus could not determine if they were an invitation to partake, or a warning to stay away.

It truly was a magnificent painting, if she may be so bold as to admit. Pride may not have been a virtue, but a modest artist would not be the one painting nobles.

She went to pick up her brush, when her eyes landed once more on her glasses. They had been discarded for the past few weeks. She recalled how her sweat had made them fog and become more of a hindrance than helpful. Yet now, when she was so close to completing, she felt that she needed to get everything exactly right.

Venus placed them on her face, and the whole world came into focus. Blurs of motion faded away into crisp, clear vision. There was one minor difference; the frames had rusted in places, which made the glass fade and darkened over time, giving everything a slight pink hue.

Even so, Venus decided that the clearness in her eyesight was worth the tribulations. Now at last, she picked up her brush and looked forward to the countess.

The countess looked less pale with these glasses on, the pink hue of their tint brought her down to a more earthy glow, making her cheeks almost appear flushed and those bright lips which had captivated Venus' attention earlier, now only appeared to be a pair of lips. Venus glanced back at her painting, and how it reflected the countess perfectly with the glasses on. Yet when Venus took them off, and saw how pale her painting became, she wondered if she could recreate what she saw when she wore these spectacles.

She had never done that before. She had only ever captured from life, exactly as she saw it. She thought about her bias — how in the dim light, this countess carried about her an aura of death as if it were smoke clouding around her character. Yet with the glasses on, and with the knowledge of those tears, she was far more palatable.

Another glance at the countess, and Venus determined that she could be deemed as beautiful. There were no blemishes on her skin, but that had been what she found so uncanny in the first place. She was almost *too* perfect. Too smooth, too wrinkle free. Was there such a thing as being so beautiful that the pendulum swung back and made it unappealing? Frightening, almost?

Her stillness, to the point where she did not even appear to be breathing. Venus wondered, if the countess had instead been a statue, would she be so afraid? Or would she admire the work of the sculptor, be enchanted by the very same details which as of now had her so on edge. Was she such a lover of art that a person who deviated from convention caused such disruption in her?

The countess was ultimately the final critic. Venus could only supply her artistic endeavors, and in her opinion, adding the tint her glasses gave only enhanced what she saw in the noblewoman.

The countess shifted her gaze once more, eyes focusing on Venus. This startled the artist, who realized she had been staring for far too long without actually painting. She hid behind her canvas as her cheeks burned. That was the effect this woman seemed to have on her.

As long as it got done. She would be free, succeed or fail, if she just finished... So, she picked up her paints and began to add shades of reds and pinks to the white she had been using for the skin tones.

It started small, just some blush added to her cheeks, her lips darkened, but as she continued, Venus began to notice details in the countess which she hadn't prior. Like the shine in her hair, or how her black ice eyes became more of a rich brown. Her uncanniness had melted, and she sat there, a beautiful woman.

It was down to the last few characteristics. A shine here on the earrings, the necklace, the headwear and the eyes. A few more flecks of yellow on the flames, a pinch more glow around the countess and...

It was complete.

Venus didn't believe it at first. Her eyes ran over the painting, top to bottom, bottom to top, certain that she was missing something. Here, she had been expecting a strong sense of relief, but as she sat, remaining inside the room of her torment, she found this revelation to be rather anti-climactic.

Still, it wasn't truly over until the countess saw and gave her answer.

She stood.

"It's finished, mistress."

The countess gave a slight nod, so small Venus almost believed she imagined it, but it was just enough for her to know that she had been heard. When it became apparent that the noblewoman had no intention of standing up from her chair, Venus went back to grab her canvas.

She had to use the utmost caution in lifting it up, since the oils would remain wet for quite some time. Her stomach lit on fire at the thought of dropping the painting now, ruining everything. By some grace she did not know she possessed, she managed to walk it over and turn it around without causing a single smudge.

At first, the countess gave no indication of her reaction. She merely tilted her head, eyes wandering over the painting as Venus' had only moments ago. She stared into it, and Venus stared at her, trying to read her face. That face which she had become so familiar with.

The countess let out a sigh. Over these many weeks, Venus had rarely heard her patron's voice, and it sent a shiver down her spine. She had never heard a sigh like that, so deep and resonated. As if she had just let out her last breath before her soul escaped her flesh.

Then, she took the canvas from Venus, seemingly with an ease and strength which impressed the artist. She brought it over to the fireplace, dangerously close to the flames. Then she set it down in the corner.

The countess turned back to Venus. She was smiling. Something that Venus should have been familiar with, but this one was different. It looked as if the countess' face was splitting, and then Venus realized what it was. She was smiling so hard that her mouth crinkled, and her eyes squinted.

She ran over to Venus, a sight so unexpected that the artist raised her arms in protection. But the countess still managed to bring her in close and embrace her. Her touch was cold, sharply so, but the room was warm enough that Venus almost found the hug to be refreshing.

"Oh, you have done it!" The countess cried. "Oh, at last! It's finally over!"

That last phrase rang in Venus' head. Yes...it was truly over. No more sleeping on this hard floor, with the dim lights that hurt her eyes. No more stealing away to the greenhouse just to feed herself. No more nights of only her and the countess.

She had succeeded. Where so many others had failed, she — Venus — had managed to find success.

She had never received such a reaction as this. Even with the highest form of praise, there was an aura of...expectations. To be embraced by a noblewoman, was... she didn't have words for it.

The countess pulled away, but kept one hand on Venus' shoulder, giving it a small squeeze. She looked at the artist, a softness in her glance now. It made Venus' cheeks burn again, and the embarrassment of that made them burn harder, but there wasn't much she could do.

"Thank you," the countess said.

Venus smiled, which she realized she hadn't done in so long.

"Of course," was her reply, then after a moment. "It was an honor, mistress."

The fiery sensation was back in her stomach, and yet it was different. Her torment was over, yes. But now, she was expected to leave. To never see this countess again. Despite her previous reservations, Venus felt as though she could bear to paint this woman again. Perhaps even a couple of times.

The countess had not been her tormentor — no, she had been an ideal model for any painter and had allowed Venus her needed breaks. It was merely this room, with its intolerable heat, dim light and hard floors, that Venus could never paint in again.

"Well...I shall..." she pulled back from the countess, whose hand still resided on Venus' shoulder. "Make my leave, then."

The countess' lips pursed as she tilted her head. "Why?"

Venus did not know how to answer such a question. It was seemingly a simple one, being only a single word, and yet it held weight to it.

"Is that not..." she thought about her words carefully, attempting to avoid offending the countess. "What is expected?"

A sound rang out then. It echoed and bounced off of the walls, reverberating around the entire room. At first, it was so profound that Venus' instincts were to assume it had been the church bells she spent all this time not being able to hear. Yet as the sound continued, she came to realize that it was coming from the countess herself. She was laughing.

Her smile was wide and broad, cutting more wrinkles into her too-perfect skin, giving her features a sense of warmth. She was beautiful.

"I know not what is to be *expected* of an artist of your talents, especially given that you are..." her eyes ran up and down Venus, as they did in the great room when they had first met. Venus felt everything inside her freeze up into stone. The countess cleared her throat. "Well, given your *circumstances*. What is your name?"

"Faucher." She answered. "Venus Faucher."

"*Venus...*" the countess bit down on her lower lip, allowing her teeth to vibrate the *V* as her tongue rolled over the *E*, accentuating the *N* and *U* until finally reaching the *S*. That was where her tongue held the longest. As if her name were a poem that the countess was trying to memorize.

"It's lovely." She stated. Venus muttered a type of thanks. "You must join me for dinner."

"Oh!"

She was caught off guard by the concept of the countess needing to eat. She was also caught off guard by the invitation in general. For a brief moment, she worried that the countess was going to pay her in dinner rather than currency.

"I couldn't impose..."

"I insist."

Had she any right to refuse?

Venus gave a small nod. "Very well."

Chapter 4

Eva

va, age twelve, stared up at the chapel from the branches of the peach tree. She plucked at one of the riper looking fruits and bit into it. She chewed slowly, savoring it as juice spilled down her chin. She would have to wash her hands twice before supper tonight, but it was worth it.

'Is sitting up here worth being caught?'

Art was not easy for her to come by. She had seen a few paintings in her life, as they were being carried inside of mansions and other fine homes, but once they were in these places, they were off limits to Eva. Only the chapels, with their stained-glass windows and sculptures, allowed her into a world she was so fascinated with.

It didn't matter what her motivations were, she knew how it looked to both sides. Gadje never liked Romani to stay around anywhere for long, but especially not at their churches. All she knew was that, when the winters came, the Gadje priests and pastors were suddenly more generous to her people. Then the rest of the year, they feared and shunned them.

On the other side, her people would also warn caution of her fascination with chapels, but it wasn't the sermons or the hymns which interested Eva — it was the windows.

The stained glass, which told stories with their bright colors and vivid details. Occasionally, she tried to listen in as an attempt to hear the stories and match them to their windows, but the stone walls kept everything far too muffled. More often than not, she merely sat in her peach tree and tried to imagine how the artist had made such pieces.

How did they color the glass? How did they cut the glass? How did they weld it back together? How did they make a picture, let alone a whole story, from one image?

She broke down the pieces in her head, imagining herself cutting glass into a variety of shapes, until she was able to pull them all together into a face. She and the figure of Christ stared at each other, and she thought to herself *"just how did someone carve you into existence?"*

Sculptures were a bit simpler to understand — at least those were just stones or mud. It was the imagery which came with them that tickled her brain. The frightening gargoyles these artists had designed. They were meant to terrify the common folk, yes, but what did it say about the men who brought them into existence?

She had tried her hands at sculpting before, by using thick mud and molding it into shapes. All that had done was ruin her dress and sent her mother into a frenzy.

Eva set the peach in her lap, then took out her sketchbook and a piece of charcoal. She opened it up to a blank page, then rested her eyes on the image of Christ. Up until this point, she hadn't summoned the nerve to try and sketch him. But she needed to practice more with humans, especially faces. And she was tired of only ever drawing her family.

The figure on the glass window was not wholly realistic, at least not to the extent which the statues were. It had a certain style to it, something that made it very distinct. This was what she aimed to mimic in her rendition. So, she didn't blend in her usual shading, but left it sharp and hard, and made the facial features more angular.

She had finished the head and was just about to move onto the body, when she heard a voice. It was far off, but loud and angry, and sounded as if it were coming closer. She didn't recognize the owner, but it didn't take long for her to realize that the shouting was directed at her.

"Get down from there! What do you think you're doing?"

She peered over at the Gadje who was yelling. For a very brief moment, she wondered what authority he had over this situation. He was not family she needed to obey, nor did he look like any official. But Gadje didn't need proper authority to assert dominance.

Silently, Eva climbed down, the remainder of her peach set between her jaw. Once on the ground, she removed it from her mouth and gazed at the Gadje, asking with her expression if it was alright for her to leave now.

He pointed to the tree. "How dare you steal so close to the house of God!"

"But I wasn't stealing."

It was a mistake to challenge him, yet the line of defense slipped out before she could stop herself. She turned her gaze to her feet, a supplicating gesture.

"Watch your tongue!" At the *T*, spittle dripped from his lips.

Eva watched in disgust as it hit the ground. He made a grab for her sketchbook and yanked it from her grip before she had a chance to react.

"What's this, then?"

Eva felt her cheeks becoming hot. Not even her family had seen every single drawing she had produced. All of her failed experiments, the disastrous proportions and unfinished sketches. Things meant only for her eyes, now in the dirty hands of this Gadje man.

Once he reached the last page, her incomplete work of Christ, he paused. Eva had no idea what he might be thinking. Was it blasphemous to draw out Christ? If that was the case, then why put his image throughout a church for all to see?

Perhaps it was only blasphemous when *she* did it.

He slammed the book.

"You're lucky I don't report you! I doubt it's just you out here, snooping around the church! Where there's one of you, there's many more! Your kind never travels alone!"

On and on he went, and she just stood there, head bowed, taking it. Her family was indeed close by, but that was simply due to the fact that she never wandered far from her camp, and it was a small town. There were more Gadje here than Roms, making *her* the one surrounded, not him.

She stood there as he continued to call her filthy, heathen, hell-borne. She didn't really understand the latter words, but she knew the term 'filthy'. Eva stared at his feet, which had been barely covered by broken up shoes, revealing his cracked, bleeding toes caked in mud. It traveled up to his knees. There were spots on his side, where he had no doubt wiped off even more dirt.

His hands, which were still pointed in her direction, shared the same state as his toes. The sight of his fingernails, filled to the brim with muck, made her own itch. She doubted this man was willing to clean his hands before a meal, let alone twice, as she planned to do.

At last, his ranting came to a stop, and she rose up, careful to avoid eye contact. They didn't like to be looked at directly.

"My apologies, sir. I shall leave now." It was far more grace than he deserved, but she knew better than to try and aggravate with arguments. She held out her hand. "May I have my sketchbook back, please?"

"You think I'm going to give back your stolen goods?"

Eva tried to explain that the sketchbook wasn't stolen, that in fact her mother and aunts had saved up for quite a while just for her to have this. Prior, she only had scraps of paper or drawings in the dirt. Despite this, her family saw how diligently she returned to her craft, honing her skills even with the obstacles. This sketchbook was the single most important object in her possession.

But the man didn't listen. Eva felt a hand grip at her bicep, nearly engulfing the entirety of her upper arm. It was a firm, tight grip which caused her to cry out in pain and shock. She closed her eyes and waited for the man to strike her.

A moment passed, and then another, and once more until she felt compelled to peek through and see what was happening.

His hand had indeed been raised, no doubt with the intent of hitting Eva, but it was being held. The man was now caught in a grip himself. She looked over at her apparent savior.

Everything about the man seemed sleek and new, as if he were freshly made, to the point where his skin all but shined in the daylight. This new man, this new Gadje, was much more finely dressed than the other holding onto her arm. There was not even a speck of dust on his shoes or jacket. She noticed that he wore a pair of gloves, as if disgusted to be touching the man with dirt in his fingernails.

"Now, now..." he stated, barely above a whisper, but they had both gone quiet. In fact, she couldn't even hear a bird, or the singers in the church, or a gust of wind. The whole world had gone quiet for this man. "Surely you have better things to do rather than pick on the likes of a young child?"

He peered over at Eva, yet she felt no comfort in his stare. It was slow, one where his eyes didn't travel over her, but rather stayed fixated on her own eyes. She suddenly felt scared to blink. It was impolite to look Gadje in the eyes, however she feared what would happen if she turned her head.

The new man let go of the first.

"My apologies, Baron..." he replied, letting go of both Eva and her sketchbook, the latter falling onto the ground. He rushed off, head lowered.

The new man walked over, and Eva almost wished the first man would come back. At least his hatred was familiar. She had no idea the intent with which this new man, this "Baron" had in mind for her. He took a step forward, and she a step back. He noticed this immediately. Instead of stepping forward again, he planted his foot in place, as did she.

It was then that the Baron noticed the discarded sketchbook. Eva felt tears pricking at her eyes. It was bad enough that one Gadje man had touched her beloved sketchbook, but two?

How could she object, though?

He peered through the pages, eyebrows tightening as he examined its contents. She couldn't see the page he stopped on at her current angle, but it could only be the unfinished Christ. He closed it and turned to her.

"What is your name, child?"

She dared not give him her real name. She prayed to be interrupted, by her family, by the church, anything. But nothing came. Just as the world hads silenced itself when this man first spoke, it was now still for his conversation with her.

"E-Eva..."

"Eva..." he repeated. The name trailed off of his tongue and into the breeze. "Do you know who I am?"

She shook her head. She could tell he was rich, but all rich Gadje looked the same to her.

"I am Baron Cellier de Durand."

He bent at the abdomen, taking a bow in the smallest of measurements. The gesture shocked Eva — when had a Gadje nobleman ever bowed to a Rom, let alone a young girl?

He must not have been pleased by her reaction, because when he pulled himself back up, he frowned.

"Do you not know me?"

How could she know him if they had only just met? She wanted to say as much and point out how Gadje nobles looked the same to her, but something told her he would not appreciate either comment. She simply shook her head. The Baron pursed his lips and gave a tight, little nod.

Then he gestured, "where do you live, child? Shall I give you a ride home?"

She didn't want to tell him where her family was camping. As scared as she was, she would not allow a betrayal to her people. But what could she do in this situation? She didn't know.

On impulse, she turned around and ran.

She did not look back. She was convinced something would happen if she did. She would run and run and run, then look to see if she were being followed, and the Baron would be right there at her heels.

The temptation was strong, however. Every footstep she heard, every clang of a horse's hooves, every shriek from another Gadje, made her believe that she was in fact being chased.

Finally, she ducked out of the city line, past the pair of gates, into the countryside, where all was open and free. Only then did she pause long enough to catch her breath. She couldn't see her family's caravan yet, but she knew the area.

There, laid by a brook, was her favorite fallen branch. She smiled as she climbed up, arms outstretched as she walked one foot in front of the other. Just as she was about to make her final move, however, she heard a quick, loud whistle. Too quick to be the wind, but not like any bird she had ever heard.

With great hesitance, Eva slowly began to turn her head and see what was behind her. There, at the edge of the city, stood the Baron. He held up her sketchbook, waving it slightly as if to urge her back over.

Then, he touched his fingers to his lips, then held out his hand to throw it at her. He took another bow and left.

Chapter 5

Venus

The countess had to lead Venus over to the nearest bedroom. She had referred to it as Venus' room, although she could hardly fathom why. Perhaps she was to spend the night after dinner, which seemed customary enough, but the thought of sleeping one more night in this place sent a spark of fear straight to her stomach. Even if it were in a room, even if she were given a bed, all she could think about was the ache in her muscles from that hard floor.

The room was laid out so that on the wall opposite the door lay a large, canopy bed. On either side were a pair of side tables and windows. The countess had stated that she was allowed to wear anything she found in this room, before leaving her alone.

Venus' immediate instinct was to rush over to open the curtains and allow any amount of sunlight into the room. Yet once she had them pulled back, she realized that the room remained just as dark. She peered back through the window and was greeted by a thick wall of vegetation. Mixture of greens and reds, with a peculiar shine to them. Amongst them, large mouths with pointed teeth.

Venus felt the urge to move them out of the way of the light. She tried to aim below the mouths to where the stems grew, but as soon as her hands touched the plant, its sharp teeth slammed closed. She let out a small yelp as she recoiled away.

Was this some sort of security? So far, there was no one else here, so the countess had to take measures to protect herself. Venus supposed she might pluck up the courage to ask over dinner.

She set off in search of candles, or anything that would allow her to see better. Especially since she noticed that this room had no fireplace of its own. She went to one of the side tables and opened the drawer. To her relief, she immediately spotted a tall, virgin candle. As she lifted it out, she felt how smooth and cool the wax was. She ran her fingers over its surface. Then she looked back in the drawer for matches but found none.

Her hand went further back into the drawer, covering every inch of it, yet found nothing. She went to the other side table and was met with the same result.

She sighed with great exasperation. Was she to dress in the dark? Was the countess' eyesight so sharp that she didn't notice how dim the lights were? Then Venus recalled her little trick at the beginning of her journey. She took out her glasses and put them on. The room didn't become brighter, but the fuzziness of the objects around her faded, and that would have to make do for now.

Without further distractions, she opened up the wardrobe and began peering through the dresses. They smelled of dust and furniture polish. They didn't reflect any fashion trend she had seen in recent years. It was difficult to determine what color each were, as they all held the same shade in this lighting. Ultimately, it probably didn't matter what color she picked.

She was, however, a little disappointed to discover that the dresses were one piece. It didn't come as a surprise, though. Her own was a skirt and blouse, the line between covered by her apron. She selected the dress which looked the least uncomfortable. The skirt still fluffed out and she knew she would have to hold the dress up while she walked, but the sleeves were not as ornate as the others, so perhaps the top half of her could relax.

She realized the mistake in this way of thinking as soon as she slipped on the dress. Its bodice was much lower than anticipated, evident by the amount of exposure her breasts now faced. She grabbed the laces to the corset, knowing that if she tightened it too much, it would make her cleavage even more prominent. Yet if she let it slack, there was the risk of her popping out altogether.

She was expected to eat with the countess alone, or at least she had assumed that. What would the noblewoman think were Venus' intentions in such a wardrobe selection?

Venus suddenly found herself laughing at her exploits. What was she so worried about? The countess sent her here to borrow a dress, she picked one out. She might find a mild amusement in her choice but would most likely be uninterested in what Venus looked like in it.

Although, if she *did* care, Venus did not think she would mind...

She turned her attention to her hair, and wondered how she should fix it up. She had redone the simple bun several times throughout her stay here but had never given any thought to her appearance. It hadn't mattered until now. And that was when it struck her that she had never seen a mirror in this place.

Granted, she had only been in two locations up until tonight, but this was a bedroom. Surely there had to be something, even a hand mirror, but she knew from her previous investigation for matches that there was none. She fixed up her hair with muscle memory as best she could, then set her glasses back on the table. Wearing them to dinner would be like wearing her apron — they were a tool she used for painting, nothing more.

She took a deep breath and headed to the stairs.

...

The dining hall was much grander than was, strictly speaking, necessary. Even for a noblewoman, but especially one who lived alone. Or at least, Venus assumed it was grand. The candles along the table were the only light source in the room. Even the cloth which covered the table was a deep, dark shade of red, blending into the shadows so much that the candles appeared to be floating.

That was what coated the rest of the room — shadows. The darkness consumed the dining hall so much that Venus couldn't even make out the walls, as if she were in a vast pool or emptiness, with only the candles and countess in her seat to serve as a reminder that Venus was, in fact, inside of a room.

The countess sat on the other end of the table, so far away, Venus could barely make out her glass of wine. Her own cup remained empty.

It was then that she began to wonder who would be preparing the night's meal. Did her cook live elsewhere, and come only in the evenings? But if that were the case, Venus would have seen them by now, and she would not have had to resort to eating up the greenhouse.

Her head had been spinning with so many questions since she had first arrived, she had almost forgotten how dizzy it made her. She resolved to remind herself that it was only one more night in this place, and then she would leave forever, including all of her unanswered questions.

There was a loud *snap* which rang throughout the dining hall. It made Venus bolt her head straight up, as if she anticipated being struck by lightning. But she saw only her countess, fingers held into the air.

A large, silver platter was brought to the table. It had happened so quickly that Venus had failed to see who had delivered it. She peered around anxiously from side to side, wondering just who the other person in these walls was.

The countess snapped again, and more dishes were brought to the table. Venus strained her eyes but saw only the vague outlines of hands as dinner was placed down. Did these hands come attached to bodies? Did these bodies speak and ache and bring life into this silent, dark house?

When one of these hands came close enough to Venus to pour her wine, she let out a small gasp. It would have been louder, but she swallowed it down. The arm stretched out from the darkness, like a tendril from the shadows. The hand itself was dark, and yet Venus could see right through it. She could see the wine in the bottle being poured through its grip.

It took a moment afterwards until she felt brave enough to look at her plate, but she realized right then how starving she was. To her surprise, the food looked immaculate. Some type of bird, skin cooked into a deep, brown crisp. More vegetables but seasoned and boiled down. And then some sort of strange, white squares. Venus poked at these, thinking they were a type of bread. She peered up slightly and noticed that the countess had become still again. Watching her.

She didn't want to appear rude, so she stabbed at one of the little squares with her fork and inhaled it before her instincts could tell her otherwise. It was then that she recognized the taste of potato. But the texture was different, not dissimilar to bread, as she initially suspected. How interesting to cook it like this.

"How do you like it here, Lady Venus?" The words echoed around the room.

Venus paused. In truth, she hated it here. This was the first time she put it into words within her head, but it was true. She despised this place, with its cold, hard floors and dim lights. The strange plants which guarded every window. And a mistress who never seemed to rest or eat.

Even now, Venus noticed that there was no food on her own plate.

"It's a lovely home," she answered, the fib slipping off of her tongue with ease. "Very rich in its history."

The countess let out an amused sort of hum. She took another sip from her glass. "My family has lived here for many generations. The sarracenia plants which still grow here, were named after us."

Ah, so that was one of the exotic plants Venus had seen.

"What is the significance of this plant?" she asked, hoping she didn't come off as impertinent.

"It's carnivorous," she said as if she had just shared the world's greatest secret. "It lures in insects with its bright colors and secretions. Once its victim comes close enough, they fall into a pit of acid and are digested."

What a horrifying idea. She had never heard of a plant which ate insects, that seemed to go against the very nature of plants.

"What made your family want to grow such a thing?"

The countess smiled, but bit at her bottom lip and moved her gaze, as if mulling over her next words. Venus' eyes remained on her lips, watching as it pulled out from under her teeth, popping back into place.

"Oh...I guess you could say we felt a certain *connection* to it."

Venus didn't understand, but she felt no need to pry.

"Where is your family now?"

She hadn't meant for the question to come out, but now it was there in the open. She couldn't bear the secrecy of this place or her hostess any longer. She had to know at least one thing about the woman she had been painting.

"Long gone, I'm afraid." She did not sound afraid. "My mother and I were the last of us. And now it's just me."

That pang of pity came back with a vengeance. Venus was struck now with thoughts she hadn't allowed herself to think about in years. Thoughts of her own family, their traditions, their meals. Once again, she felt a sense of kinship towards this countess. Different walks of life, for certain, but not everyone knew the burden of being the last of a line.

"I'm sorry to hear that," Venus said, unsure if her pity was wanted or appreciated. When the countess did not reply, she then asked, "and you never married?"

"Why in the world would I do that?"

A part of Venus wanted to protest. But she understood the sentiment. The countess was living comfortably, with everything under her own name. In her position, Venus would also be hesitant to hand all that over to a husband.

"You're frightened of me."

The statement hung in the air like a criminal from the noose. Venus had just placed another one of the potato breads into her mouth, and now she did not wish to be done with it. She would have kept it in her jaw forever if it meant not responding to what the countess had said.

Alas forever was over in only a few moments.

"W-what?"

"Don't try to lie," the countess went on, taking another sip of her wine. "People are often afraid of me. It hangs over them. The way they act, speak, even the way they breathe tells me the truth."

She kept her eyes on her wine glass, and ran her fingers over the edge, which created a high pitched yet not unpleasant sound. She no longer seemed to be addressing Venus.

"It's fascinating to read people like a book. Do you know, you can tell when the bourgeoisie marry below them? There's a way which noblemen act that you have to be born into. When they marry and dress up their spouse, you can still see the poor person behind the fanciness.

"I think they're aware of it, at least. I think they can also read this because they can read me. People see me and know I am to be feared, even if they are unaware of my title. It's the ones who aren't afraid which torment me. I can't get a read on them, and yet, they seem to easily dissect me."

The countess sat there silently, then. Venus was unsure if she was meant to respond.

"I see, mistress." She answered, hoping it was a generic enough acknowledgement.

Venus didn't care if the countess kept talking. It would be if she wanted a response that the artist would find herself in trouble.

The countess gazed into her wine as if she were trying to scry from its contents. Venus looked into her own wine, contemplating doing the same. She stared at her reflection, watching it move and morph inside the liquid. The first time she had seen herself in weeks. She looked tired. Her eyes had sunken in and developed the faintest shade of purple beneath them. Her cheeks had hollowed in a bit, making the bones stick out.

It was then that she noticed she had been given white wine as opposed to red.

"I don't tell you this to give off the wrong impression," the countess went on. "I know you are afraid of me, as well, you should be. The whole town fears my title."

Venus was not intimidated by the countess' power, even though she kept a safe distance and responses short. She had served nobles before; she knew how to handle them the way an animal tamer understood dangerous beasts. It was everything around the countess which unnerved her. This place, the plants, the lack of real light. The lack of real life, for that matter. As though the garden around the building were sucking it out and keeping it for themselves.

"But I do have an offer which you should consider."

Now that got Venus to look away from her wine glass.

"What is it, mistress?"

The countess took another sip, letting Venus know that she was in no hurry to answer, and that they were acting on her time.

"I want you to be my official painter."

Venus' throat went dry. Stay here? The rest of her life, painting in this dim light, with this unnerving countess? Her first reaction was to reject the offer, but three things ran in her mind simultaneously.

One was the most obvious — her threat. If Venus was not tactful, what exactly was this noblewoman capable of? The food, which still sat in front of her, had been handed off by nearly invisible, clearly inhuman sources. Were they still here, hiding in the shadows, listening to how this conversation would play out?

Second, and most selfishly, was the title the countess had used. *Official* painter. Venus thought back to the reason she had left in the first place. She did not know what she had anticipated. She did not know if she would succeed or fail, and what would happen afterwards. She had merely wanted to paint.

Yet she *had* succeeded. More so, she had succeeded where several other artists had failed. And now she was being offered the position she had coveted for years. Yes, this place was dark and cold, it made her skin crawl, but had she been truly happy before? And would she be able to find success like this again?

The countess was right. This was an offer she *should* consider.

The third and final thought was less of an idea and more of an emotion taking form. That strange connection she felt between the two of them. That underneath their differences, they had something in common.

These thoughts swirled around in her head and pooled down into her stomach. She could taste the potato-breads sneaking back up her throat.

"Your answer?"

Venus was brought back to the room. "Can I...may I think about it?"

"It's a simple question," the countess retorted, slamming her wine glass down onto the table. "Yes or no. What is there to think about?"

Why was the countess in such a hurry for an answer?

"Then..." Venus treaded lightly over the subject. "May I ask some questions? About the role?"

The countess did not give a verbal response, but she dipped her head slightly to give a nod of encouragement.

Venus thought of where to begin.

Which question would be the least offensive to her? She decided it would be best to start with self-reflection. To gage with whatever it was the countess found so fascinating about her.

"Why me?" she asked. "What did I do differently from the other artists which pleased you so?"

It was a question which had plagued her mind. Once again, the countess took a sip of her wine.

"Do you really doubt your own skills so much?" She replied as she pulled away her glass, licking up at a single drop pouring down her chin.

The flash of tongue was a surprise to Venus. Most noblewomen would have used a napkin rather than make such a display.

"It's not that," she replied. She began to shift her hands together. "I'm just curious."

She heard the countess let out a sigh. A long, whoosh of air as she reclined in her seat.

"Do you know your mother, Venus?"

That was the last question Venus was expecting. What a full question it was, indeed. So much so that she began to truly ponder it — *did* she know

45

her mother? There was a time when she would have said yes, easily.

"Well?"

"Yes." She replied, opting to take the question on face value.

The countess hummed. "And have people ever remarked on your resemblance to her?"

One had, yes.

"They have."

"Then perhaps you can understand," she brought her hands up, gesturing towards herself. "Imagine, if you will, a lifetime of never seeing your face. You can touch it, memorize all of your features, but the only true visual you have is the woman who gave birth to you. And she is the most beautiful woman to have ever walked the earth."

Venus didn't know if she thought of her mother as beautiful. She didn't think she was ugly, but she had also never given the matter much thought. Her mother had looked like her mother. That was it.

"So, what do you do, you hire a painter to capture that beauty." The countess went on. "For your mother, there is success. You can see plain as day that the painting is equally beautiful. And you have also been told your whole life how much you look like this woman. So then, why is every painting commissioned for yourself utterly plain?"

Something about the countess' words stuck out to her. What had she meant by a lifetime of never seeing her own face?

She was on the verge of asking this herself, when the countess continued, "surely you must at least understand what it is like to not be seen as wholly yourself."

The words stung, even though Venus could not quite articulate why.

"What...what do you mean?"

The countess gave her a look which implied that this was the wrong thing to have said.

"Come now, don't play coy," she replied. "You think I'm ignorant of the implications of being a female painter? You think there have been many before you?"

Venus knew of other female painters, she had trained alongside them. But it was one thing for a woman to learn how to paint. It was another entirely for her hobby to be taken seriously.

"Was I..." she didn't know where she found the courage to ask. "Some sort of a last resort then?"

The countess chortled, a most unbecoming sound for a noblewoman. Then her voice rose into a full-on laugh. It echoed around the room.

"It's a good thing you worked out, isn't it?" She asked, smile larger than Venus had ever seen. "Which is why I'm so determined to have you on my staff."

The air went dry, so much so that Venus felt compelled to take a drink, less she coughed. The wine dribbled, then she picked up her napkin and wiped at her mouth. She felt the tension in her muscles, and while her stomach was in knots, she decided she would rather do something with her hands than sit idly. She picked up her silverware and began to cut into her food once more.

"Although..." the countess continued. "I wouldn't quite say that. I had my doubts regarding a female painter, certainly. But I thought that maybe you could see something that the others couldn't."

Venus swallowed down another bread-potato. "What do you mean?"

"You know what I mean."

She heard the scraping of wood against wood. She looked up to see that the countess had stood up from her seat. Her heart pounded against her ribcage, trying to break free, and somehow, as the countess moved slowly towards her, Venus felt that the noblewoman knew.

"You can feel it, can't you?" The words were a whisper, but Venus heard clearly. The countess was halfway down the table's length at this point. "The similarities between us."

Venus opened her mouth, only to be greeted by silence. Her voice was trapped inside her throat, caught between her lips and her heart. When it was finally released, there was a crack to it.

"I'm sorry...I don't understand."

There was no response, because there didn't need to be. They both knew it was a lie.

And then, the countess was at her side. Or rather, looming over her. One hand was on the chair, and the other on the table, dangerously close to Venus'. The pulse inside of her wrists quickened, she didn't understand why. The countess had been closer to her earlier when she had embraced Venus. But this was different. The hug earlier had been a sign of comradery. This was...

The countess leaned in closer, so Venus could feel her breath against her cheek as she spoke.

"You see something in me which others don't..." her breath was the only warm thing about her, the rest of her body soaking up the warmth around it like the sun evaporating water. And yet Venus' body felt as though it were on fire. "And that frightens you."

Venus realized that she was indeed afraid. Of what, she could not pinpoint. She only knew that her own breathing had increased, deep and heavy, trying to mask out how loudly her heart was beating. Her bosom swelled inside of her corset, and she thought about earlier in the night, when she had pondered over the countess' reaction to her choice of attire. What was she thinking now, staring down at Venus, with her chest exposed?

The worst part was that she did not want this to end. The rush of emotions flooding inside of her, filling her up with more adrenaline than she had felt for years. Perhaps even ever. She didn't know what she expected to happen. But she wanted it.

"Have you thought over my proposal long enough?" The countess whispered, her lips right at the top of Venus' ears.

Venus thought about how she had run away from her last residence. If needed, she could run away from here, too. She thought. But would she ever be offered another opportunity such as this?

"Well then... yes."

"Good."

There was a tingling sensation against Venus' neck. She tried to peer down but found that she could not move. The feel sensation trickled up and down her throat, filling it with heat, caught somewhere between pain and rapture.

Then it was over.

The countess moved away, heading back to her seat. Venus was left there, breath coming out in big, heavy gasps. And the feeling that something was now missing inside of her. As if the countess had reached into her and hollowed out her body, leaving behind the husk of an artist.

Only one thought remained in Venus' mind.

'What have I done?'

The countess had resumed her place at the table and picked up her wine glass once more. Yet when she went to take a drink, the wine appeared...

...stuck. At first, Venus thought the light was playing tricks on her eyes, but the countess tipped her head back, and still the wine refused to move, desperately clinging inside the glass.

She inspected its contents, before throwing it to the side. It must have hit a wall, because Venus had jumped at the sound of glass breaking, but it had been swallowed in by darkness.

"I need a fresh top off," the countess announced. She raised her eyebrows. "You?"

Venus looked down at her own glass, white wine still halfway full. She declined the offer. The countess took no offense, and raised her hand to snap again. Venus braced herself to once more see those disembodied hands.

Yet instead of a bottle, they brought out a large, silver dish, and placed it in front of the countess.

"A curious name you have," the noblewoman said. "Venus."

She didn't understand the change in subject matter, but she held her tongue.

"It surprises me that you were unaware of my carnivorous plants. In particular, my Venus fly traps."

Even though she had no way of knowing which was which, Venus pictured the plants with the sharp teeth and jaws that snapped shut, and she knew these were the plants the countess was referring to.

"My name is Greek." She answered.

She hoped the countess would not ask any follow-up questions to her statement, that she would have no interest in learning anything more about Venus' family. Fortunately, that seemed to be the case.

"I am aware," the countess replied, her fingers tapping. Not in a hurried manner, as one might do out of impatience or stress, but rather, her fingers moved down slow and deliberate. One at a time, hitting the table with precision. "A sarracenia and a Venus, all under one roof."

For the first time, they shared a smile. Venus appreciated the context enough to be in on the joke.

"But Venus," the countess went on, interrupting her thoughts. "Make no mistake about your place here. I extended an invitation, and you accepted. Never forget that."

Her fingernails hit against the table once more. The strumming of it vibrated against the table. Venus thought she could feel it all the way from her side, but it must have been her mind playing tricks. Still, the sound of it was steady and loud.

It rang inside Venus' ears, until she realized that she could no longer hear her own heartbeat. She panicked but couldn't move.

Why couldn't she move?

Thump.

Thump.

Thump.

"And never..."

Thump.

Thump.

Thump.

"Forget why it is you fear me."

A shadow hand stretched out to the table, over the silver platter, and removed its cover. Venus looked with curiosity, anticipating another bird or perhaps a pig. At first, that was what her brain had concluded she was looking at, for that was an answer which made sense. What she was actually looking at, however, took her much longer to comprehend.

It simply could not be real. It was too wrong to be real.

Yet no matter how many times she blinked, the image did not change. And then she truly began to react. Her mouth opened as her jaw went slack. Once again, no sound came out. Still, her lips opened as if her jaw were broken, and then her voice came, loud and clear as she screamed into the night.

Displayed on the table was a human head.

The skin was yellow from decay, its mouth sunken in so the individual teeth were each visible. The tongue flopped over like a slug, and the eyes were curled back so the pupils hid behind the skull. Even then, they were more red than white.

No thoughts were cohesive inside Venus' mind. They were more like half-formed conceptions, hardly even words.

She continued to sit there and scream as the countess raised a new glass, smiling wide.

Chapter 6

Eva

Eva drew with a stick into the dirt as her two aunts tended to dinner. She was meant to help with this chore, but only her mother demanded immediate assistance. Her aunts, it seemed, were the only adults in Eva's life who still viewed her as a child. She did not wholly care for this, but when they allowed her extra time to draw before chores, she took advantage.

Still, she kept the stick drawing to herself. She had yet to tell anyone about the sketchbook, and she planned to keep it that way. There was a close call once, when her cousin had asked her to draw an interesting looking frog perched near the brook, but she had managed to convince him to skip rocks instead.

She thought about going back to town, finding the man — the Baron — who had taken her sketchbook and asking for it back. But when she thought of the way he had looked at her, she became so ill at ease that she couldn't move.

Her mother's voice could be heard approaching, and Eva moved quickly to scrape over the sketch with her hands and feet. She ran around the caravan to greet the three women.

Immediately, her mother's reaction was that of exasperation. "Why haven't you been helping?"

"But I was helping." The lie was reflexive, even though she knew it wouldn't work.

"With such filthy hands?"

Her mother walked over and took hold of her wrists, inspecting them. Eva looked at her aunts, who bowed their heads in silence.

"What were you doing in the dirt?"

"I was trying to make clay statues again."

She had thought long and hard about the excuse. It was the best one she could think of, but she knew she only had a few instances to use it before everyone would start to notice that these alleged statues never manifested.

Her mother sighed.

"Eva, please, keep your art in your sketchbook. That's why we bought it for you."

She let go of her wrists, and Eva turned to walk over to the stream to wash them off. As she left, she could hear her aunts talking.

"You need to let her express her creativity, she has a gift. We all know this."

"It doesn't come along every generation. You," her aunt said in reference to her mother. "You make beautiful jewelry, but I have never seen you sketch the way she does. And so young. Where does she get it from?"

"Her grandfather was a woodcarver and blacksmith," answered her mother. "He made all sorts of things that way."

Eva knew this to be true. She herself had many small, wooden trinkets lying by her head at night. She liked to think that they were her grandfather's messengers, watching and protecting her.

She wished she had known her grandfather long enough for him to have taught her. She had tried her luck with woodcarving, but to no avail. She had cut herself multiple times, and even when she managed to finish something, it never looked the way she wanted.

"What about on her father's side?"

This stopped Eva dead in her tracks. She tilted her head back, trying to get her ears closer to the conversation without moving her body.

"My husband was no artist," her mother answered. "You know that."

"No," her aunt replied. "Not him..."

Every drop of blood inside Eva chilled, causing goosebumps to take over her skin. Her aunt went on, but she never heard the rest.

"Eva!"

Her mother's angry voice shocked her out of the trance, leaving her standing on the earth once more.

"What are you still doing here?" Her mother came around the caravan, bending over as she scolded Eva straight to her face. "Supper needs to get done, and you are filthy!"

Eva muttered some apology, but it was hardly audible over the memory of her aunt's voice, saying over and over again:

'No, not him...'

...

Later on that night, Eva found herself lying on her back, eyes wide while everyone else slept on. Her brother snored, her sister occasionally spoke nonsense in her dreams. And her mother slept soundly, as quietly as the dead.

Her aunts were most likely asleep in the caravan besides theirs, with her cousins bundled up between them. All asleep. All but Eva.

None of them had the plague she had encountered this afternoon. None of them had the questions which had been stirring around in her head for hours.

Eva tried to think back to her father, or the man she had thought of as her father. He had lived long enough for her youngest sibling to be born, and then that was it. His soul had been demanded back. She did not have distinct memories of him, but there were fragments.

She remembered the pitch of his laugh, low and melodious. He never chuckled, not in her memory. He either laughed heartily, or not at all. She remembered him smoking his pipe at the end of the day, and the way he would pat her back when she sat down beside him.

Eva turned her head and glanced over at her siblings, who she realized must have known even less about the man.

'No, not him.'

Just what had been meant by that? Eva did not doubt that her mother could have had other suitors prior to marrying, but if she understood the phrase correctly, then Eva's father had not been her mother's husband. Which made no sense, and she must have misunderstood her aunt.

But what else could it have possibly meant?

Her brother gave out an especially loud snort, causing Eva to jump. For a brief moment, she wondered if her worries and thoughts had transcended past her mind and into the room. She turned away from her family and forced herself to think of something else. She thought of climbing trees, catching fish, the shape of a person's face — and every time her thoughts went back to her aunt's words, she shoved them back so hard until her body eventually wore itself out enough for sleep to drag her away.

...

The rest she got did not prove to be fruitful. Eva awoke the next morning feeling more tired than she had the previous night. Everything she did was automatic – her body moving her around, getting dressed, eating breakfast, helping her siblings...all the while, her mind was miles away.

No one seemed to take notice, until they had begun to wash the dishes, and she sat there with a single plate in the water, unmoving, for several minutes.

"Eva," her mother inquired, voice gentle. "What's wrong?"

Eva stuttered, sounds coming out of her mouth without constituting as actual words. She almost dropped the plate she had been holding. She set it aside before attempting to continue.

"I..."

It made sense to ask her mother directly what her aunt had meant yesterday. But how could she? She measured her options.

Would the scolding from her mother be worth the knowledge gained? Would it be only a scolding? Would it be knowledge she actually wanted?

More pertinently she did not have an alternative answer to give. Her head had been empty, save for this burning question.

She wanted to think about anything else.

"Yesterday," she started. She stared up at her mother, who returned the gaze in expectancy. "What did auntie mean when..."

As if summoned, her aunt began to yell out to them. They turned to see her, skirts pulled up high as she ran across the land to them.

"You need to come quick!" She addressed only to Eva's mother, who immediately stood up and ran back to the caravan.

Eva remained seated at the brook, turning her head towards her family's camping ground. She had anticipated one of her siblings or younger cousins to have been injured, or a fire broken loose.

What she saw was much worse.

There was a carriage. A fancy, expensive looking one. Even though there was seating for one, maybe two passengers at the most, it was still larger than her family's whole caravan. It loomed over them like an omen.

And out from the mouth of this carriage, stepped the Baron.

Eva's heart quickened to the point where she felt dizzy. Her cheeks flushed and her stomach threatened to empty itself. She thought she might faint, and vaguely, she wished she would. It would be an escape from this moment.

Instead, her legs kept on moving, so that the carriage and the Baron became closer and closer. The ringing in her ears rushed louder and louder, screaming at her, begging her to turn around and run. That was when she realized it wasn't her own thoughts yelling, but her mother.

"You cannot be here!" She pointed to where the city ended. "Get out!"

Eva had known her mother to be headstrong and strict around her family, but she could not believe the force which she used against this man of power. Her mother, who had sold trinkets and begged from Gadje, who had thanked and smiled even when they spat at her, who did what she had to do to keep her children fed.

This woman was now red in the face, her eyes squinting with tears, spittle dripping from her mouth. Her hair stood up a little, as if trying to make her appear bigger than she was.

Her features resembled less her mother, and more the gargoyles on the church.

Eva managed to walk up behind her, the anguish inside her residing slightly as she felt a sense of protection. The Baron, on his part, gave no visible reaction to her mother. He did not see what a force of nature she was and instead treated her the way all Gadje did — as a nuisance.

"I'm so sorry, madam," he replied, his voice cool and measured.

It was the first time Eva had heard his voice since their last encounter, and it immediately made the world colder. She had her head facing downward, wishing she could sink into the ground. Even then, she knew he was staring at her.

"I don't mean you intrude on your...lovely home. But you see, I am merely here to return this."

Eva heard a shuffling sound, but still she did not look up. She knew what he was handing over to her mother, and the expression she would be wearing while collecting it.

"Your daughter is very talented," he went on. "Tell me, who is her teacher?"

There was silence, so heavy that Eva could feel it pressing down on her shoulders. Even her mother had been shocked out of her voice. Then, finally, there came the small reply.

"She has no teacher."

Eva did not recognize this woman. First, a gargoyle, and now a mouse. Was she to protect Eva from this man, or not? Perhaps out of disappointment, or anger, Eva found the courage to look up. Her mother's hands clung to her sketchbook, showing the veins beneath the skin. She too had her gaze lowered, now.

"None?" He lifted his voice to give the impression of surprise, but the way he stretched out the word indicated his falsity.

"We are more than capable of teaching our own children!" Her aunt yelled over. Eva noticed how they kept a considerable distance, despite the venom in her words. She began to wonder where her cousins and siblings were, but she got her answer when she spotted little, spying eyes between the caravan sheets.

The Baron paid her aunt no mind. "You let a talent like this go to waste?"

What did that mean? Her family had saved up a long time for that sketchbook. They sometimes told her she spent too much of her focus on it, and needed to attend to chores, but how was that a waste of anything?

There was a gasp, so foreign to Eva's ears that she did not realize right away that it had come from her mother.

"Don't mock us!" She cried, a single tear pouring down her cheek. "Just leave!"

"Now, now, my dear woman..." his eyes shifted back and forth between Eva and her mother.

They had been called worse things, but there was something especially disgusting about him referring to her mother as his 'dear woman'. As if he had ownership over her. Gadje saw them as less, but Eva had never heard them call her family property.

"I come bearing an offer, one which I think would suit you and your... humble family."

Her mother gritted her teeth, and Eva wondered how much her tears were from fear and how much from anger, that she was somehow the gargoyle and mouse all in one.

"The girl deserves a proper teacher," the Baron went on. "She is not going to find that here."

For some reason, the first image to come to Eva's mind was her grandfather, how she had always believed he could have taught her ways to improve on her skills. Then, it occurred to her, she didn't really know why she wanted to improve her skills. She had her own personal ambitions, of course, but what exactly was her ultimate goal in the end? At most, she gave her sketches to her family members as gifts, which they always appreciated. The walls of her aunts' caravan were decorated with them. But the supplies had only ever cost her family money.

There had been times in the past when she had asked her mother if she could sell her sketches off to Gadje the way they sold her bracelets. But her mother had correctly predicted that they would not want their portraits drawn by a Romani girl.

Then she understood why her mother had accused the Baron of mocking them. Eva had two strikes against her in the art world – what would a teacher accomplish besides an even greater cost?

Still, despite the logic of the situation... Eva considered it. She imagined learning the secrets Gadje painters seemed to possess which made their work seem more dynamic than her own. She could learn how to accurately capture a human face, and understand what she was doing wrong when hers still looked like lines and shapes on paper. Oh, to even have the opportunity to use *paints*...

He held out his hand to her mother, which caused them both to recoil. Eva's fantasy died as she recalled the strong distrust she felt towards this man.

"May we speak alone?" He asked her mother.

"Get out."

"Madam, hear me..."

"Get. *Out.*"

Eva heard her mother yelp before she saw what happened. His grip had wrapped viciously around her arm, so that his knuckles stuck out from under his gloves. He pulled her in close.

Just as Eva had not recognized her mother while she had been shouting, she now did not recognize this man. His face was contorted with anger, jaw and eyes jutting out, bottom teeth showing as his lip flared back.

Two gargoyles were fighting over...over...*her.* Why were they fighting over her? What did this man want?

His words came out in a quiet snarl. "I have every right."

Her mother struggled in his grip, but when that proved futile, she stood up straight and matched his tone. "You have no jurisdiction."

He let out a laugh, so loud and unexpected that both her mother and Eva flinched.

"Who taught you that trick?" He asked, smile still broad. "You think you're impressing anyone because you know a big word? What else can you do?"

Her mother remained silent, but her eyes hurled daggers. At last, she ripped away from him. The spot on her arm which he had been grasping was now red.

"Fine, then." The Baron relented, his voice and face returning to its calm demeanor. "Let's have the girl choose then, shall we?"

Her mother's eyes went wide. "No...no please, don't!" She turned to Eva. "Run!"

At first, Eva's legs would not obey. She understood the word, agreed with it, but still she stood there. Then, something in her brain clicked, and her feet began to move. No sooner had she turned around, however, did she hear the Baron speak again.

"Stay where you are, child."

The fear of him pinned her in place, but tears began to form as an atonement of her betrayal. Eva did not turn around, unable to face either of them. She could hear her mother's sobs behind her.

"She was bound to find out sooner or later," said the Baron. "Now you tell her. Or I do."

More sobs was the only reply he received. The moments dragged out, as if time were purposefully being stretched to give more than its fair share. Eva begged and begged for it to end. For this man to go away and never come back.

"Very well. Child — "

"No, no..." her mother said at last. The tears were still evident in her voice. "I'll do it."

Eva heard crunching noises, and then a hand placed itself gently on her shoulder. It burned, searing, as the rest of her body numbed. It felt as if the spot being touched was now the only part of her which was real.

"Eva..." her mother said, voice cracking. She begged her to stop what she was doing, what she was about to say. "You were trying to ask me earlier, weren't you?"

'Please...' Eva wailed internally. 'Don't.'

"It is time you knew the truth..."

Eva thought about how her skin had always been paler than anyone else in the family. No matter how much time she spent in the sun, her skin never darkened as theirs, and by winter months her efforts were for naught. How her eyes had been a brighter brown. How much thinner her hair was.

"This Ga— this man. He is your father."

And there it was. The secret kept from the whole world. Now out in the open, as real as the earth and the air.

Eva felt weightless. As if these words could not possibly be true, but if that were the case, then she should not exist. So, the universe was pulling her away, in different directions, undoing its mistake.

It wasn't until the tears started falling that she felt her body around her again. It was some time before she felt her mother's embrace against her. And it was still some time more before it sunk into her that if she was still here, then those words must be true.

"I will leave you some time to decide," the Baron stated.

He was not compelled to tears. The earth had not slipped from him, time had not slowed down. How could the universe be so biased?

All Eva could think of at that moment was why. Why had this man come? Why had he ripped apart her world so vehemently? What did that make her?

Both she and her mother turned to watch as the Baron got back into his coach. He gave them one last look.

"Think about my offer," he said. "This is no life for one of my own."

With that, he closed the door and took off.

Chapter 7

Venus

Venus had not gotten out of bed for three days. At least, she assumed it had been that long. She had lain awake and fallen asleep three times, and that was her only measurement. She didn't want to sleep — every time she closed her eyes, she saw rotted, leathery skin and rolled back eyes — but she had no energy for anything else.

Her appetite had left her, as well. She had gone three days before without eating. Eventually, the sharp pain would dull down enough to be ignored, but she didn't even feel that much. She feared she may never eat again.

During this time, the countess did not come to check on her. At dinner, once Venus had managed to stop screaming, she had excused herself from the table and hurried up to her bedchambers. She had not seen her new mistress since.

She wondered if the countess knew she was alive, or moreover, if she cared.

Venus closed her eyes in exhaustion, then immediately ripped them back open as her mind played back the memory of the head yet again. Was that to be her own fate, then? Had the countess lured her here to simply allow her to expire in a guest room, to then feed off of her head? Her words plagued Venus' thoughts.

'Never forget why it is you fear me...'

There was a strong possibility that this was the case. Venus could only hope to beg her mistress to leave a window or door open so her soul may escape. An eternity trapped inside this place would be torture beyond words.

However, if the countess had wanted Venus dead, then why not kill her already? Venus had to remember that she had pleased the countess with her painting. That was her true use — deliver to the countess what she demanded, or die.

A bitter huff of a laugh managed to run past her lips. Wasn't that always the stake she was dealt with? Give the nobles what they wanted or perish trying. Well, she was never one to give up so easily.

That said, she had no intention of staying. The countess was not human; there was no alternative. Venus could not expect to be safe here forever. Escape would not come easily; it would take time and resources. She had to figure out each and every move before making them yet never arousing her mistress' suspicions.

And again, she had reminded herself that she had already pleased the countess. She just had to keep on pleasing her in the meantime. This gave her an idea. With a sense of renewed energy which she hadn't felt in days, Venus sat herself up and pulled the sheets off of her. She walked over to where she had left her apron.

She still had yet to find any matches for the candles, but her eyes had grown used to the darkness. A quick rummage through her pocket had confirmed what she had already known — she was running out of paint.

Asking the countess if she would be permitted to town to gather more supplies was a risk in many aspects. At best, the countess may insist on having someone else bring them to this place, or there was a slim chance she already had more supplies tucked away. At worst, she would grow immediately suspicious and...

Venus couldn't finish the thought.

She got dressed and braided back her hair as best she could and then made her way out. As soon as she left the room, however, the first flaw to her plan occurred to her. She had no idea where the countess was.

Or rather, she had no idea where her bed chamber could be located. Venus peered around the darkness, recalling how the first time she had come here, she made the assessment that the rooms each circled around the great room below, save for a single hallway which led to the fireplace. It was no bedroom, but —

A gush of inexplicable wind flew by, tickling her skin. She recalled the hands and their invisible owners within the shadows, and she became afraid.

Without a second thought, Venus raced down the hallway. As she ran, she imagined those hands reaching out for her, grabbing on and pulling her into the darkness, trapping her soul inside her corpse for eternity. She kept her eyes forward, on the door which still lay slightly ajar, showcasing its fiery contents.

She slid right into the door, and it swallowed her inside the room. The light, while still dim, was much brighter here than any other room, and it took her eyes a moment to adjust. As water began to leak from them, Venus pulled off her glasses and wiped them away with her sleeve.

"I was wondering when you would come out," a voice said coolly.

Venus thought she would be relieved that her search for the countess had been so brief, but that was the furthest from the truth. She put her glasses back on and looked up at this woman, who never slept and placed rotted heads on her tables. The smile she was giving Venus now was the same one she had given at that dinner, as she had watched Venus scream and scream.

The imagery still did not make sense to Venus. Even though she had witnessed it herself, she could not fathom that this was the same woman she had painted for weeks on end. This woman with her strange, hypnotic stare and bright red lips. This woman whose beauty was an acquired taste, but once discovered, could not be unseen.

Venus had watched many ugly things happen in her life. Why couldn't she believe one more?

"My apologies, mistress," she said once she had caught her breath. "I was umm..."

"Do not bore me with petty details," the countess interrupted, turning away from Venus to stare above the fireplace. "I had no less of an expectation from you at dinner, but it is important for you to understand who you are dealing with. There are few who know of my family's true nature and remain alive. Consider yourself at the highest honor."

By whose authority was this honor given? That had not been the first time she had asked this question. Nobility seemed to think there was something special inside their blood to appoint them to higher status. But who was *their* appointed?

She said nothing but bowed her head as she inched closer to the countess. Every step made her heart beat louder, until she was close enough that she was certain the countess could hear it. Right on cue, the noblewoman gave a small smile, and Venus felt ice in her blood at the prospect of her being able to read thoughts.

Would her plans of escape be for naught, then? No, if that were the case, the countess would have already done her in. This was a game. Venus just had to play along.

"Thank you, mistress." She answered. "I *am* truly honored."

They stood there a moment, both staring up at the painting. Venus did not know what the countess saw when she looked upon it. If she was admiring the craftsmanship or merely her own perceived reflection. Just the sight of it caused Venus' arms to ache. Her muscles remembered the process they had to endure for this painting, all of those nights sleeping on the hard, cold floor. She saw smudges of paint, smeared together in an attempt to create something.

And yet, even she had to admit, this was her best work. She had spent days to weeks prior on projects, but never before had she slaved towards something the way she had with this painting. Her sweat and blood, even her very soul, poured into every drop of oil. It had been the closest thing she had ever come to giving birth. Now it was here, not to please the world, but rather to please the monster standing next to her.

"I look forward to painting more for you," she started. The countess turned and gave a smile. A small one, but more genuine than her previous. "However..."

At that word, the countess' smile faded, and her eyebrows narrowed. Venus swallowed. There was no turning back.

"I am running low on paints." The countess' brows relaxed, and at that, Venus felt her heart vaguely return to normal pace.

"Of course," her mistress replied. "It is only to be expected. We shall leave for town by nightfall."

Venus felt herself sigh heavily. It had worked? Just like that? The countess hadn't even put up a fight. For the first time, she felt a shred of hope. Then, a revelation. It couldn't be that simple. The countess was not so stupid. A poisonous plant looks ripe for a reason.

Then, a second realization washed over her. The countess had said 'we' shall leave for town.

But Venus must have misheard. This was a simple chore, nobles did not bother themselves with such things. In an attempt to make sense of the situation, Venus momentarily forgot herself and thought that perhaps the mistress had meant the other servants would be joining her. Then the memory of disembodied hands came to mind.

The room began to spin, and Venus felt her feet give out beneath her. She outstretched her arms to find balance. She took in greedy gulps of breath and pushed these thoughts from her mind. The only way she was going to be able to endure this was by focusing her attention on survival.

The countess had her gaze fixed on Venus. Not with a look of concern or even annoyance. Instead, half of her lip was raised with amusement. As if Venus was putting on a parlor trick for her.

Venus was quick to pull herself back up, and continue the conversation at hand.

"Excuse me, mistress, perhaps I misunderstood... did you say that *we* will go at nightfall?"

"Yes," such a simple and blunt answer. And yet such a burden of complications it carried.

Was Venus' leash meant to be so short? How was she meant to respond? What reaction was the countess anticipating from her? Was it safe to keep asking questions? Or should she simply accept the explanation, and go back to her room to think?

"You are doing it, again..." the countess observed.

"Hmm?" Venus internally scolded herself for the mumble. Some nobles became offended when responses were made with colloquial sounds over words. But it was an instinctual reaction. "I beg your pardon?"

The countess gestured at her own head. "You are overthinking things."

Venus could feel her cheeks becoming hot. Half from embarrassment, but also out of fear. This revelation that the countess was picking up on her mannerisms did not bode well for the young artist. She decided it was best to speak her mind, rather than leave the countess to wonder and come to her own conclusions.

"I am not accustomed to my patrons joining me in the task of procuring supplies, is all."

The countess chuckled. Her red lips parted wide, and her throat shook as the hollow sound of it rang out into the room.

"Look at you," she commented. "Using such big words."

Revulsion twisted inside Venus' guts. Here was a woman who would place severed heads on her tables, passing judgements. Venus did her best to swallow it down, but the sickness merely switched into anger.

"In truth," the countess went on. "I don't often go into town, but it is good to make an appearance once in a while. Did you know," she suddenly became excited upon this next phrase, similar to a child becoming excited over the prospect of a treat. Her black ice eyes shone, and once again Venus felt her brain disconnect the person standing before her with the person who was at dinner three nights prior. "That once, I had been gone so long, that there had been a rumor going around town that I had died?"

She laughed again, her pitch higher and giddier. The joy of it was infectious, and Venus could not resist the smile which sneaked across her face then. Until she began to wonder just how long this countess would have had to refrain from social interaction for such a rumor to start.

"When I made a public appearance, I could see the disappointment in the crowd's faces!"

Venus had remained in the countess' company until her hunger demanded attention, and it was once more to the greenhouse for her. The seasons had changed, making the earth far colder than when she had first arrived. Yet the greenhouse remained the same, warm and inviting. Offering her nourishment and comfort. Her only friend here.

Then, she merely sat in her room and thought of escape. She had opened the windows once more, hands running through the plants, looking for a weak spot. But alas, they were far too thick for her to reach past, and even when she tried, the mouths shut so quickly and forcefully that her hand sprang back each time.

When that venture proved pointless, she once again investigated for matches. She checked every corner of her room, taking advantage of the little shreds of sunlight peeking through while she could. She even got down on her hands and knees, leaving no corner unchecked. Nothing.

At that point, the sunlight had begun to fade, and she knew it was almost time to meet back up with her mistress. She rummaged through the closet once more for a coat, then headed to the stairs.

It was not until she stepped outside that she realized this was the first time she had seen the front yard of this place since her arrival. Back then, she had come in the morning, and yet the sun seemed to have greyed out and died.

Now that it was night, the moon reflected off of everything, creating such sharp contrast between the shadows and light. The statues, still beneath their planted imprisonment, seemed to be staring at her. Watching her every move.

She walked down the stone path towards the gates, a sight which both horrified and relieved her. One day she would walk past those gates and never come back in. At least her horse was safe at the farm she had left it in.

Her mistress stood at the mouth of the gates, her own coat and hat on, complete with a veil. It would have hidden her features, but her skin was so bright that it gave her away. Especially her bright, red lips.

So entranced was she by the vision, it took Venus a bit of time to notice the carriage which awaited them. It was a luxurious piece indeed, made from dark oak and well-kept details carved intricately into the sides. More of those carnivorous plants clung to its side. It was rather on the small side, however. Venus stared and wondered how the two of them were meant to fit.

Yet that was not the strangest part. What Venus found most peculiar was the lack of horses attached.

"Are you coming?" The countess asked, forcing Venus from her thoughts.

Dare she ask? Would her mistress see the question as a blight against her intelligence? Venus found she could not contain her curiosity.

"Forgive me, mistress. But..." she gestured toward the front of the carriage. "How are we to be pulled into town?"

The countess did not laugh, but Venus still spotted the red of her lips curl up.

"Now don't you worry about that," she stated.

Her fingers snapped, and the door burst open. She stared at Venus expectantly. The artist felt her feet plant themselves into the ground with such firmness, they might have sprouted roots. Still, she knew she needed this and tried to convince herself that this carriage could not have been more dangerous than the place she had been staying in. She stepped inside.

The seats were hard and cramped, as she had anticipated when she looked from outside. Just like the manor, it was somehow colder inside than out. So much so that Venus kept her hands clutched around her elbows for warmth. Her breath showed heavily before her, like her very soul was trying to leave.

The countess was quick to follow, sitting with far more ease than Venus. Her fingers snapped once more and the door slammed shut, causing the whole carriage to jump slightly. Venus stared at her mistress, wondering what her next move would be.

The countess merely gave a tap against the front of the carriage and said the words "carry on."

There was a loud crash outside. At first, Venus believed it to be thunder, even though she hadn't felt any rain. She shrieked as the carriage rocked back and forth, fearing that there were people on the outside, trying to get in.

But the countess remained still, save for the sway of the carriage, which against her appeared a gentle, ocean wave.

The wheels began to turn. It started slowly, as though it had not moved in quite some time. A newborn learning to crawl, it went only a couple feet from their starting point. Then, filled with renewed confidence, it took off.

Venus was pulled back into her seat. It was as if the wind was bellowing down, keeping her in place, despite the fact that the windows were closed. No, it was more like tugging. The seat was pulling her in, begging her to never leave, but to stay always.

The turns were worse. The curtains on the windows had been drawn, and Venus could not reach up to open them. This meant that she could never predict when the carriage would suddenly veer to the right, or the left, which caused her body to jerk violently every time. Her abdomen seemed to remain in place, but her upper body was flung about, her arms and head hitting harshly against the carriage's unforgiving wood.

When she felt that she could bear it no longer, that her skin must surely be black and blue, it all came to an end. The stop was not a slow easinge, but as blunt and sharp as the corner turns. Venus had felt herself lifted up in the air as the rear wheels found their place back on the ground.

Even when the countess had raised herself up and made way for the door, Venus sat there, hands tight in her lap as she breathed deeply. She didn't believe that the ride was over, that somehow this was also a trick, a way to lower her guard so it could rip off again with such ferocity that she would surely die.

It took her mistress turning back to her, black ice eyes and red lips clear still under the veil, to get Venus' attention. She willed Venus to get up with one look, and yet the artist could not budge. Her brain simply did not connect back to her body, and she wondered if the two had been pulled apart from the ride.

Then the countess' face softened. A sad, pitiful smile came across her face, and she held out her hand as one might do for a child who has scraped their knee. It took a moment of struggle, but Venus managed to raise her hand and place it into her mistress' palm. Her fingers shut around quickly, and the chill radiating off of her shocked something inside of Venus, so that she was able to get up.

The countess pulled her in closer. Despite the cold, Venus wanted to venture in. She could see those bright red lips parting beneath the veil, showing teeth as white as her skin. Her black ice eyes blinked, once, twice, and again.

Then she opened the door, and they stepped out. Once the countess had reached the ground, she released Venus' hand. She was left at the opening of the carriage, warmer but with a heavy sense of emptiness to her.

She did not dwell on it too long, however, because her gaze was caught by the night market. The town looked so different, lit up with torches and candles, the vendors out on the streets with their tables.

Her mistress did not stop to wait for her, and Venus pulled up her skirt to run after. As they walked into the street, the people of the town halted at the sight. A hush had settled over them as they stared in wonder at the Countess Luchia de Saracennia.

The noblewoman paused, acknowledging the shift in the atmosphere and her influence on it. Although Venus stood promptly behind her, she could sense her mistress' smile. It was the way she lowered her head slightly, a way to draw emphasis towards her red lips. Venus wondered if anyone could see them under the veil as she did.

Then her mistress took a step forward. The crowd had taken a considerable step back. The streets became clear of humans within a matter of seconds, parting like the Red Sea for her to step into. Venus did her best to keep up behind her. All the while they walked, she could hear the whispers of the town.

She could only make out a few words here and there, mainly *"she"*, *"what is"*, *"who is"*, and *"returned"*. Venus supposed she should have anticipated such a reaction. She didn't dare to glance towards them at first, but curiosity got the better of her. To her great relief, no one seemed the least bit interested in her. They had eyes only for the countess.

Even that began to worry Venus. Why had her mistress chosen to take them to such a place?

She doubted anyone here would be keeping oils. The only time she had seen paint like that was at more exclusive reserves. She could make the oil herself if needed. The gardens within the greenhouse did not house any of the plants she needed, and Venus was certain she would have spotted them by now. She could buy them dry and make the oil immediately, and then also buy seeds or roots so she could grow more.

The only thing she could not reproduce were the pigments. Those would require certain rocks and minerals, some of which were rare and difficult to find. Which made them very expensive, but if her mistress was willing to pay...

It was then that her thoughts shifted course. In her state of habit, she had begun to think as a painter only. She would not stay long enough to grow her own plants. Still, it may help to maintain the illusion to her mistress.

From the corner of her eye, she spotted a table selling herbs, and she immediately headed towards them, not thinking to check if her mistress was following.

"Do you have flax or linseed?" she asked.

Then, she got a good look at the person sitting at the table.

"Oh," Venus exclaimed. "It's you!"

There sat the young Romani girl who Venus had bestowed a peach to, weeks ago. The girl looked back, eyes darting up and down Venus.

"And it's you," she replied.

Although they were strangers, Venus felt so relieved to see some sort of familiar face that a smile broke out, followed by a cracked and dry laugh. She cleared her throat.

She opened her mouth again to speak, but the girl interrupted,

"I've got flax, but no linseed."

Venus nodded. It was a start, and she was not about to leave this booth now without paying for something. She fished around in her pockets while the girl huddled and wrapped the herbs. Then, to Venus' dismay, she realized that she had no more coins.

Having been trapped inside the manor for so long, never having to use money for her food and lodging, and having a countess as a patron, she had almost forgotten how the real world worked. She had no more peaches to give, and nothing to trade. Without any other option, she peered into the crowd for her mistress. The search was brief, for the instant she turned her head, there she stood.

"Venus," she said. Her voice was quiet, but over the silence of the crowd, it could be heard for miles. "What are you doing?"

The artist floundered. Her cheeks heated up as she lowered her gaze to her feet and fiddled at her apron.

"I was buying flax, mistress. For oils. But I haven't any money…"

The countess let out a cackle, which caused an uproar of murmurs.

"Darling, I have a supplier. We're going to him directly. There's no need for you to mingle around with vagrants…"

Venus felt her cheeks grow hotter, but not with embarrassment. Her eyes shot hot daggers into the countess as she boldly brought her gaze back up. If her mistress gave any indication that she noticed the fury before her, Venus did not see.

A few coins from someone like the countess would mean to this little girl the difference between a warm place to sleep, or a cold one. A night with a full stomach or an empty one. Yet *she* was the inconvenience.

But what could she say in opposition? Her mistress seemed to consider this, as she tilted her head. Waiting for Venus to give her an excuse. Then she turned to the little girl.

"Child," she stated. "Come here."

The girl looked to Venus, then at the countess, and back to Venus once more. Silently asking for a way out of this. Sadly, Venus had nothing to give. She gestured towards her mistress and felt her own heart break at the small betrayal. There was a long pause before the girl finally backed up her chair and stood up, making her way around the table and between the two women.

She kept her eyes on the ground as she waited before the countess, who stuck out her hand. At first, Venus thought that her mistress might have held coins in her palm, but a quick look revealed that there was nothing.

"I have always wanted to have my palm read." She said, and again Venus

71

felt a stinging sensation deep within her bones.

Must she be so blatant in her mocking?

The countess continued to outstretch her hand, going back into that state of stillness which Venus had become so familiar with. It must have frightened the little girl, for even now she hesitated. She reached out, and then pulled her hands back in, before attempting once more to take hold of the countess.

Her tiny fingers barely wrapped around when someone called out;

"My lady!"

Just like that, a man was standing between the countess and the little girl, arm striking down to shoo away their touch. His uniform announced him to be a guardsman, but it wasn't until he turned to glare at Venus that she recognized those red eyes. He peered at her, too, either in trying to place her in his memory, or to once again wonder as to what she was. Venus returned his glare, either way.

"What is the problem?" the countess inquired, her tone cool and soft.

The guardsman turned back to her, his aggressive energy dissipating.

"Forgive me, my lady..." he motioned towards the little girl. "This thief was in the process of robbing you."

"I wasn't!" The little girl yelled out, and Venus immediately felt tears in her eyes, as if someone had slapped her firmly across the face.

'No, child, don't speak! Don't give them the excuse!'

But the countess laughed. It was her dry, hollow laugh, except Venus could not determine who it was directed at until she spoke once more.

"Robbing *me?* Who would dare?"

An arrogant question, but one which might help the situation. It was a fair point to consider, even though Venus wished that her mistress would explain that it was she who had called the little girl over. It was foolish thinking, however, and she knew it.

"You cannot trust these people, ma'am." The guardsman went on. "It's a tactic they use. One will divert your attention, while another comes up from behind."

Where was this supposed partner in crime, Venus wondered. The countess laughed again, quieter than before, as though something in his words rang true to her. Venus looked to her, eyes pleading, hoping that beyond all measure, her mistress would at least take pity on a little girl. For her to recognize her power in this situation, and to acknowledge her innocence. If only once, just once, mercy could be shown to them, let it be to her.

It was hard to read the exact expression the countess wore while under the veil, but she was at least no longer smiling. She also was not looking at Venus, but rather, had her gaze fixed on the little girl, who in turn kept her eyes down. Her hands were at her side, unclenched, to show that she had nothing in them.

Venus wanted to approach her, say what she was thinking out loud, try and persuade the countess. But the guardsman stood between them, a warning that she could only make things worse with her interference. Why – why did they have to endure silence, and let their fate be put in the hands of others?

His patience, however, was the first to wear out. "Ma'am, what would you like to do?"

A soft hum came from the countess, and Venus noted how her lips became thin as she pressed them in contemplation.

"I am... not sure." She answered.

Her answer terrified Venus. This could be over, for better or for worse, but her mistress instead chose to drag it out. Like the thread of life being pulled slower and slower for a person so close to death, making an eternity of every second before at last ending their suffering.

"Not sure, my lady?"

She turned her gaze from the little girl to the guardsman.

"I am not sure if I want less of her in the world, or less of you."

Her words hung in the air, as thick and tangible as the fog hanging about them. The three of them stared at her, each with a different interpretation of what she had just said.

The guardsman spoke up first, again.

"I am... sorry, ma'am, I do not understand?"

"You care about your own laws, and I shall care about mine." She stated, as if she were explaining an obvious concept. "I do not believe there is a living soul who would dare steal from me, but I care not for the affairs of men." She walked past him then, and over to Venus. "Occasionally, a few of you prove your usefulness to me. Arrest the child, if you are so keen to, it matters not what I say. However, my painter here seems fond of her, so I

73

shall play no part in this."

Venus could only stare at her. Between salvation and damnation, she was not sure where this answer lay. Yet with her so close again, Venus felt her skin grow cold, but her soul grew hot. Looking at her now, seeing past the veil to her face, she had gone from the upper class back to Venus' muse once more.

Venus did not know what she wanted, did not know how she could forget the little girl in a moment's notice by just being in proximity to her mistress. And yet that was what happened. Her mind simply would not turn the three into one — the artists' muse, the condemner, and the murderer.

How was this woman who had infuriated her now turned into something so enticing?

Then her mistress placed a hand on her shoulder and turned Venus away. The action should have engulfed her completely, but instead it woke her up. She turned back towards the little girl, who stood helplessly, joined by the guardsman in being dumbstruck.

Even as they walked away, the countess still did not remove her hand, and it did not take much longer for Venus to succumb to her spell. It was easier to give in. It was easier to focus on her beauty and this strange feeling than the brokenness of the world.

Venus looked over at her, transfixed by her features once more, calculating them in her mind, the shapes and colors of the countess. She wanted to paint her again.

As they made their way down the street, a shriek rang out. Venus bolted her head around in time to see the guardsman bring down his club. The little girl screamed as he continued to strike her. She raised up her arms as a meager attempt of protection, but it meant that they received the brunt of his blows.

She continued to scream, only stopping to cough, and when she did, the streets began to glisten with red. Venus took off, running towards them, when suddenly her feet stopped. The wind had been knocked out of her body by the sudden refusal to move. She looked back to see her mistress, hands gripped firmly around her forearms.

"Let me go!" She had meant for the words to come out as a plea, but the anger in her voice had made them a demand.

She saw the countess' eyebrows raise with amusement. Venus tried to break free from her grasp, but it was like iron chains had been wrapped around her. The countess did not budge.

"We must keep on schedule," she explained calmly. "The sun will be up soon."

"I have to help her!"

This time, her words came out like begging. She stared back at the gruesome event, praying for someone, anyone, to step in and stop this cruelty.

The guardsman finally stopped hitting the girl, only to then grab the scruff of her neck and pull her upward. Venus let out a meek, scared little sound.

"I will take care of it," her mistress replied, yet as she spoke, she began to pull the both of them away.

Venus shrieked and fought. He was dragging the little girl away, now. She had to break free, she had to save her.

"I will take care of it," the countess repeated.

Chapter 8

Eva

Eva hadn't slept in three days. She stopped drawing, despite having the sketchbook returned to her. She could no longer bear to look at it, let alone hold it. Just the thought of it made her feel unclean.

She barely helped with the chores, which earned her the frustration of everyone around her. It was not that she lacked the desire to help. She simply lacked the energy for it.

Most of her days were spent with her sitting about, watching the clouds roll by. It didn't seem fair how unaffected the rest of the world was by this. How it could all look the same and move the same as if nothing had happened, meanwhile Eva no longer knew if her soul was attached to her body. Or if she had ever known her soul at all.

What was she to call herself, then? Was she still to keep the Rom traditions? Keep herself clean, her skirts low? Could any of it possibly clean out the Gadje blood inside of her?

She had a fantasy playing out in her mind. One where she took a knife and sliced at her hand, draining out half of her blood, so she could feel like herself again. Whoever that was. But Eva was not brave enough to attempt it, no matter how fervently the images played out in her mind.

She hated that man for coming, but the hatred she felt towards him was baseless. The real betrayal had come from her mother. The woman who had carried this dark secret inside her belly for months. The woman who had nursed her, clothed her, named her. The woman who had given her shelter and taught her the ways of their people.

The Baron had been unclean, yet her mother had forced that onto Eva.

The only time Eva got up to move was whenever her mother came near, for just the sight of her filled Eva with rage and sadness, a mixture of emotions too great for her to feel, so she either felt nothing or everything at once.

One day, she sat by the brook. The gentle noises it made with its turning helped to drown out the endless questions her mind wrestled with. She started to wonder, though, if it was deep enough for her to put her face into. If she could spread her whole body along it, let it wash over her again and again, if that would at last make her feel clean once more. She reached out her legs and dipped her toes into it.

The water was cold. So much so that it sent a chill up to her knee, and she jerked back. Then, it was as if something had snapped in half inside of her. Like that one touch from cold water had woken her up from a long, deep sleep. This touch was the first physical sensation she had felt in days.

She moved closer to the brook, dipping her legs in even deeper, welcoming the waters' cold sting against her skin. She began to laugh at the sensation, and once the laughter started, she could not stop. On and on it went, her lungs forcing it out of her like a cough. Louder she became, laughing harder and harder...

"Eva?"

Her laughter did not die immediately, but rather, it transformed into short huffs of breath, until at last she became silent. It was only then that she turned to face her mother.

She stood there with a container full of dishes for washing. She kneeled down next to Eva but did not encourage her to leave the water. Instead, she took out the first plate and began to wash it.

Eva watched her, acknowledging that this was the most she had seen of her mother since that day. How, in her mind, her mother had become a wisp of color and shades. But here, so close, she could see the little details which made her all the more real. The loose strands of her hair, the wrinkles on her face, the marks along her arms where the sun had kissed her.

Deeper still, she could smell her mother's scent. The smell of flax and spices. The smell of soap and sweat. Then the distinct smell which could only be described as her mother's. It brought back a flood of memories into Eva's mind, and suddenly she could not connect this woman with her betrayer.

Even so, she continued to silently watch on as her mother washed the plate.

"Why bother?" She asked bitterly. "I am making the waters unclean. I make everything unclean..."

She thought of her poor younger siblings, and her cousins, and how she had been sullying them unintentionally her whole life. Her family, her home, all of it tainted, because of her.

"Listen to me." Her mother's words were sharp. She did not touch Eva, but she came close as she looked her straight in the eyes. "You have never been unclean. You are a Rom, and my daughter. That man is not your father."

At the words, Eva became weightless. The stream could have carried her off in that moment, up to the clouds above, she was so relieved. But then her mother continued.

"He is the reason I became pregnant, but he is not your father."

How could her mother be so cruel?

She washed at the plate harder, even though she had been working on just the one this entire conversation, and it surely must have been finished by now. Still, she scrubbed away at it with such ferocity that Eva feared it might break.

"Why did..." Eva began to ask, for she was not so young or naive as to not understand where children came from. "Why did you let him, then?"

Her mother stopped washing the plate. She leaned over that brook, staring down into its waters. Eva wondered what was going through her mind when it occurred to her that what she had been staring at was her own reflection.

"I didn't," her mother said at last.

Eva did not ask her to elaborate, even though everything inside of her begged to. She let her mother breathe in this silence as she planned her next words.

"I was a dancer. Before any of you, before I met my husband. I would dance along the Gadje streets, with my cousins. Their husbands played instruments for us. Of course, Gadje would ward us away, but it was nothing we couldn't handle. We made enough to keep ourselves fed, that was all that mattered to me. I thought I was safe. I felt safe. Then there came that day.

"I knew who he was. I knew he was a powerful man, but I didn't think he would pay us much mind. Powerful Gadje only ever give us a glance or two but mainly keep their eyes on their own pockets. This one, however, stood around. He watched us as we danced. I thought it was a golden opportunity. I thought, if we can impress him, we will make enough to feed ourselves for a month.

"The others did not seem so enthused, but we danced on. What else could we have done? The only thing Gadje hate more than suspicious Roms, are Roms becoming suspicious of them. We were about halfway through the routine when I noticed something strange. I didn't want to admit it at first, I felt I was giving myself too much flattery. But he seemed to stare only at me.

"I gave him a smile, or two, and perhaps I shouldn't have. I was only thinking about the prospects. I was only thinking of feeding my family. After we had finished, he approached me. I thought he was going to give us a handsome sum, but instead he told me to come and walk with him. I didn't know how to refuse. Some of the husbands protested. I can't remember what they said. Eventually, I had no choice. I knew what he wanted, I wasn't stupid.

"We stepped inside his carriage, so no one would see us walking the streets. He didn't take me to his house, his wife was there. It didn't happen right away. At first, we were going for a ride around town. He asked me strange questions, but I can't recall them anymore. I only remember how I felt when he asked me then, and how strange I thought they were.

"Then, he gave me a drink. I'm not sure why. He already had me right where he wanted me, but I guess that wasn't enough for him. At first, I only pretended to take sips from it, but he checked the flask. I haven't had a drop of alcohol since that day, I can still remember the way it smelled. Sometimes, when I smell others drinking, I feel so sick that I have to lay down.

"He grabbed me, held me down, and forced it into my mouth, then held my lips shut until I swallowed. I fought him...up until I could no longer. I woke up on the streets, a long way from home. I never danced again."

As her mother spoke, she stared out past the brook, down to where the sky met the earth. The plate hung in her limp hand, forgotten. Eva had seen her mother like this only once before, back when her husband had died. Is that what had happened to her? Had a part of her died in that carriage?

Had a part of her died when Eva had come into the world?

She wanted to ask her mother something but realized she did not have the courage to. And her mother continued to say nothing.

Eva bent over, gently took hold of her mother's hand, and took the plate from her. It was only then that her mother began to cry.

...

Eva tried to find contentment in drawing what was around her. Placing her focus solely on her art helped to keep her mind from thinking of less pleasant things. It didn't heal the wound she felt, but it acted as a type of tourniquet.

All the same, the lands around them were far blander than what she could find in the city. She had no interest in sketching caravans or rocks, she had already drawn her family members numerous times, and woodland creatures never held still long enough for her to finish.

She flipped through her sketchbook to her incomplete portrait of Christ. Eva placed her charcoal to the paper, wanting to attempt to draw from memory, but the details were hazy in her mind. She drew them on anyway but then hated the sketch once she was done. The half which had been drawn with reference had detail which far outshined the newer parts.

She slammed her sketchbook shut and threw it gracelessly into the caravan. The charcoal stained her hands, but at that moment, she didn't care. How much dirtier could it truly make her? She balled up her fists and wrapped her arms around her legs as she pulled them in, resting her face into her knees.

"Eva?" Came a little voice. She looked up to see her two cousins staring up at her. "Are you coming with us to town today?"

The question was enough to coil her stomach. She felt something rise inside her throat, burning it. Then that man — the Baron — his face became so clear in her mind, his details, in such high clarity that not even the face of Christ could evoke. He might as well have been standing in front of her.

"No," was all she managed to say.

"Eva," they went on. She shushed them, not wanting to hear the question again. "Eva, why don't you draw anymore?"

What did they mean? She just had her sketchbook out. She had been studying the land around them for the past few days. Did they not see her working on those? She said as much, but they persisted.

"But those are little things. You don't come into town anymore to draw the church faces."

She tried to give them a reassuring smile, but she could hardly make those muscles work. "Sometimes people decide to draw different things."

They shrugged, seemingly losing interest as they ran off for one last game before the trip. That was when Eva noticed her mother behind them, arms folded across her chest, but without aggression. It was as if she was holding herself together. She approached Eva with careful footsteps.

"They are right, you know." She said, looking as though she wanted to sit down next to her daughter, but settled for standing in front of her. "Your soul is not in your work anymore."

Eva snarled at her, an act which previously she would never have dared. But there was nothing more her mother could do to her, and how dare she mock the one thing that kept her mind occupied.

Her mother simply sighed. "Eva, you listen to me, and you listen well. Even if you should never speak to me again, and you never heed my words again, you listen now. That man took several things away from me. You think I know nothing about what you are going through?"

Eva didn't answer.

"You cannot let this man take from you, too," she went on. "I don't know why he chose to come here and tell you the truth after all this time, but if you give up on everything that makes your soul, then you are giving him power over you."

Eva didn't understand. He was a Baron, he already had power over her, over all of them.

"Why did he have to be the one to demand the truth?" she asked, catching the shock in her mother's eyes. "Why didn't you tell me yourself?"

Her mother's mouth opened for her to speak, but no words came out. She closed her lips, and stood there with contemplation on her face. Then, she shook her head.

"There were so many times when I tried," tears were forming, but Eva remained unmoved. "I was never sure if you were ready to hear it. It was my own fault, I accept that. I wanted to protect you as long as possible. I was selfish. I'm so sorry."

Eva tried to recall if she had ever heard her mother apologize to anyone, let alone to one of her own children. Perhaps to her husband, but the memory of it was more fantasy than anything. This should have been a significant moment, Eva should have felt tears herself at the words. But instead, her insides were hollow.

Maybe the Eva of yesterday would have been touched by this exchange, but the Eva of today was not.

If her mother had had her way, how long would she have taken to tell her? Would she have waited until Eva was grown, married, ready to bear her own children? She would have allowed Eva to soil their blood as well?

Her mother was looking at her with anticipation, expecting a response.

"So?" Eva asked. "Was I ready to hear it?"

These did not seem to be the words her mother had wanted to hear, and it showed as her eyes faded and her brows knit.

"You tell me," she replied, her tone becoming harsh once more.

Eva got up from where she was sitting, prepared to walk away from the conversation.

"It shouldn't be up to me."

...

The days and weeks dragged by, simultaneously feeling too slow and too fast. Eva wanted there to be a pause in time, and yet, she also wanted this to pass. She didn't know how she would recognize when this era of her life would be over, if ever, but she craved it with all of her being.

She still mostly sat around by herself, not really contemplating anything, but rather, allowed things to happen around her. The whistle of the wind, the chirping of the crickets, the crackle of the fires...they went on without her.

She had not picked up her sketchbook since the conversation with her cousins.

Then, one day, they woke up to find her mother sick. Her siblings were prodding at her to get up from sleep, but she would only shake her head and pull the covers up higher. Eva got up herself and placed a hand on her mother's forehead. It blazed against her skin.

Some part of Eva which had been frozen until now began to melt. A great distress fell upon her. She had not forgiven her mother, but she had not wished ill will towards her.

She was struck with a thought. A horrendous, inconceivable thought. As soon as it had formed inside of her head, she had begun the work to kill it. But alas, it remained in her mind like a plague.

What if her mother was to die?

Eva looked at her siblings. Two small, fragile things who depended on their mother for everything. She thought of her aunts, how they were a touch older, their hair already starting to grey, and their movements a little slower. What would become of them if her mother was no longer here?

Would Eva have to be the one to care for them? She realized at once how selfish the question was, as she watched her mother lie there suffering, and all Eva could do was wonder how this might impact on her life.

But it was a question she had to ask, because it would inform her next move.

She hadn't felt the need to move in some time. Now, it was the only thing she could think about. Eva got to her feet, and climbed down from the caravan.

"What are you doing?" asked her siblings. "Where are you going?"

"To town," Eva replied as she fitted on her shoes. "I'm going to get medicine."

"We have herbs and tea here!" they protested.

"Yes, have our aunts boil some," she reached over to where her sketchbook and charcoal lay. "Get something into mother's stomach before the day grows hot. But it won't be enough to save her life."

"How will you get medicine?"

She did not answer, she merely tucked her sketchbook beneath one arm, and set off.

The town was busy with activity. Eva scouted out, looking for a corner to stand by. There were few spots they frequented, and she tried to guess which one may prove most profitable at this point in time. When she at last made her selection, she opened her sketchbook to a blank page.

"Excuse me, sir," she called out to a man passing by. He had a woman on his arm. "Would you like your portrait drawn?"

She held up her book, which seemed to earn the amusement of the woman, but the man only frowned. Eva tried to flip the pages, to show them in earnest what her capabilities were. But the man shook his head and pulled his companion along.

"It's one thing for a woman to think she can draw," she heard him say. "Let alone one of *them*..."

His companion laughed before they turned the corner. Eva felt her stomach fill with a burning sensation, but she swallowed it down with a smile as another pair of Gadje walked by. She gave her offer, and they turned her down.

She went on like this for quite some time, with most Gadje ignoring her, some declining with less than magnanimous vigor, and once a man threw a small rock at her, which she had shrieked at.

When the sun reached the high sky, she found herself ready to give up. She looked down at the sketchbook itself. Paper was not cheap, especially bound together like this. Perhaps she could pawn it off or trade it...

"Good afternoon." came the voice she had dreaded most to hear.

Eva could not bring herself to look up at him, but she turned towards his direction. All she saw were his freshly shined shoes and the bottom half of his cane. She attempted to return the greeting, but it came out as an unintelligible mumble. The Baron did not seem to mind.

"Dear girl, what are you doing on the streets like this, all alone?"

The question would require more effort in her response. She held up her sketchbook, as if that alone could answer him.

"I'm selling," she said, then realized the phrase made little sense without context. "Portraits. I'm drawing portraits to sell."

"Let me see how many you have done this morning," he didn't hold out his hand as much as reach over to take the sketchbook, but Eva stepped back.

"None," she replied with great haste. "None yet today."

She finally managed to look up at his face, pleading with her eyes for him not to try that again. He nodded and pursed his lips. Then he turned slightly, placing a foot up as if preparing to leave. Eva held her breath with anticipation.

"Come, child," he said, gesturing towards himself. "Walk with me."

Her heart sank. She peered around, looking for places to run. But she knew if she did that, she would be informally banished from the town forever. And she still did not have any medicine for her mother.

She remembered the story her mother had told her, how he had led her away. It was then that Eva noticed he had no carriage. It would appear that he intended to walk with her, out in the open. Granted, she was not naive enough to believe that Gadje would help her should she be in danger. But she also knew that powerful noblemen had a strict regimen regarding their reputation. He may not wish to tarnish it with violence.

What did this man want from her? Her...father? The word felt so foreign in her head. She needed to call him something else, the title did not seem fit for him.

Still, she stepped over to him, and the two began to walk down the street. Although they were side by side, she kept a considerable distance. Particularly from his cane. Eva kept her eyes darting about, keeping them on any open opportunities she may need to run. She could hear whispers around them, which was both a comfort and a concern.

Then, she began to recognize the route they were taking. Another left, then a right, and they would be at the church. Sure enough, that was where they stopped.

The Baron pointed up at the windows. "Your drawing of Christ, have you finished it?"

Eva bit her bottom lip, unsure how to phrase it. She supposed saying that she had wasn't technically a lie, so she stated as much.

He held out his glove-covered hand. "Give it to me. Let me see."

She stared at him for a moment. He wanted to hold her sketchbook, but not so much as to do it with his bare hands. She wondered what they must look like under there. The secret deeds he had committed, concealed by a stitching of leather.

Eva held up her sketchbook and he took hold. He flipped through it from the beginning, although he appeared to show no interest in the other drawings within. When he at last stopped on the one he had been searching for, his eyes loomed over it, sponging up every detail.

Eva realized that she was holding her breath. She inhaled quietly, not wanting to alert the Baron of her anxiety. She did not know why she felt this way. What did his opinion on her work matter? Yet despite the logical part of her mind saying otherwise, she found that indeed, she wanted his approval. As though it would prove...something.

He turned back to her, pointing at the sketch. "You forgot yourself, didn't you? Some of this is quite remarkable, and yet there are parts which wouldn't be worth wiping up filth with."

The words stung.

"I tried to remember the details, but I couldn't..."

He brought his cane up and bashed it against the cobble streets, causing a crack so loud, nearby birds were startled away.

"Try!" He repeated. "Try! If you cannot do something right, then do not do it at all!"

He threw the sketchbook, and it landed gracelessly on its spine, spilling open and showing off the face of Christ. Eva ran to pick it up, nestling it in her arms with the same care as one would give a newborn.

How the anger filled up in her then. How dare this man take her from the corner to the church, just to insult her work and toss it aside. The weeks she had wasted lying inside the caravan, letting life pass her by. She doubted very much that he had let the encounter impact his life so greatly.

Consequences be damned, she stood up to face him.

"I am doing the best I can with what little I have! If you could do half as well, then prove it to me now!"

He stood there staring at her long enough for her to regret the words. As he raised his cane so it now rested in both palms, she backed down and began to apologize. Her eyes darted around, searching for escape, but it was so open that if she ran he was sure to follow. Even if he didn't, he knew where she lived.

Eva bowed her head as she anticipated the blows soon to come. Better to get it over with now than suffer his wrath later. While she waited, gaze fixed firmly on the cobblestone, all she could think about was her mother. The woman who had raised her, lying sick in bed, most likely on her way to the grave.

She could see her aunts now, pulling her out into the open, letting her die in the fields so her soul did not become trapped inside her corpse. But she would die with Eva's anger latched onto her. She would carry for eternity the thought that her daughter hated her.

Eva felt tears in her eyes.

'Oh, mother...' she thought. *I'm so sorry it took me so long to realize I don't hate you. I was angry, yes, and that anger may never go away, not completely. But I do not hate you. Please don't die thinking that I hate you...'*

Her thoughts were interrupted by the last sound she had expected to hear. The Baron was laughing. A full throttle, hearty laugh. The kind that stops a man's breath. Eva found the courage, or rather the curiosity, to look upon him.

"Child!" He bellowed, a smile still broad on his face. "I do love your spirit! Come, come! Grab your sketchbook, and we shall have a closer look!"

Eva did not move. She tried to understand his words. She knew what they meant as a sentence, but she could not have heard them correctly. He made it sound as if they would be heading inside of the church.

"I cannot go in there," she replied, and immediately regretted speaking on two fronts.

One, was her phrasing. It wasn't that she was physically incapable of entering the church — she did not know if the Gadje God was the kind to strike lightning at the Roms who entered His domain. They certainly talked about Him as if that were the case. But whether it was Him or His subjects, she would not be welcomed within those stone walls.

Secondly, and this was the more important of the two, she had disrespected him again. She was not foolish enough to believe that his patience — or his amusement — would give her a pass every time.

But he looked her over her, as if he was truly considering her words. At last he nodded. "True. Yet I think they will make an exception for me. I have a friend inside who I greatly wish for you to meet."

Did he not understand? How could she make him understand? Gadje did nothing to benefit the Roms.

"My mother is sick," she said before she could stop herself. The Baron turned and raised an eyebrow, suggesting that he needed more of an explanation. "I came here to trade for medicine."

"Trade?" he repeated.

"Well, my... my sketchbook is all I have. I figured if Ga- if the villagers did not pay for portraits, I could sell the book itself..."

Before she realized what was happening, he stood in front of her. Inches away. She had never noticed before how much he towered over her.

"You listen to me, child. Never, under any circumstances, doubt your gift." He raised an arm in the direction of the church. "Now, a meeting with my artist friend will not take long. And afterwards, I may be persuaded to have you sketch something for me. Especially if it helps out your poor mother."

The way he said that final word implied detestation, as if he had swallowed something bitter. Yet Eva was the one who felt sick to her stomach.

"It would be a far better use of your time than standing in the streets," he pointed out. "Unless you favor your luck, with the... *villagers* as you put it.

Eva thought about her mother at home, shivering under the covers, her aunts most likely spoon feeding her tea and soup. A heavy weight rested in her chest. Then she thought about the Gadje man and his companion, how they had laughed at her.

She had betrayed her mother by admitting her illness to the man who had hurt her. And accepting his money felt like even more of a betrayal. Yet, she agreed with him — if he was indeed prepared to pay her for a sketch, wealthy man that he was, then it would save precious hours Eva could not afford to gamble with.

So, with nothing else she could do, she followed him inside.

To say that she never wondered what was within a church would be a falsity. She had only ever imagined a giant room where people stood around and sang. Much to her surprise, she was mostly correct.

There were seats in rows, which she had not anticipated, and they all faced the giant cross at the end. Pierced onto the cross was the Christ figure. It was not the first time Eva had seen this image, but it was grotesque, nonetheless, even more so than the gargoyles above the chapel. Why would Gadje want to see a carving of a dead man displayed in front of them?

In front of the cross itself was a small crowd, two men and a woman. She squinted her eyes, and realized she recognized a pair of Gadje as the same man and woman who had laughed at her on the streets. Alongside them was a man in white robes holding incense. Eva recognized the smell as frankincense. She knew the family who grew and sold it.

The man in the white robes was saying something in a language she didn't know, and after he had finished, the Gadje put gold coins into a bowl. So that was why they never seemed to have anything to give to starving Roms. When they turned around, she turned to look at the windows in an attempt to avoid making eye contact with them.

Yet as they continued walking down the aisle of the church, Eva allowed her curiosity to get the better of her. She had never been so close to the stained glass before, and from this proximity, the colors were even more vibrant, and the details more extravagant. Her fingers felt an itch which they hadn't in such a long time.

She wondered how long the Baron intended to keep her here, if he would allow her one sketch before departing.

"Ah, Jacques!" The Baron cried out, his arms outstretched. The third man, who Eva did not recognize, smiled and sauntered into the embrace.

As the two men exchange pleasantries, the other pair of Gadje walked by. Eva thought they looked at her, given that their footsteps ceased as they neared her, but she still did not peer over to confirm. Eventually, from the corner of her eye, she saw their shadows pass and fade.

"Come here, child," the Baron demanded, snapping Eva back into the room.

She did as she was told.

The Baron held out his hand once more, presenting his friend as though they were meeting royalty. "This is Jacques Faucher. A brilliant artist, and the friend I wanted you to meet."

The man called Jacques took a small bow, and Eva felt herself heat up. She suddenly felt as if her most embarrassing moments were placed before the three of them and were up for debate. Here this man was, not only a Gadje but a real artist. And he was bowing to *her*.

Eva gave a little curtsy, which made both the men burst into laughter. She frowned, not understanding why. She was only trying to be polite.

"The Baron," Jacques began as soon as he stopped laughing. "Has told me about you, little one. Says that you show promise."

Eva didn't know how to respond. Her family had always complimented her work, believed in it. But none of them were artists, as this man was. Would she come across as conceited if she agreed? Or defiant if she did not?

"I...I wouldn't know, sir."

Her words were so quiet that at first she thought they had not heard her. But when she turned up her gaze, she saw that they were chuckling once more. What in the world was so funny?

"Come, come," Jacques said, gesturing grandly with his hands. "Let me see."

Eva held out her sketchbook for his inspection. Unlike the Baron, Jacques did not skim through until he found her sketch of Christ. Instead, he stared long and hard at each page. Eva felt her stomach rising into her throat again.

What would happen if he did not approve? Would the Baron rescind his offer of paying for a sketch? How much time did her mother have, now?

But deeper down, far further than Eva wanted to admit, she longed for his approval, even without the incentive of helping her mother. This was the first time a real artist was looking at her work. The first time a trained eye would give genuine feedback.

"Your construction is rather simple..." Jacques began. He flipped back and forth between pages. "Proportions are fine. Very close attention to detail. Your light sources are...confused."

"Confused?" she asked. "Light sources?"

He walked over and bent down to her, presenting one of the sketches she had done of her cousins. "You see how you have the shadows at the back of the arm? But then you have shadows at the front of the face."

"That's what he looked like!" Eva protested.

"Perhaps, but you need to find balance..." from his pocket, he produced his own piece of charcoal, wrapped in a handkerchief.

In a blank corner of the page, he drew in a crude mimic of her cousin. At first, it looked like a handful of lines in the vague shape of a boy sitting, but with a few more strokes, darkening up the back of the arms and face, it began to take on a more dimensional form. As if it were lifting off of the paper.

Her jaw simply dropped open. She analyzed just what exactly he had done to achieve this effect. Jacques smiled, but for once did not laugh at her reaction.

"So?" The Baron stepped in, interrupting their moment. "What do you think?"

Jacques stood up and walked back over to his friend, carrying the sketchbook with him. "She certainly has talent. She reminds me of myself when I was a child. I would be happy to teach her."

Teach? What was he talking about?

Eva recalled the day the Baron had barged into their camp, and demanded the truth from her mother. He had said something about Eva not having a proper teacher. Why did he seem to care so much?

"I can't," she said hastily. "My mother... I only came back to help my mother, I do not have time for lessons..."

The Baron held up his hand. "I will buy all the medicine you need for your dear mother."

The relief Eva felt was short lived. She anticipated a catch.

"If you agree to let Monsieur Jacques teach you in the ways of art."

Again, Eva was at a loss for words. Why would a Gadje, even her own... *father...* want to help her with this so fervently? Once more, she thought of that day when he had come to her family's camp and had told what a talent he thought Eva was. How her mother had accused him of mocking them. Was that his goal, then? To train her like an animal for the amusement of him and his friends?

It seemed too elaborate for such little rewards, even from a Gadje. Yet at the moment, she could think of no alternative.

Then she thought of her mother, suffering, and wondered how much time she had wasted already. Of course, the only answer she could give was yes, but once she had the medicine in her possession, what was to keep her from breaking her word?

Aside from the fact that the Baron knew where she lived...

Then, most selfishly, she looked over at Jacques, who was still holding her sketchbook. He had kept it open to the page he had drawn on. They were simple scribbles, ones he had done in under a minute, yet they far outshined her own, even though she had slaved away hours on every detail. What secrets did he possess, that it came so effortlessly to him? What could he tell her so that she may do the same?

Eva opened her mouth and said the only option she knew she had. "Alright."

The Baron clapped his hands, looking rather pleased with the outcome. Jacques handed the sketchbook back to her.

"We shall start the day after tomorrow."

Eva tried to hide her sigh of relief as she collected her sketchbook back. At least that gave her a little bit of time to figure out what to do.

Jacques bid them both adieu and left through the back entry of the church. Eva overheard him greeting what she assumed was the man in the white cloak. As she realized that she was once more left alone with the

Baron, now inside a secluded area with only the stained-glass windows as witnesses, she silently begged for the artist to return.

The Baron took a step towards her, and held out his arm. "Shall we, then?"

She did not know what she was meant to do. She stood there, staring at him.

"Little girl, are you so simple?" His tone was stern without being cold. "Latch onto my arm so I may escort you to the apothecary."

He could not be serious. He may have persuaded a single friend to give her the time of day, but there was no conceivable way he meant to walk arm in arm with her out on the streets, where everyone could see. This must have been a trap, but where it led to, Eva could not conclude. So, she took hold of his arm.

The pair of them walked out of the church, onto the streets, and down a ways until they reached their destination. As Eva had suspected, many a whisper happened around them as they sauntered through the crowds. She noticed, once more, the Gadje and his female companion within the mix, staring at her with...not revulsion, but some form of morbid curiosity. Eva herself could hardly create sense around it.

The apothecary had many shelves of jars. Once inside, Eva let go of the Baron and looked around.

"Don't go off too far, now." He commanded, and against her will, Eva couldn't help but think how much he had sounded like her mother just then. She shook it off as Gadje paranoia trying to ensure she would not steal anything.

She recognized all of the contents within the jars — lavender, chamomile, mugwort. Again, she had known the families who harvested them. They used to provide herbs, teas and medicine for her family's camp. Oh, how she could have used their knowledge today, but they were not around anymore.

The Gadje guardsmen picked them up one day on charges of "selling illegal substances" or "illegally selling stolen goods" Eva could not remember which excuse they had given. They survived, thankfully, and rumor told, they had even escaped prison and gone north. That second part was never verified, but it made for a happy ending, in a way.

She hadn't known what had become of their garden until now.

She turned her head at the sound of coins hitting wooden countertops. The Baron was still discussing affairs with the shop owner. Eva prayed for him to finish, so she might finally return home, give the medicine to her mother and put this whole day behind her.

Until the day after tomorrow, when Jacques expected her back.

Eva swallowed down the thought, determined to come up with a plan before then, when another thought crept into her mind. What if the Baron insisted on escorting her back to camp, as well? What if he forced her to walk arm in arm, so everyone could plainly see her betrayal? Would her mother even accept what Eva gave her, or would she rather die than take help from this Gadje man?

She looked around at the jars which had been on display. The herbs which had been stolen from her people, now packaged and sold to Gadje. For the first time in her life, Eva was tempted to reach out for one and run away. Would it still be stealing if she was merely giving it back to her family?

Then she heard the Baron's voice once more. What would he do? Come after her? Would the store owner run, too? Shouting threats and profanity over herbs which were not his to sell? And then what — would her family then have no means to purchase much needed medicine? Forced out of the store because of the actions of one, desperate girl?

Eva felt a hand on her shoulder, and she jolted. The Baron stood behind her, holding not one, but two jars out to her. She did not hesitate in taking them, so frightened that he may somehow change his mind and rescind the offer. She had no pockets to place them in, and it was difficult to balance both the jars and her sketchbook, but she managed.

She stood, then, waiting for his next instructions. Waiting for him to tell her that he would be escorting her home, where she would have to think of an explanation for her family in regards to this entire day.

"Go on, then," was all he said.

Eva tilted her head, anticipating more.

"Leave," he insisted. "Run home. Help your mother."

Again, Eva did not hesitate. She took off like a shot towards the door, before the Baron could change his mind. She stopped only once she reached the door and called over a 'thank you' as she opened it.

"Meet me at the church, day after tomorrow." He said this as though it were a warning.

Eva nodded. Just before she exited, however, she noticed the shop owner from the corner of her eye. He had a small, wooden box on the counter, and as soon as he saw her looking over, he was quick to hide it. She did not give it much thought before she turned around and left.

...

Her aunts brewed the herbs and fed them to her mother by spoon. An hour later, her fever broke. She was still too weak to leave the caravan, but at least she was finally sitting up.

"I don't know what came over me..." her mother said, pulling the blankets down and allowing the evening air to cool her sweating skin. "I haven't been around anyone sick, to my knowledge."

"Could you have caught it while being in town?" Eva asked.

"Perhaps..." her mother speculated. "But if Gadje were getting sick, we would have heard something."

Eva was going to suggest that maybe her mother had eaten something she disagreed with. They had discovered she was allergic to hazelnut, and as a result, the family had not eaten any for years. But Eva was old enough to have remembered that night. How swollen and red her mother had been, coughing and sputtering. However, those did not seem to be her symptoms now.

"I do hope it isn't anything catching," her aunt replied, handing over another cup of tea. Her mother was able to take it and drink for herself now.

"At any rate," she said, taking a sip. "I feel much better."

Eva smiled, genuinely feeling her body calm down after being on edge for the majority of the day. But one little niggle remained, like a singular weed in a garden patch.

What on earth was she to do about the Baron?

Chapter 9

Venus

T
he countess had a vase filled with her carnivorous plants brought to the room with the fireplace. Or at least, Venus assumed she had her disembodied hands fetch it for her, she highly doubted the noblewoman would have brought it herself. Then again, she had gone to Venus' room to call upon her. Quite eagerly, the artist noted.

She had big plans for Venus' next painting. Because of course that was the prominent thing on her mind. Of course she thought no longer of the other night, when they had witnessed the guardsman beating an innocent child. Why would she?

Meanwhile, Venus could not close her eyes without seeing that poor little girl. The face of the decapitated man had been replaced in her mind with a new horror, and one that struck a much more visceral chord than the prior. Venus had not known the man who had died, just the inhumanity shown towards him was enough to cause terror. And while she did not know the little girl any better, she was alive. She was not a detached thing to be placed on a table, she was a living person.

At least, Venus hoped so.

She walked around the countess and her plants, sketching out her studies, and tried to focus. After all, her mistress had claimed that she would take care of the situation at hand, but Venus suspected greatly that this had only been a means to calm her down.

She could still feel the spots on her arms where the countess had gripped her so tightly. They had bruised, in fact, and had gone from a deep purple to a dark yellow. Venus wondered if the mark her mistress had given her the first night of their contract remained on her neck. She had yet to find a mirror, and it was too dark to see into reflective liquids. But she felt it, little bumps when she scratched her nail across. She wondered if the little girl had seen, if the guardsman had, if they understood what it meant.

"I hear that the princess will be returning to town..." her mistress mused. Venus merely hummed in recognition. "She had been married to a king in another country, but apparently he died and his brother usurped the throne," the countess continued, apparently not pleased with Venus' lack of interest.

But the artist had never been one for royalty gossip. All it meant for her was more or less invites to whatever balls her patrons were hosting that season. But she supposed that her mistress had no one else to tell this to.

"When will she be arriving home?" she asked as a means of appeasing her.

"Oh... summer, I believe?"

Vaguely, Venus contemplated the movement of time in this place. It had been spring when she had first arrived, so it could not be far away from summer, now. She still found it difficult to give the matter much thought, especially since she was already attempting to clear her mind of the previous night. She found herself sketching the plants more than the countess and reasoned that she had already memorized a good portion of the noblewoman. All the same, she wanted to show her efforts.

She wanted to please the woman who decapitated people and thought nothing when children were beaten.

She could bear it no longer.

"Mistress..." she said, looking up from her sketches

Apart from her mouth turning downward, the countess did not move. Venus decided not to wait for a cue to continue.

"When you said...last night, when you said you would 'take care' of the guardsman. What did you mean by that?"

She expected a scolding. A warning in regards to her impertinent behavior. But it was better than sitting here with the weight of it on her shoulders. Besides, her mistress being cross with her was the least she deserved, after what that little girl had to endure. Venus almost wished the countess would strike her just so the guilt would ease in the slightest.

But that was not her mistress, and Venus should have known better.

Her mouth went from a tight frown to a broad smile, and she let out that hollow laugh which Venus had become so accustomed to. Why did this woman find everything Venus said to be humorous?

Then again, her laugh did not seem to reflect Venus' words, but rather as though the countess was pondering her own private joke.

"I am glad you brought it up," she said jovially. "You will see tonight, when I invite the guardsman over for dinner."

Whatever weight Venus had been feeling up until that moment had suddenly dropped. Not from relief, but rather as if it had gained ten tons to it. She longed to ask her what that was supposed to mean as well, but for some reason she restrained herself.

Instead, she asked the other question weighing on her mind. "And what...of the little girl?"

The countess tilted her head and raised her irises into the upper right corner, a manner imitation of her pretending to remember something.

"I'm sure she's still alive. The guardsmen don't get any pleasure from killing quickly."

Then all that weight went from Venus' stomach to her throat, as she fought with every inch of herself not to vomit right there. While she wished and prayed for the little girl to be alive, the thought of her being tortured in a jail cell until death came to claim her regardless was of no comfort.

Venus thought back to what her mistress had said, about having invited the guardsman to dinner. She did not know if she would be able to stand in the same room as this man, let alone be expected to sit and dine with him. She contemplated telling her mistress that she had taken ill. It was not a complete lie.

But the thought of that man coming here, eating a lovely dinner, and then being on his merry way filled her with such fury. For indeed, she did not anticipate her mistress to actually be on her side. The wealthy help only themselves.

Therefore, it was up to Venus. She had no plan, but allowing this man to walk from his crime blameless could never be an option. No, she had to concoct something for his punishment... for his demise. Yes, for what else would he do except go forth and beat more children, and perhaps worse. The world would be better off without a man like that.

But what did Venus have to accomplish such a task? Her art tools could cause an injury, she was aware, however she did need to consider his height and weight compared to her own. She contemplated the idea of poisoning his food with her oils, but it would be far too easy to trace the crime back to her. No, she had to be clever about this in order to prevent suspicion. Her victory would mean nothing if she ended up imprisoned.

But wait – poison may be just the perfect route to take. The house was surrounded by plants, surely at least a few would be disagreeable to a human. And with the countess being as strange as she was, it certainly wouldn't raise suspicions towards Venus if the food which was served had been contaminated.

Venus could not help but feel a pang of guilt. She did not necessarily feel ill will towards her mistress, at least not to the level she felt towards the guardsman.

"You seem deep in thought," her mistress mused.

Her cheeks began to burn, and she damned herself for it. She placed her glasses on as a means to hide it, though she suspected it did little beyond highlight even more how red her skin had become. Yet she could not bring herself to pull them off.

"Just focusing on the painting, mistress."

She let out a small chuckle, the vibrations of it bouncing across the room and straight down Venus' spine. "You are lying, but it's alright. All will be revealed later."

Venus nodded, but did not comment on the countess' riddle. She could not worry about that at present. For now, she had a dinner to plan for.

...

Lunchtime was her excuse to finally go down to the greenhouse. She searched throughout the plants, but the majority appeared to be edible — vegetables, fruits, herbs. Then she spotted the carnivorous plants in the corner. Venus walked over to them and gave them a quick inspection. This was the one with the mouth, the one her mistress said shared Venus' name. Its teeth stuck out like needles and glistened within the limited sunlight.

While they may eat meat, that did not necessarily mean they would be harmful to humans. A vision ran through her mind of having a plant large enough to swallow a man, then she would need to merely push the guardsman in. She could even claim that he fell.

Alas, as impressive as the plants were, they had hardly the size to take down a mouse, let alone a man. The countess had said they ate insects. They must be doing an impeccable job of it — she had never seen so much as a house fly since being here.

Then she spotted another set of carnivores. These were taller, almost vase-shaped, with lips that curled out at the top, as well as a lid. These were the plants her mistress said had been named from her family. The Sarracenias.

She leaned over towards it and looked inside. Beneath the lid, she could see nothing except for more of the plant. She did not understand how it "ate" its prey. The other ones at least had teeth. Venus shuddered at the thought of this plant chewing down on something, opening and closing its mouth, teeth covered in blood.

Then she noticed that one of the Sarracenia had its lid shut. She peered at it, through the light, as one does when inspecting eggs. She saw a dark, indiscernible blob. It might have been an insect once, that was all she could say about it. Until she noticed it was surrounded by liquid.

Venus peered back into the other head with its lid open and confirmed once more that there was nothing. Yet the one with the closed lid was full, not only of meat, but with a thin, clear juice.

That must be the poison it used to kill its prey. Venus smiled, feeling a sense of relief for the first time that day. She began to stroke at the plant, particularly around its top, trying to coax it open. When that didn't work, she wriggled her fingernails beneath what she could of the lid and pried it open. The plant fought her, like an animal that did not want to give up its meal.

At last, however, she was able to rip it open. She kept her fingers inside to prevent the lid from closing again. She became coated with the liquid, and she felt a nauseating sense in her stomach, unsure if it was directly from the poison or her own paranoia. Her eyes peered around until they fell onto a couple of ceramic jars.

Without removing her fingers, she bent down and reached out with her foot, running her toes uselessly across the jar nearest to her. She curled her ankle, attempting to knock it over enough so she could grab onto it. Her efforts seemed in vain until finally it fell on its side. She pushed her foot into it and dragged it across the dirt floor to her.

She spread the plant open further with her fingers, and poured the liquid into the jar. The black blob slid down as well, but she stopped it in its tracks. It smelled horrible and oozed against her fingers, forcing bile to rise into her throat. She threw it to the side.

Once she had the poison, she wiped her fingers on her apron, determined to wash them properly before heading back inside. Then she realized she did not have a proper place to hide her new treasure. With the top being exposed, placing it in her pocket was not prudent.

While she doubted that her mistress had moved from her spot, she suspected that the shadows lurking about this place were not to be trusted. She decided to keep the jar inside the greenhouse for now, with plans to make an excuse to return. She would say something about wanting fresh fruit for dessert and offer to collect it herself. She would need to be careful with the timing and would have to be early enough before the cooking — however that process worked here — so as to slip the poison into the dinner somewhere.

That would all come later. She set the jar down, back on the floor where she had originally found it, and headed back inside, where she would be expected to paint this afternoon as if nothing else was on her mind.

...

Venus was very careful in her selection of a dress to wear that evening. Not that she cared for her appearance in the presence of such company, but one dress in particular came with more folds than the others, and a large sash around the waist. It would be perfect for concealing a small jar inside.

Once laced up, she opened the door to immediately see that her mistress was waiting on the other side. She let out a rather loud gasp, then apologized for nearly bumping into the noblewoman.

The countess tilted her head and gave that small smile. "I thought perhaps you might want to take another trip to the greenhouse before dinner. I know how you prefer it to the dining hall."

Venus' throat went dry, but she could not quite name the reason. She supposed it was due to embarrassment over her discomfort having been pointed out, and she was tempted to rebuke it by saying that it was not the food which had upset her that evening. Yet she kept her mouth shut, for her mistress had presented her with the perfect opportunity.

She nodded and made her way past the countess. Venus continued down the hall, when she had the sudden urge to turn around. An inkling of a feeling sprawled down her spine, and she spun to see her mistress close at her heels.

The countess continued to smile, her eyes widening, silently asking if something was wrong. Then realization washed over Venus. Her mistress *knew* what she had been planning. She was going to follow Venus into the greenhouse to ensure that she did not go through with it.

At first, Venus wondered how exactly the countess had figured it out. Had she been right in assuming the shadows were her spies? Perhaps Venus had simply taken too long and had earned the countess' suspicions organically. Or — and this was the most troubling thought — her thirst for revenge was simply too clear on her face.

She wondered what she would be able to do. If there would still be a way to sneak the jar into her dress and make a dash for the kitchen. But if the countess knew this much, Venus had no doubts that she would anticipate such a move.

What then? Just proceed with the dinner as planned? Sit and pretend to eat as this vile man sat beside her, blood on his hands, no matter how many times he washed.

She felt her heart begin to race with anger once more. She thought of the little girl, her whole reason for putting this plan into motion to begin with and knew then that she could not allow this man to walk away unpunished. Even if Venus faced dire consequences, she had to avenge that poor girl.

When the two at last reached the greenhouse — Venus held open the door for the countess to enter — it occurred to her that this was her first time seeing the countess in this place.

It was a strange thing to come into her mind, but the image of the noblewoman inside the glass house — inside Venus' personal sanctuary — was quite a shock to behold. Although, it was after sunset, and there was not much light left to see. Still, she watched as the countess sauntered around, inspecting her fruits as they hung off of the branches.

She looked at them with satisfaction, but no hunger, as Venus would look at them. When she walked over towards her carnivorous plants, Venus felt her blood run cold. Would she notice how one of the Sarracenia had a lid which had been pried open?

Venus closed her eyes and imagined the little girl. Not being beaten, for that memory had plagued her thoughts long enough. No, she imagined the girl at the stand, face full of determination, packing up the requested herbs as if it were something she had done a hundred times over, because she probably had. A self-sufficient girl, not unlike Venus herself.

The anger boiled her blood again, and she stood strong.

Her mistress paid no attention to the inner turmoil Venus was feeling but kept her gaze on her precious carnivores, and as she did, Venus took a step forward. Not a noise was made as she did, her skirts had barely even rustled, so small was her step, yet she remained glued to the spot until she was certain that the countess had not noticed.

Then she took another, bolder step. Another, and she was closer to her destination. She kept her eyes fixed on the countess, and the back of her head.

Venus' feet were hardly leaving the ground, the grass beneath her brushed against the soles of her shoes. Then, her toes were stopped temporarily as they pushed into a pebble. From what Venus could feel, it was a small, insignificant thing. Not even a full rock. Yet it went tumbling forward. It rolled out past her skirts and bounced, landing along a nearby ceramic jar and hitting it with a profound *clank*.

Again, Venus froze in place, as her mistress turned to look at her.

"Did you need something?" she asked.

Venus shook her head, mouth too dry to form words.

"You haven't picked anything to eat yet." The countess walked towards her, and Venus felt the urge to step back. Always the urge to step back, to get away. "Have you grown tired of my garden?"

The artist shook her head once more. She attempted to swallow as a means to coat her throat, but this only made her cough. The countess turned and picked at a flower, which Venus recognized as lavender.

"Here," she said, holding the small bundle out to Venus, who accepted. "Let's brew you a tea."

She put her hand on Venus' waist and escorted her out of the greenhouse. Venus had to fight every urge in her body not to turn around for a glimpse of her jar.

She felt the countess raise her hand up to Venus' shoulder and give a light squeeze.

"I'm sorry you're feeling under the weather," she said this very close to Venus' ear, so that the artist felt her breath. It was as if a breeze had breathed into her ear rather than the countess. Despite that, she felt her face grow hot. "Some tea and rest will help. I want you at full strength for this dinner tonight."

It seemed to be that when times came where Venus felt she could not be angrier with her mistress, the noblewoman would show a much softer side of herself. Times like these once again made it difficult for Venus to create the mental connection between the woman who had a decapitated head on her dining table, and the woman who was prepared to brew her tea as a means of comfort.

Or when she stood so close to Venus, the artist once more became entranced with her strange beauty. Her skin was so pale, it seemed to glow in the fresh moonlight. What colors would Venus have to mix together to achieve such an effect? Times like these were when she felt that she could paint the countess forever.

That was when the wave of guilt washed over her so hard, she nearly fell over. A little girl was in prison, most likely being tortured, and Venus had just left behind her one means of retribution. How could she possibly be thinking about... painting?

Before she could collect her thoughts, Venus found that they were both suddenly in the kitchen. Or at least, she assumed it was the kitchen — she had never actually been inside it until now. But there was an oven, countertops and cabinets, dusted and rusted well beyond their use.

Venus anticipated the countess instructing her on where the kettle was, yet instead she pointed to a chair and gestured for Venus to take a seat. She held out her hand at that moment, and Venus placed the lavender into her palm.

The countess then went into the cabinets herself to pull out an arrangement of sorts — pots, pans, metal and ceramic. Venus watched silently, waiting for her actions to make sense, however she only then started to pull out the silverware. Venus began to wonder, how often had this woman made anything in this kitchen?

"Mistress, do you..." she wanted to choose her words carefully, but the sight of the countess rummaging between different sized spoons had become far too bizarre to intimidate her. "Do you...not know how to make tea?"

The face which her mistress made then was one Venus had never seen displayed before. Her lips were tight and pursed, somewhere between a frown and a pout. Her eyes were wide, despite her eyebrows being furrowed, and her pupils dilated. Even her cheeks puffed out a little, completing the image of her as a small, spoiled child.

Venus could not hold back then — she gave out a thunderous laugh. She tried to cover her mouth with her hand, which was of no use. The laughter poured out of her, so much so that her sides began to ache.

"What's so humorous?" the countess demanded.

"Nothing!" Venus insisted, in between large gulps of breath. When her laughter at last began to slow down, she continued. "Nobles are so... important. They have so much to do, I forget that they...need help with the mundane."

The countess relaxed a bit, lips still pouting. "My mother never taught me how to make tea..." she started, her voice and tone low. Suddenly, everything stopped being funny to Venus. "I didn't think it would be that hard, it's just water and leaves, but..."

Venus got up from her seat and walked over to the countess. She wanted to place a hand on her in reassurance, yet she felt that might not have been her place. So she kept her hands wrapped around her waist instead.

"Did your mother ever teach you?" the countess asked.

"She did," Venus answered quickly, trying not to dwell on the memories. "Yes, I've brewed tea many times in my life," she looked over at the countess and noticed another new expression, with an emotion she could not quite put her finger on.

Her eyes looked both longing and angry. Could it be that she was jealous? Of the fact that Venus' mother taught her something that the countess had never learned from her own? That sense of kinship filled her up again.

"I do appreciate the offer," Venus went on, redirecting the subject. "But I wouldn't want to cause you any trouble."

The countess attempted to smile. At least, that was what it had looked like. One side of her lips had curled upward before immediately falling back down, so that it might have been more of a spasm than anything else. She shook her head.

"If I thought it was troublesome, I would have called on my wait staff to take care of it. I just wanted to do something nice for you, since it seemed like you were not feeling well, and I really need you to attend this dinner..."

Venus had not been anticipating the outburst. While granted, yes she had been confused by the gesture the countess was putting forth, she couldn't deny the way her heart had melted because of it. She outstretched her arms, then pulled back, so the two of them were standing there, in an almost embrace. Venus remembered the first time the countess had hugged her, back when the portrait had been completed. She still remembered the weight and shape of this woman around her.

The countess reached forward and returned the gesture, completing the embrace. Venus felt the breath leave her lips, as she could not decide if she felt relief or confusion. And she hated herself for it. She hated that she could not make up her mind. Or that she kept becoming distracted from her goals for this evening.

In a way, she almost wished the countess was crueler, at least towards her. Then she could feel hatred in its fullness instead of this complicated wave of emotions.

As the two began to pull apart, Venus wondered if there was still a chance to talk to her mistress, to convince her to understand her plight.

"Mistress...?" She began. The countess gave a half nod in encouragement. "Listen...about the little girl? From the other night? What will become of..."

"Oh honestly!" The countess interrupted. Her tone was for the most half part playful, but not without a twinge of annoyance. She batted her hand in the air as though trying to shoo off a fly. "Still going on about that, are you? What is your fondness for this girl?"

"Fondness...?" Venus would be the first to admit that she had almost no maternal instincts, despite her more nurturing manner, but did most people not pity children? Was it not normal to feel compassion for those smaller and more helpless than oneself?

"What do you find so entertaining about her?"

Entertaining.

Now she got it.

This was still a game to the countess. She, a woman who had grown in great privilege, who had no responsibilities. What does an adult like that do except play with those around her? Of course, she would only see the little girl as a type of pet.

"Well?"

Venus couldn't answer. She knew she would say something she would regret, and if something happened to her, there would be no chance for the little girl.

"Forgive me, mistress." She said with a small curtsy. "I spoke out of turn. It won't happen again."

She had already started to walk backwards, closer to the door, when she mumbled something about being right back and then rushing outside. She ran to the greenhouse, never once turning back. She feared what she would find if she did.

Once she reached it, she flung the door open and rushed inside, to where her jar still lay sitting. She picked it up, gave a quick inspection to ensure that the poison remained inside, and then went to place it inside her dress. Just as she had lifted up her skirts, however, a cold hand grabbed at her wrist. She gasped, but managed to keep a firm grip on her jar. That is, until the countess pried it away from her.

"You do know these juices wouldn't be poisonous, right?" Her mistress said, holding up the jar. "At worst, it would merely get the guardsman... drunk. And I don't want such a thing to happen for dinner."

Venus did not allow herself time to think. She simply reacted by yanking herself away, surprised when she had been able to on the first try. The countess must not have been using much force.

Then Venus stood there, debating her words. After all, she could not possibly be more of an expert on the plant which had gotten its name from the countess' family. Still, she wanted to believe it was a lie. She wanted to believe that there was a means to make that man pay for what he had done. Yet she had been caught red-handed. She had failed that girl.

The only thing she felt then was regret. Regret for taking this position and allowing herself to become part of the countess' world. Regret that she had born witness to what had happened to an innocent child and had done nothing to help. Most of all, a thought which had not truly crossed her mind previously, she felt regret towards never learning this little girl's name.

She closed her eyes as the tears began to roll. Oh, to have risked herself for a child whose name she did not know. That girl would never know what Venus had done to try and make things right. She only prayed that someone left a window open so the little girl's soul would not spend an eternity trapped inside her corpse.

The countess touched her again, gentle this time, taking hold of Venus' wrist and pulling her forward.

"Come along, then." Venus gave no reaction to the gesture. "Let's get ready."

...

Venus sat at the table and stared into nothing. She vaguely heard the sound of the doors opening, but she made no move to look. Two figures came into the dining hall, and Venus eventually recognized them. The countess took her seat at the opposite end of the table. The guardsman took a place near her, leaving Venus alone.

"I am pleased that you were able to make it here tonight," her mistress began, lifting up her wine glass between her fingers.

"I must admit..." he began, his tone much lighter than any Venus had heard him use on the streets. He sounded humble, almost flustered. How had this man been the same one to beat a child? "I was surprised by the invitation."

The countess nodded. "You actually have my painter to thank for that."

Venus thought she saw him eyeing her again, that same confused look he had before. She wanted to sneer back at him, but her face would not move.

The countess snapped her fingers, and the noise rang into the halls, so loud that Venus actually flinched. Her first true movement since she had been made to sit down.

The invisible hands made their debuts, placing the food and wine before the three of them. Venus had expected the guardsman to be in shock at the sight of hands appearing from the darkness with no noticeable bodies attached, but he hardly paid any attention, focusing instead on the smiling noblewoman sitting by him.

Venus did manage to see that her mistress' cup had remained empty.

She looked down at the food before her. She supposed that any other day, it might have looked appetizing. The color of the vegetables was bright, the meat was supple and juicy. But the thought of putting it in her mouth and swallowing was enough to churn her insides. Even the smell ruptured within her. When the room began to spin, she feared she was going to faint.

"So what exactly is her title, then?" The guardsman inquired, pointing at Venus.

"I have already said," the countess answered, still holding up her empty glass. "She is my painter."

"Of course, teaching lessons, I presume." He cut a large chunk of meat and shoved it into his mouth. Even from her distance, Venus could see the drool roll down his chin. "But what is she, really? A lady-in-waiting?"

"No. She paints me in a rather satisfactory light."

"Countess Sarracenia, if I may... you are powerful and deserving enough of a genuine master. You should not need to settle for amateur work."

Amateur — her?

He had never even seen her work. He knew nothing about the years of study she had dedicated to the craft. She doubted this man had ever been in the presence of a 'master' painter, but that did not matter. She was a woman, and that was all he would ever see.

"I *did* hire a genuine master." The anger in her mistress' voice was evident, and Venus could not help but feel a small amount of satisfaction from it.

The guardsman paused, as if to wait for her to continue. Instead, they both just sat there, with him staring awkwardly at her cold gaze. She let him fester in the moment for a while longer, before releasing him at last with a turn of her head. He still waited another pause before resuming his meal.

Admittedly, Venus felt a little disappointed at the progression, or lack thereof, with the conversation. She would have rather liked to have heard the countess defend her skills. Yet that gaze had been all she had needed to shut this man up. The sad part was, he would never see the irony. He was trivializing the skills of one woman while acknowledging the power and privilege of another.

She wondered what that power must be like, the ability to shut down men who were considered lower class. Not that Venus believed in such things. Money and power, blood... from her perspective, everyone was human. Well, perhaps the countess herself was not, in fact, human, but she had done nothing special beyond being born into her family and title.

Venus did not envy her status. She did not want the ability to control the lives of others. She only wanted the singular ability to shut men like this up.

She tried to tell herself it did not matter, that she had more important things to concern herself with this evening, but she could not help it. Another fire had stirred within her, one which, she realized, she had not felt since arriving at this place. Since she had met the countess.

"Will you not be dining with us, your ladyship?" he asked, interrupting Venus' thoughts.

The countess gave her empty glass a shake. "Does this bother you?"

Immediately, the guardsman was full of contrition, insisting that he had intended no offense towards her character. The countess gave out that dry, hollow laugh of hers, and Venus could not resist the smile breaking out across her face. It was just so thrilling to watch this man squirm, and more than that, she even began to feel the smallest bit of hope. Perhaps the countess really did bring him here to give a proper punishment. Stripping him of his title, or something of the like.

"How are you enjoying the meal?" The countess asked. The guardsman nodded, hardly looking up from his plate. "Good, I am pleased. I actually am rather famished, myself," the countess confessed, at last setting her glass on the table.

Venus anticipated for her to snap her fingers once more and have it filled, but instead she stood up from her seat altogether.

"But there is something I must ask you to do, first."

The guardsman stood up, leaving his silverware behind with such haste, they clamored against his plate with great chaos. What remained of the meat dripped red with blood, pooling up into a puddle beneath itself.

"What is that... your ladyship?" he said, those last words in between a clearing of his throat.

The countess took a step closer, and he took a step back. Venus found herself about to laugh. She had never seen anyone react the same as she had.

'*This is what you get,*' she thought. She strangely felt her appetite begin to return.

"You will apologize to my painter."

Venus did not know what demands her mistress had prepared for the guardsman, but it certainly was not that. She stood up herself then, a complete bodily reaction as her mind did not understand what was happening. Was she completely in the wrong about this entire night? About this whole situation?

The countess was so strange. What noble person went out of their way to ensure an apology to someone under their employment? Perhaps she felt that her own pride had been wounded with the comment. Still, Venus would have thought that she might demand an apology towards herself, not to the artist.

The guardsman looked equally confused, face going back and forth between Venus and the countess.

"I beg your pardon...?"

Here he paused, eyebrows raised, asking for an explanation, because she could not have meant what they thought she did. Even Venus found herself silently asking the same thing.

"You have been very rude to my painter since the start, and I demand that you apologize to her, at once." Her voice did not raise as she said this, yet her tone had such bravado that her words echoed around the room.

Again, the guardsman looked back and forth between the two women, remaining still in his spot. "Forgive me, your ladyship. But I do not understand?"

At that moment, there was a sharp, quick sound that rang into the night. It startled the guardsman so much that he tumbled backwards. Venus looked up to see that the countess had raised her hand where his face had been. She thought he had been slapped, but then Venus took notice of the blood on her mistress' nails. Sure enough, when the guardsman rose, his face had been adorned with three, long streaks of red.

"I will not ask you again." Her voice still did not rise, but the anger in it was clear. "She stands right there, at the end of the table, you need merely walk over. You understand that much, do you not?"

"My, lady, please hear me!" He begged, keeping a hand on his wound. "There is something not right about that woman! I knew it from the moment I first saw her! I didn't recognize at first, but when I saw her the other night with that little — "

Venus could no longer restrain herself. She lifted up her skirts and marched over to the two of them.

"Where is she?" Unlike the countess, her voice *did* rise, high above them to the ends of the ceiling, if they could be seen. "What have you done with her?"

The look he gave her was a cross between confusion and hatred. The hand which was not pressed to his cheek curled into a tight fist has his jaw jutted out. His cheeks turned red as his eyes darkened. But Venus had no fear of him, and he knew it.

She stood right up to him, wondering if she too would strike him across the cheek. Perhaps give him a matching wound on the other side. Would her mistress punish her for such actions? Venus could not deny the excitement brewing deep inside of her. So this is what it was like, when men lost their power.

Even though he knew what was expected of him, the guardsman remained silent, save for a deep coughing within his throat. Venus briefly wondered if he was perhaps choking on something, and the thought brought a smile to her face.

"Here," she said, picking up his glass of wine and holding it out to him. "Have a drink."

She caught the eye of her mistress, who returned her smile. The countess gestured towards the glass, which the guardsman reluctantly took. He swallowed the entire contents in a single gulp. He still stood there, sputtering and swallowing, pounding on his chest with his fist. Then, finally, he began to relax once more and took another cold look at Venus.

"Well?" The countess said. "We are all waiting. This could be over and done with, depending on how cooperative you decide to be."

He stood up straight, taking in a large breath of air. He looked Venus in the eye, but as he said his words, the gaze lowered down to their feet.

"I... apologize." The phrase came out so mumbled that if Venus had not known what he was being made to say, she would not have been able to understand it.

"For?"

"My lady, you cannot mean to — "

"For...?"

He let out a sigh of annoyance. "I apologize for underestimating your painting abilities. They are clearly suited enough to have impressed the Countess de Sarracenia."

Venus nodded, feeling tears start to swell in her eyes, with no explanation as to why. "And the little girl?"

"What about her?"

Venus did not hold back her fury and indeed struck the man across his other cheek. He did not shriek as he had when the countess clawed at him, but the sound it made and even the stinging of her own palm were both quite satisfying.

"Is she safe?" Venus demanded, unable to remain in her delight.

"She is alive, if that's what you mean."

It was time for Venus herself to let out a sigh of relief, although that hardly seemed to be the appropriate phrase. It was as if her very soul had lightened.

"Then she must be released," Venus said, turning to her mistress, unsure if she was making demands or asking for a favor. "Given a trial, at least."

The guardsman, cheeks both red, not from his own fury but from the two women around him, raised an eyebrow in confusion. "What on earth for?"

Venus cried out and went to lunge at him.

But the countess was quicker.

She grabbed him with one hand, and slid the other across his throat, piercing into the flesh and causing blood to pool out in droves. Venus found herself stepping back now to avoid the sprays. The guardsman screamed into the night. His wailing was eventually drowned out by his own blood, and that was when the countess opened her mouth.

She curled back her lips to reveal that two of her upper teeth had grown considerably in size, but Venus did not have time to admire the trick before the countess plunged them both into the guardsman's open wound. His mouth hung open in horror, lips quivering as though he was on the verge of tears. His eyes shot out so far from his face, Venus anticipated them to fall to the floor.

Eventually, his skin turned pale. Very pale. Almost as pale as the countess herself. Then the light from his eyes left, and Venus knew that he was dead. The countess dropped the corpse unceremoniously to the ground, where it landed with a heavy *splat*. She then looked up at Venus. From her nostrils to her waist, she was drenched in blood. The expression on her face was unreadable, until her white teeth showed past the red liquid in a wicked smile.

Venus returned the grin. That was when the countess moved past the corpse, so quickly that Venus had no time to react. It wasn't until the countess had her arms wrapped around the artist and pulled her in close that Venus even registered what was happening.

Her mind went blank again as the countess leaned in and pressed their lips together. Venus did not fight it. Instead, she opened her mouth just slightly so the countess was able to take her upper lip between her own, giving it a gentle tug as she did.

Venus could taste iron on her tongue, but she did not care. In that moment was only pure ecstasy.

Eventually the countess pulled away, still grinning past the gore on her face. She had never been more beautiful.

Chapter 10

Eva

The next thing Eva knew, she was waking up on the day she was meant to meet back up with the Baron and his artist friend. She had yet to create a plan to get out of it. She could not ask her family to go yet — it was not the season for them to migrate, and they would ask her questions.

In her darkest moments, she contemplated running away. Head to a new city altogether, far from the Baron and his ugly truth. And far from her mother. But she knew that could never be a true possibility. So, what was a Rom girl, age twelve to do?

She pulled the blankets off of her, washed her face and got dressed. After a light breakfast and packing her sketchbook, she announced that she would be heading into town.

"What for?" Her mother inquired, for nothing got past her.

Eva had nothing prepared, but the words slipped out of her mouth of their own accord. "The herbs I got the other day, the shop owner traded them to me in exchange for labor. I'm going back to help him this afternoon."

Her mother nodded, clearly not convinced, but she said no more. As she returned to feeding the younger children, she gave a small flick of her wrist, a sign that Eva had her permission to leave.

Once in town, she made her way to the church. She slowed her pace, for a running Rom always caught unwanted attention. Her gaze was also kept down to her feet, as she avoided the Gadje she passed on the streets.

When she finally arrived, she looked around and saw very few attendants. She knew that Gadje typically arrived at the church on Sundays, and this was the middle of the week. But there was no sign of the Baron.

She dared to release a sigh of relief. Perhaps he had lost interest in her, or feared his reputation was on the line. Maybe she could return to her family and never have to think about that man again.

Just as she began to feel lighter, however, she heard the familiar sounds of hooves and wheels. She did not turn around to see who she knew was approaching.

"I'm so glad you made the right decision, dear child." He announced, placing a hand firmly on her shoulder, squeezing it far too tightly.

She gave a small nod in acknowledgement.

"Come," he gestured, not towards the church but to his carriage.

Eva planted her feet down, wriggling out of his grip. His face distorted into a sneer, but she remembered her mother's story about his carriage.

"Papa?" came a little voice. Eva looked in the direction from where she heard it.

Peering out from the carriage, was a small, pale face. She had the same eyes as the Baron, but a different nose and mouth. Her hair was also a sickly yellow, nearly matching the color of her skin, in contrast to the Baron's black streak of hair. The color of her dress was also lacking, as if too much saturation would cause the girl to melt. If Gadje could afford to pay for more pigments, why did they refuse to use them?

Eva looked down at her own clothing, which was rich and vibrant. Her shirt, sewn by her aunt. And her skirt, a hand-me-down, but one which had been restitched by her mother. Clothes woven by her family out of love.

She remembered when she had finally been old enough to be no longer considered a child, how her shirts and skirts were washed separately, unlike her younger cousins and siblings, who could still wash all of their clothes together. Eva had felt like such an adult that day. Strange, how she had forgotten this sense of pride.

She wondered if the Gadje girl's dress had also been made by beloved family members. Or what type of clothes and customs would indicate that she was no longer a child in the eyes of society.

The young Gadje girl looked at the pair of them, as if awaiting permission to come out of her confinement. The Baron granted this request by holding out his arm in her direction.

"Yes, come, my dear! Greet our guest!"

Eva looked up at him. What did he mean by that? They were out in the open, not at his personal property. She was no guest. But it seemed to be what the other girl needed to hear as she stood from the seat and descended down the little flight of stairs.

She approached the two, eyes on the Baron, and then on Eva. The girl looked like a ghost, even more sickly up close.

"Dear child," the Baron continued, placing a hand on Eva's shoulder once more to indicate that he was referring to her. It was then that she realized, despite him knowing what her name was, he had yet to use it since their first encounter. "This is my daughter, Venus."

Eva blinked as she looked back at the other girl. She did not know why this fact came as such a shock to her — it made perfect sense. Her mother had told her that the whole reason he had lured her into the carriage was to keep the gossip away from his wife, and Eva supposed she couldn't believe herself to be his only... child.

Yet the two girls appeared so close in age. The Gadje girl may even be a year or two younger than Eva. This man could keep his hands to himself so little?

The Gadje girl — Venus — gave a small curtsy, albeit a forced one, as the strained look in her mouth and cold stare of her eyes indicated. Eva began to wonder... did this girl know exactly who she was? Or did the Baron lie about Eva's existence? Did his daughter believe that Eva was some type of charity case? Did she look at her with such disdain because she did not understand her father's interest?

Or did she know exactly what her father had in mind? Well, at any rate, that made one of them.

Eva returned the curtsy, then she looked up at the Baron, anticipating his introduction of her. But instead, he merely led both the girls towards the carriage, while discussing how pleased he was now that the two of them had met, and that they would be off to collect his artist friend.

Eva still found herself hesitating to enter the carriage, but a look from Venus reassured her. She reasoned that, as despicable a man as this Baron must be, he surely would not try anything too treacherous in front of his own young daughter. Eva had to believe in his humanity, at least that much, because she had no other choice except to step inside.

She took a seat next to Venus, and the Baron sat opposite to both of them. He stared down at the pair and gave a most unpleasant smile. Again, Eva wondered just what exactly she had gotten herself into.

When the carriage started to pull away, it ran over a sizable rock, and the current it caused to the wheels was enough to place Eva's stomach in her throat. The continuing movements made her dizzy, but she held her own well enough.

The Baron pointed at his daughter. "My Venus draws, too. Takes lessons from Jacques, as well, matter of fact."

Eva nodded, unsure of what she was meant to say to that. She knew that nobles paid to have their daughters taught things like art or music. They never actually performed with their talents, however. Her mother had told her that possessing skills like that made the daughters more marriageable.

"But she does not have your gift," the Baron continued, shaking his head to emphasize his point.

Eva looked over to see Venus bowing her head in shame. Was that his angle, then? Did he wish Eva to teach his daughter how to sketch? She doubted she could be a better teacher than Jacques. Or maybe he wanted a pupil around as encouragement. Even so, Eva felt that there must be other Gadje children more suited to the role.

Eva did begin to calm down at the potential prospect, however. It still did not make much sense to her, but at least she had more answers as to what the Baron wanted from her than she had prior. Drawing had always come so naturally to Eva, it could not be that difficult to learn. Perhaps some people just needed more time, but she was certain that the Baron's daughter would pick up on it eventually.

She once more looked over at Venus, and offered a small smile, as a means of reassurance. The girl curled up her lip in a sneer as a response, and Eva shrunk back. The Baron reprimanded his daughter, but he did so in between amused laughter.

"I'm sure you two girls will be thick as thieves by the end of all this!"

The end? How long was she expected to stay? Eva could not possibly be here for more than an hour or two if she was to return home without suspicion.

She leaned forward, prepared to voice her concerns, when she realized she did not know how to address the Baron.

"Excuse me, sir..." she went with the most generic answer she could think of. "Um, just how long are these lessons going to take? My family doesn't know where I am, and I need — "

"Of course, of course!" The Baron said, waving up an arm to interrupt her. "We will have you back safe and sound by this afternoon, no later! You have my word!"

...

The Baron's manor was larger than even the church. Eva did not see the point in its size, if it was only a singular family living inside. Particularly one where not every member of the family even resided. That was another aspect to Gadje life which she had never understood – how could they bear to be away from their families? Granted, most of her mother's sisters had been married off and left to their husbands' homes. But how quiet would such a large house be without cousins running about.

When they stepped inside, the walls reeked of Gadje. She did not comprehend how a house this large could still be so stifling. Did Gadje enjoy sitting in their own stink?

Still, the architecture was well designed, and Eva took appreciation in the artistry she saw around the house. Vases and glasswork sat among the furniture, in different shapes and sizes. Eva stared at a large vase holding flowers, and she wondered from where the artist had gathered the clay.

There were many paintings and tapestries displayed on the walls. She had seen her mother and aunt create embroidery before, mostly on their clothes, and always small pictures, like animals or flowers. They had occasionally tried to teach Eva, but she would fumble with the needles and give up.

The paintings were all other Gadje. Most likely members of the family, and again, Eva could not help but wonder where they had gone, that there was no room for them inside such large walls. Though, perhaps, they understood that any stationary place, no matter the size, was a prison of its own.

The Baron took note of her staring and began to explain the origins of the subjects. Histories of his uncles, grandfathers, cousins. He apparently had no brothers, as one had died in an ice-skating incident, and the other stillborn.

"Where are the women?" Eva asked.

The Baron laughed, and she had wondered what was so amusing. Surely even the Baron must have been born of women, and not just his grandfathers.

"You are forward-thinking!" He praised. "Just like me!"

Eva did not know what words she would use to describe this man, but forward-thinking was not a phrase in her vernacular. She was not sure she would use it to describe herself, either. She had only asked a question.

She thought back to her own sketchbook, and how often she had sketched out her mother, aunts, her sister and female cousins. How the feminine face had always come easier to her than the masculine. That was why the Christ figure had intrigued her so much – there were no men in her life, but she saw his face so often, she wanted to make an attempt.

The Baron patted her shoulder, hard enough to snap her out of her thoughts.

"Come," he said. "Jacques will be here soon. Venus, you as well, come along, my child! I'll have some tea made."

They went into the kitchen where more Gadje were bustling around, cutting vegetables and meats. That would explain the smell, then. The Baron approached a larger Gadje woman, giving instructions for the tea, she was quick to oblige.

Venus took a seat at the table, Eva then followed suit. She stared over at the little girl opposite, wondering if she was meant to ask any questions, or start a conversation. Eva had never been one for social idleness. That had been the beauty of having everyone around her being either older or younger – they were typically content with hearing about whatever she had on her mind.

And Eva did indeed have many questions on her mind.

"Where..." she began. "Where is your mother?"

"My mother has been dead for three years."

The answer was stone cold, as if it had been said countless times before, and the soul behind them had died years ago, as well. Eva felt her stomach drop. Mostly from the guilt of having asked such a painful question, but also in her guilt of feeling a sense of relief. It meant there was one less Gadje around to become enraged with the current circumstances she found herself in.

"I'm sorry," she said, then without thinking, "my father died when I was very young."

"No he did not." Venus, who had kept her gaze on her hands, suddenly shot her eyes up. Her stare burned into Eva. "Your father is mine. He stands in this kitchen, now."

Eva took in a small breath. So, she was aware of the truth, then. The two of them sat there, acknowledging their sisterhood. Yet the thought did not fully form inside of Eva's mind, that she was just as much connected by blood to this pale, Gadje girl as she was her own siblings. She tried to look into her face to see any resemblance, but just as she had with the Baron, she saw very little of herself in Venus. Perhaps their eyes were the same shape, or the way they pouted was similar... that seemed to be about it. Or maybe that was all Eva was willing to look for.

Eventually the tea was brought to them, piping hot, alongside lumps of sugar. Eva waited until Venus helped herself before feeling it was appropriate to do the same. She held up the cup, blew away the steam, and took a sip. It tasted of lavender and chamomile, a very relaxing combination. Exactly what she needed to help settle her stomach.

The Baron sat down at the head of the table, placing him between the two girls. He started rambling about something, Eva thought it might be more about his family line, but she could hardly pay attention. Instead, she found herself looking outside the window and watched as the sun moved across the sky.

"Excuse me," she said, regretting the words once she realized that both the Baron and Venus frowned at her for interrupting. "Will your friend be here soon? It looks to be nearly noon, already."

The Baron peered out the window himself. "Ah, yes. I see what you mean! Not to worry, I'm sure Jacques will be here any moment now!"

As if on cue, there was a knock on the door. It was such a coincidence, Eva wondered if it had been planned. The Baron got up from his seat, apparently finding the arrival too important for his staff to attend to. Eva could hear him at the front of the house, greeting the new guest with great bravado. She recognized the other voice as that of the artist.

"Father says you have talent," Eva heard the whisper from across the table. She turned to see Venus leaning in very close to her. "Is it true?"

Eva blinked at the sudden realization of the close proximity the two now were. "I... I suppose so. That's what most people tell me, but I've never had a lesson, so I really don't know..."

"Don't let them see." She said these words with utter seriousness. The callus nature she had previously shown to Eva had melted away, and here she was, confiding an important secret to a friend.

The word felt too strong, despite the fact that there were stronger words to describe their connection. But the need to share this information was vital to Venus, Eva could tell.

"Why?"

Before Venus had a chance to answer, the two men returned to the kitchen, laughing at some unheard joke between them. Venus sat upright in her chair once more, teacup in her hands so quickly, Eva had not even seen her pick it up. She mimicked the motions, taking her own cup into her hands and sipping once more. The liquid had cooled considerably, and that made it much easier to swallow down.

"Jacques, you remember little Eva from the chapel the other day?" Eva sputtered on her tea at the sound of the Baron stating her name.

She was once more standing in the town square, when this man was larger than life, and playing with her name on his tongue as though it were an exotic sweet. The terror she had felt then came back to her as well, and she nearly dropped her cup. Somehow, she managed to place it back on the table, albeit rather loud and forceful, but in one piece. All eyes were on her as she continued to clear her throat from the tea.

"Yes," Jacques answered, at last. "Of course, of course."

"Very good," the Baron responded, giving a firm pat on the back. He turned to his daughter. "Venus, you will escort Jacques and Eva upstairs to begin your lessons."

She nodded, and slipped off of the chair in one, graceful movement. She sauntered over to where Eva still sat and held out a hand. Eva was not sure what to do in that moment. She did not trust anyone around her, even with Venus' confession earlier. Above that, she had never willingly touched a Gadje before.

Granted, Venus' hands were far cleaner than the farmer who had yelled at Eva the day she had first met the Baron. But she also wore no gloves, like her father. Eva would have preferred that, at least. No one had scrubbed their hands prior to sitting down for the tea, so she tried to argue that she would need to wash later anyway. She had to convince herself that the safest route was to be obedient. That it was best to remain on Venus' good side.

Besides, could there really be anything on her hands dirtier than the blood they shared?

Eva reached out and took her hand, which lacked any calluses her family had from hard work maintaining their upkeep. A hand which had never dug into the ground, or washed plates in a river, or caught their own food. Eva felt a sense of both pride and jealousy swim inside her like electricity.

Venus led her out of the kitchen, with Jacques close behind. They wandered up the stairs until they came into a wide, open room. There was a small couch, a table with a litter of books on it, and two canvases with easels by the only window. Eva could not help but think it was such a waste of a room. There was no need for a whole separate part of the house to be dedicated to crafting, only. This could just as easily be done outside.

Still, as she approached, she became enchanted by the scene. The tight weaving of the canvas, the luxury of having an easel. Eva had always balanced her sketchbook on her knees, which cramped her back and neck after so long. More so than that even, the sight of paint dazzled her.

In her family, colors were saved for clothing and jewelry. Not once had she ever had the opportunity to create her art in color. The possibilities ran before her, playing out in her mind's eye. So lost in her thoughts, she ran right up to the easel and placed her hands on the jars of paint.

She was met with a loud crack and a sudden searing pain at her knuckles. Eva looked up to see Jacques holding a stick of some sort. She rubbed at her injuries.

"You will wait until given permission," he said simply.

She thought she must have apologized as she bowed her head and walked back over to her mentor. She stole a glance at Venus, but it was not returned. Venus stood at his side; hands folded before her lap. She kept her gaze firmly on the easels ahead, but not with the same excitement Eva had displayed. She looked at the supplies as though they were a lifeline to grab.

Eva wondered how many times her hands had been whipped before she became the ideal student.

"You now have my permission to sit."

Venus walked forward first and took a seat at the stool before one easel. Eva hesitated, fearing being whipped again, despite the invitation.

She was not averse to pain. Her mother had hit her before, when she disobeyed. So had her aunts. But only ever with their hands. They needed to show her when she had done wrong so she would learn the ways of this world. That was not why this man had struck her. He did it because he could.

Eva took a seat.

"Have you ever worked with paint before?"

Since he did not address her by name, it took Eva a moment to realize he was speaking to her.

"No," she began, but he interrupted before she could continue.

"Then do not be hasty. Paint is not a thing to be wasted. It takes precious time to make and should not be used merely for practice. If you do not create a masterpiece with it, then you have wasted it and must start over."

She nodded, although she did not understand his words. How would she improve with paint if she did not practice?

Jacques handed over several small pieces of parchment to both girls. Then he walked over to where the small table sat. He picked it up and placed it between the girls. Then he brought over a vase of flowers.

"Here is your subject for the day."

He gave no other instructions, but Venus immediately picked up her charcoal and began to sketch, turning her head from the canvas only to look at the still life. Eva found herself disappointed. She had wanted to learn to draw people as she had seen Jacques do.

Flowers had never been her strong suit. A single one, perhaps, but they all came with so many petals, she would get lost in the details. And this vase held a multitude of flowers.

Jacques struck again, not at Eva, but at the table housing the vase. The sound was loud enough to make both girls flinch.

"Get to work." He demanded. "Once I have approved your sketch, you may paint."

Eva picked up the charcoal and began to sketch. She started with the vase itself, drawing out its curves and design.

"No!" Jacques yelled. He grabbed at the parchment and ripped it from her hands, crumpling it before tossing it to the ground. "You waste time on the details! Record as much of your subject's shapes as possible, worry

123

about detail later! Again!"

Eva sat in shock by what had just happened. She stared down at the crumpled parchment. After he had ranted about being wasteful. When she hated her own sketches so much that she tore them from her book, they would be used for fire kindling. And she had not drawn on both sides, there would have been plenty of room for a second attempt...

"Again!" Jacques shouted.

Eva moved in submission, doing as she had been told. This time, she drew a rough outline of the vase, then circles where each flower would be drawn.

"No!" Once more, Jacques grabbed the parchment and crumbled it. "You are still wasting time on the details! Figure out your entire shape first, then move to refinement! Again!"

Eva put the charcoal to the paper, but she did not begin drawing until she caught a glimpse at Venus' sketch. Jacques had yet to snatch away her parchment, after all. On the other girl's parchment, the vase and flowers had been made one, in only a few simple lines. The shape almost resembled a fan, where the upper part represented the flowers, and the lower end the vase. From that shape, she had sketched out calculations, which informed her of where the flowers would be. Although she was sitting opposite Eva, the accuracy in her sketching was apparent.

The strangest sense came over Eva then. Had the Baron not complimented her sketching? Had he not said that his daughter did not possess Eva's skill? She felt disappointed in herself. Never before had she met someone her own age who performed better at drawing than herself.

A loud crack against the table shocked her back to reality.

"Again!" Jacques shouted.

It went on and on, where Eva would try to please him, only to have him rip the parchment from her hands once more. When she had run out, he struck her hands again, calling her the wasteful one. Venus had been able to move onto painting after her first sketch, while Eva remained in her seat to watch.

Venus, taking pity on her, handed over the remainder of her own parchment pieces. Jacques stepped forward, as if in preparation to stop her, but she shot him a look to remind him of who exactly she was, and he backed down. Eva gave a small smile as she accepted the gift.

Once more, she attempted the motions she had seen Venus perform. A few simple lines to help her calculate the whole, big picture. It occurred to her then how, despite the many different flowers in the vase, they all created one, cohesive shape. The giant fan which Venus had drawn. It would be easier for her to determine where the flowers were placed if she started like this.

"Good," Jacques stated, so quietly that at first Eva had not heard him.

She smiled to herself. She could not help it, after hours of being yelled at, and her knuckles sore. She kept up the momentum, dividing the fan into smaller bits before drawing circles where each flower went. She did this part very slowly, determined to get each flower exactly right.

"Good," Jacques said again.

Only then did she begin to add in the smaller details. Admittedly, now that she had done the more mathematical aspect of the sketching, it no longer felt intimidating to draw out each of the petals. It was almost enjoyable, even.

At last, she handed over her sketch to the mentor. She felt the smallest fear that he would crumple it once more, until she realized that this was the first time today when he had not simply snatched it from her. He took it and glanced over it, staring intensely. He nodded on occasion from time to time. She swallowed, awaiting his answer.

He gave it back to her.

"Very good. You catch on quickly. It took Venus a month before she started to understand."

Eva's relief on his approval was short lived. She did not want to look over at Venus, but her eyes turned before she could stop them. The other girl's pale cheeks had burned a bright red. Eva cleared her throat and addressed Jacques once more, attempting to assuage Venus' embarrassment.

"Does that mean I can go ahead and paint?"

Jacques drew in a deep breath through his nose. "I hesitate to say yes, since you are still such a novice, but I was instructed to train you as quickly as possible, so, I suppose there is no time like the present."

Eva did not understand anything he had said beyond his approval for her to paint. She became excited, spinning around the chair to face her canvas.

Except, when she did, she at last got a good glimpse at the window and saw that dusk was upon them.

She stood up. How long had she been here? Had she truly become so absorbed in her sketching that she had neglected the time? What on earth was she to say to her mother?

"I must go," she announced, fleeing from the room before either Jacques or Venus could prevent her from doing so.

The stairs leading back down spiraled, and Eva was in such a hurry that she became disoriented, hitting against the walls and nearly tripping. When she finally got to the bottom step, she needed a moment to compose herself before locating the front door. She ran to it and had her hands on the latch before she noticed the Baron standing right next to her.

He was leaning against the doorframe, completely at ease. Eva glared at him but proceeded to try and open the door. Yet despite her efforts, the latch remained closed. That was when she turned her attention back to the Baron.

"You lied to me!" She screamed, fear of retaining dignity and politeness gone. "You said you would take me home at noon!"

"I did indeed," he replied, voice as cool as the evening air. "Yet I don't recall you stepping away from your lessons to come and fetch me. I am a very busy man, I cannot be expected to remember every detail."

Eva's cheeks began to burn. She looked down in an attempt to keep him from seeing.

"I need to leave," she said through gritted teeth. "Where is the key?"

"You are free to leave anytime you like," he stood from the wall then, towering over her. "But there is a reason I lock the doors at night. It's hardly safe for anyone to be out at this hour, let alone such a young girl."

"Then take me back in your carriage!"

"You want your family to see that?"

Eva's jaw dropped open. So, he *was* observant. Then he must be aware that she had lied to her family about her whereabouts.

"They'll find me..." she continued, with far less confidence than she had a moment ago.

She had no doubt her family would be worried and out to look for her. But the little ones could only handle so much, and she did indeed fear for the group of women who raised her walking around at night.

"If I may," the Baron redirected. "You will have to come clean to your family regardless. You may as well stay the night and clear out in the morning, when it is much safer to do so."

Eva tilted her head. She recognized the trap, and yet, it did make sense. She would have to confess her lies, and she would face severe punishment no matter what. Her family would certainly be looking for her, but the needs of the little ones had to outweigh that at some point. Her mother would say how resilient Eva was, and how she would make it on her own.

The last thing Eva wanted to do was stay in this house. However, she knew the journey on foot would not be safe and she needed to get home to her family.

She could wait until everyone in the manor was asleep, and then sneak out a window, or some other door, surely the servants had their own entrance...

"Alright."

The Baron clapped his hands together and started to ramble about how she would sleep in the guest room and borrow clothes from Venus. Eva flinched at the thought of wearing Gadje clothes, particularly borrowed ones that had not been washed in who knows how long. Yet she nodded and allowed the Baron to escort her back up the stairs and to her accommodations.

...

That night, Eva was awoken by the nearby clock tower. She laid in bed, eyes wide open, counting the chimes, which let her know it was midnight. She began to lift up the covers. This she did with the stealth of someone who was being watched, even though she had been the only one in the room when she came to bed.

The room was so dark, only lit by the moonlight in the window. Even if someone else were present, would they truly be able to see her moving about? Eva did not risk it and proceeded to take off the covers very slowly. When she was free at last, she stood up and walked over to the window.

She lifted it open and peered down. The room was on the second floor. Eva calculated, looking at every roof, every brick out of place, to determine if she could climb down.

She peeled off the Gadje nightgown and retrieved her own clothes.

Before putting them on, she lifted them to her face and inhaled deeply, taking in their scent. The smell of her family. The smell of her home.

Eva removed the covers off of the bed completely and tied one end to the bedpost. She flung the rest of it outside the window, and once more calculated before her next move. It had seemed like such a simple plan only a moment ago, but now, in the second before actually performing it, Eva found herself frozen.

One small error could leave her badly injured. If she waited too long, she would miss her chance. Dawn would be approaching soon, and who knew how long before the servants came about.

She swallowed, took a firm grip of the sheet, and began to climb down. Immediately, she lost her footing and began to slip – the side of the house was much smoother than she had initially anticipated, and the bottom of her feet struggled to grasp onto anything. Her body leaned further back, being pulled down by the weight of her head and the speed with which she was plummeting.

Eva almost let out a scream, almost let go of the sheet, but then she forced her body upward. Too quickly was this action performed, and she found herself slamming against the wall, pain shouting in her arm, leg and temple. Once more, she almost let out a scream but managed to choke it down into a stifled cry instead.

Once she realized that she was still hanging on, still alive, Eva found the strength to push forward. She moved much slower now due to her injuries, and her arm especially yelled out in protest. She may have sprained it, she thought. Despite this, she pressed onward, until she was just a jump away from the ground.

Then it was over. She was outside, in one piece, more or less. Eva could not resist the smile forming across her face. She had succeeded! She was going to escape and run back to her family! She would tell them the truth, not even caring what punishment lay before her at home, as long as it was home she was bound for!

Back to her aunts and cousins and siblings. Back to her mother.

Eva turned and spotted the gate which encased the whole manor. It was no doubt locked, but she felt confident in her abilities now to climb it. She ran, as best she could, smile still broad against her face despite the pain her body was in. She was so close, so close! Soon to be free!

Then, a more terrifying realization washed over her — she had no idea where she was.

She had been so focused on surviving the initial carriage ride here, it had not even crossed her mind to look out the windows and take note of where they were going. Even if she managed to get past the gates, she would have no clue where to go. The thought was enough to freeze her in the middle of the yard.

What would she do? What would she do?

She tried to convince herself that she was a Rom, that traveling was in her blood. But she was also part Gadje.

No, she could not stop now, not when she was so close.

Then Eva recalled the clock. That had been what had originally woken her up. She knew that it was in the center of the town, and that it would ring every hour. It might take all night, but if she followed the sound of the bells, she would eventually make her way back.

She had nothing else to lose, so up to the gates she went. Once she was close enough, she was delighted to see that she did not even have to climb over – the bars were spread wide enough that she would be able to push herself through.

She was free.

The pain in her arm and leg had not subsided, but it didn't prevent her from running as fast as she could manage. She looked back, once, enough to see the manor shrinking behind her. She paused only briefly when she turned forward and saw that before her there was a thick forest. She had not realized it had been there upon her escape. The image of wolves and snakes ran across her mind.

Even without the threats of predators, how was she to prevent herself from getting lost within the trees? But then she remembered that if the carriage had come through this way earlier, then there must be a path. Eva walked up and down between the trees, peering into the darkness as best she could, until she saw a stretch of ground between two large oaks. At that moment, the clock struck again, signaling a new hour.

This thought frightened Eva — she hadn't realized she had been out so long, already. Without another ounce of hesitation, she ran into the woods.

The trees looked sharper at night, their branches leafless and outstretched, like old and bony hands. She tried to keep her gaze on the ground, where the path remained open, but she kept on imagining one of those hands reaching out to snatch her away in the night.

An owl hooted above her, and she let out a scream. Her first one of the night – loud, unabashed, and full of terror. It echoed all around them, frightening the owl enough to make it fly away. It had become more afraid of her than she of it. Guilt mingled with embarrassment. She told herself that she needed to be more vigilant, if she was ever to get out of these woods alive.

That was when she heard it.

Footsteps.

Not a single pair, but several, pounding away at the ground.

Directly behind her.

Eva was not sure what to do. Her mother had always taught her that if a dangerous animal approached, not to run, because it activated their primal instincts and caused them to strike.

The correct action to take was to walk away slowly, never turning your back until the animal was out of sight.

But this creature, whatever it may be, was already behind her. The footsteps did not seem to be running, but they were distinct in their path. And they were coming closer.

Eva took a step forward. Then another. And another. She tried to keep herself from picking up the pace, tried to keep her footsteps even, to match the creature behind her. Then, her foot caught onto something. Before she realized what was happening, she had fully stepped onto and snapped a twig in half. Just like her scream, the sound echoed around them.

The creature began to run.

As did Eva.

She continued to keep her eyes on the ground, trying to avoid any more twigs or rocks that may trip her. She did not look up to see how far she must be from the village at this point, nor did she dare to turn around.

Still, she could hear the creature from behind, eager in its pursuit.

Eva then began to wonder – what would happen, should she veer from the path, for a moment? If she took shelter behind a nearby tree, and allowed the creature to run past her, would it stop to find her?

There were risks, but in the moment, nothing scared Eva more than whatever it was chasing her. She dove from the path and down into a bush.

Her skirt became caught within its thorns, leaving her partially exposed. Eva gave it a tug, but it would not give. She yanked some more, harder and harder until the fabric ripped and she was free. She stayed low to the ground and crawled behind a tree. She pressed herself into its trunk as she waited and listened.

She did not look out to check, for fear of being caught, but the footsteps became louder, until they sounded like a storm of thunder approaching her. She shut her eyes tight and put a hand over her mouth to cover up her gasps and heavy breathing.

She thought for certain that at any moment, this creature was going to reach out and grab her. It would be smart enough to know where she hid, smell her out, and claw its way around the tree to where she sat. Tears pricked at her eyes as she prepared to die.

The thunderous footsteps came in all their glory, and just as quickly, left in a blaze. Eva could hear them becoming more and more distant. Still, she remained behind the tree until she heard the sound no more.

It was over.

Eva crawled from the bush, spotting the ripped edge of her skirt among its branches. The embroidery had been torn and ruined, she saw. She sighed, mourning its loss before finally getting back onto her feet. She brushed the dirt off of herself and began to look around the path. She peered up and down and realized that she no longer knew which way she was supposed to go. In the dark, both sides looked the same. Panic began to set in.

Then the clock struck again, telling of the new hour.

Eva ran in its direction. The tiniest specks of dawn soon began to tease the sky, and the ground below her became easier to see. At last, she felt confident enough to keep her eyes forward, and see where she was headed rather than where she was.

Eventually, she saw more trees parting, and beyond that she saw buildings and bricks along the ground. So relieved at the sight, Eva started to laugh. She was tired and sore, but she ran to the village, almost skipping. The sun was peeking out more, and as she left the trees, it bathed her face in the most satisfying warmth.

She only stopped to catch her breath once she had officially made it out of the woods. Then she walked over to a nearby well and gave its rope a tug.

She was glad to see a bucket attached to it and continued to pull until it was at the top, and she took a long gulp. The water was so cool it burned at her throat, but she didn't care. She drank and drank until she felt her stomach begin to distend.

Then she let the bucket fall back down inside and turned to rest against the well itself. She was still determined to get home, but surely it was safe enough now for her to rest her eyes.

She was not able to close them, however, before she spotted the carriage with the Baron inside.

He smiled the instant he spotted her, and at once her tiredness left her body. Eva stood up and tried to run, and find somewhere to hide. She even considered going back into the woods for shelter, but as she moved, pain shot through her leg as the muscle cramped.

She cried out and fell over. Immediately she went to rub at it, begging the pain to leave as she watched the Baron approach her. The pain only barely subsided by the time he was close enough to eclipse her into his shadow.

"I had a feeling you might try and run away, despite my warning." He said, the smile never faltering. "That is what you people do best, isn't it?"

Eva sneered as best she could without wincing, but she prioritized tending to her leg.

"Come then," he went on, bending over and offering his hand. "If you are that determined to leave, to shun my offer and my gifts, then let's return you home."

"I'm not going anywhere with you!" Eva meant for this to come out louder, but her voice was hoarse from all of her running and instead came out more as a whine than anything. "You are a liar!"

He recoiled his hand, and for the first time that morning, his smile faded. He looked at her with cold, black ice eyes. Dead eyes, soulless eyes. And Eva felt her confidence waiver just a little, as she felt fear start to overcome her.

But the Baron simply bent down on his knees, so they could look at one another face to face.

"What exactly is it that your mother has told you about me?" He said this in a gentle, soft tone.

Eva did not want to tell. She had already betrayed her mother so much.

Besides, he already knew, she didn't understand why he was making her tell him again. Yet she did not want him to become angry.

"That you tricked her into your carriage," she said, hating herself for it. She opened her mouth to continue, but all that came out were sobs.

The Baron nodded. "I see. It's no wonder you have no trust in me, then. I can hardly say I blame you. But Eva," once more, she flinched at the sound of her name on his lips. "Your mother is the one who kept this a secret all your life. I told you the truth almost immediately. Everything I've said to you has been true. I got you medicine, I have provided lessons to help you with art..."

"This?" Eva demanded, holding up her hands to showcase her bloody knuckles. "How does this help me to be a better artist?"

"Art is about discipline. You have a natural talent, yes, but without discipline, you will never be able to hone all your skills. The sketchbook you brought is almost full, isn't it?"

Eva hadn't even realized until that moment how she had left her sketchbook behind at the manor. Honestly though, at this point she did not care if she never saw it again. That thing had caused her nothing but trouble ever since she had met the Baron.

"I can offer you as many sketchbooks as you like. As many charcoals. Paints, canvases. You could even learn to carve, if that is what you wish."

"Why..." there were so many questions running through Eva's mind, but they had left except for one. "Why...do you want to give me so many things?"

He opened his mouth, but then closed it into another smile. Not like before, not the cold one she had seen so often. This one changed his entire face. Made him look like a different man. A kinder one. A gentle one.

"My dear child," he replied. "Is it really so hard to understand why I want to get to know my own daughter?"

That was the first time it had been said aloud. The word had felt like a slap to the face, despite how gently it had been said. Yet Eva found she could not rebuke him. After all, he hadn't been the one who had lied Eva's entire life. That had indeed been her mother.

She had been denying this half of herself for so long, she hadn't even considered that his motivation would be so simple. It had been so long since she had received fatherly love, though.

"I still need to get home," she said, but in a much gentler voice, one matching his own. Her leg cramp had at last subsided, and she pulled herself up. "I need to let my family know that I'm safe. Maybe...maybe we could convince my mother to let me visit you more often."

What was she saying? She didn't want that. Yet she could feel the truth within her words. She felt almost obligated to give a type of compromise to her... to her father. The word stung, but she may as well get used to it. There would be no ridding herself of him, she knew that now. Maybe she could strike a middle ground. Find a way to be with her family and his.

She didn't think she would mind seeing Venus again. In fact, it had been nice to be around someone close to her own age. Someone else who could draw. It had been the first real challenge to her talent Eva had faced.

"By all means," the Baron replied, once more holding out his hand.

This time, Eva accepted, and he pulled the two of them up.

They headed towards the carriage, alone. Eva had not expected Venus to be there, but her presence was sorely missed. Still, as soon as she took a seat, she scooted over to the window and drew back the curtain. Even as they rode off, she did not falter in her observations. She needed to ensure that they were headed in the right direction.

As they reached the center of the town, her nerves began to settle, but it was not until they reached the outskirts that she truly started to become excited. She was going home this time, no tricks. Consequences be damned, anything to see her aunts and cousins and siblings and her frustratingly wonderful mother.

She could not see her camp from the angle the carriage was at, but she recognized the landscape around it. She smiled, before telling the Baron that they were in the right location, and he signaled for his horseman to stop.

Eva nearly fell out of her seat, anticipating the reunion so much that she stood before the carriage had come to a complete stop. She didn't care, and rushed out before the Baron could object.

As soon as she opened the door and stepped out, she paused. The sight around her had stunned her so completely that she could not comprehend what she was looking at.

Her campsite — the caravans, their animals, her family — were gone.

Chapter 11

Venus

T he countess had escorted Venus upstairs to a bathroom she had never seen before. Not that Venus had much use for indoor plumbing — waste should be outside of the house, where it belonged. But inside this room was a lavish, ivory bathtub, already filled to the brim with water. Hot water, if the steam billowing from the top was any indicator.

The countess stood between Venus and the tub and began to undo her corset. Venus stayed in place, wanting to turn away in shame, but somehow knowing that she was not meant to.

Lace by lace, the countess stripped off her dress and allowed it to fall to the floor. Next, she reached up and pulled the pins from her hair. It was only then that she turned around to look at Venus. Her black hair engulfed her pale face. Moonlight in the night sky.

Except for the blood which still remained dried upon her mouth and chin.

"Come along," she said. Not demanding but inviting.

Venus still remained unmoved. Her skin prickled as she shivered, freezing despite how warm the room around them was. She had never been one for baths, either. Sitting within your own filth hardly sounded like an effective way to become clean. Flowing, streaming water or sponging down had always been her preferred method.

But she was not going to get that tonight.

Moreover, and this was the part she truly could not rationalize, she wanted this. The strange beauty of this deathly creature before her. How she fascinated Venus so. Especially now, lips still caked with the blood of the guardsman.

The blood which also stained Venus' lips after their kiss.

She could still taste the countess on her. Not the coppery taste of the blood, but the sickly-sweet flesh and saliva of her mouth. How soft her lips had been pressed against Venus. How she hadn't even minded the cold from them because her own skin had been flushed so hot.

Had the countess not indeed delivered on her promise? She could hardly begin to judge this noblewoman, after she herself had spent the entire afternoon plotting the demise of the man.

Suddenly the horror of her mistress began to subside. Even the thought of the head on the platter began to dissipate in her mind. This woman was clearly not human, but did that make her evil?

She fed on blood and flesh, but did not most humans do that to animals? Venus herself had caught and eaten a fish prior to coming here. True, a fish was nothing in comparison to a man, but if her mistress was above even humans, was she to be denied the food she required?

Perhaps it was simply the natural order of things.

And right now, this woman, this non-human woman, wanted Venus to join her in the bath. Slowly, Venus began to undo her own laces. Then there they both stood, naked as the day they were born.

The countess reached out, and took a gentle hold of Venus' hand, and led her across the room to the bath. She entered first, lowering her body into the steaming waters, and then led Venus inside as well.

It did feel good to be surrounded in heat, for once in this drafty place. Venus brought her knees up to her chest and took notice of her mistress, who at the moment seemed more interested in combing through her hair than washing off the blood. She did, however, swipe at her jaw with her tongue from time to time.

"What..." Venus hesitated to ask the question, but she could not have been in a more vulnerable position, so what else could she possibly have to lose? "What are you?"

The countess smiled, small and soft, anticipating this question since the beginning.

"My race of people is far older than humans," she began. She continued to run her fingers through her hair as she spoke. Little flecks of white poking past that dark mess. "The olden days were far more peaceful. We did not know of hunger, then. But we did know loneliness. We were thrilled when humans came to be, like a child waiting for a new sibling to be born."

She reached forward, dipping her hands into the tub, allowing the waters to pool up within her palms. She brought it up to Venus' face and rubbed it into her skin. Venus looked down as the clear water turned pink.

It did feel good to have the blood washed, even though the sight of her body being in the same water it was falling into made her extremely uncomfortable.

She focused instead on the touch of her mistress, waiting for her to finish the story.

"Where did we all come from?" Venus asked when the countess remained silent.

"Does anything alive truly remember? One day we weren't here, the next we were. Who can say how? But we tell each other stories," she reached for a bar of soap, and handed it over to Venus, who took it graciously. "Some believe that humans come from God," she went on. "And that my people came from the Devil."

"I know the feeling..." Venus stated before she could stop herself.

The countess stared at her a moment before a smile broke out and she laughed. "I knew I sensed a kindred spirit in you! I knew it the moment I first learned your name!"

Something about that statement made Venus' stomach churn. Were they truly alike? Yesterday, Venus would have thought not. In fact, even just this morning she thought the pair of them could not be more opposite. But as she had observed, the countess had committed a murder which Venus herself had planned to carry out.

She did not think of the countess as evil for this act. Was it because Venus herself was evil?

She shook her head. She was letting bad memories disrupt her logic. She did not come from the Devil, and she doubted her mistress had as well. Those were rumors other people created about them so they could feel superior.

Then why would she feel a connection to someone like Venus? Beyond her art skills, she was nothing special. Resourceful, certainly, but she had never dazzled a room. She was not so beautiful that people stared. She was not so clever as to find ways out of bad situations she put herself in.

She was simply...a person.

"What are you thinking about?"

Venus looked up to see that the countess had washed the blood off of her own face. Now the waters were a deep red. She wanted to jump out of the tub, go to a stream and clean herself properly. Yet she stayed in place.

"Do you know how often I wonder that?" her mistress said. "How often I see you lost in your thoughts? It's like you're not even in the room anymore."

"I'm sorry..."

"Don't be sorry, just tell me what's on your mind."

Everything was on Venus' mind. How would she even begin to explain?

"I suppose..." she started, trying to find a good anchor. "I'm wondering what we do now?"

"About what?"

She couldn't tell if the countess was genuinely confused or merely playing a game. Venus decided to indulge her, regardless.

"With the body."

The countess tilted her head, implying that her confusion was indeed real.

"Won't he be missed? He worked at the castle, did he not?"

Then her lips parted once more into that smile. "Oh, Venus! The court knows how I feed! They're not going to mind if one little guardsman goes missing! In fact, they'll probably be grateful I have selected someone so replaceable!"

Venus sat stunned. They knew? The other noblemen, the Queen and King...they all *knew*? And they simply allowed this to happen, they allowed her to dine upon humans? Humans who were "replaceable".

That really should come as no surprise to Venus. Was she truly horrified? Or was she jealous? Jealous that a creature who fed on human blood was seen as more worthy of respect than her. What had Venus ever done beyond being born? Why did the world hate her so?

"I'm surprised you haven't asked about that little girl yet,"

This snapped Venus from her thoughts. "W-what about her?"

She hated herself for the question, this should have been the first thing on her mind. Why was the attention of her mistress so distracting?

"Well, now that the guardsman who put her away is gone," the countess said, an amused tone to her voice. "She is free to go. I thought perhaps we could bring her back here, to the manor."

"Here?" Venus repeated.

"Yes."

Venus thought about a child being trapped in this place. With little food and even less sunlight. Only carnivorous plants and disembodied shadow hands. A child would surely go mad within these walls. Why on earth would the countess want her here? Venus could not imagine that she would have the patience required in caring for children.

Besides, Venus could not think of anything crueler than pulling the child from her family. Roms were not like Gadje, they valued their time with their children. Being apart from them was a form of torture.

"Mistress..." she began.

"Sarracenia."

"What?"

"That is my name, I would like to hear you say it."

Venus swallowed. Suddenly the room felt even warmer, stifling so. "S-Sarracenia, if I may say, I don't feel that it would be proper for us to bring the girl... here. I think it would be better to send her back home to her family."

Sarracenia tilted her head, musing over the concept in her mind. She bit her lower lip, caressing it beneath her teeth, which somehow always managed to stay pearly white. The lower lip moved slowly from beneath them.

Then, she nodded.

"I suppose that makes more sense. At any rate, I only offered as a means to please you. But if that's what you want, then that is what you shall have."

Venus sighed in relief. "Thank you,"

Sarracenia smiled again. "I shall have to look for a more suitable pet for you another time."

...

They had exited the bath, but Venus could not remember what

happened next. All she knew was that her clothes were back on her body — a body which still did not feel clean — and that she had returned to her room.

Her hair was still damp at the edges, and it clung to the back of her shirt. Venus undressed into her nightgown. She felt cold all over, even as she huddled beneath the blankets. She should have been happy. The little girl was going to be released and returned to her family. Venus had done that. Venus had done the right thing.

Except, she had done nothing.

Sarracenia had been the one who had done everything. Who had arranged for the guardsmen's execution, and for the release of the little girl. All Venus had done was appease her. By painting her portrait.

That was the only thing Venus was good for... painting. This whole situation was based solely on luck. She had been lucky enough to find the one person willing to indulge her pleas. Even if it were for less than honourable reasons.

Venus tried to tell herself it did not matter. What mattered was that the countess had the power to free the little girl and she was using it to do so.

Yet why did Venus' skin still crawl?

She supposed that, when she was in that bath water — the disgusting, red bath water — and the countess had instructed for Venus to use her name, the artist had felt...well, she had felt that sense of kinship once again. More than that, however.

She had felt like an equal.

Just for Sarracenia to go and make that comment she did. Why did they always have to do such things? She saved one little child at the behest of her favorite employee, but would she even care to look at any of the other prisoners wrongfully locked up? Or perhaps it was Venus' fault for believing in such notions as a noblewoman with noble intentions. Why did she have to be so naive?

Thoughts of Sarracenia in the tub, fingers running through her hair, hands washing Venus's face came rushing through the artist's mind. How their lips had felt pressed against one another.

Venus pulled the covers up higher. She tried to reassure herself that she would feel better in the morning when they went down to the prison and saw firsthand the little girl let out of the cell.

Yet it was to no avail. She pulled herself from the mattress, taking a blanket with her and wrapping it around her shoulders. She walked over to the window and looked out as best she could past the aggressive plants, and to the moon.

She had the sudden urge to be outside. To be out from these walls, and down beneath the sky and her stars. Venus went to turn the latch. She glanced at the plants, and their sharp, drooling teeth.

She told herself that it was a farce. That they ate nothing but insects. Besides, she had seen what true terror looks like. She flicked her wrists against them, sending them off to the side as she walked out onto the small balcony.

The air smelled of rain, and she drank in its scent. The moon shone its heavenly light against her face. Despite the chill in the air, Venus no longer felt cold. Instead, she was comforted to be out in nature once more.

Truthfully, she wished to be on the ground, with her feet in the grass and dirt. But her room was too high up for the journey, and she did not care for the idea of going back into this place to climb down it. No, she would be content in this moment with the moon and the breeze.

She was not sure how long she had stood there. Time was still when one kept their body as such. The night carried on, however, and she began to feel tiredness seep into her. As she turned to head back inside, though, something caught her eye.

A shadow was moving down below. Venus looked over, trying to determine what it was. She did not anticipate that anyone would be bold enough to intrude on this place with this countess, yet what other explanation could there be?

She leaned over the edge of the balcony, and upon closer inspection, saw that it was her mistress, Sarracenia. The countess walked alone on the ground, still fully dressed.

When did this woman sleep? Venus began to wonder. She supposed she should not judge too harshly, considering how she was also up rather than being in bed. But she at least had her nightgown on.

Sarracenia approached the gates, and she stood there with her arms outstretched. Venus expected the gates to open, by some unforeseen mechanical device or magic. But instead, her mistress simply continued to stand there.

Then, Sarracenia's body began to convulse. Her arms remained out in the air, but her spine shook profusely, causing every part of her to move in rhythm.

Immediately, Venus shot up, concerned that her mistress must be having a seizure. Before she turned to head inside, however, she noticed something else. Something unexplainable.

Sarracenia began to shrink. Her hands curled back at an impossible angle and sunk deeper into her arms. The same must have been happening to her legs because she decreased in height. Her skin even began to darken, and Venus wondered if she had caught fire somehow, and was turning to ash. Yet where were the flames?

Eventually, her mistress stood there no more, and in her place was a large, grey bat. It laid on the ground, shifting its head from side to side. Then it lifted its body up, stretched out its wings, and took off into the night.

...

Venus woke up the next morning convinced that the previous night had been a dream. Not the part where the countess had murdered the guardsman, that still felt real. It was everything afterwards. The bath, the conversation, the transformation.

Venus' head must have been full of wild imagery to combat the stress she was putting herself under. Or perhaps the plants she had been cultivating the evening prior had impacted her senses. Yes, that had to be it. Fumes from poisonous plants and having witnessed Sarracenia kill a man before her in an admittedly violent way must have caused her mind to have fantastical visions.

Even though Venus noticed how her room was slightly brighter that morning due to some of the plants having been pushed back. She closed the curtains and noticed that her fingernails were caked with a dark substance. She sat down on her bed and began to pick through them one by one, cleaning out what appeared to be brown gunk.

Venus recalled her urge to wash, how last night she had not felt clean. She recalled her dream of being in a bath of blood. The stream, where she had caught her fish before arriving here, would be quite a walk but it was the only moving body of water she knew of in this area.

That would have to wait. What mattered now was going down to the prison to release the little girl. Venus threw herself from the bed and rushed to get dressed, not caring which outfit she chose and doing only the bare minimum in terms of grooming.

Then she set off to find Sarracenia.

The first place she checked was the same place she had always seen her mistress in — the room with the fireplace. Yet as she opened the door and stepped inside, it became immediately apparent that the countess was not present. This put Venus in quite the conundrum. The only other place she could think to check was the dining room. But what if she was not there, either?

Was she to check every last room? The size of this place suddenly felt very daunting to Venus. Such a task could take hours, potentially days, and it was precious time she could not afford to lose. She did not trust that the other guardsmen would respect the countess' wishes indefinitely.

That was when Venus noticed something in front of her easel. She walked over and saw what it was. There had been laid two pieces of parchment, both rolled up. One had a wax sealant on it, and the other had tiny writing against the side. She had to tilt her head to read that it said 'Venus'.

She picked it up and unrolled it.

'My dearest Venus,

I know how impatient you are. No doubt, as you read this, your plan was to run about my castle until you found me, so we can go down to free your little pet. I know I cannot trust you to wait for nightfall, when I will be able to walk outside.

Rest assured that I have taken care of everything. You need only present this note to the head of the guards, and all should go as planned.

I will see you tonight, darling.

Yours eternally,
Countess Luchia de Sarracenia'

Venus looked down at the second parchment. There was a curiosity as to what it could contain but opening it would risk breaking the wax sealant. She would need that to serve as proof to legitimize the document, whatever it may be.

She placed down the parchment which had been addressed to her, a shiver crawling up her arm as she did so. It frightened her that Sarracenia had predicted her actions so exactly. Was Venus truly that easy to read?

This would be a matter she would worry about later. For now, she grabbed the second parchment. Her painter's apron hung on the easel. She pulled it off and slipped it on, not caring how it clashed with her dress. She placed the parchment safely into the pocket of the apron and headed out the door.

...

Venus was unsurprised to see that the carriage did not wait for her outside of the gates. Even if it had been there, she doubted that she would have the nerve to use it, despite her desperation to get down to the prison as soon as possible. She truly needed to get her horse back. When this ordeal was over, that would be her next move.

For now, her safest bet was to walk. If there was anything of note that afternoon around town, she had not witnessed it. However, as she continued into town, her eyes wandered over to where the palace stood. Even from her distance, she could see what a powerfully large structure it was.

She vaguely recalled her mistress telling her that the princess was to be returning home. In the moment, Venus did not understand why this memory came back to her, yet she was grateful for the information.

Finally, she stood before the steps of the prison. The guards outside gazed at her, and Venus could not tell if they were trying to understand why a woman in mismatched clothing was arriving at a place like this, or if, once again, they were trying to determine something about her in their minds. Either way, it was a look she had become familiar with.

"I am here to release a prisoner," she stated, going back and forth between the two in order to look both of them in the eye. She had no clue what the proper protocol for such an event was, but she felt it would be best to appear confident. She pulled Sarracenia's note from her pocket. "I have an official request from the Countess Luchia de Sarracenia."

That seemed to get their attention. They turned to one another and whispered into each other's ears. One left his post, while the other kept his gaze on Venus. He gave an awkward, little nod and a half smile. Venus was unsure what to do with the gesture, so she returned it with her own awkward curtsy. Soon afterwards, the second guard returned with a third. This one wore a different uniform, more ornate than the two in front of the door. He must have been someone in charge.

He was very tall, yet he did not turn his head towards Venus when he peered over at her. Instead, only his eyes moved to look down upon her.

"I understand that you have... an official *request* from the countess?"

He said the word 'request' as though it left a sour aftertaste along his tongue. Venus bit her lip. Would they believe her?

"Yes." She stated plainly, then held up the parchment. "Here it is."

He took it into his hands and inspected it. His gaze darted back towards Venus on occasion, and he ran his fingers over the wax sealant, as though he was trying to detect any evidence of forgery.

"Well, the seal is indeed official..." with his satisfactions met, he went ahead and broke it.

Venus was rather curious as to what the note had to say, what one needed to say in order to gain the compliance of the guardsmen. But he held it so close to his face that she could not even sneak a glance. As his eyes wandered lower down the page, his face became increasingly pale. His jaw opened slightly and she could hear his breathing pick up. Before she could blink, he had folded up the parchment and placed it behind his back.

"Well, now..." he said, a false smile wide across his face. "Everything appears to be in order. Let us..." here he cleared his throat. "Let us proceed!"

The doors were opened, and Venus was led inside. The dimness in light matched that of the place she currently resided in. Except that instead of the smell of rot, there was an odor of piss and mold which lingered throughout as much as the screams wafting in the halls did. Venus felt the urge to wash after merely walking around. She tried to keep her eyes down, to watch her feet as she walked. She did not want to look upon the other prisoners in here.

'I'm sorry,' she thought. 'This was all I could do.'

Soon, the guard leading her stopped in front of a cell, and only then did

Venus have the courage to look inside. The sight of the young girl was both a relief and an utter disturbance. The scant amount of clothing she had been given, the mud and blood caked against her arms and legs, or what remained of them, at any rate. She had not been down here so long that starvation would hold a permanent effect on her body, but her face had still been hollowed down, with only the shadows under her eyes giving her skin any color.

Yet, she was alive.

Venus stifled a cry. She covered her mouth to hide the fact that she was smiling, afraid that it may be considered inappropriate under the circumstances. The guard pulled out a ring of keys from somewhere, and placed a large, iron one into the lock. It clicked, then the door opened, but the little girl did not walk forward.

"Come on, then!" He barked. "Don't you know freedom when you see it? You wanna stay in that cell? Huh? Stupid child!"

Venus walked up to him, and placed a hand on his chest, silently telling him to move to the side. So taken aback by her brazen attitude, he did as instructed. Then she stepped into the doorway and called over.

"It's alright," she said softly. "I've come to get you out of here. Let's get you home, and back to your family."

Still, the little girl hesitated. She stared at Venus, then the guard, and the iron key in his hand. As if she were anticipating this to be a sort of trick. Venus could not deny that she felt the same level of anxiety. That at any moment, the guard would change his mind, grab Venus herself and shove her into the cell alongside the girl. But she put on the sincerest smile she could muster.

"You remember me, right?" she asked. "I was there, at the night market, when you... well, I talked to the lady I work for. She's a very powerful lady, the countess, in fact. I convinced her to let you go, because you hadn't done anything wrong!"

'Quickly,' she begged internally. 'Quickly, let's leave before they do change their minds. They cannot be trusted to keep their word.'

The little girl must have sensed Venus' growing concern, because she suddenly bolted towards her with so much force that she collided straight into Venus' torso. It nearly knocked her over, but she managed to stand firm. She could feel her dress becoming wet and realized that the girl must have been crying against her. The girl was getting mud and stains all over Venus' outfit... and yet, at that moment, she had never felt cleaner.

She reached around and gave the girl a pat on the back. Their bonding was all too short, as both of them sensed the guard's disdainful gaze. Venus took hold of the girl's hand and escorted her down the hall. As they walked, other prisoners cried out, begging for release, pleading their innocence. Again, Venus kept her eyes on her feet, and her grip on the girl tight.

The sunlight blinded her as they stepped back outside. It caused tears to flow, which she wiped away. She checked behind to ensure that the girl was still there, despite the fact that she could feel her grasp even then.

They did not linger on the premises.

Venus ran the two of them down the flight of stairs and across the streets. She made sure the prison was out of sight before stopping so they could catch their breaths. The girl slumped down to sit on the stone streets, and Venus wished she had been patient enough to have grabbed the girl something to eat before heading over.

"Where does your family camp?" she asked. The sooner she returned the girl to her family, the better, she told herself.

"West," was the answer, as the girl remained seated. "Out past the town boundary."

Venus nodded. "You will have to lead me."

The girl stood up, and held out her hand, which Venus accepted. Then the two of them were off.

"What's your name?" she asked, suddenly aware of the fact that she had been referring to this person as only a little girl.

"Maria."

'Maria,' she repeated in her mind. It was a name which seemed fitting and yet unexpected at the same time. It was not the name Venus had pictured in her head for the girl. But it was nice to finally know what it was.

"And what's yours?" Maria asked.

"It's Venus..."

Maria turned back to her with a look somewhere between amusement and bewilderment. "Really? I've never heard of a name like that before."

"It's Greek."

"No, I know that. I know the story. She came out of a shell, didn't she?" Maria turned her head back once more to see Venus nod in response. "Yes, just not the name I had expected for you, that's all."

"What name would you have expected for me?"

Maria shrugged, at least as best she could with one arm tethered to Venus. "I don't know. Maybe after a flower or something. Pretty like, you know?"

"Well, to be truthful..." Venus began. "My mistress carries these plants which – "

Maria stopped dead in her tracks then. Venus almost stumbled over her. She turned back around, all amusement gone from her expression.

"That woman is a monster, you know that, don't you?"

Venus stared at Maria for a very long time. She did not know how to answer. The countess had been the one to set her free, after all. Had killed her assailant. Did she know that?

Would it have made a difference? Would admitting to the young girl that the man who had brutalized her had met his own demise in an even more gory murder? Would she be so keen to hold Venus' hands if she knew how the artist had then bathed with the murderer?

Then what did it say about Venus, that she was so hesitant to agree?

Venus peered around, as if she somehow anticipated eyes to be on her. As if she had expected her mistress to be watching her, sensing the betrayal. Her mistress, taking the shape of a bat, ready to fly out from a corner at any moment, prepared to scratch out Venus' eyes.

But there was no one and nothing in the streets except for the two of them.

Venus turned back to the little girl and nodded.

"Aren't you afraid?" Maria asked.

Again, Venus hesitated, but not nearly as much before answering. "Yes. All the time."

"Why don't you leave?"

Venus thought the same thing she had been thinking for the past several years. "I have nowhere else to go."

"Stay with us, then."

The statement came out so naturally, so immediately, that it took Venus a moment to process what had been suggested.

"What?"

"With my family. I'm sure that they would let you, at least for a little

148

bit. To thank you for saving me."

Venus had no doubt about that. The offer did in fact sound enticing. People – beyond her mistress or guardsmen. Surely a few hours would not hurt if they would have her. She nodded, and Maria led the both of them back to her campsite.

It was a large mass of land, covered with caravans and horses. Clothes hung up to dry and music played in the air. The bright colors of the clothing everyone wore was such a refreshing change of pace from how bleak everything at her mistress' manor was. The smell of hot food being prepared made her mouth water.

Everyone seemed to be staring at them, but it wasn't like how the town people stared at her. These stares made sense. After all, Venus was a stranger here, holding hands with a young member of their group.

Finally, they came across a humble looking caravan near the back. There was a man chopping firewood, and a woman staring into the dying flames.

"Mama!" Maria cried out. "Baba!"

The two looked up. The woman stood as the axe fell from the man's grip. Little heads began to poke out from the caravan. The family started running towards them, arms outstretched. It was only now that Maria let go of Venus and rushed off to accept their embrace.

For her part, Venus stood back and watched. Tears spilled from the parents' eyes as they kissed their daughter's cheeks. The younger ones bounced and laughed and asked such a large variety of questions that they blended into one another. Maria smiled.

Venus knew, in this moment, seeing this family reunion, she knew that she had done the right thing. And if that made her a monster too, well, then so be it.

She had begun to turn around to walk away, when Maria took notice and called over to her. She approached Venus once more, her family at her heels.

"This is the woman who set me free!" She exclaimed, pointing.

Venus felt her cheeks grow hot. Maria's mother walked up to her with her hands raised. She placed them both on Venus' cheeks and gave each one a kiss.

"Bless you, child." She said, her breath smelling of bread and spices. "Bless you for bringing back our child to us."

Her father came over and said more or less the same thing. "We must repay you, please dine with us tonight!"

In her world, declining the invitation until it was insisted upon would have been considered courteous. But in this world, she knew that the offer of food was not given lightly, so she accepted at once.

They all sat down by the fire, washed their hands in a basin, then began mixing recipes into bowls. Venus herself was handed a ceramic containing flour and water. She reached inside and gave a squeeze. It poured between her fingers in the most delightful way. She rolled the dough around the bowl, occasionally pressing against it with her palm. She had always preferred to do things with her own hands. From her paintings to catching or finding food, it was far more satisfying when following up hard work.

On and on this method was repeated, until her hands were caked in the mixture. She stopped a moment to pull some of it off, and that was when she noticed it. There, right between the nail of her left ring finger, was a small, dark smudge. Venus was quick to flick it off so far that she did not see where it landed. She stared at the bowl now, hesitant to get back to work.

She had sullied this family's meal. She had mixed the bread they needed to nourish themselves with the blood of the man who had tried to tear them apart. How was she to complete the kneading now?

Maria mistook her pausing as a sign of completion and took the bowl from her. Venus opened her mouth to object, but what could she say? As Maria placed the loaf into the fire and gave Venus a smile, she found that she hated herself. Now this family would happily swallow down tainted bread.

That was what made her a monster. Not her association with the countess, but her own cowardice.

The sun soon began to set, and the meal was served. Venus had no appetite, but she sampled everything, including her bread. She deserved the knowledge of being unclean. Not that she had been clean since arriving at the countess' door.

Other members of the group sat with them, sharing stories and myths, singing songs as the night air drifted over them more and more.

"Where do you come from, miss?" Maria's father asked Venus.

"France," she answered. "I spent most of my life there."

He nodded, as though expecting this answer. "And what is it that has brought you here?"

Maria shot her a look, one which begged Venus to lie. The artist gave a half smile. There was no point in hiding the truth.

"I took up a commission from the Countess Luchia de Sarracenia."

There was a pause so the only thing which could be heard was the crackling of the fire.

"The countess?" Someone in the crowd repeated. "The vampire?"

Vampire. The word rang through her head, as she recalled when she had asked the countess what she was. All this time, there had been a name for her.

"And you survived?" Another asked. "How on earth did you escape?"

Escape? Is that what she was doing? She looked around, realizing that no one here was expecting her to leave. That did not mean her welcome to stay was a permanent one. Still, it had not been her intention to escape when she agreed to the invitation.

Wasn't it? Why wouldn't it be?

Isn't that what she had longed for, during those nights on the cold marble floor, in the dim light with nothing but raw vegetation to eat? Her muscles still held the memory of that time.

Hadn't the countess made herself fearful back then? That's what she had said, when their contract had been first negotiated. To never forget how much she feared her. Venus was afraid. Wasn't she? The countess had killed people before her. Venus should fear her, right?

Yet, as she looked into herself, Venus knew the truth. She was more afraid of what she was becoming than anything Sarracenia had done.

"I...I didn't," she answered when at last she noticed how everyone had gone quiet to stare at her. "She let me go."

"Why?"

Venus gestured towards Maria. "To free her."

"So you will go back?"

The question struck something inside of her. What would happen if she did not return? The countess would be out of a portrait painter, one she had sought for so long, but it would not harm her. Would not kill her. It would be a betrayal, yes, but it was not the first, nor even the biggest, Venus had ever committed.

Something did not feel right, however. If it was this easy for her to walk

151

away, why would Sarracenia even allow her to leave? Why not force her to wait until nightfall and go with her to ensure a return?

"I have nowhere else to go," she replied.

Even though she knew it was not coming, she prayed for the invitation to remain here.

There were murmurs about the fire then. They were discussing amongst themselves what to suggest. Maria's father switched places with his daughter, sitting close to Venus.

"They say," he whispered, giving a glance to Maria, warning her with his eyes not to listen. "That she keeps the corpses of her victims in a dungeon down below. Their souls cannot escape the walls. They remain there, trapped."

Venus shivered. She had not seen what had been done with the guardsman's body, nor the head from her first dinner there. Everything seemed to appear or disappear, with no source or destination.

"I do not know," she said. "What the countess does with the bodies."

His eyebrows furrowed, and he drew in his lips, but he said nothing and nodded gravely.

"Can you not go back to France?" someone called out.

"No." Venus answered bluntly.

"Another country, perhaps? They are always looking for artists, everywhere!"

"Yes. Artists who are men, though."

There was a hush around them once more. As if they suddenly understood her tether to the countess.

"Marriage?" Another suggested. "A pretty thing like you should have no troubles securing a good match."

"I am already married," again she was met with heavy silence.

"The princess!" Someone else shouted. "She will return to this land soon! She will need a tutor!"

Now *that* was an idea. Actually, a rather good one. If there was a noble more powerful than the countess, it would be the princess. However, there was no guarantee that she would want Venus as anything in her court. Then of course, there was the risk. The one which followed Venus around her entire art career.

"Thank you," she stammered. "Yes, that...that just might work."

There was a collective sigh of relief and a round of applause. Once the matter was settled, instruments were brought back out. Everyone was on their feet, dancing. Venus stayed by Maria's side, designating her spot as a chaperone for the children. It was fun to play around with the little ones, letting them grab her hands and skirt, pulling her this way and that.

There was a prick against her neck. Venus swatted at it, assuming that an insect had bitten her. But it only increased, feeling more like a burn than a bite. She was confused, then. Had an ember from the fire been kicked high enough to get her on the neck?

She began to rub on the spot, and felt the two puncture wounds her mistress had given her the night she had agreed to the contract. The more she touched them, the harder they burned. But taking her fingers off was worse. Then she had nothing else to focus on but the pain. The heat increased so much that soon her fingers could not bear it. She crouched down, head in her hands, crying out. The children gathered around her, soon followed by the adults. They asked her what was wrong, but she was in so much pain that she could not speak.

She lifted up her hair to reveal the accursed marks.

"It's a sign from the vampire!" Someone yelled out. "She has been bitten! Get her!"

Suddenly many hands were upon her, grabbing at anything they could reach. Her shoulders, her arms, clothes or hair. She screamed out in protest. Underneath the noise, she could hear Maria crying out.

"No, let her go, she's my friend!"

The flames licked at her feet, but they were nothing compared to the soreness she felt in her neck. She almost welcomed it, as a means to end the pain.

Everything stopped.

The noise, the pulling, the burning. Time had paused to allow her a moment to breathe. Unless she was already dead, and this was the afterlife. Venus thought bitterly how she had died many years ago.

Yet the grip on her arms remained, and she could feel the heat of the fire, and realized she had been pulled back enough that they no longer reached her skin. She peered around to see that everyone was looking up in the same direction. She followed their gaze.

There, standing upon the caravan, was Sarracenia.

153

Venus could not help but think about the fact that there was no way the fabricated roof could have supported the countess' weight. She almost appeared to be floating.

The countess crouched down slightly and lept into the air. Her dress billowed out, making her appear even larger than she was. As her feet reached the ground, everyone stepped back. Cries were let out as the hands on Venus' arms let go.

Sarracenia paid no mind to the crowd, despite their jeering at her. She looked only at Venus, her expression far more cross and cold than the artist had ever seen on her before.

"Perhaps I should have made myself clear," she stated, quietly but not calmly. "You and I are in a contract together. Did you forget?"

Her teeth snapped when she said the '*t*' in that last word, making them flash and showing off her fangs. Venus had no words. A lie would only put her more at risk, and the truth would only harm everyone around her.

Everyone.

Everyone around here had just tried to kill her. They had tried to shove her into the fire, because of a mark she had no control over having. Sarracenia had been the one to brand her the mark, but they were the ones who had branded her a monster.

They were right.

Whatever power or magic the countess possessed, it was clearly enough to keep Venus in her place. Not even a princess could save her from someone like that. If a princess would even have her.

Her golden cage.

Venus looked over at Maria, who had tears in her eyes. Such a young girl, with so much on her shoulders. More weight than such a small age should bear. Venus pitied her.

She turned to Sarracenia. "I am sorry, mistress. I won't leave again."

This seemed to satisfy her, as she began to smile once more. She held out her hand and Venus accepted it without hesitation. No one tried to stop them from leaving the campsite. They shouted out many harsh words, but they were toothless.

Venus saw that she had not been the only coward. She had been caught in a village of them.

Chapter 12

Eva

Eva, aged sixteen, sat in her bedroom, waiting for her sister to come in and announce that they should be getting ready. Her little sister was turning fourteen, and their father wanted to present her to the world tonight. They were holding a party at their estate, with dinner and a long guest list. The servants had been preparing for the evening all week, endlessly cooking and cleaning. Eva and Venus had entered the kitchen many times for sampling but were sent away with scraps and red wrists.

Eva was looking forward to finally being done with it. Not that she would let it show — she would be there, smiling happily for her sister as she danced with all the eligible bachelors their father deemed worthy for her.

She was not jealous, exactly. She truthfully had no interest in being married, settling down and having children. It sounded rather tedious. Perhaps that was her father's viewpoint as well. For whenever she inquired as to why Venus was being presented at age fourteen when she herself had not been two years her senior, their father would change the subject. He told her to remain focused on her lessons. That was where her future lay, not with worrying about engagements.

Eva always found herself content after these conversations. Nothing was more important to her than painting, not even this family, although she would never admit it to them. It was merely the principle of the matter which bothered her. Their father had never publicly claimed her as his daughter. When others asked, he said she was his ward, a distant relative with nowhere else to go. She knew how the truth would shame his name, but she wished he would not make it so blatantly obvious. If she was such a burden, then why not find somewhere else for her?

Her bedroom door knocked, then opened as her sister stepped inside before being given permission. She had always been like that – announcing her presence whether it was expected or not. Eva did not mind, she was used to it. Besides, it was always a gift to see her sister come running in with a wide smile.

"Are you ready?" Venus asked as she lept onto the bed. It dipped under the weight of her, causing Eva to bounce and lose the charcoal she had been fiddling with.

"No," Eva replied, looking down at her plain dress and apron, hands covered in soot. "But you look just about."

Venus was already in her ballgown, yet she still wore curling ribbons and her feet were bare. She was most likely here to beg Eva for help with her hair, as she always claimed that Eva was better at it than she.

Before she could even get the first word of pleading out of her mouth, Eva was off the bed and over to the small wash basin which sat in the corner. She rubbed the warm, wet cloth over her hands until the water turned grey and her hands were clean. She wiped the remaining excess off onto her apron and then turned back to her sister, who had already moved over to the vanity and sat on its stool.

"Are you excited?" Eva asked, knowing the answer was obvious, but wanting to allow her sister the chance to release some of her nerves.

"Yes! It's going to be a wonderful party! I can hardly wait to go dancing and finally try that feast which has been cooking for the past week! Did you know that father had cakes imported all the way from..."

"And..." Eva interrupted as she curled her sister's hair around her fingers. "The suitors?"

Venus suddenly became very quiet. Her whole demeanor shifted. She looked down at her waist, twisting her fingers.

"I can't possibly find a husband in only one night, right?" She replied. "These sorts of things take time, don't they?"

Eva did not know, but she wanted to calm her sister down. "I'm sure father will be certain to find you the best match possible."

"But what if the best match is the one furthest away?" Her voice cracked, and Eva worried that tears were soon to follow. "What will I do if I must move so far from here? From you?"

Eva turned her sister around and knelt forward so they were eye to eye.

"We are blood sisters. We will always be connected, no matter how far apart we are."

Venus' lip quivered, in spite of this, she nodded. She wiped at her eyes and inhaled deeply. Eva stood up, expecting her to turn around so they could finish with her hair. Instead, Venus looked back up at her with a strange expression.

"Is that how you feel?"

"What?" Eva responded, though she feared deep down that she knew the question which was to follow.

"About them? Your old family?"

Her stomach dropped. She never quite had the words for when the subject was brought up. A million phrases and thoughts ran through her head. Not a single day went by without her thinking about her family. Yet when asked about them, the words would get stuck deep inside her. As if keeping them in were the only thing which held her together, and that if she released them into the world, she would break apart completely.

Where had they gone? Why had they left her behind? Did they think about her during these past four years? Or did they find out where she had been and who she had been with, and decided that she was no longer a part of their family?

Were they even alive?

Venus stared at her expectantly, but Eva only stood there, trying to stop the tears from running down her face.

"L-let's keep getting you ready..."

...

Eva had never been one for parties. To her, they were loud and aggressive. People running about, sharing useless gossip to give their lives meaning. It might not be so bad if it were held outside. Under the moonlight, with the fires going, smoke reaching the stars. In the grasp of nature, she would understand what it was they were celebrating. Instead, the parties her father threw were inside these insufferable walls.

Always so crowded, so loud, and hot. Yet leaving her so lonely. No one seemed to take any interest in her, at least not to her face. When she first arrived, she had been the talk of the town, but not in a positive light. Everyone knew what a scoundrel her father had been in his youth. A little girl showing up unannounced at his doorstep? The gossip and intrigue had gone on for months.

She had heard all of the rumors. Some were deadly close, those being about her as his daughter, which he always denied, and which the sting never faded from. While others were more ridiculous. Like how he had traded a piece of land for a son but was swindled and got a second daughter instead. Or that his wife had died from embarrassment about her, even though she had died long before Eva had come into the picture.

Logic did not matter. It was in good fun, and who cared if it was at Eva's expense?

She sneaked her way over to the table where drinks and snacks had been laid, determined to make a plate for herself and then retreat back to her room. She searched for her father in the crowd, to be certain that he had seen her make her obligatory appearance and she was therefore free to exit.

Instead, she spotted her sister in the crowd, amongst three rather devious looking young men. Venus was laughing and talking animatedly to each of them. Eva smiled a little. May one of them prove to be a loyal husband.

She turned her gaze a little more and at last spotted her father amongst his own small crowd. This time, it was the people around him doing the laughing. When the two made eye contact, he grinned broadly and gestured for her to come over.

'*Oh God.*'

What could he possibly want?

He knew she was no good at parties. She placed her plate back on the table and grabbed a glass of wine instead. She did not need comments about her eating habits from the guests. Eva made her way to her father. He introduced her to his friends, who she did not recognize, and she gave a small curtsy.

"It's very lovely to meet you, young lady," one of the men in the group said.

Eva smiled and thanked him, but all she noticed were two things. One, every man standing before them was extremely old. Even older than her father, whose hair was still as black as the day she had met him. Then secondly, next to each man stood a female companion. This could not possibly be a marriage proposition — unless they had sons who were not present — so what did her father mean by having her introduced to them?

As if reading her mind, her father pointed down to where Venus stood, still talking to the three young men. "Those are the sons of these fine people..." he then went on to state their titles. A duke, a marquis, and a count.

Alright, so her father had answered one inquiry, but her head was still full of questions.

"Your father tells us you have quite a talent with painting," said the man who had been introduced as the marquis.

Suddenly Eva felt herself become very excited. "Oh, yes! I–I mean, he does tell me that. I think I'm good, but not in a conceited or proud way, just...enough to keep practicing."

She took a large sip of her wine. Her father had been promising her to secure commissions. He said that it was taking some time because she was such a young woman. Eva did not think of herself as so young when her own little sister was being set up for marriage. But people cared which hand held the brush for a masterpiece. So the prospect of her finally having commissions did not weigh easily on her soul.

"Several of her paintings are displayed around the manor, if you would like a tour." Her father continued.

The group agreed, and they were off. It took a little bit of navigating to get past the large crowd, but they eventually made their ways into the parlor. Her father led them, then, with Eva close behind. The first portrait they came upon was one of her father himself, which she had done as a birthday present. He was standing next to his desk, a proclamation sitting on it, awaiting his signature.

She opened her mouth to discuss her technique and symbolism, but her father interjected.

"As you can see, the use of shadow here guides the audience's eye towards the center of the painting. The particular stroke of the brush combined with the oils also gives it a sense of texture."

The group nodded.

"What is it you are about to sign in the painting?" Asked the man who had been introduced as a duke.

"A proclamation of land," he said proudly. "It is meant to depict me securing more for the kingdom. Notice how the expression is very serious, showcasing the momentous aspect of the occasion, and the power it exerts..."

Eva did not understand why her father spoke of this event as though it were one which had truly happened. He had been trying to buy off this piece of land for months now, but the current owner was unrelenting. She thought he might appreciate the gesture, even a fabricated one, for his birthday.

Then again, she did not know why he was talking about her painting. True, she knew her place as his daughter, but if he was to advertise her as a material painter, then why was she being pushed to the side?

The group gave her very little acknowledgement, she noticed then, and they moved onto the next one. The following was a portrait of Venus alongside her favorite horse. Eva had wanted to paint her atop the creature, riding it with the wind in her hair. A powerful image of joy. Yet she had been warned by both her father and Jacques that such a display in a painting would be too masculine and would cast her sister in a bad light.

So instead, Venus stood next to her horse, brushing its mane. Her face was turned to the audience, a smile across her lips.

"Here you can see that once again the shadows draw the attention to the center of the portrait," her father explained. "Yet notice the much lighter use of paint here. The lack of color has the subject almost glowing in an angelic manner,"

That was just the way her pale sister looked to Eva. She never thought of it as angelic, simply pale. It seemed to impress the crowd, however. One of the women commented on how the tone in the skin reminded her of the moon, which Eva took as a compliment. She opened her mouth to discuss how she blended the paints in order to create this specific glowing effect, but once more, her father interrupted her.

"If you will take notice of the soft, gradual transition between the shades of paint in order to obtain this effect..."

Eva found herself becoming a little annoyed. Not only from having herself be interrupted, but also by a man who she had never once seen pick up a brush. He may have studied art – she heard him and Jacques discuss such matters. But unless he actually picked up the skill for himself, how was he to truly discuss the efforts put in?

She realized she should have been used to this by now. That her father always insisted he knew what was best for her and Venus, and that people simply took men more seriously than little girls. On and on he called them 'little girls', despite their developing bodies.

When Eva had lived with her family, she had been considered an adult as soon as her clothes had to be washed separately. Her mother may have scolded her to keep her in line, but never had her mother talked over her, especially about art. Her aunts too would ask her questions and give her space to explain her technique and thought process.

The thought of the women from her former life came back to her so fiercely in that moment. She could recall the feeling of their calloused hands, the smell of the spices on them as they cooked. She could see the wrinkles in her aunts' smiles and eyes. She could hear their voices as they sang lullabies to the children.

Abruptly this place became suffocating. The stale air which never held the fresh scent of the outdoors. The people who were obsessed with jewelry and finery yet bathed in their own filth. Who sang only hymns and never anything she knew from childhood.

"Dear, what on earth is the matter?"

Eva blinked as she looked up at her father. She felt the tear roll down her cheek and wiped at it quickly.

"It's nothing..." she stammered, although her words were unconvincing. Everyone heard the hesitation, and if not, they surely heard her sniffling as she regained composure. "Something in my eye..."

Her father's face softened in a way which she rarely saw. It was the face that told her deep down inside, he must have been a good man. For what sort of monster could make a face as gentle as this one?

Every time she thought she was past this...

Then her father turned towards the crowd and raised his eyebrows, as if to suggest that Eva's feminine wiles had got the better of her. That was what he always claimed to be the problem. The other members chuckled at the gesture, wordlessly agreeing.

"Why don't you head back to your room for the night?" he asked. "Get some rest?"

The last thing she wanted was to be in her room alone with her thoughts. Not to mention how embarrassed she would be to leave early on her own tour. Surely these people would not take her seriously as an artist if she could not even handle discussing her work. Not that she was doing much discussing, in general.

"No," she said. "I will stay. There are not so many more of my portraits around the halls, anyway."

"But many sketches in the art room," her father stated, more to the crowd than to her. They nodded, as if they might be interested in seeing these as well, and Eva found contentment in that.

"Do you have any self-portraits?" Another one of the women asked.

Eva found herself stunned by the question. This was the first time all evening that anyone had asked her a question.

"We do not permit the study of vanity, countess." Her father answered, interrupting her yet again.

Eva conceded to the statement. He had never allowed her to look in the mirror and study her own face. Unbeknown to him, however, she had done small studies in her own time. At the vanity in her room, she drew her lips in various poses. Her nose at different angles, her eyes and all of their expressions. Simply because it was easier to study her own face rather than constantly ask such things from others.

The woman who he had addressed as countess scoffed at the remark. "Every artist has a self-portrait! How else will she be remembered in history?"

Remembered? She merely wanted to get through life. She only longed for commissions because they were her ticket out of a marriage contract. She had never been ambitious enough to think that anyone would care to hang up one of her paintings in a church or manor and recall her fondly, even after she was dead and gone, to write her name in a history book.

Was it possible to long for more? Was it possible for her to stand amongst the greats, and be remembered herself? She looked at her father. She had anticipated pride from him, knowing that some people thought that his daughter was worthy of fame. Yet his expression showed only disdain.

"She has no reason to paint a self-portrait," he repeated. He brushed at the air, gesturing for everyone to turn around. "Come, let us head back. My daughter will need me to start the toast, soon."

...

The remainder of that evening had been rather uneventful. Eva stayed long enough for her sister's birthday toast but then did in fact go back to the table, fill another plate of with food, and retreat back to her room.

Her mind was uneasy that night. A seed had been planted inside of her and it was growing quickly. Was it truly vain of her to want this? *Should* she want it? Why not – if men were allowed to chase fame and fortune, what was so different about her own pursuit?

She tried to remind herself that this was merely the opinion of a singular woman. No one else in the group had agreed with her. What's more, no one had in fact offered her a commission. Nothing had actually changed.

Except for her views on herself.

...

The next day at breakfast, Eva played with her fork around the pair of eggs on the plate before her. Her sister was noisily crunching down on a piece of toast.

"I didn't sleep a wink last night!" she proclaimed, a smile wide on her face as she wiped crumbs from her lips. "I think I danced... until around three in the morning."

Eva nodded, attempting to offer up her own small grin. "I didn't sleep last night, either."

"Up drawing, I presume." Venus said this without malice. She was aware of her sister's aversion to social gatherings. She took a bite from one of her own eggs. "That's our little artist, always working towards perfection!"

Eva gave a bitter laugh but then went ahead and asked. "Do you really believe that?"

Venus stared at her, mouth full of egg.

"That if I work hard enough, I could produce something perfect?"

Venus took a hard swallow before speaking. "What I mean is... you hone in your craft so that it is perfect to you. I never believed that the goal of art should be perfection, only God can achieve that..."

"But could I make something meaningful to this world?"

"What is bringing this on, so suddenly?" Then Venus' eyes grew wide. "Did someone finally offer you a commission?"

This question made Eva turn down her face, back to her eggs, which she had accidentally stabbed too hard so they began to run over to the edge of her plate.

"No..." she answered, attempting to clean up the yolk with her napkin. "Not exactly, it was just something one of father's friends said. That every great artist should be remembered."

Her sister did not respond. The silence lasted so long, Eva eventually felt compelled to look up. Venus had set down her utensils and gave Eva the expression a mother would wear when telling their child that they were not getting a pony for their birthday. She sighed and reached out for Eva's hand.

"Sister... we're women." She said, "we have limited options."

"What is all of this for, then?" Eva demanded. "Why do we take lessons, over and over until our knuckles bleed? Why do we stay up for countless hours mastering? Why slave away at every painting?"

Venus rubbed at her closed hand and tilted her head. Eva realized her mistake in saying 'we'. While Venus did sketch from time to time, she had found skills elsewhere, and had not continued serious lessons with Jacques as Eva had.

"Of course, I think that you're talented. I think that you could go on to be one of the greats. Maybe... I don't know, maybe you could become a lady-in-waiting, teaching lessons to a powerful noblewoman. There would be no shame in that."

"I would not be considered the artist," Eva countered. "Just the teacher."

"I know that it isn't fair, but it's not up to us. The world is ruled by men."

Eva pulled her hand away.

"The world is ruled by men?" she repeated. Venus nodded. "Then why is it that every day, my people are restricted more and more. Every day, we send our leaders to talk to yours, and every day rights are denied us. Men who work hard to feed their families. Men whose labors are used but never given credit to. Sister, we have far more in common with those men than any who 'rule' this world."

Venus opened her mouth, then closed it once more and bit at her lip. She poked at what remained of her toast without actually picking it up.

"I didn't say it was fair," was how she replied, not making eye contact with her sister. "But Eva, why do you still refer to them as 'your people'? It has been years, you are one of us now. Father has brought up your station significantly – why is that not enough for you?"

Eva wished she had been more shocked, angrier. In truth, however, the only person she blamed for this current conversation was herself. How could she ever expect her sister, who had been raised in Gadje privilege, to understand what she was talking about?

Finally, Eva leaned in close, whispering her response. "You are still your mother's daughter, even though she has been dead these last several years."

She could see the tears form in Venus' eyes as her words sunk in. They stung deep, as Eva had intended.

She felt no pride in having said what she had, only the satisfaction that for a second, her sister saw her.

Venus got up and left the table, her seat out and food abandoned. Eva stayed where she was. Her sister would be angry for the rest of the day, she knew. But she would come to forgive her in time. They were each other's only friends.

Her father came in shortly afterwards. He was humming as he entered and completely ignored the mess Venus had left behind as he approached Eva.

"Marvelous news, dearest daughter!"

She perked up at his words, dropping her own fork. It clattered against the table loudly, dripping yolk around it. He didn't seem to mind, though.

"The count, whom we spoke with last night," her father started. He took a rather unnecessarily long pause here, as if her anticipation could possibly grow any bigger. "Has agreed to ask a cousin of his to commission you!"

At the word 'commission', Eva felt her excitement reach its peak. It rose up so much that she could no longer sit but had to stand up. Her face must have glowed, for she felt her cheeks flush.

At the same time, though, it mixed with confusion. A cousin? Did the count not want a commission himself? Considering he was the one who had seen her work... what about the countess?

She had been the one to think so highly of Eva last night. Did she not want a commission herself?

Her father was standing there with his arms outstretched, waiting for her response.

"This is..." she stammered, then forced a smile back on her face. "Such an honor! Truly, I can hardly believe it!"

He clapped his hands together. The noise was so loud that it made her jump. She wished he wouldn't do such things when he got excited.

"Excellent!" He exclaimed. "Now, his cousin is a duke in Germany, which means we shall — "

"Germany?" She repeated, her tone undeniably flat.

He looked at her and frowned. "Let me finish, dear. Don't you know that it is rude to interrupt? Have I taught you nothing?"

Eva slunk back, her head bowed.

"Now then — yes, Germany. So the two of us shall need to leave soon, perhaps in a day or two so I can get my affairs in order."

"Leave? Both of us?"

"Why, yes!" He said this as though he were appalled, but she knew his theatrics well enough. "I can't very well send my daughter out to Germany alone!"

Why did she need to go anywhere?

"But...the count only said that he would ask his cousin," she pointed out. "We have not heard word back yet, or even if word has been sent."

Her father folded his hands across his waist. She waited for him to tell her that this was true, that they should not be hasty. Perhaps in a month they would hear news and then set off on this strange journey.

Those were not the words he had for her, however.

"My dear," he hissed. "Do you understand how much I put on the line for you, everyday of your life?"

Eva looked at him but did not respond. Always, always with the theatrics. Why couldn't her father ever just get to the point?

"Do you know what they say about you, the other nobles in town?"

Of course she knew.

"Then you know what has become of my reputation since allowing you to stay. Do you know how difficult it has been to even arrange a match for Venus, your own little sister, because of the rumors spread about our family?"

It did not look like he was having a difficult time last night when she had captured the attention of three young men.

"And yet, I keep you anyway. I took you in as my own child, which you are. I upgraded you from the life of a vagabond to that of a young baroness."

Did she have that title? That was what Venus had always been called, but her father had never publicly claimed Eva was anything more than a ward he had taken in.

If her family had still been at their campsite, she would never have...

"Do you not understand what a golden opportunity this is? A recommendation for a commission. In your state, and with our reputation, this is monumental! But a letter can only get so far on its own, especially with the duke not having seen your work." That had been the point Eva had attempted to make. Why did he even treat their agreements like arguments? "So yes, dear daughter of mine, we shall travel to Germany post haste to seal the deal."

She still had so many questions. A trip like that could take weeks, potentially even months if the offer was accepted and she indeed needed to paint for the duke.

"Who will look after Venus?"

True, her sister was no longer a child, but she could not cook, and was very naive. Eva's worst fear was one of those three young men returning and taking advantage of their father's absence.

"The servants will tend to her needs, as they always do." Eva tilted her head, and her father must have understood her fears. "And I have asked Jacques to stay to look after anything else which needs tending to."

Eva did not understand. "Wouldn't it make more sense for Jacques to go with me? He is, after all, my tutor, and..."

"Nonsense, my dear!" Her father roared. "What kind of parent would I be if I allowed my child to travel across countries without proper supervision?"

What kind of parent was he to leave one of his children behind?

"In that case...could Venus come with us?" Her father opened his mouth, but for once Eva felt emboldened to continue. "The journey will be quite long, and we know no one there, it would be beneficial for me to have some company, don't you agree?"

Her father did not answer right away. Instead he put a finger to his chin and mused over the idea. Eva did not want to feel the sweet sense of relief just yet. After all, he had not made up his mind.

"I can see your point," he said at last. "Very well, then. Venus may come along. I have not yet made any propositions to the families who have inquired about her, anyway."

Propositions already?

Now her sister would surely forgive her — Eva had just bought her more time.

...

The sisters rode in their own carriage while the men — her father had insisted that Jacques now join them, too — were in the one ahead. Eva did not know who would be looking after the manor since their trusted tutor was now in attendance, but her father had said not to worry. She doubted that he left the affair to be settled by solely the servants.

So many memories resided within those walls. But the only good one was sitting in the seat across from her.

"Isn't it a little strange?" Venus asked. Eva perked up to show that she was listening. "For the four of us to be going like this? I mean, if the goal is only to even convince the duke to take on the commission. Will he even be expecting us?"

Eva held tight to the portfolio she had fashioned. None of her paintings, they were too fragile, but a collection of her finest charcoals. Venus' concern struck deeper than she had expected. She imagined the four of them arriving, only to be turned down immediately. The duke not even bothering to look at her skills.

She did not know how she would be able to handle the rejection. She told herself to be strong, but if this trip came to nought, something inside of her would definitely break.

"Father knows what he's doing," she answered, unsure who she was trying to convince.

"Do you think a duke's manor will be much bigger than ours?" Venus asked, changing the subject. "Even a German one?"

Eva did not understand what it mattered that the duke was German. To her, there were only Roms and Gadje. And now, she supposed, wherever that left her.

"Can't say that I know," Eva replied. "My family stayed in France throughout the summer, and we would travel south in the winter."

Venus looked like she wanted to ask more but held her tongue. Eva had a feeling she knew what her questions were, however. She had said before on

168

many occasions how she could not imagine spending life inside of a caravan, without a "real home", as she put it. Eva had always pitied her for this. With only their cold and distant father for company, Venus had never known a real home in her life.

...

They made one pit stop, which Eva and Venus both agreed was a waste of time, but their father insisted that it was meant to be a treat, intended for Eva's birthday, and that it would serve as inspiration for the task to come. Eva thought that was presumptuous. Besides, her birthday had passed over a month ago. At least, her real birthday had. She tried to recall when the one she gave her father was to come, but it eluded her every year.

They drove down to a museum. Suddenly, Eva felt herself becoming excited. She had been to small galleries, a handful of chapels, and had been allowed to watch master painters at work. But this was to be her first time in a genuine museum.

"Can you imagine?" She said to her sister. "Seeing the greats from the past?"

Venus nodded, clearly not sharing in the enthusiasm. Eva thought that was a little unfair, considering they had just had a grand ball for her. All the same, when they arrived at their destination, Eva did not hesitate to leave the carriage. She had made her way up to the door before even her father and Jacques had.

She could not decide what she was more excited for. The paintings, which were sure to be inspiring, or the statues and other forms of art, pieces which she rarely saw. She could hardly wait for the rest of her family. At last, the others caught up to her, and they went right on in.

The first thing which caught Eva's eye was a painting, on a canvas far larger than any man. It was a depiction of a Bible story — Eva could never remember which one. What she *did* notice were the vibrant colors, the heavy use of shadows, and the perspective. How the position of each character, the drama of the blood being splattered, and their emotions, told a story. A single frame of oil could write novels. It took her breath away.

She stepped in closer, and the swirls of the brushstroke became even more evident. It always amazed her how, up close, the blobs of paint were apparent, and yet from far away, even on such a large scale, they became a face, a person, a story.

Her companions had to drag her away in order to see the rest of the exhibits. Each one was more impressive than the last. Oils, acrylics, charcoal and marble. Ancient pieces, modern pieces. She memorized the details and broke down the techniques in her head. They made her fingers itch.

By the time they had left, her head was spinning with ideas. New experiments to try, new subjects to tackle.

There had been just one aspect of the visit which had dampened her spirit. It was one she had expected, because it was what society had expected, but now that a seed had been planted in her mind, she could not help but feel its sting. All the artists she had seen that day had been men.

"Do you think that my work might one day hang on those walls?" she asked.

"Do you really want me to answer that?" Venus responded, fanning herself, suggesting that she had a headache. Eva gave her a look which let her know that she wanted to engage in this conversation, so Venus sighed. "Perhaps on the walls of someone else's house. Maybe even someone of great nobility. But on these walls? Don't get your hopes up."

"Do you think walls like that would host any woman at some point?"

"I don't know, Eva." She leaned back and attempted to fall asleep.

The rest of the journey had taken days, which made them stop at hotels for the night. Both Eva and Venus quite enjoyed the second hotel they had stayed at. There had been beautiful tapestries on the walls, and even an impressive fountain outside. It was grand, and they had a nice time walking around looking at it. Their father had granted them permission to wander about outside, as long as they stayed within the confines of the hotel.

The girls did not hesitate. It was a rare treat indeed for the two of them to be allowed to wander without an escort. Especially when that escort tended to be their art tutor.

They never felt like they could walk around and chat about whatever fancies two young women such as them might have.

Eva took a deep breath, as though it were the first she had taken in years.

"The sky seems less blue, here," Venus commented.

Eva looked up. She had smelled the hint of rain when she had inhaled.

"It's because of the clouds."

"Oh, I hope it doesn't pour while we're out," her sister complained.

"Maybe that's why father let us go off on our own. Because he knew we would have to turn back."

Eva had said these words absentmindedly, but Venus did not refute them.

She did, however, spot a flower vendor close by.

"Let's go have a look!"

Eva hesitated, "I'm not sure…"

"Just a look won't hurt!" She pointed to the ground. "We are still within the confines of the hotel."

Eva could not stop herself from snorting at the poor excuse. But she agreed, what would it hurt? They approached the cart, and Eva made a mental list of the flowers she recognized. Lilies, daffodils, lavender. Each was in full bloom, ripe with color and shape.

Venus marveled at the roses. Those had always been her favorites, mainly because she never had any issues with identifying them, but also because she found them so romantic. She had once said that the best love stories always had roses in them.

Then they turned into the cart and looked at the person selling the flowers. At first, they saw only a young woman with her back to them. But when she spun around to greet them, Eva saw a face very much like her own.

It was her little sister, now grown. It had been years but one never forgets the faces of their family. She recognized Eva too, for she paused and allowed her jaw to drop open.

"E-Eva?" She stammered, confirming the suspicion.

Eva suddenly leaned in close, as if to reach out and grab the girl.

"Where are they?" She demanded, her voice desperately ragged. "What happened? Where are they? The others? Mother?"

Venus had stepped back. She said something about how Eva was frightening her, but the words fell onto deaf ears.

Her Rom sister did not answer. She stood there with her mouth still agape.

"I…I don't know…" she said at last.

"What do you mean you don't know?" Eva's voice had risen, so that a few people in the crowd turned in their direction.

"Where have *you* been?" Her sister countered. "You left one day and never returned! We searched all night for you!"

"I came back the next morning!" Eva protested, not sure why she was so angry at having finally seen her family member again. "By the time I arrived, you had gone! Why? Why had none of you remained?"

"We were arrested!"

By now, there were active onlookers of the scene taking place. Venus again pleaded for Eva to leave, that they needed to go, but Eva would not even turn to look at her. Finally, Venus took off on her own.

"What did you say?" Eva replied once she and her Rom sister were alone.

The two leaned in closer, at last calm enough to speak in lowered voices.

"We were arrested," her sister repeated. "I don't really remember the details. We came back, after searching for you. I was so tired, and it was so cold. I was half asleep, and then, when we got home, something woke me up."

Thunder could be heard in the distance. Eva felt the first few drops of rain hit the top of her head, but she did not move.

"Loud crashes..." her sister continued. Her eyes were wide and glazed over, hands shaking. She was no longer inside the cart, but back in that night so long ago. "Gadje men. I think they had been waiting for us. I don't remember how many. I just remember our aunts screaming, and our mother trying to beat them off. They set our caravans on fire..."

Eva reached out and placed her hands on her sister's shoulders. She was not nearly clean enough to touch her — having lived the life of a Gadje herself for the past four years — but she couldn't help it. For the first time since that day, she held another Rom in her grasp. And not any Rom, but her little sister. Her true little sister.

Then it settled in Eva like a bag of rocks how she was only as connected to this sister as she was to Venus. She had no right to think of her as more 'true'.

"It's alright," Eva crooned, knowing it very much was not. "What happened next? To everyone?"

Tears fell down her sister's face then. "They separated us from the boys, first. Our brother, our cousins. Our mother and aunts screamed out for their children from behind the cells..."

It hurt every inch of Eva to hear these words. She had wondered what had happened to her family. Part of her, as sick as it was, felt some relief in the knowledge that they had not gotten up and abandoned her. Still, it did not make the image of them locked away in cells any easier to swallow.

"They took our aunts next. Said they were too old. It was just me, our cousins, and mother."

At this point her sister had burst completely into tears. Eva felt them in her eyes, as well. She knew she was not going to get the rest of the story, no matter how patiently she waited. She stood there, holding her sister as they cried together.

"By the time they let me out, I was alone," she went on. "Some traveling Roms took pity on me and invited me to stay with them. I have no idea where the rest of our family is."

Eva nodded, taking it in. Of course, she wanted to believe that everyone had survived. That they had found kin and were making a life for themselves to endure their separation. She wanted to believe that her mother would not have gone down without a fight.

Her sister had landed on her feet, so what were the chances that the rest of family had as well? But the sinking reality was, she had no way of knowing where they were, if they were even alive. And truthfully, at least a few were probably dead.

"You are still here," Eva replied, trying to put on a bold face. "You survived, and it is so good to see you again! I never thought I would, after..."

"Yes," her sister said, voice filled with venom. Eva let go of her with a speed she did not know she possessed. "After you had run away. To what, then? It was that man, wasn't it? That Gadje man. Our aunts led us away that day, but I saw him! And you never forget when a Gadje comes to your camp! Look at you! You look like a Gadje yourself!"

Eva sank back in shame. Raindrops began to fall on her head again, with more ferocity. She wished that they could wash her clean, wash her of the years she had spent in idle luxury while her family wasted away inside prison cells. She wished they could wash away her unclean blood and make her whole.

"Please..." she began to beg. "Please, don't do this. Our family is already broken, we have found each other again, let's...let's..."

She didn't know what to say. Should they run away together in the vain hope of finding the rest of their family? How would the two girls survive on their own? How would she provide for her little sister?

The decision was made for her, however. Her sister had stepped back, eyes dark.

"I don't know you."

Eva stood there, stunned. The world beneath her cracked and crumbled, leaving her weightless and floating. Then it started to spin, the rain in her eyes blurred her vision.

She thought she heard the voice of her father, yelling out her name. She thought she felt him grab at her arms and drag her away. She thought they headed back inside of the hotel, warm and dry, while her sister remained outside in the rain.

Eva didn't remember any of it by the next morning, however. Her whole world began and ended with that phrase.

'I don't know you.'

Chapter 13

Venus

A ball?" Venus repeated, looking up from her canvas to stare at Sarracenia directly.

Her mistress, of course, never moved during their sessions, but when she spoke, she did it so quickly, and only when Venus was in the thrall of concentration, that she never actually saw her lips move.

"Yes," the countess replied, once she realized that Venus would not return to work without a proper answer. "It has been a while since I've had people in my manor. Real people, born of high class and sophistication."

Venus knew the words were meant to be an insult to the guardsman, but they stung past her skin as well.

"What is the occasion?" Venus asked, returning to her work as a means of distraction.

Perhaps it was her birthday? If creatures like her celebrated such things. It was a cruel thought to have, Venus felt. Sarracenia *did* have a mother...

"Isn't it obvious?" the countess teased. "You, of course!"

Now this made Venus stop, so abruptly in fact, that the brush stroked the wrong color on the canvas. She looked at the countess' arm, now an angry shade of red above the elbow.

Fortunately, oil took days to dry, and she would be able to scrape it off. "Me?" she said, setting down her brush. "Whatever for?"

Upon realizing how thoroughly she was distracting her artist, Sarracenia moved from her spot and walked over. Venus was quick to pick up her scraper and clean away the mistake she had made. Better to have her countess think her more behind than planned as opposed to being prone to accidents.

"For your brilliance," she said. "So everyone can see how true beauty is captured on canvas."

When was the last time she had heard that description of her work, if ever? The countess wanted to show off her work, as her own. There was no one else to give credit to. Everyone would come and see her for who she truly was.

She thought of the guardsman, and his words when the countess had explained who Venus was. How he believed that only a man could be worthy enough to paint her mistress. Only a man could be worthy enough to paint a woman. How ironic. Was that how everyone would see it? Would they find flaws in her work that would have gone undetected for a male artist? Would they criticize and jeer?

Perhaps not to the countess' face, out of fear, but certainly under their breaths. That same type of whisper which nobles somehow did not perceive but Venus always did. Those born of noble blood were not used to being spoken of unfavorably, so they never developed the ear to listen.

"Well?" Sarracenia stated, her tone more than a little annoyed. Venus had to learn to stop regressing into her own thoughts like this. "What do you think?"

She did not understand what it mattered to the countess, she clearly felt it was a good idea, so the ball was to happen.

"I... I'm honored," she said, which was not altogether a lie. "That you would think to do something like that for me."

Sarracenia smiled. "Greatness should be celebrated, don't you think?"

Venus nodded, unsure how else to respond. Her mistress sighed.

"I'm bored with posing now,"

Venus had a difficult time believing that. This was their fourth painting together, and nothing seemed to please Sarracenia more than looking upon the beauty she perceived herself to be.

"Let's go for a walk then, shall we?"

It was always difficult for Venus to tell the time of day from inside this place, but she had developed her own sense of rhythm and routine. She had already feasted upon eggplant and carrots for dinner, and given how energized the countess must be if she would rather walk than pose, it must be pretty late into the night.

Venus set down the rest of her tools, then took off her apron before hanging it to the side. The countess held out her arm, which Venus wrapped her own around. Once more, even though her mistress' skin was cool to the touch, she felt her own start to heat up. She never got used to the level of intimacy between them.

The two of them headed out down the hallway and into the great room. Venus tried to picture it, lit up and hosting a horde of people. She was almost excited about the prospect of there being life inside of this place beyond her, Sarracenia, and the shadowed hands.

To feel the warmth of this place for once...

Sarracenia led them both down the stairs and out the front. Venus had expected them to walk out of the gates and into town, walk around the shops or head to the night market. But the countess turned and the two walked deeper into the grounds. Venus had never actually walked anywhere among the grounds of this place beyond the front walkway and the greenhouse. She had never realized how imposing the building was.

Many towers, bricked together into a giant square of protection, shielding a grand opening in the center. Such a waste of space for only one person. Two people.

She was now all the more determined to get her horse back.

"Mistress..."

"I've told you not to call me that."

"Right. My apologies. Sarracenia?"

"Yes?"

"Would you be..." she tried to think of how to phrase it. "Wholly opposed to me bringing my horse here?"

"I did not know you had a horse." The question was so genuine, lacking so completely in her usual teasing tone, that it caught Venus off-guard.

She went on to explain that she had traveled by horse but had rented space for it at a local farm, as she did not know if she would be able to tend to it while painting. Sarracenia gave her a sly smile, as if to imply that it was bold of Venus to presume that there would not be staff around here adequate enough to care for her animal. Venus swallowed but said nothing. They both knew it was a good call.

"Well, I suppose I did offer to let you keep a pet here, didn't I?" The words made Venus' blood boil but she smiled and nodded, thanking her mistress.

As they traveled deeper into the grounds, Venus recognized how this was the area where she had spied her mistress' transformation. The thought made her recoil involuntarily.

"What's wrong?" Sarracenia asked, pausing them to do so.

Venus inwardly scolded herself for being so obvious. "It's nothing, just the cold..."

She could tell that her mistress did not believe her, but she said nothing and the two continued their walk. Venus *did* wonder if she should ask about that. Or if it was something Sarracenia would naturally bring up. Considering this was a woman who had killed in front of Venus, would the subject of transformation be so taboo?

Venus had been frightened that night, however, that may have been due to the unexpected nature of it. She knew very little about her mistress. Now that she could anticipate it, the thought did not seem so unusual, after everything she had witnessed up until this point. Maybe that was even why Sarracenia had brought her out here tonight.

"This place was not always so empty," Sarracenia stated plainly, breaking the silence the night had held. "It used to be a safe haven. My family, my kind, had roamed freely."

"What happened?" Venus asked, now intrigued.

She could not exactly explain why she had such a deep interest in learning more about her mistress, beyond that it would be useful to understand the full scope of her creaturehood.

But the countess merely shrugged.

"I don't think this world is equipped to handle the likes of us. Too many started to question the purpose of bringing children into the world when we are already immortal."

Immortal? Venus had not known that one. She logged it into her memory, although a detail such as that would not be one easily forgotten.

"Your mother must have had her reasons for wanting you," Venus half asked, half reassured.

Sarracenia gave out a bitter laugh. "My mother was the one person I could never learn to read. I swear, she made me as a mockery. A version of herself that could not compete. I was a pretty bauble she could admire when she pleased, to be ignored the rest of the time."

The countess gazed ahead as she gave this confession, as if unsure if she were telling it to Venus or to herself.

"When she died... I admit, a part of me was glad to finally be alone. Without her... staring. All the time, staring at me."

"How did she die?"

Sarracenia looked at her with alarm. Then, her eyebrows furrowed down and she scowled. She pulled away from their entwined arms.

"Do not think that I would be so careless as to inform you on how exactly my kind expires," she hissed.

"No, no, mistress!" Venus pleaded, bending in submission. "Forgive me, I lost myself in thought. I only meant to add to the conversation. My own mother... I know not if she lives, or if she died many years ago."

"So you asked me out of pity, is that it?"

"Kinship, really." Venus took a deep breath, thinking over her next few words carefully. She could feel her pulse begin to rise. She had seen the countess angry before, but not like this. The anger she was displaying ran deep and was not to be taken lightly. "There are times when I think us so much alike. I can relate to the struggles you have described, to some extent, at least. The best I can while being a..."

"A human?"

Venus nodded but kept her head bowed. Then she heard something which brought neither comfort nor concern, only added confusion. She heard her mistress scoff. Very slowly, Venus lifted her gaze to peer upon her.

"Yes, I suppose I should only expect so much from a human, after all," she went on.

She held up her arm again, which Venus was hesitant to accept. Her fears of what may happen upon rejection proved to be greater, however, and she returned to having her arm wrapped around Sarracenia's.

"You are very brilliant with your painting," the countess continued. "That is your role here. I should not expect you to be as equally talented in every area."

The insult burned. "I... I'm sorry, mistress."

"Don't be. Our conversations have been some of the most fun I've had in ages. It has been so long since I have spoken with anyone besides a nobleman come to try and swindle me out of my fortune..."

Venus had a difficult time thinking any aspect of the countess' life could be less than luxurious. Even though she found this place to be a waste of space, it was a much grander home than the general population could ever wish to live in. Truthfully, she could probably home the entire town. Then Venus began to picture it – the entire town, its villagers, placed inside here as an easy feeding spree for the countess to go on. Every night, no one knowing who would be next. She shook her head.

"Still cold?" Sarracenia asked.

"Yes..." Venus answered automatically.

The countess nodded. "It's alright, we won't be out here for much longer."

"Why are we out here, again?" Venus asked, unsure if she truly wanted the answer.

Yet, she felt that the sooner they got on with whatever fancy her mistress had at present, the sooner she could return inside, and retreat to her room.

She never thought there would come a time when she longed to re-enter that place again.

"I have another proposition for you," Sarracenia began. She stopped so suddenly in her tracks that Venus stumbled before catching herself. The countess chuckled at this. "You see, I have been giving it a great deal of thought. You said so yourself, yes? How we have a kinship?"

Venus had just said those words, yes.

"Do you think of us as equals?"

This made her furrow her brows. "No," she said eventually.

"Why not?"

"Well, because..." she did not know how to answer. She had been too presumptuous before and it had angered Sarracenia, something Venus was not keen to repeat. "As you said, I am only human."

Sarracenia's eyes widened at the response, as though it were unexpected. She must not have realized how little gold, class or status meant to Venus. She was merely the patron who allowed the artist to live off of her skill. It was transactional, nothing more. It did not give her power over Venus. Her supernatural abilities, however, Venus held with slightly more respect and regard.

Then, in the full moonlight, Sarracenia's fangs became present and reflective as she smiled broadly.

"Oh, how you amuse me so!"

Her grip on Venus' arm tightened. She was becoming aware once more just how close the two of them were standing next to each other. And she felt very cold.

"I do agree, though," her mistress carried on. "We will never be true equals so long as you remain a human."

Venus nodded. It may or may not have been the appropriate response to the observation, but she honestly could not determine which.

"That is why I want to offer you the chance to become something more."

She must not have understood correctly. Each word had made sense to her on an individual level, but strung together into that particular phrase... Venus could not comprehend it. Or rather, she did not want to comprehend it. Because if her mistress had indeed meant what those words were implying, then...

Venus stepped back, somehow managing to break away from her mistress' strong grip. She must have anticipated this reaction, because she simply stood there and smiled, unperturbed.

"It is a lot to take in, I understand." She replied, folding her hands before her. "I am not expecting an answer tonight, only the consideration."

What was there to consider? The answer would obviously be a no. Venus did not fear death. She did what she had to do in order to survive day by day, but when death inevitably came knocking at her door, she would not hesitate to let him in.

Not to mention the prospect of having to eat other humans in order to maintain immortality. Humans dying for the sake of her own cowardice. All for what – so she could live on, and transform? She still did not know the full extent of Sarracenia's powers, but they could simply not be worth it.

The blood of others was not worth what she would gain.

"Mistress... Sarracenia... please, I – "

"Think deeply on what it is you will gain." Her mistress said plainly. "What exactly it is that I am offering. It is not just about immortal life. It is also about retaining eternal glory."

Venus did not understand what she meant by that. She opened her mouth to say something, but no words came out, so she shrugged pathetic and clueless.

"I recall the way that man spoke of you. The guardsman. How he said you were not worthy enough to paint my portrait." Venus' hands balled into fists at the mention. She could not help it. Sarracenia must have noticed. "I know that it makes your blood boil, to be underestimated. And as I have said before – how many women have I commissioned prior to you?"

Venus swallowed hard. "None."

"None..." Sarracenia repeated. "You think that coincidence is lost upon me?"

Again, what was the right answer to give? Where was she going with this? Venus wished her mistress could, for once, skip the preamble and state her point.

"How many other women are out there, exactly like you? Other women who paint to their heart's content, and yet never see a profit off of it. Women who are allowed to be tutors or ladies-in-waiting. Women who never get commissioned simply because of how they were born."

There was more to it than that, Venus knew. It was not just because she was a woman. It was because when people looked at her, they could not decide if they knew what she was. She wondered if Sarracenia had ever experienced this. If everyone in the town knew what she was, or if it was only spread by rumors. She recalled what the Roms had said about her the other night.

"In a world where everyone imposes their expectations onto you," Sarracenia went on. "You have to decide what it is you want out of life. So, what *do* you want, Venus?"

Normal things, really. A roof over her head, meals everyday. A chance to do what she loved. Venus did not think herself ambitious, despite her clientele, but nobles were the only ones interested in and capable of paying for her services.

Is that what the countess wanted to hear, though? That this would be how Venus planned to spend an immortal life? In pure simplicity? That never seemed to be enough for nobles, they had a taste for the exotic, and soon all of life became merely a pursuit of that.

"Well?"

"I — why?"

"Why what?"

Venus shrugged, then brought her hands up to gesture around her.

"Why...everything? Why me? Why offer this up?"

There was silence between them. Then, Sarracenia stepped in closer, but for once, Venus did not back away from her. Instead, she allowed the countess to come in close.

"Do you really think of yourself as so unworthy?" she asked. "You must have thought you had something to bring to the table. Or you would not have replied to my letter. It wasn't even intended for you, but your husband."

Venus nodded at this statement. She had no way to refute it.

"I will admit, I was surprised when his wife's services were offered up in his absence, but at that point I was desperate. I thought to myself, 'why not? It could not possibly be any worse than the others, and if it is, then it might be entertainingly so'!"

Venus felt her cheeks grow hot despite the cold night air. She did not know why these words embarrassed her so. She had been aware of how her mistress had underestimated her at first. Still, to hear them spoken out loud, despite the outcome, made her feel very small.

"Then you proved me wrong." Sarracenia continued. "Do you know how often that happens?"

At first, Venus had thought this to be a rhetorical question, but then Sarracenia kept staring at her expectantly. "Not too often, I assume?"

"You assume correctly. But it's something you are used to, aren't you? People have underestimated you for your whole life. So you've had to work harder than everyone to show what you are capable of."

It surprised Venus to realize she had tears streaming down her face. She wiped at them with her sleeve. Her mistress kept right on speaking.

"How many times have you actually been able to showcase your abilities? How many times, despite your efforts, has the world allowed you to present what you can do?"

Venus did not know how to answer that. She had in fact painted for many nobles in the past. The countess was hardly her first patron. It was just that...

"You are the first," she answered before she became too lost in her own thoughts.

This reply seemed to please her mistress, as she gave a slow smile and a very small nod.

"Exactly. I could give you more, Venus dear." The countess said her name so rarely despite their arrangement, that it sent shivers down her spine every time. "You deserve more. Don't you think?"

She didn't know what to think. She never did when it came to her mistress. Her thoughts always became so cloudy.

No — it couldn't be worth the price. But then she thought about the people in the village. She thought about the guardsman, who had herded Roms like cattle. Who had beaten and imprisoned a young girl. How she had wanted him dead so, so badly. How she had plotted his murder once given the opportunity to do so.

Then, she thought of the Roms themselves. How the instant they had perceived her as a monster, they turned their welcoming arms into ones of malice. She could still feel the sting of the flames licking at her feet.

She did not belong anywhere. And here was someone offering her a place.

"I...I don't have to make a decision tonight, right?" she asked. Sarracenia did not give a verbal answer, only a more profound nod. "Then I shall consider it. It is a tremendous offer, I do not wish to take it lightly."

"Of course..." Sarracenia replied, closing the distance between them completely and taking Venus' arm back into hers.

They began to walk towards the doors, and Venus felt herself relieved at the idea of being back in her own room.

"Let us see how they react to you at the ball," the countess stated. "Let us see how they treat you now, as a human. As a woman. And then afterwards, you may make your decision."

Chapter 14

Eva

B y comparison, the manor at which they arrived seemed rather subpar. It was still an impressive size, but the garden was overgrown, and it had no statues around the yards. Eva supposed that was why they wanted to have an artist come in to freshen it up.

They were greeted at the door by a maid. Venus had to hold in her laughter at the sound of their accents. It occurred to Eva then how rare it must be for her to hear the way other people talk. They were escorted inside, and from there were split into two groups again.

Both men would have their own rooms, while the girls were meant to share. Eva doubted that this house lacked the room capacity for the two of them, but she was here on official business, so who was she to question their host?

The maid led her and Venus down the hallway. The room was nice enough, decoration wise, but it was smaller than either of their rooms back at home. The girls gave each other a look, sharing the same thought.

The maid then gave instructions on when to be ready to attend dinner, when to be in bed, and to not leave the room once lights were out. Immediately, Eva imagined the type of Gadje souls wandering about the hallways of such an old and drafty place. She imagined them handling the doorknobs until at last finding one open, desperately searching for a window. But in all likelihood, the maid probably meant that the master of this house did not care to be disturbed at night.

Did he have no children of his own, then? Was that why this place was so miserable? She wondered what that must be like, to live such a lonely existence, even one surrounded by luxury. Then she shook her head, attempting to turn down her assumptions. She knew nothing about this duke, other than that he was a potential client. That was all he had to be, and that was all she needed to focus on.

"What are we to do, now?" Venus asked, abandoning her luggage and lying flat on the mattress.

"I brought a deck of cards," Eva offered.

Venus rubbed at her head. "I'm rather sick of being indoors, aren't you?"

Always.

"I don't know if we're allowed to go exploring,"

"Oh, surely outside is fine!" Venus protested, sitting up.

Truthfully, Eva had very little interest in exploring the premises. She doubted it would be any more impressive than the house itself. She also saw it for what it was — a distraction. A waste of time. Her nerves were already on edge at the prospect of meeting a potential client. Yet remaining idle was not a more appealing option. She would rather be gathering information on this duke whom she might be painting. That was when she got the idea.

"Want to do something even more fun?"

Venus looked up at her with interest. "Go on."

Eva did not answer. Instead, she gave a mischievous smile and crept over to the door. She opened it just enough for her to peer outside with one eye. Only then did she turn back to her sister to whisper.

"How about we take a peek at the duke's bedchambers?"

Venus' mouth dropped open with the largest grin Eva had ever seen on her. So scared was she that her sister would begin to laugh in loud hysterics, that she waved up her arms in protest. Venus simply put a hand to her mouth and covered the quiet hiss of a chuckle.

The next thing they knew, they were both out into the hallway. They had no sense of direction, but the manor was only so big, and of course whichever bedroom they discovered to be the biggest must belong to the duke. So down they rushed, aimlessly full of vivacity.

Around the corner they went, only to discover the maid on the other end. She was readjusting the curtains and had her back turned to them, allowing the girls a chance to hide back behind the wall.

Venus mouthed the words *what do we do?*

Eva peered back over to the maid and gave a shrug. The hallway, she realized, was a dead end, meaning that she would have to return in their direction. As this thought occurred to her, footsteps were heard approaching them. Fiercely, Eva pointed to the nearest open door and both girls ran into it. Eva had to fight the urge to slam it shut, knowing that the noise would alert the maid.

The girls stood directly behind the still ajar door, backs against the wall. They saw her shadow approach, then stop. The girls held their breaths. They had no idea what sort of punishment would await them if discovered disobeying direct orders from the start. Her father would scold her for acting so childishly when they were here on official business. He might be so angry in fact, that he never assisted in securing a commission for her again.

Then, the maid reached out, shut the door completely, and walked on by. They waited until her footsteps faded into the distance before letting out the breath they had been holding in. Then the two burst into light giggles, trying hard to keep quiet while also being unable to stop.

"Abigail, is that you?" came a voice from the corner.

Both of them jumped and turned to see an old man in the corner, gazing out the window. He spotted them before they even had a chance to run. His eyebrows rose in surprise, but he did not appear angry.

He lowered the pipe he had in his mouth and spoke again. "So sorry, lovely young ladies, I thought you were...well, never mind."

Feeling a little encouraged by his gentler approach, the girls stepped away from the wall and approached him. Eva's eyes wandered around the room. The walls were decorated in floral paper, and the sheets upon the small bed were a faded pink. On top of the covers were stuffed animals and a doll with golden curls. This did not appear to be the suite of a duke, yet the man himself did not look like a servant. His clothes were much finer, if older and worn. His hands looked clean and soft, rather than covered in dirt or callouses.

"We're the Baron's daughters," Eva began. She could see from the corner of her eye that Venus was silently begging her to stop talking, but the introductions had to start somewhere. "We just arrived from France. We wanted a look around."

The man nodded, taking in her words. "Yes, yes, the artist my cousin has told me so much about."

His cousin? So this man must be the duke, then. He wasn't at all what Eva had been picturing. For starters, he was much older than the man Eva had met at her sister's gala. And he seemed rather unintimidating. She had her share of questions, however. What was he doing in a room like this, alone? Did he not intend to see his guests?

"Indeed," said Eva, a little quietly. "That's me."

This made the man look up. At first, his eyes were wide with surprise, and Eva did not know if it was due to her age or her sex, but either way she felt the pang of anger. Then, his face softened into a deep smile.

"I can see now why my cousin had you sent to me," he replied. Eva returned the smile, even though she did not fully comprehend his words. "What is your name, child?"

"It is Eva." She responded. Behind her, Venus cleared her throat in a less than subtle manner. "And this is my sister, future Baroness Venus Cellier de Durand."

Her sister gave a small curtsy, and the man made a type of exclamation which seemed to be mock admiration.

"Well, welcome both of you to my humble abode! I do hope you forgive my lack of manners; it has been some time since I've received guests in the house..."

He walked towards them, arm outstretched, and the girls waited for him to approach. Just as he was about to lead them out, however, the door burst open and in stormed the maid.

"What are you two doing out of your room?" She demanded, eyes narrowed. The girls went to answer, but when she saw who was with them, she shrank back. "Sir, forgive me, I had given strict orders for them not to — "

"It's quite alright, Agatha..." the duke reassured, waving around his pipe so that the remaining smoke faded out. "Lord knows how long it's been since this room had young women in it."

He opened his arms and ushered the four of them out. Eva managed to take one last look at the bedroom before the door had shut behind them. Her eyes fixed on the small stuffed animals residing on the bed.

Her father and Jacques were quick to join them, both with the same apologetic yet frustrated nature that the maid had demonstrated. Just as with her, the duke laughed both of them off. Then, he invited them for an early lunch. Eva's family seemed pleased with the gesture, but she could not help but notice the forced smile the maid gave.

Part of her felt satisfied in knowing that she and her sister were getting out of this situation without consequence, but some other part of her felt pity that a kind gesture came at the expense of someone else. Still, there was nothing she could truly do about it, so she smiled and followed everyone else down to the dining room.

The table was large enough to seat all of them, with the duke at the head of the table, the men on either side of him, and then Venus next to Jacques and Eva next to their father. The lunch itself was rather bland, consisting of poached eggs, toast and salads. Eva suspected that she had been spoiled by her father's extravagant taste over the years, even though she had been unfamiliar with most of the dishes when she first started living with them.

She hoped that the duke did not ask how she liked the food — Eva had difficulties with lying, and her honest tongue would come out before her flattering one. She bit into her eggs and quietly swallowed down the yolks.

"I must say," the duke started once the food had been passed out. "I was rather hesitant at receiving guests, but my cousin spoke so highly of the talent your daughter possesses..."

"Oh yes, sir." Her father began, wiping yolk from his lips with his napkin. "She has been training hard for years, under our own Jacques, here."

"Indeed..." the duke did not look up from his food as he spoke, that is, until he turned to look directly at Eva. She looked back up at him, as well. "My dear, I have lived a long and rich life. Everything around here, I built from the ground up."

She knew there was no way that could possibly be true. He must have inherited this land from his family. Or he married into the title. Perhaps the house was built from scratch, but by others, under his supervision, and who knows how low the pay was.

"I have lived a life in pursuit of comfort," he went on. "And yet, there is something which has been missing from my life. Something only an artist can achieve."

This intrigued her. She sat up straighter and gave a small nod. The duke surprised everyone by getting up from his chair. They were about to follow suit, then he motioned with his hands for them to remain seated.

Hesitantly, they did as instructed, all the while watching him walk closer over to Eva. He pulled something from his pocket and handed it over. It was a carefully folded, but very old looking piece of paper.

Eva picked it up and realized that it was a sketch. She recognized one figure as the duke himself, and next to him was a woman holding a baby.

"My wife, Elizabeth." He explained, pointing at the woman as though she could not have guessed who he meant. "I had her portrait done as a wedding gift before her passing, she had a very weak heart you see, but here..." he pointed down at the baby. "This is my Abigail. Her passing was most unexpected. She did not inherit any of her mother's conditions, and in fact the doctors said that she was an exceptionally healthy young girl. I wanted to wait until her debut before having her portrait done..."

He said all of these words as though this were a story he had told many times before. That sort of somber recollection only the elderly looked upon their life with. Yet, at this last phrase, he paused, and she heard him inhale deeply, as though attempting to stifle something back.

"Tragically, she lost her life at only age twelve. Riding her favorite horse, the beast had become spooked, and she fell into the nearby river, where she drowned." He moved his hand from the sketch to Eva, and placed it on her shoulder. "What I am asking of you is a favor to an old man. One which I imagine will not be easy, since there will be no model, but if you could even indulge the idea, I will pay you handsomely."

Eva looked up at him. She was so moved by his sorrow, that she would have done him a favor for free, if her father would have ever allowed such a thing. She had a feeling she knew what the request was to be, but she encouraged him to voice it, regardless.

"What would you like me to paint?"

"Since my daughter died before I could have her portrait painted, I have not seen her face in many decades. I never got to see her face grown into the woman she should have become. I ask that you work with me, and the memories of an old and lonely man, to recreate what she may have looked like at about your age."

Eva nodded. "Did you daughter look very much like your wife?"

"Eva..." her father began, as though she had asked a rather impertinent question.

"Yes!" The duke answered, rather enthusiastically. "So very much

190

alike!"

Eva smiled. "Well, then the portrait you have of her shall come in handy."

The duke smiled, almost bouncing with exhilaration. He picked up his sketch once more, and was about to lead Eva out of the room to begin at once, when the maid came in with their dessert. Reluctantly, he sat back down.

...

The canvas and paint were set up in the drawing room. The main decoration of this place was the large, oil portrait hanging above the fireplace. The subject was a lovely woman with golden curls — was every Gadje woman a blonde? — and light blue dress. The woman had a pleasant face, with soft cheekbones and lips which suggested gentleness despite their lack of smiling.

Eva did not start with the canvas. Instead, she pulled out her latest sketchbook and opened it to a fresh page. There were two wooden chairs next to a small table, as well as a couch, but the duke sat in neither of those. Instead, he paced around the room, discussing in great detail the appearance of his daughter.

"Now, she had her mother's eyes," he began. "But larger, full of youth. Although, I suppose if we are to draw her as older, they would be not quite so large?"

At first, Eva had been very excited at the prospect of the project. She would be bringing the dead back to life. Yet as the duke continued to ramble on the description, the feat of the task at hand became more and more apparent. She drew the faces of a dozen girls, all with various details so small in difference, the measurement for them did not yet exist. Then she drew a dozen more. Another dozen after that.

The duke was very patient. He did not reprimand Eva as he critiqued her work, rather he mostly criticized himself for not having the 'memory he used to have.' Eva was grateful that her knuckles were at peace.

Perhaps, she thought, she was thinking about this the wrong way. The duke wanted to see a girl he had no memory of – the teenager his daughter never became. She looked up at the portrait, at his wife who was older than maidenhood but still very young indeed. Maybe she simply needed to

191

reverse the clock a little more. She drew her own rendition of the oil portrait, but lifted the eyebrows a little more, enlarged the eyes, rounded out the cheeks, and pursed out the lips. This girl did not look like the many previous attempts, and did not really fit the many memories the duke had rambled on about. However, she did look like her mother.

"How is this?" Eva asked, holding up the sketchbook.

The duke came over and gave a look. His eyes squinted, and his head tilted, and for a very long time he said nothing. Eva began to lower the sketchbook, worried she had offended him with her bold take. Then, his face split open into a wide smile, and he nearly jumped back on the heels of his feet.

"Bravo, young lady!" he declared with triumph. "You've done it!"

Eva felt her chest swell with pride beneath the relief that was washing over her. At last, this customer of hers was satisfied. She set down the sketchbook and picked up the canvas. Next to this, painting seemed like the easy part.

The duke finally sat down in one of the chairs, but not before bringing it over so that he could observe what Eva was doing.

"She was a lovely girl..." he said in that far away, dreamlike tone of voice which let Eva know that he was not truly speaking to her. "So lovely..."

"Tell me more about her. What was she like?" Eva insisted, knowing that this would be the best way to preoccupy him while she worked. She was not accustomed to having someone other than her tutor watch as she painted. She was not entirely sure that she enjoyed it, but given the circumstances, she felt that this was excusable.

"Oh..." the duke began. Eva expected him to talk about her looks or her charms, instead he went with, "headstrong. Very stubborn, just like her mother. Moreso, even. Abigail had the strength to live in ways Elizabeth never would have dared."

Eva turned back to the mother's portrait. Nothing about it seemed to suggest sickness, as the duke had mentioned. She wondered how much of this rendition was also an exaggeration. How much of the way his wife looked did he truly remember, and how much was just this painting.

"How do you mean?" she asked.

"Well, her taking up horse riding, for one thing. If Elizabeth couldn't ride in a carriage, she walked. Or simply refused to go." He laughed at his own words, as though he were telling a joke. Eva smiled to be polite. "But not my Abigail. She did not want the confines of this estate to keep her spirit locked up. Her words, in fact."

Eva nodded. Since he spoke so highly of her hobby, she wondered if she should attempt to finish this portrait with Abigail atop of a horse. "My sister enjoys horseback riding. I've always been too afraid myself, but I — "

"She should have exercised more caution." The duke went on. At the tone of his voice, Eva decided it would be best to not place Abigail atop a horse. "Do you ever warn your sister of that?"

"Pardon?"

"Your sister," the duke replied, as though that in itself was the explanation. "Do you ever tell her to exercise caution when riding?"

"Um... well..." Why had she turned to make the conversation about herself? Why could she not have stuck to asking him the questions about his daughter? "I...feel that my sister is cautious enough when she rides."

The duke shook his head. "They could always be more cautious..."

He went back into his routine rambles, but it still took Eva a bit to stop shaking. She did not understand why his words had gotten to her so deeply. The thought of her sister, meaning Venus, being so careless in horseback riding that she would fall over in an accident and die... she supposed it was enough to shake anyone.

Then she thought of her other family. Her first family, and how likely that many of them were dead. Not from horseback riding, or anything done for leisure, nor by accident, but by the brute force of those who claim the right to make the laws.

Eva tried to bring herself back into the present moment, yet how could she? Would it be alright to ask for a break? They had been going at it for hours now on the sketch alone. Or would the duke be too excited at the prospect of a finished painting that he pushed her onward? Surely, both of them must sleep at some point, even though the thought of lying in bed with these thoughts was the last thing Eva wanted to do.

Fortunately for her, the duke let out a yawn himself.

"It is late, and candles will need to be lit soon. It is best we continue in the morning, when the light is at its peak."

Eva agreed, or rather, she did not argue, as she collected her sketchbook and charcoals before heading out of the parlor. The duke invited her to dinner, but she had no appetite. Instead, she scurried back to her room and opened up the sketchbook to a blank page.

She stared into it for a very long time.

Then, she picked up her charcoals and put them to the paper. A circle at first. She always began with a circle, as a means of measurement. It would not do to make the subject too big on the paper. Some people, like Venus, preferred to start with small details, such as the eyes, as a way to build from the ground up. But Eva preferred to have a concrete beginning before moving forward.

Soon, the circle had a more organic shape. Not quite perfect, intentionally asymmetrical. Then it had a nose, very distinct in its shape. Then thin lips which never smiled. Finally, a pair of eyes which could be soft or cold, depending on who the conversation was with or about. They were always squinting at the sun, but they came to life when the flames of the evening fire were lit. Then Eva drew in the hair. Wavy, but tied back, with stubborn strands sticking out on all sides, refusing to be completely tamed. Just like her soul.

When she finished, Eva looked down at the face she had not seen in years, and for the first time since that last day, her mother looked back at her.

...

They continued on like this for quite some time. The duke would sit and watch as Eva painted away, commenting on details here and there — no, her cheeks did not have so much blush to them, or her eyes were a softer blue. Overall, she enjoyed listening to his stories. They helped to pass the time, especially when she needed to wait for the oils to dry before moving on to the next set of details.

Sometimes, they just sat in the parlor for hours, sharing stories and jokes back and forth. It reached a point to where, when she returned to her painting, she felt as if she too knew Abigail. That this was a dear, long-lost friend whom she had not seen for some time. Eva noticed the impact this had on her brushwork, how she was gentler and more careful in response.

She also realized how much she began to look forward to her sessions with the duke. How she could not wait to listen to the next humorous or dramatic story or have him repeat some of her favorites. Eva had not known many Gadje men in her life, but out of all of them, this one was her favorite.

When finally came the time in which she realized she was adding the last of the details, Eva felt a heavy pang in her heart. Would that be it, then? The duke would get his painting, Eva would get her payment — money meant little to her now that she lived under a rich father — and then return home, never to see her friend again?

She felt all of this so deeply that she began to cry.

"My dear Eva," the duke inquired as they sat together. "What on earth is the matter?"

Eva wiped at her tears. "Oh, I was only thinking. About how soon the painting will be done, and how my family will leave, and we will never see one another again."

The duke gave her a long and thoughtful look. She wondered what it was he pondered over. Did he feel the same way? Or did she pour her heart out to the sentiments of an old man whose feelings did not go past his family?

"My dear Miss Eva. You have given me what I haven't had in decades."

She waited for him to continue, but he only looked at her with expectation. She gestured towards the painting.

"No, no!" he reassured. "Well, yes, that. I can gaze upon my daughter's face once more, and I have you to thank for it."

He rested his hand on her shoulder. She looked down at it, at its wrinkles which told a story, at the dirt between his nails, which had grown over so much that he could no longer clean them, and at the slight shake of his wrist.

"But also the company you have provided over this time. For being a presence this household has not seen for decades. For going along with the sentiments of an old fool and reminding me once more of what it's like to have a daughter within these walls."

Eva felt tears begin to prick at her eyes. Why had her own father never said these words to her before? He had given her flattery, yes, and in truth she got her way more often than not, at least as far as painting or other pretty things caught her eye. But up until this moment, with this duke, there had been something between the two of them which Eva had not been able to name before. It had always felt as though she were property to her father. An asset to be acquired.

Here, with the duke, her presence was enough. Simply being here with him, providing company was enough. She was enough. She placed her own hand over his and gave it a rub with her thumb. The tears flowed freely from her eyes at this point.

"Thank you..." she tried to say, but it came out more as a subtle whisper.

He seemed to understand, giving her another smile. "Which is why, I have a proposition for you."

This caused Eva to straighten up slightly. The tears still dripped from her cheeks, but new ones stopped in their place.

"What is it?"

"As long as you don't mind continuing to indulge the sentiments of an old fool," here he took his hand back, as though it were necessary to emphasize his point with it. "Then I would like to ask your father for permission to hire you as my family's official painter."

Eva blinked. "I..." she stammered. "I don't know what to say..."

That would mean that she would get to stay here, with her friend, listening to stories while painting every day. She would be employed, earning commissions regularly, doing what she loved most in the world. And that was far too wonderful an option for her to deserve.

"Say nothing, for now." The duke replied, his tone becoming more somber. "Merely think it over for the night, and if you remain interested by morning, I shall have a talk with your father regarding the arrangement."

Eva nodded, a smile breaking wide across her face. She stood up, understanding now why the duke always did that when becoming excited. Then, unable to contain her emotions any further, she leaned over and wrapped her arms around him, pulling him into a tight embrace.

"Thank you!" She proclaimed. "Thank you, a thousand times, thank you!"

He gave her back a light pat, and she took that as her cue to let go. She gave the duke one last smile, and an awkward wave, before heading off to bed with a much lighter heart than the night previous.

During slumber, she dreamed of her new life. Of the paintings she would create, and how the hours would pass by with just her and her new friend. She dreamed of the parties they would hold where the duke would sing her praises to guests, and where she would be allowed to discuss her own techniques without being constantly talked over.

She was woken up very early the next morning, ripped from her dreams like a drowning victim pulled from the water. She sat up in her bed, drenched in sweat and breathing deeply. Venus stood over her, eyes red with tears.

"What?" Eva asked. "What is it?"

"It is the duke," her sister sobbed. "He died last night."

...

The funeral was small, but not cheap. The duke had only a small number of friends who were still alive to attend. They came with their wives, and a few of their grown children, and that was that. Eva knew none of them and they did not know her, and the proceedings thereafter did not change this aspect. They said their prayers, sang the hymns, and said farewell in their own way, parallel to one another.

When the time came for them to approach the coffin, Eva could not bring herself to look inside at first. She did not want to see her friend lying there, eyes closed and skin waxy yellow. In her mind, she wanted to keep him as the spry, excited old man who nearly jumped when he felt so compelled. A man who had been so full of life.

But then she thought about how this would be the last time she would ever see him. How this very afternoon, they would be closing that casket and burying it deep within the ground, so he was nothing more than a memory and a headstone. That thought filled her with such grief, she felt compelled to look down upon him.

It was not as bad as she had feared. The make-up put on him helped to hide how yellow his skin had become, and with his eyes closed, he appeared to be sleeping. His face was calm, peaceful, yet somehow this made it all the worse.

There must have been a mistake, he would surely rise up at any moment, he had to be merely sleeping, he had to. But as Eva was escorted away by her family, she knew that she could no longer deny the truth.

She turned around to face where her friend laid one last time, and whispered, "I'm glad you are with your wife and daughter once more..."

...

They did not return home immediately afterwards, rather they stayed behind to look over the affairs. Eva did not fully understand how that burden had become theirs, but her father had insisted.

Lawyers came over the next few days, as well as a few family members Eva recognized but did not engage with. They had long discussions with her father over tea, about the distribution of the duke's assets, what to keep, what not to keep, who would receive what and what was to be done with the unwanted possessions. It burned her heart with anger and sadness. Had her friend become only a collection of things to be passed around?

She had to remind herself that it did not matter. Her friend was now a corpse in the ground, and his soul was free, reunited with his family. He was at peace, at last.

It did not lift the ache she felt in regard to their deal. She felt guilty whenever she pondered over it, how there was still a part of her which remained disappointed that she would never be able to live the life he had promised to her. They had not even been able to propose the idea to her father and ask for his permission.

Venus seemed strangely distant, as well. Eva tried to tell her sister some of these things in confidence, but every time she tried to catch her alone, Venus would wander off as though summoned by another. Perhaps the funeral was hitting her hard, as well, although Eva did not see why it would.

Maybe it brought back terrible memories of her long-passed mother. Eva did not know if Venus had ever attended any other funerals besides that one. Perhaps she wanted to avoid Eva crying about the duke because it would simply be too painful for her own soul to bear. This was only speculation, but Eva had no other conclusion for her sister's mannerisms.

Then one morning, she heard her father talking in the parlor with the lawyers and family members. She had been passing by on her way to breakfast, when a question was asked that stopped her right outside the door.

"And now, what is to be done with the paintings?" It was a man's voice, one she had come to associate with one of the lawyers. "These were his most prized possessions, but they hold mainly sentimental value."

How dare this man be so disrespectful to the artwork. She had slaved over hers, and she had no doubt that the artist who had painted his wife had done the same. To say that their value lay only for the duke was beyond insulting.

She heard her father's voice.

"Perhaps they would be of more value if the artist were made aware? Then they may be sold off as a collection or to a museum."

"That is true," the lawyer replied. "Who is the artist for this piece, then?"

A woman answered and given that Eva did not recognize the name being spoken, she must have been referring to the painting of the wife. They discussed a bit further regarding the artist, asking where he lived, and what compensation he may require should they sell the piece off. It eventually was decided that it would be best to simply give the painting away to a relative, that the late duchess may have a distant cousin or two who may be interested.

Eva felt her heart beating ever faster within her chest. They had to discuss her painting next.

"And as for the painting of the daughter?" The lawyer went on, and Eva stopped breathing.

"Well, I should hope I know the artist," her father replied, in that manner which suggested arrogance. Eva fiddled with her fingers as she waited for her father's testimony. "It is the entire reason for our stay at this estate. The artist is I."

Everything froze.

Time itself stood still as it had so many years ago when Eva first learned the truth about her father. It paused without malice, giving her a chance to catch up with it. To catch up with what was happening around her.

Voices were talking, but she could not hear what they said. What did their words matter, after what her father had just proclaimed? She must have misheard, she must have misunderstood. There had to be a mistake.

When she could bear it no longer, Eva stormed into the parlor. Six shocked faces stared up at her, including her father's, and Jacques, as well. Eva looked at her tutor first, eyes borrowing into his. Surely, he would not allow such a lie said? After all of their training together? Those endless nights when he whipped against her knuckles. Had he no shame, then to call out her father?

Her father... she turned to him next, gaze still so full of hatred. And she did hate him in that moment.

"Father..." she seethed through her teeth, tears threatening to come back in full force. "What is the meaning of this?"

All eyes turned to him, and he stood to walk over to his daughter, immediately escorting her out of the room. Before he even managed to shut the door behind them, she was yanking herself out of his grip, spinning around to glare at him.

"How dare you!" She snapped, ignoring his gestures for her to quiet down. "You cannot take credit for what is mine!"

"Eva, dear, of course that's not what I am trying to do..." he reassured, venturing to take a few steps closer to her, in order to place hands on her shoulders, but she did not allow him to.

He cleared his throat and took a momentary glance back at the door to the parlor.

"You have seen the types of people who are in there, they are old fashioned. They will not believe that such a painting could have been produced by a young woman."

"I am here," Eva interrupted, finding enough control to lower her voice. "They can see proof for themselves, if they need it."

Her father nodded. "I have no doubt of that, dearest. But even if you were to do that, all they would do is demand a lower price. Now, what I am offering is for your piece to hang oin the walls of a museum, with every bit as handsome a commission as the duke was offering."

"He was my friend," Eva responded, not caring how clearly it irritated her father that she had interrupted once more. "He was old fashioned, and yet he did not mind me being so young. Or a woman."

Her father stared at her a moment, before letting out a long sigh and reaching into his pocket. From there, he produced a pipe, not unlike the one she had seen the duke use when first meeting him. Nostalgia panged in her heart. Her father lit it and inhaled deeply before letting a giant puff of smoke surround the air. It even smelled like the duke, and Eva could feel her anger wash away into sadness.

"I just want to do what is best for my daughter," he went on, his words breathing leftover smoke in her direction. She stifled a cough. "If you feel that you could go in there and prove yourself worthy of not only their acknowledgement but also their approval. If you feel that you can convince a group of lawyers and noblemen that a painting by a woman is deserving of wall space within a museum, then by all means. Present your case."

Eva looked in the direction of the door. She wondered what was being discussed in there, while the two of them spoke to one another. She wondered if suspicions were rising, if anyone in there was wondering about the truth of her father's words, or what role Eva had in this.

Or perhaps they simply thought this man had gone out to deal with his difficult daughter. They were most likely spreading rumors about her, even if only to one another. And what of Jacques? Was he in there, holding his tongue until his friend came back in?

"You think it's good enough to hang in a museum, don't you?" she asked, unsure why that was the first question to come to mind. Her father cocked an eyebrow at her. "Because that is the truth, it is a painting by a young woman. But you still think it's good enough to hang in a museum, don't you?"

"Of course!" He exclaimed once the meaning of her question became clear to him. He placed a hand on her shoulder, and this time she did not shudder away from his touch. "Of course I do, that's why I am fighting so hard for your case! It isn't *me* you have to convince of your talent, it's the rest of the world. A world which can be so cruel to its women. Especially those of... lesser blood."

Eva wanted to retort that his blood flowed within her veins as much as her Rom blood did. That it was his very same blood which had made her feel so unclean for so many years. To this day, in fact, she longed to rip it out of her. She said none of this, for deep down, she knew that he spoke correctly. That it would not matter if she proved to these nobles and lawyers that she was the true artist, they would indeed demand a lower price for the piece.

"Besides," he continued, taking another puff from his pipe. "You know that most museums do not even permit female artists from displaying work. How would it feel to have all of those weeks of toiling wasted, just for your painting to end up in the corner of a rubbish heap? Don't you think the memory of the duke and his daughter deserve better than that? Don't you think *you* deserve better than that?"

Lord, she hadn't even thought of that. Was that why there had been no women artists in the museum they had visited before their arrival? They simply were not permitted? Is that why her father had pushed commissions onto her, because that would be the only way her work could get any recognition or payment?

Except she would not be receiving any recognition. The money to be given was most likely going to go to her father, now. Yet he could not have predicted the death of her friend, the duke. He was only trying to make the best of an imperfect situation.

"Just this once?" she asked. "Because they are so old fashioned? Next time, we find patrons who are more open-minded, like the duke. Who would not mind that their portraits are painted by a young, Romani woman?"

Her father pursed his lips and nodded. "Of course, my dear, of course! I would do anything for your happiness!"

The two of them returned to the parlor, and as expected, a group of eyes stared upon them as they returned. For her part, Eva sat down quietly and allowed her father to finish up the negotiations. She felt nothing as a price was given. It was as if the price of her very soul had been called out, and a handshake later, it was sold. It would hang in a local museum for the time being, as other arrangements were to be made. Eva tried not to imagine her work along the walls, bearing her father's name in the description.

She also tried not to pay attention as the party went on with the discussion, but when she heard one of the family members request going over details for a commission, her ears perked up. Would her father admit the truth now? Surely he would have to — it was not like he could carry on the pretense. He had also promised that this would be the only negotiation made under these false pretenses.

Yet as she listened in to the conversation, her father seemed very bold in his decisions. He stated how honored he would be to work with another set of nobles, and that his family would pack right away for the journey. It did not make sense to Eva. Just what was his plan, then? Would he reveal the truth once they arrived at the new location?

She looked over at Jacques, unsure as to why he was not speaking up against his friend. He must be aware of her father's lack of artistic ability and understand how ludicrous this arrangement would be. But then he stood up and approached the noble her father was talking with and shook his hand.

"I have yet to introduce Jacques," her father stated, patting the other man's back. "My future son-in-law."

The phrase jolted inside of Eva. Future son-in-law? They were old enough to be brothers, what on earth was he talking about? Then Eva thought about how distant Venus had become as of late. How she never seemed to be able to focus on a given conversation. Eva had assumed it was due to the funeral, but could it be that…?

No. Absolutely not. Her father would want a good match for his daughter. A man — a young man — of promise, with high prospects. Not a broke artist whose only job was tutoring said daughters. He could not possibly think of arranging such a match.

Eva found that she could bear the conversation no more. Not a single person looked her way as she arose from her seat and exited the room. She did not pause until she had made her way back to the bedroom she and her sister shared. A part of her was relieved to see Venus sitting there, for Eva would not have known where to find her, otherwise. The relief was short lived, however, when Venus turned to show the red in her wet eyes.

Eva approached her and took a seat on the bed.

"Is it true?" She asked, wondering if she needed to expand upon her question.

Venus seemed to understand, as she nodded. "I was told a few days ago, right before the funeral, in fact. I just… with everything going on, I could not find a way to bring it up. And then doing so made it feel all the more real…"

"But father cannot be serious!" Eva protested. "Of all the men in the world, there are surely younger, richer ones who could make a better match!"

Venus provided no answer. Her mouth hung open as she attempted, but she only burst into a single sob before the tears sprung down her cheeks. Eva knew that this was not the time to conspire or plot. For now, her sister needed comfort. She leaned over and wrapped her arms around her as best she could and let the younger girl cry into her. After a moment, she ran her hand softly through Venus' hair and shushed her lightly.

"It will be alright…" Eva said. "No matter what happens, I will remain your sister. We are in this together."

She did not know how honest her words could be. If Jacques remained, then they could all live under one roof. But if he decided to take his little wife away, then there was next to nothing which Eva could do to prevent it.

Yet these were the words Venus needed to hear right then.

"You are the only sister I have ever known," she said to Eva between sobs. "Nothing will change that, we will be together, no matter how far they may try to tear us apart!"

In a moment of weakness, Eva was tempted to tell her sister about the proclamations their father had made in regards to her painting. She just wanted to tell the truth to someone who would understand her frustration and lack of action. It would have to wait until later, though.

"Exactly," Eva replied, grateful that her sister understood what she was attempting to say. "We will stay sisters, and we will stay together. No matter what."

Chapter 15

Venus

V enus had been doing everything in her power to avoid her mistress. The day after their walk, she had gone out to the farm to collect her horse. A strong sense of comfort washed over her at the sight of the animal, who in turn, seemed to be equally pleased to see her. A pang of guilt stabbed at her heart at the fact that she had not come to collect her animal earlier, but she felt even more guilty over the idea that soon it would be trapped in that abysmal place with her.

This thought did not prevent her from returning on its back, however. She needed an ally.

The night of the ball would be upon them soon, and she had not yet given her answer. It had been difficult to evade her mistress altogether, as she was still required to paint her on a regular basis, but fortunately Sarracenia seemed to have no interest in discussing the topic while Venus was at work.

At dinner, she refused to dine with the countess, feigning a headache most nights, or insisting that she should remain working on whatever progress she had made that day. Then later on, she would sneak down to the kitchen and her greenhouse to eat. She would then go and visit her horse and ensure to provide its fill of food as well.

The rest of her time, she spent outdoors. Now that she knew her way around this place, at least a little, she wanted to take advantage of the natural sunlight while she could, both walking and riding her horse. The warmth from the distant star always calmed her nerves, as though it were a barrier shielding her from the countess. Eventually, however, the sun always stretched out its course across the sky and would set in the west. She inhaled deeply and then headed back inside for the evening posing.

To her relief, and mild surprise, once Venus reached the inside of the fireplace room, she found it empty. While it did concern her that she did not know where the countess presently was, Venus appreciated the moment of pause before having to spend another evening praying that Sarracenia did not ask the question Venus feared she would.

As she waited, she began to go through her recent portfolio. The original painting hung up proudly above the fireplace still. Then there was the latest finished piece, containing Sarracenia with her name-bearing plant. Now were two unfinished pieces that Venus went back and forth on, depending on which one her mistress wanted to pose for. One was of her holding a chest, the contents within, Venus did not know. The other was her standing with a skull in her hand. Venus did not ask for the origins of this article.

She looked at all of these paintings, the mountain of oils, the monotone of its subjects, and wondered how she had managed to convince herself that she could spend an eternity finding the countess to be an interesting study.

She knew that she would turn down the offer. There was no way she could bear doing this forever. Did her feelings even matter, in the end? The countess would never let her go as long as she could hold a brush. If not for all of time, she would surely spend the rest of her life within these walls, until she died naturally or the countess found favor in her no longer and killed her off.

Her worst fear was that either way, her death would happen within this room, with its closed windows, trapping her soul inside forever. Venus had more than once, in a fit of paranoia, gone around the room to attempt and open the glass, but the windows in this room were small and high, far above what Venus could hope to reach, even with the stool she sat upon. Her heart constantly sank being in this room.

"Well?" came a voice, the only voice, startling Venus out of her trance. "Shall we proceed?"

Sarracenia sauntered across the floor and took her place in the chair. Tonight would be the painting with the mystery chest. That was fine enough for Venus, as she much preferred it to the skull. She picked up her brush.

She was still laying down the flats of this painting, with the shading on the face blocked out. She wanted to finish the countess first before moving on to the other details.

"Our ball is a few nights away," the countess spoke. Venus silently prayed that the conversation would stay on the subject at hand and not turn to anything more dangerous. "Are you prepared?"

Venus opened her mouth. The countess had not asked for her input regarding the ball before.

"I suppose as ready as I'll ever be."

Sarracenia pursed her lips, and Venus felt a chill down her spine at the fear that she had answered incorrectly.

"None of the dresses you own are suitable," her mistress stated. Venus was almost tempted to point out that they were in fact *her* dresses, and that Venus owned very little within these walls. "You must come to my bedchambers for something to wear."

Out of all the surprises this evening had to offer, this one was by far the largest of them. Venus did not even know where the countess' bedchamber would be. She had difficulties picturing her mistress asleep in any capacity. When the countess was not in her line of sight, she secretly thought that she merely... ceased to exist in a physical form. That rather, she would become like vapor, and hide within the walls, eyes constantly on Venus.

"O-of course, Sarracenia." She answered, then added. "I would be honored."

In truth, she did mean that last part. The countess had shown her many intimacies; a luxury found so rarely with nobles. She doubted that many had seen the bedchambers of the Countess Luchia de Sarracenia. And lived.

Then, another thought crossed her mind. Would the introduction to someplace so intimate, so secretive, be the countess' way of asking Venus for her answer?

Was her intention to corner her within the bedchamber and demand for her to choose? Or make an answer for her?

Venus swallowed. She could not reject the invitation now; she would have to hope that Sarracenia merely meant to present her with a dress.

The rest of the evening carried on in silence. Venus had attempted to stretch it out as long as she possibly could, but at a certain point her arms ached, and her eyes would not keep themselves open. The countess could see this and made a comment.

"You are falling asleep, come. Let us go to my chambers before you are too tired to walk."

Venus already was too tired to walk. She could have fallen asleep right in that spot, or on the cold, hard floors as she had so long ago. Yet her mistress came over and took hold of her hand and pulled her along the way.

They walked down the hallway, and a part of Venus began to wake up as she tried to calculate where this bedchamber could possibly be located. She had begun to explore the outside of this place, but everything inside save for the kitchen, dining room, fireplace and her own room remained a mystery.

She had no desire to try and find anything within these walls. But inside a place quite this large, so overwhelming, where would one put the bedchamber for the nobility who owned it?

Venus received her answer once the two of them stopped at the top of the stairs for the great room. Again, she pictured it full of life and people, a reality in just a few days. Then, the countess took a step forward, and Venus was prepared to descend the stairs. Except the pair did not go down, but rather, their steps led them higher and higher.

At first, Venus was under the impression that her exhaustion had caused her to hallucinate – that she was caught in the middle of a dream. But as the two continued, she could not deny the way her feet fell against nothing, and the thrill that went through her body as they went.

Then, she looked up at the ceiling for the first time. There was a radial design upon it, with sharp angles and arms stretching out from the center. It took her mind a moment to recognize what it resembled – a spider's web.

The countess held out her arm, which made her let go of one of Venus', causing the artist to shriek at the sudden lack of support. This did not last long, as the countess took hold of a door which Venus had not been able to see at this angle. She gripped the handle and yanked it open, forcing Venus inside before following her.

Venus was so surprised by the action, that she landed on her hands and knees. She coughed, lightly at first, but her throat did not clear, and they became more frantic so that her eyes began to water.

There was no light, so the first thing Venus noticed was the smell. It was old, and musty, the way elderly people sometimes smell. But there was also something beneath it, a putrid, rotten smell she could only catch with every other breath. She felt her stomach quiver, even more so because of the journey they took to get up here. Between her exhaustion and nausea, Venus genuinely worried that she would pass out.

Then, a small flame lit right behind her. She turned her head to see that the countess was holding a large, white candle in her hand as she walked in closer. Venus was at last able to look around.

The old smell was explained by the dust which clung to every surface, including the floor. Venus immediately stood up and wiped her hands against her apron, caring too late if such an action would offend the countess.

She continued to peer around and saw that cobwebs also hung along the walls. There was a small table in the corner – or at least, it would be a corner were it not for the fact that the entire room was circular – where the countess had produced her candle. Next to that was a wardrobe, where Venus imagined the desired dresses were residing. But as her eyes peered around, she saw no other furniture within the room.

Save for one piece directly in the center. There, lay a large, and ornate coffin.

Venus felt herself shiver at the sight of it. The concept of death itself did not make her uncomfortable, yet to see such a piece inside of a bedchamber was enough to be unsettling. It was more than that, however. It seemed to be calling to her, enticing her to step closer. It reminded her of the way the carnivorous plants blossomed into such a rich red to lure insects in. Or the red in her mistress' lips, hypnotizing her. This coffin was whispering sweet nothings out into the air, tempting her.

Venus feared what could possibly lay inside of it, but she also felt that if she laid hands on it, her very flesh would burn off of her bones.

"Come along," the countess interrupted.

Venus turned, grateful for the excuse to no longer have to look upon the dreaded coffin. As soon as she walked away, the whispers stopped, and she was left with a lump inside of her stomach.

Sarracenia placed the candle down on the table before opening the wardrobe. Venus was unsurprised to see a cloud of dust wafting over the air as she did so and had the foresight to stay back a moment longer before joining her.

The countess placed a finger to her chin and tilted her head, mocking the concept of her thinking hard over a decision. Because it would be her decision, and her decision alone. Venus was there as a prop, a doll for her to dress. This knowledge did not stop Venus from peering deeper inside of the wardrobe, however, and inspecting the options.

She saw a maroon dress with large, puffed-up sleeves which she felt might be the most comfortable one. There was also a midnight blue one with soft- looking material. However, once she had spotted a dress with a low-cut front, she had a feeling that this would be the choice of her mistress. Instinctively, she placed a hand against her torso, as if to protect it for another moment more before being subjugated to wearing an outfit against her will.

So she was rather surprised when instead Sarracenia reached out for a black dress. Venus tried to think of the last time she had worn anything black. It must have been at the last funeral she had attended. The countess pulled it out and held it up. Venus took notice of how similar it was to the dress Sarracenia wore herself, and for some reason, this caused the pit in her stomach to drop even more.

She said nothing as the countess handed it over to her and then proceeded to stare at her expectantly. Venus took the dress, gave a small nod, and then turned around. She was not entirely sure why she was so shy about undressing in front of her mistress, considering the two of them had shared a bath together before. She supposed however, during that particular time, she had been more focused on other things — such as washing the blood from her body — to really think about the awkwardness of being naked and in close proximity to her patron.

She told herself that she turned around because she wanted to avoid judgement in how clumsily she took off her clothes. At first, she had no idea what to do with the dress itself. She could not hold onto it and untie her ribbons at the same time. But she did not want to put it on the dusty floor, both for sanitary reasons and also to avoid the perception of rudeness.

As if reading her thoughts, Venus suddenly felt two hands along her back. Completely void of voluntary reactions, she let out a shriek in surprise. She heard a small giggle behind her as the countess pulled at her laces and then helped her out of the corset.

Venus already felt so exposed despite the fact that no amount of skin had been revealed by the action. She hoped that her mistress did not continue, but these thoughts were in vain as she then felt the laces of her skirts being undone. They fell to her feet. Venus refused to let her blouse be removed as well.

She stepped forward and placed the dress in front of her before placing her feet into the middle, then pulled it up to her waist. Next, she pulled the blouse off of her arms and over her head. She was quick to bring the rest of the dress up and wrapped her arms behind herself for the laces before it was even completely on.

She spun around to face the countess, longing for her approval as quickly as possible so that she may leave. But the countess remained silent. She tilted her head, less in a mocking manner and more in a way which suggested genuine contemplation. It was in the stillness of this moment that Venus looked down upon herself.

She was met with a full frontal look at her cleavage, and she watched as her breasts heaved up and down with every breath she took. She was not startled by the sight — this was how the countess preferred to see her. Looking at herself lower, she was once more drawn in by the similarities of the details within this dress and the one Sarracenia wore. They seemed to be the same, save for the lack of red within Venus' version.

She stood up straight with her chin held high, before hitching up the skirts and giving a curtsy, trying hard not to come off as sarcastic with the motion. This seemed to please Sarracenia, as her smile grew.

"Yes, this will do nicely."

Relief washed over Venus. At least she could end this encounter sooner rather than later. But she began to feel sick again at the thought of a ballroom full of people seeing her in such attire. Perhaps it was hypocritical for her to care how other people saw her in a physical sense, but this was a party for her sake, at least according to Sarracenia, and Venus did want to make a good impression. Would people really look at her, dressed like this, and take her seriously?

Would they regardless? Once more, Venus thought of the fact that it was Sarracenia alone who saw her artistic talent first.

She turned in a few directions before Sarracenia was satisfied enough for her to change back into her own clothes. When she was finished, Venus' hand was taken again, and the two headed out of the bedchamber. Sarracenia remained an escort until the pair had returned back to Venus' room.

Even as she entered alone and closed the door behind her, Venus paused for a moment and pressed her ears into the entryway to ensure that her mistress indeed walked away. When she was certain that she was at last alone, she took a moment to let out a deep breath. At least her mistress had not asked for an answer tonight.

...

Time between then and the night of the ball washed away as quickly as water. The next thing Venus knew, she was standing in her room, lacing up the corset of her loaned dress, before pinning up her hair. This was the most difficult part to do without the use of a mirror. She continuously pressed a hand against her scalp to determine if any strands were out of place. When she found them, she added another pin. Hopefully it looked acceptable enough.

She prayed that the lighting for the ball would be as dim as it normally was, so that her appearance would be less noticeable to the guests. Venus did stop to appreciate the irony in how she was now relying on the lack of light this place had.

Once she felt that her hair was as pinned up as physically possible, she smoothed out her dress, cleared her throat, and headed out the door. Part of her had been anticipating her mistress to be on the other side, waiting for her with that quiet demeanor she carried around with her, but Venus had opened the door to an empty hallway. A voice down the corner answered her question — her mistress must already be out, preparing for the arrival of guests.

Venus pictured the disembodied arms, stretching out from the shadows, placing every decoration and hors d'oeuvres from God only knows where. She shuddered at the image of it. One would think she would have grown used to the arms by this point, but without ever having learned their origins, Venus found the mystery to them still as frightening as the first night she had laid eyes upon them.

She picked up her skirts and ventured out into the night, following the sound of her mistress' voice. She had never heard the countess speak so loudly before. She was not surprised to hear the command and authority in her voice, as this was a quality she had regardless, but Venus had been accustomed to hearing her speaking in low, almost whispers. In a bizarre way, she found her yelling almost refreshing.

Sarracenia was standing at the top of the stairs to the great room, pointing from side to side as she instructed on the arrangement of everything. Venus hesitated to look down once she had moved close enough to look but in the end, her curiosity got the better of her. As anticipated, the arms were straggling about below them, moving as franticly and as desperately as cockroach legs. The sight nauseated Venus, and soon she had to force herself to look back at the countess.

Her brows were furrowed and her lips pressed together with concentration. Her eyes traveled over the great room with such precision that Venus doubted she had even been noticed.

"When will the first guests be arriving?" She asked, then chastised herself for the question. Sarracenia was deeply focused, it would be best not to interrupt her flow.

Yet the countess surprised her by giving a straightforward answer. "Around an hour or so. The food has been prepared, it's just a matter of placing everything."

Venus struggled to imagine the exact origins of the food the countess had prepared. In nights prior, she had assumed the countess had a storage room of sorts to keep items in, but to procure such a feast for a large group, she would need to secure a bounty. Venus thought that she may have heard voices at the door the other night, perhaps a butcher or a delivery, but she could not be too sure.

Her mind had been preoccupied with other things. She had to tell herself that this had been the case, however, because she could not bear to ponder on any other possibility.

"Is there anything I can do to assist?" Venus asked then.

"No," the countess replied, reaching out an arm and pulling Venus in close. "Just stay here. Keep me company."

Venus nodded, hoping that the shiver across her skin went unnoticed. "Of course."

The room was lit with a handful of candles surrounding the area, which made the room appear even larger as they cast shadows along the enormous walls. As Venus had suspected, however, the light remained dim, so that the shadows were the most distinguishable aspect.

Two rows of tables lay at either side, the assortment of food and wine stretched across them. This allowed most of the space to remain empty, save for the smaller table sitting directly in the center of the room. Propped up against it was the original portrait Venus had painted of her mistress. It lay proudly among bushes of Ssarracenia and Venus fly traps.

The arrangement gave the guests plenty of room for dancing. Venus wondered how the countess intended on providing music for her guests. She pictured the disembodied arms playing instruments, and she could not decide if the image was disturbing or oddly hilarious.

The first of their guests arrived not long after that. Sarracenia introduced them as the Viscount and his wife, as well as their two adult sons. Sarracenia did not let go, even when the Viscount took her hand and gave it a kiss. Venus found this to be peculiar. She tried to determine if the Viscount and his family demonstrated similar thoughts, but their faces displayed only the largest of smiles.

"Come," Sarracenia said. "You have the privilege of being the first to gaze upon the masterpiece."

The group cooed in excitement, the wife had even clapped. The anticipation seemed so false to Venus. Nobles see paintings all the time, and by far more famous artists than Venus. What warranted such a strong reaction, other than being desperate to please the countess?

Venus thought to herself that, perhaps some people would be curious as to who the artist was that had at last satisfied the Countess de Sarracenia — but that there may be many more who were here solely to say that they were in the presence of such a powerful countess. Then she wondered how many of them would truly care about the painting itself, let alone acknowledge her.

The Viscount took out his spectacles in order to give it a closer inspection.

"Excellent use of brushstroke."

Venus felt her heart swell the smallest amount with pride. She waited with her breath held for him to continue. But as he kept looking on, all he did was nod on occasion.

"I never had much of a head for painting," one of the sons remarked. He had detoured to one of the buffet tables before regrouping at the painting, and he now had a glass of wine in his hand. "Father made us take lessons, but I was never any good at it."

"The colors are nice," the other son remarked. "I like the lighting, it's very... what's the word... atmospheric?"

"Thank you!" Venus stammered out, regretting how clearly her desperation for approval was.

"Quite a likeness," his wife pointed out. Venus turned and smiled at her, trying to persuade her to continue, but she was focused on the countess. "It truly captures of your beauty."

"Thank you," Sarracenia replied, and was the first one to give a glance in Venus' direction. "I thought so, too."

"I remember when you were still a young girl," the wife went on. She gazed back to the painting; however it was clear that she was too deep in reminiscing to be actually looking at it. "You were the spitting image of your mother! What a woman Bianca was..."

"Yes," Sarracenia interrupted. The whole room could hear the annoyance in her voice. "I have been told many times before."

The silence hung in the room like a mist, filling up the air so that Venus almost choked on it. She could feel the grip on her arm tightened. It made the skin under the countess' touch start to sweat. It was not only her, however, as she could see droplets of perspiration begin to fall from the Viscount's forehead. He took out a handkerchief and wiped it away. His wife fiddled with her hands, unsure if she wanted to say anything more or remain silent. She avoided eye contact either way. The son who had the wine glass took another long gulp.

As the tension was reaching its peak, there was another knock on the door. Every human in the room let out a collective sigh of relief. Venus was then twirled around in an almost violent fashion as the countess strolled the two of them down to answer it.

And so was the repetition of the night. Nobles appeared, Sarracenia brought them to the painting, they said a few hollow words of praise. These comments were reflections primarily on the countess' beauty, while a minority would state something regarding the technique. These were largely the same — that she had a good use of brushstroke — the more she heard it, the less she understood what it meant. The way a painter moved the brush against the canvas had little to do with the overall quality at the end of it.

None of them seemed to know what to say in detail. They must not have been art enthusiasts. Venus tried to assure herself that eventually someone had to come in and give it proper attention. Why invite so many people who, in their own words, did not 'have a head' for painting? Yet as more people poured in and came to see the painting of the hour, the shallower the comments became. Often, they did not even bother with remarking at all, only nodding or humming, before making yet another comment about how beautiful the countess was.

Not one of them looked Venus in the eye. They did not care. They truly did not care about the proof in front of them, the testimony of the countess, that she — a woman — had painted this piece.

Venus began to pray that the last of the guests had already arrived, so she would have an excuse to walk away. She would say that she wanted to get supper, even though the last thing she felt this evening was hunger. Anything to step away from this extremely disappointing situation.

"Has everyone been accounted for?" she whispered to her mistress after the latest group walked away.

"We're waiting on one more family," Sarracenia replied. "Officially, at any rate. The princess may make an appearance, but I never did hear back about the invitation..."

Venus nodded. A visit from the princess would be a high honor, and she was still interested in meeting her. However, if her presence was not for certain, then this moment may be her only chance for hours to step away.

Venus gave the arm which gripped hers a light tap. "I'm rather hungry."

Her mistress let out a giggle. "Of course, go on."

Venus did not fully realize how tight the hold had been on her until she was let go. The air around that spot felt instantly cooler. If the flesh there were capable of breathing, it would have been taking heavy gulps at the moment. It took every inch of her not to rub at the area. Instead, she thanked her mistress, before walking over to the buffet.

No one paid any attention as she stormed over, save for a few who realized that the countess was now alone. Venus turned only once to see them crowd upon her like vultures. To her credit, she took it very graciously — smiling that dazzling smile of hers, laughing when others did, and moving so delicately.

The first thing Venus picked up at the table was a glass of wine. White wine. She took a long gulp. It burned her throat, which made her cough.

She was not accustomed to alcohol, however the heat it gave her insides was rather sensational. Her muscles suddenly felt less tense as she ventured another, significantly smaller sip. It still burned, in a pleasing way like the flames of a fire on the coldest night of the year. Her glass was halfway finished before she decided it was time to select her dinner.

"What a remarkable painting!"

The words perked her ears up immediately. She spun around to see the admirer. From where she stood, she could only see the back of his frame, and the faint outline of a shadow.

"Look at the details! How the light captures the facial expressions without revealing too much! As though the painting itself were inviting you to learn a secret the subject was keeping!"

A smile beamed across Venus' face. At long last, someone who appreciated art! Her mistress approached the gentleman first, dipping behind the frame as the two of them spoke in much lower tones. Venus made her way to them.

Lost in the praise, and slightly swaying from the sudden consumption of alcohol, Venus did not recognize the voice at first. As she ventured closer, it was as if a buzzing had gone off in her ear. A nagging, almost screaming sensation for her to run in the opposite direction. She ignored her own warning and stepped around the painting's frame to come face to face with her father.

Venus stopped dead in her tracks.

The Baron Cellier de Durand paused as well, though his expression was less surprised than the one Venus most likely wore. Indeed, he looked at her rather expectantly, having recognized her work instantly.

Sarracenia tilted her head, giving a curious expression. "Venus, dear, you look as though you've seen a ghost."

She said this with a teasing tone, and it was then that Venus began to move. The shock inside of her was twisted around into pure terror, although who she was more afraid of, she could not be certain. Was her mistress trying to imply a truth she had already known? Or was this her usual manner of playing with Venus? If she did know, what was she going to do about it? And if she did not know... how long until she did?

More than that — what was he doing here?

They had traveled much in her youth, yes, but he was a French man, and here they were in the middle of Italy. Did he come looking for a new deal and happened to find her, or was this meeting intentional from the beginning? Terror mixed with the wine and threatened to rise up her throat. Venus coughed again, covering her mouth with her hand but unable to keep her volume down.

"I have to go..." she said as the room began to spin. "I have to..."

Another grip on her arm. One far more firm than that of her mistress, with a hand much larger than hers, as well.

"Nonsense," her father said, his tone deceptively lighter than his hold. "I came all this way to see your painting, I must discuss your work."

"Oh please do stay!" Sarracenia begged.

Venus stared at her. She held her hands folded in front of her chest like a child begging for a few more minutes of play. It was pathetic.

She tried to pry herself from her father's grip, but he did not budge. The room was still spinning, and she closed her eyes to try and straighten herself out. Granted, fainting right now would be the perfect excuse to escape this moment, but she feared where she might wake up.

No. No.

Her father could not do anything to her now. She had escaped him, and no matter what, she was staying here. The countess would not allow him to take her away, truth or no truth.

It did not prevent him from leaning in close and hissing into her ear.

"Did you really think I would never find out?"

Venus returned her gaze to the countess and pleaded with her eyes. Sarracenia stood, apparently clueless for a moment, before her eyes fell completely on the grip this man had on her artist.

"Excuse me," she said, reaching out and giving his knuckles a tap. "That's her painting arm you are holding."

Her father dropped his grip immediately. Venus felt no qualms about rubbing at the spot this time, glaring up at him as she did so. He did not seem as tall as she had remembered him being the last time she had seen him.

"My apologies," he said to the countess, not to his daughter. "I get a little overly enthusiastic about art."

The countess nodded. She raised an eyebrow towards him. Then she addressed Venus.

"The princess will be here soon, I am certain." she stated, and reached past Venus' father and held out a hand to her. "Come, let us go and wait to greet her."

Venus took hold and the two took off before her father had a chance to protest. This did not prevent her from turning around to ensure that they were not being followed. Her father met her gaze and kept his eyes on her as they traveled further away, but he remained in place.

A few of the guests attempted to grab the countess' attention, and she paid them no mind, not even giving a verbal excuse to her indifference. Venus was grateful for this — she did not want to entertain these people again. The countess continued to lead them both out of the great room, through the front doors and into the yard.

The cold air hit Venus with sharp precision, and she knew that her shivers were far from subtle. That was when the countess pulled her back in, although it did little to help, considering how cool her skin was, as well. Venus pulled in close, though, desperate for some sense of comfort.

"So are you going to tell me what that was all about in there?" The countess asked, under her breath despite no one else being around. Her words created vapor around her lips.

Venus knew this conversation was to happen at some point. She supposed it would not hurt to share at least half of the truth.

"He is my father," she stated, her own words creating vapor around them as well.

The countess nodded. "I had assumed a past connection like that. You have different surnames — because of your husband?"

"Yes," Venus went on. "My husband was set to leave for your place, but I... I knew that I was the more skilled of the two of us, so I went ahead and left before they could stop me."

This part was less true. While she did not lie in saying that neither of the two men in her life would have wanted her to leave on her own for a commission, she had intercepted before they had a chance to read the letter. They had known nothing about the request, she had been sure of it.

Sarracenia let out a laugh then, filling up the space around them with her breath. "Oh, you devious little thing, you!"

Venus could not resist smiling as well. It was a bit humorous that she had gotten away with what she had. That she had been determined to succeed so badly, she stole the opportunity from another.

"You are not afraid of him, are you?" her mistress asked, tone shifting.

The smile on Venus' lips fell, and she turned to look Sarracenia in the eye. "I... am unsure. It startled me very much for me to see him again."

"I never met my father," Sarracenia said with a shrug of her shoulder. "It was only ever my mother and I. Although I did always believe that she had something to do with it. His disappearance, I mean. Honestly, I think the only reason she married him was to get me."

Venus nodded in acknowledgement, although she did not know how to respond. To fully suspect that your mother had killed your father...

Then again, who was she to judge?

"Did he treat you poorly, then?" Sarracenia asked, once more catching Venus off guard. Was her switching between subjects an intentional ploy, or did she truly not understand how to keep a conversation when she was not the center of it?

Venus gave a shrug herself then. "I suppose you could say that. He never beat me or anything of the sort, but we... had disagreements about my art, and his word was law in his house."

"And you felt you deserved a better life?" The countess let out another laugh, but a small and bitter one. "I often wondered if that was how my mother felt. If that was why she did away with my father after having me. Did he treat you worse than your mother did, then?"

Venus desperately wanted this conversation off of her. "My mother did not treat me poorly. She loved me."

"Then why marry a man who was cruel?"

Venus went to explain that her parents were never actually married, until the sound of wheels and the drumming of hooves interrupted her. A carriage pulled up to them. Venus had not seen what other guests had rode in on, but she could see how lavish and extravagant this one was.

The exterior did not appear to be made of wood, rather ivory, as it showed white under the moonlight. The embellishments were done up with blue and gold paint, dotting every inch. It looked almost ridiculous to Venus. It took no guesses to determine who the passenger of such a carriage was. They stood back and waited for the princess to make her debut.

The footman came around the front and opened up the door, holding out a hand. Then out stepped an elegant shoe, followed by an extravagant dress, and finally a soft, beautiful face. The princess wore her curls back, held fast by gold chains and pearls. She spotted her host and the artist and flashed them both a smile.

Sarracenia let go of Venus' arm as she rushed over to greet the new arrival. They took in one another's hands and exchanged a kiss on both cheeks. Venus stood back, hands folded in front, as she waited for them to finish exchanging pleasantries.

She wondered when these two would have met, considering how socially reclusive her mistress was. This was different, however. This was royalty. Arguably the only family more powerful than her own. This thought made Venus wonder if Sarracenia's reactions were out of admiration, or from a deeply rooted envy. It almost made her pity the princess, who seemed wholly pleased to be in her company.

Her mistress turned then, arm outstretched to Venus, inviting her to join.

"This must be the wonderful artist!" The princess exclaimed.

Venus smiled, not just from politeness, but also the sheer overwhelming sensation of finally being acknowledged. And by a princess, no less. In her bliss, she almost forgot about the events not five minutes ago. She almost forgot about her father.

She approached the two, picking up her skirt and giving the deepest curtsy she could manage. "It truly is an honor to meet you, your majesty."

The princess beamed. "It is an honor to meet you, genius painter! The countess has written me several letters praising your skills! I cannot tell you how much it pleases me to know that she has at last found an artist to sate her exquisite taste!" There were so many hidden meanings behind her words, she must have rehearsed such a greeting.

"You give me far too much credit, your majesty." Venus said, standing up straight once more, but keeping her gaze down. "I am but a humble painter, who is grateful to have such a magnanimous patron in the countess."

"It is your very patron who gives you praise! I am here tonight to see this painting for myself!"

Something about her words caused Venus' cheeks to grow hot. She looked to Sarracenia to take over for her. The countess gave a knowing smile, before taking a step forward.

"Right this way, please, to my family's humble abode."

The princess laughed outright at the comment, but Venus noticed Sarracenia's eyelid twitch. Venus herself had no idea if this comment was made in jest, since anyone could plainly see the vast scale of her manor.

She allowed the two to take the lead as she soaked up the significance of this moment. A princess was about to look at her painting. Unlike the previous guests — minus her father — this one seemed to have a genuine interest in seeing it. A princess, a royal family member, was interested in one of *her* paintings. She repeated the thought in her head repeatedly, but she kept losing her ability to breathe.

This moment would not have been possible without the countess. Venus watched the back of Sarracenia's head as they continued to walk. She was the first person to truly believe in Venus' abilities. Even with her hesitation at first, she had taken a chance, and now here they were. A party with royal guests here to see what she was capable of doing. Eternity was too long to spend together, but Venus would always remember the gratitude she felt towards this noblewoman, monster or not.

However, she continued to contemplate leaving Sarracenia specifically for this very princess. Did Sarracenia know this? Did she realize the thoughts that would be running through Venus' head when she invited the princess? What level of power could she possibly flex over the situation?

Venus tried to tell herself that she was being ridiculous. Of course the countess would invite a princess, especially one who had married in a different kingdom and then returned. It would have been an insult at the highest level to have neglected inviting her. That did not mean, however, that she was unaware of this potential rival.

Venus would have to tread carefully moving forward. While there was only so much the countess could potentially do to the princess, she herself did not share that luxury.

They reentered the great room, and Venus instinctively moved closer to the two women. Murmurs were spreading in a less than subtle manner around the room as the three of them stepped in. Venus' eyes darted around the crowd. She didn't see her father. She was unsure if whether this was calming or more stressful. She did not want him to see her, but she would rather know of his exact location. She almost wished the countess would take her arm once more.

They made their way to the center of the room, and Sarracenia held up her arms to gesture grandly towards her portrait. The princess let out a gasp which, from anyone else would have felt forced or exaggerated, but the way she carried herself made Venus believe this to be a genuine reaction.

"Oh, it is magnificent!" She exclaimed, stepping in closer. "Look at the details! She even captured the way you fold your hands so perfectly!" She pointed. "Do you see? That exact sparkle in your eyes? I cannot believe this was done merely with paint! It is so lifelike that I would sooner believe she painted with your own soul!"

Sarracenia chuckled at this comment. Venus was not certain as to what was so humorous about it. She was, however, extremely flattered by the princess' excitement and energy regarding her piece.

"Thank you, your majesty. From you, this is the highest honor." She gave another curtsy and longed to say so much more.

She restrained herself, though. It was important to not show too much appreciation, lest her mistress become suspicious of her plans. Then, the princess said the last thing Venus had expected. It was something that, if they had been alone, would have been the greatest phrase she had ever heard in her life. But as they stood here, countess present, it filled her only with dread.

"You must come and paint me!"

Venus' breath left her lungs. Hairs on the back of her neck stood up so straight that they began to mingle with the clasps of her dress. The countess rolled her eyes to the side to meet with Venus.

"Of course," she answered on Venus' behalf. There was no smile on her lips as she said this. "If that is what her majesty requests, I will happily loan out my artist to you."

The princess clapped excitedly. As if answering Venus' prayers for this moment to end, a group approached them and began to address the princess directly. Venus did not understand what they were discussing. It must have been important, for the princess apologized then excused herself.

Now she was alone with the countess.

She tried to tell herself that she had done nothing. She had merely thanked the princess in a way which anyone would have towards royalty. It had been the princess herself who made the request. It was the countess who had accepted.

Venus had said nothing.

She also knew, though, that none of this mattered.

"Sarracenia," she started, taking in the tension on her mistress' brows and jaw. "I don't..."

"You know there's nothing I wouldn't do for you, right?"

What did it have to do with anything? "I'm... sorry? I don't understand?"

Sarracenia sighed, but not with impatience. It was more the sigh of someone finally letting a burden roll off of their shoulders. "You gave me my heart's greatest desire."

Venus raised an eyebrow.

"I know that a painting may not mean much to anyone who has the means to see their face in a mirror," she went on, as if reading Venus' thoughts. "But as someone who has gone her entire life without knowing for certain what she looked like, with her only frame of reference being her mother, to at last know what others see when I enter a room... it is more than an eternity of money or titles could ever buy."

Venus was once more filled with the sympathy that came only when her mistress showed the most vulnerable side of herself. She wanted to reach out and take a hold of her hand, but she was not bold enough to do so. Until she saw the first tear drip from her mistress' face. Then no force on earth could stop her from clasping her fingers around that cold, soft hand.

She looked at Venus. "What is it that you desire?"

All at once, Venus realized she had been asking herself that very question her entire life. She had thought that she had wanted to paint and be acknowledged for her craft. But hadn't her mistress given her exactly that? And now what was it that she wanted — to leave this woman for the princess?

She did not want to spend an eternity preying on other humans, even if it meant she would be forever painting. It had hardly even been a temptation. But she could, perhaps, give the rest of her mortal life to the countess.

Then she recalled the head on the dinner table. The death of the guardsman — the one which she had participated in. Is that what she would spend her life adhering to?

She did not know. Perhaps she had never known. Every step she had taken to come closer to her goal had only ever caused her pain and loss. If she could live her life over again, she would still have her family. Instead, she had a patron who ate people.

It should not have been that way. If she had only been born into a world that would have accepted her as is, she would not have to resort to measures such as this.

"Well?" Sarracenia demanded.

Venus shook her head. She was on the verge of tears, and if she opened her mouth now, they would surely come. She knew better than to cause such a scene in a place with company like this.

"Countess?" a voice called out.

Venus closed her eyes and inhaled through her nostrils as her father walked back over to them. How long had he been there, standing in the shadows?

When at last she opened her eyes once more, Venus looked over at her mistress, only to see her grinning wildly. Venus had never seen such an unabashed smile across the countess' face. Her excitement rivaled that of the princess', and yet it filled Venus with dread.

'What was she thinking?'

Sarracenia held out her arms. "Ah, Baron! Just the man I wanted to talk to!"

Venus felt the bile in her stomach rise to her throat. She had to stop... whatever was about to happen. She stepped forward, taking note of the pleased look her father currently wore, when her feet stopped in place. The sudden pause caused her to lean forward and almost fall over, but she held up her arms and found balance. She remembered this, from that night at the market when she had witnessed Maria's beating. Sarracenia was holding her in place while she continued to speak with her father.

"I am glad," he went on. "I was hoping to speak with you again before the night ended."

Sarracenia leaned in close, putting a single finger on his chest. "Would you mind accompanying me to somewhere more private?"

Venus again felt the urge to vomit. Her mind immediately thought of Sarracenia lifting him up with that inhuman strength she possessed, flying them both up into the spider web which held her bedchamber.

She thought of the words her mother had said so long ago about this man she called father. She shut her eyes, but that only made the images playing in her mind worse. She could not stop herself from seeing their bodies mingled together.

"Sarracenia," she gasped out from her standstill. "Please..."

Her mistress spun around to face her. That wild, unrestrained smile remained plastered over her face, threatening to stretch out her skin beyond repair. She clapped her hands together.

"Of course, Venus dear, you must come with!"

She grabbed her arm once more, and while Venus did indeed move her legs to keep up, they did not lift of her own accord. Nor did she have the strength to pull out of Sarracenia's grasp.

The countess gestured towards her father, who admittedly looked somewhat less gleeful than he had a moment ago. Venus anticipated the two of them being lifted up into the bedchamber, ignoring the furor it was sure to cause with the guests. But her mistress must have been conscious of this, for they headed away from the center and towards the stairs, turning a corner and over to a door Venus had never seen before.

The wood looked old and worn, even more so than the rest of this place. In the candlelight, Venus could make out how thick the layer of dust over the doorknob was. It made the fingerprints on the knob all the more prominent. This door had been used very recently.

Sarracenia did not let go, even as she pulled a key from her corset and unlocked the door. The only light source came from the candles around them. Venus counted about five steps on the staircase leading down below before the rest were swallowed up by darkness.

"Come along," Sarracenia said to both of them, already pressing forward to lead.

Venus shook her head, but her body did not refuse. Her father stepped behind her as they walked. Inching closer and closer to the thick darkness, Venus could not suppress the fear she felt as she imagined there being nothing beyond that point. That the three of them would be swallowed up. Then her foot landed on another stair as she stepped down. Even though she could not see it, the staircase continued.

After this revelation, her fear became that it would never end. Her mistress was leading them down a spiral where they would be walking without seeing until the end of time. Or they were headed beneath the earth, down to the flames her Christian family believed in.

She could hear her father's breathing behind her. Big, heavy gulps which betrayed his own anxiety in a way which no words or forced bravado could hide. She heard his nails scrape against the wall as he tried to adjust his footing.

She did not have the luxury of running her hands against the wall for support, as her mistress retained a grip on the arm closest to it. Her free hand held out uselessly, flailing in the dark nothingness as the impression of someone trying to keep her balance.

Occasionally, he would trip and his foot would catch on her skirts, causing her to stumble as well. Sarracenia paused every time this happened, and although Venus could not see her expression in the dark, she could imagine the anger across her face at the interruption.

Then, just when she felt that this journey to Hades could not last any longer, the texture of the floor changed. No longer wooden, but now soft and cold, like dirt. Her feet scraped forward, but the ground remained level.

It was her father who asked the silent question, after stumbling a little to get down from the staircase.

"I beg your pardon, countess. But where exactly are we?"

Venus could not see the smile across her mistress' face, but she let out a sigh which suggested her games had begun.

"My wine cellar."

She pulled herself and Venus forward, deeper within until Venus could hear her fingers tapping against glass. It echoed around them so that the countess felt everywhere, consuming the very room they stood in. Venus could bear this no longer.

"Mistress," she pleaded. "Is there any light at all we can use? My... the Baron and I are not as adapted to the darkness as you are."

Another small chuckle. "Of course, Venus dear. I do want you to see this."

She snapped her fingers, and just like that, there was light around them. Venus looked around, and saw that there were glass bowls hung above their heads. Inside each was a candle so small, that this would probably be their last breath of life before being completely extinguished.

She barely made out the shapes of the disembodied hands as they sank back, so blended into the shadows already.

Once the source of light was discovered, her eyes wandered around their new location. It was as the countess had said — every corner and every nook was filled to the brim with shelves, each one holding a multitude of wine bottles. Something did not seem right, however. It took Venus' eyes a second longer to adjust before she realized what was so off putting about their surroundings. Every one of the wine bottles was empty.

"My family had such a fine collection back when they had first built this manor," Sarracenia began as she sauntered over to the Baron. "It was their life's work, their entire sum of wealth."

"Forgive me," her father interrupted, which Venus felt was a very bold and foolish thing to do. "I thought that your family consisted of landlords."

Her teeth dazzled in the candlelight as her smile grew. "We are. That is our wealth, in human terms. But in our eyes — " here she turned around and outstretched her hands to the collection around them. "This was what wealth was all about."

She lowered her arms then, her smile disappearing. Her gaze moved down towards her feet, and she suddenly seemed very small.

"But they squandered it. Became too greedy. We saw this as the cup which would always overflow. But nothing truly lasts forever. Not even us."

While Venus started to feel her sympathy return again, her father must have felt only confusion, for he continued to ask questions.

"I am sorry to hear that," was the line he opened with. "But why are you telling us all of this? What is the relevance?"

The countess spun around to look at him, her demeanor now full of the power she knew she possessed. Venus felt herself stiffen, as though she could try and match that energy.

"We don't bring just anyone down here," she stated. Each step she took towards the Baron made him shrink down more and more. "Only a small selection of humans are deemed worthy. And you, my good Baron, are most certainly worthy."

"Oh?" Her father responded, in a more playful manner. He even had a springy in his step as he ventured closer to the countess. He side-eyed Venus, who kept her gaze dark. "How is that?"

"Firstly, you are of nobility." Sarracenia explained. "That's always been very important. We did not want to taint our collection with common blood..."

It was Venus' turn to give a side-eye, but towards her mistress. If the countess had noticed, she did not make it clear. Her gaze remained solely on the Baron.

"Secondly, your connection to my artist."

This made her father stop in his tracks. Venus thought very briefly that she had used her powers to freeze him as well, but after a moment he continued to step forward. She did begin to wonder, should he try to run, if her mistress would then feel compelled to stop him.

"What do you mean...?" He gave a cold stare in Venus' direction, and she tried to guess what he was thinking at that moment.

"Don't play coy," Sarracenia went on. "I want to hear you confess what you've done."

"Countess, I am unsure what this woman has told you, but I can promise, that — "

"No." To call the word a shout would be an understatement. She spoke so loudly that the flaming candles above their heads danced in nervousness. "You cannot play these games, Baron. Not with me."

He looked at Venus again, this time with pleading eyes. But she could do nothing. Even if she had the ability to move, what was she to do in defiance — beyond begging his case. And that, she tried.

"Sarracenia..." she started. Her voice cracked, from the tears she had shed earlier and from the dryness of the air around them now. "Please don't..."

She tried to think of something else to say. Please don't, he was her father? Sarracenia knew that already, and it would make little difference. Please don't, she loved him? That was not true. That had never been true. Please don't, he was a good man? Also had never been true.

'Please don't, I am only human and I cannot bear to see anymore bloodshed on my behalf.'

The words did not leave her mind. She just closed her eyes and thought them over and over again.

Instead, her father continued to talk. "If you must know, yes, she is my daughter. She is here under false pretenses..."

Venus' eyes snapped open. She did not expect him to bring this up, not

229

so easily, at any rate. The Baron wiped sweat from his brow, but how in the world he would feel hot enough in this environment to perspire was beyond Venus' understanding.

"It is true, that she is my daughter," he began, his words stammering a little. "And it is true that I have a daughter named Venus Faucher. But this is not her — she is my other daughter, my illegitimate daughter, Eva."

Eva.

She had not heard her true name in so long, she had almost forgotten the sound of it. But it rang throughout the air and hit her straight into her soul.

'*Eva*,' she repeated internally. '*My name is Eva. My mother named me Eva.*'

Sarracenia did go to look at her then. "Is this true, Venus?"

Eva nodded. "It was my sister's husband who you invited. I intercepted the letter. I didn't mean to — "

The countess held up her hand to stop her. "What a shame. Venus is such a lovely name..."

Eva inhaled sharply. Of course, that would be the only aspect her mistress was upset about. That had been their first connection, at least in her mind. Eva meanwhile felt a sense of relief. No more using her poor sister's name.

Sarracenia went back to interrogating the Baron. "What did you do to make her run away?"

He held a hand to his chest incredulously. "What *I* did? How am I to know the follies of a woman's mind? One night, I'm telling my daughter to have sweet dreams, the next morning, she is nowhere to be found."

"But you were aware of her artistic abilities, weren't you?" Another step towards him. "As her father, and a noble, you must have been the one paying for her training."

He nodded. "Yes, of course I knew. I was getting her regular commissions. She always had a roof over her head, food in her belly, and a life of luxury as the daughter of a Baron. I have no idea why she would run away from it all!"

"You bastard!" Eva screamed, surprising everyone in the room, herself included. Her eyes were red from both fury and tears. "You unbelievable bastard!"

"Watch your tongue, girl!" he yelled back, pointing his cane in her direction. "I would be mindful about using that word towards *me*."

She stood there and seethed. She wanted nothing more now than to run over and wrench the truth from his throat.

"We can keep playing all night long," Sarracenia said, her voice as chilled as the room around them. "But I grow tired of your presence, and I have guests to attend to upstairs. So, either you can tell me the truth, or my artist can." She gave a small nod in Eva's direction before turning back to the Baron. "But I want to hear it from your lips. Why did your daughter run away?"

"Countess, believe me when I say — "

"Why did your daughter run away?"

"If you would just let me give a proper explanation — "

"Why did your daughter run away?"

His face contorted into a sneer, tightening the wrinkles the years had put on him. Even in the dim light, Eva could see his skin turning crimson.

"Listen here..." he hissed through gritted teeth. "I do not care *who* you are, no one speaks to me that way — !"

He raised his cane as though to strike, but the countess was quicker. Eva saw her father hit the ground, screaming out in pain before she realized what had even happened. He clutched at his cheek, but when he moved his hand to inspect his palm, she could see the bloody streaks across his face.

"Is this secret truly worth more than your daughter?" Sarracenia demanded, her hands in fists, blood trickling down the fingers which had scratched him. "Do you want to take this to your grave?"

His eyes were wide with fear now. The menace he had possessed not one minute ago had vanished. Now, he was a sniveling old man, crumpled helplessly on the floor. The first thought to cross Eva's mind at the sight was that she wished her mother were around to see him now. To look at this man who had hurt her so long ago, reduced to this. Her mother would have shown no mercy.

And yet, there was a part of Eva who hated to see him like this. If this man who had frightened and controlled Eva had truly been so pathetic this entire time... then just what was it she had feared all those years?

"Please..." he begged, voice barely above a whisper. "Please don't kill me..."

Sarracenia only smiled. He turned towards Eva.

"Please...!" He pleaded once more, his voice a little louder, moving but unable to get up. One of his ankles looked slightly twisted, and she wondered if he had injured it during the fall. "Please, Eva, help your father!"

She could not. Even if she had the ability to move, she could not stop this from happening. He had to accept what was to come.

Sarracenia stepped closer. "Why did your daughter run away?"

"I swear I don't know!"

She struck again on his other cheek. He screamed again, reeling over his stomach.

"It will be your throat next." The countess warned. "Why did your daughter run away?"

He gave a swing with his cane, but Sarracenia caught it with ease and yanked it from his hands. She tossed it to the side, into the darkness, so they could only hear it land in the distance.

"Because..." his eyes darted around, as though looking for another weapon. Or a way out.

His gaze landed on the staircase, and he crawled his way over to it. Sarracenia stood back long enough for him to get his hand on the third step, before she walked over and pressed her heel in between his knuckles. He did not have the strength left to scream, so he groaned long and loud.

"Why did your daughter run away?"

He tried to speak, but his throat was parched, and he coughed instead. "Because she is an ungrateful daughter...who cannot accept her place in this world as a woman!"

Eva expected her mistress to strike at his throat as promised, and he must have anticipated the same move for he ducked his chin into his chest. The countess merely remained in place, waiting for him to continue his confession.

"She...she did not understand...or just didn't want to accept...that people will only pay for art if it was created by a man. I let her reap the benefits of the profits, all I had asked in return was that she allowed me the best, the most logical, business practice I could offer!"

Again, Sarracenia did not move. She was inspecting him, digesting his words. Something about her being so still unsettled Eva. Like the calm before the storm, she waited for this to come to an end.

Then, Sarracenia lifted her foot and brought it back down to the floor. She grabbed at the Baron, with a strength she did not appear to possess, and threw him as a heap before Eva.

"Is there anything you would like to say in response, Venus?"

Was she forgetting her true name already, or did the countess not care? Eva did not know, nor did she think it mattered in this moment. She turned down to the mess that was her father.

He looked up at her, tears blending into his blood-streaked cheeks, lower lip quivering. She remembered being a child, longing to drain his blood from her veins so she could be whole again. How ironic that he would be getting her wish tonight. Then again, that had been all he had ever done.

She had only three words to give him. "Rot in hell."

With that, Sarracenia reached behind and clawed open his throat. The splatter hit against Eva's legs, feeling warm and heavy past her skirts. His screams lasted only a moment or two before being drowned out by his own blood, and Sarracenia knelt before him to place her mouth against the wound.

Her shoulders convulsed as she drank deeper than Eva had ever witnessed anyone do so. Between the laps of blood being swallowed were moans of pure pleasure. Her father's skin turned almost as white as the countess, and his eyes began to lose focus and glaze over.

Eva felt sick to her stomach. She wanted to close her eyes, but somehow hearing the act made it worse. This was a favor the countess was doing for her — it felt wrong to turn away from it. So she watched on as the man she once called father became no more than flesh and bone.

When it was over, Sarracenia dropped him down so that he gave a graceless thud against the floor. Eva hoped that this would not be his final resting place. She could not stand the thought of living in the same house which held her father's corpse just below her feet.

Sarracenia stood up, and Eva could see the streaks of blood sticking to her chin and down along her torso. Most likely down her dress, as well, but she could not tell against the black material. Only her teeth shone white as she smiled with satisfaction. Eva was very much reminded of the night when she had killed the guardsman.

Except this was the blood of her father.

Sarracenia held out both hands. "Let's go then, our guests will be missing us."

"Won't they be put off by our appearances?" Eva could not believe this was the question she asked as she stepped over the corpse of her father.

The countess laughed. "They know who I am. And now they know you too."

That last sentence rang inside Eva's head like a bell. Perhaps she was right. Maybe this was exactly where she belonged. Maybe this was exactly who she was.

Just as they were about to head up the stairs, however, Eva caught movement in the corner of her eyes. She would have written it off as a rat or another similar creature, except for the location from where the movement came.

It was her father's corpse. She stood there a moment longer, despite the slight tugging from her mistress, eyes fixed as she inspected closer. Right along where his shoulder was, another distinct motion. Eva gasped.

"Mistress..." she cried. "He lives!"

The countess let go of Eva's hands yet showed no signs of distress. She watched as the scene played out before them. Eva looked on as well, unable to move her eyes from the sight.

The same shoulder jerked again, too quick to be natural. Eva once again wondered if the culprit was a rat, caught underneath the corpse. She hated herself for feeling relieved at the thought. What would she even do if her father was still alive? Stand back as Sarracenia ensured that she finished him off?

Then his other shoulder twitched. Then his leg, right at the knee, bent at an odd angle. The sight sickened her, but she dared not turn away. All at once, a creature emerged. It ran across the room so quickly that Eva screamed. It had been far too large to have been a rat. In fact, it had seemed large enough to be a...

The creature returned, spreading itself along the walls, and that was when Eva took in what she was staring at.

It was the shadow of her father.

Even without his face, she could see the outline of his head and body, a silhouette she had grown very familiar with. There was no mistake.

The shadow seemed to turn its head. She could not be certain since it had no features, but a part of her knew that it was looking in her direction. With what intention, she did not know.

When its head turned back, it stretched out its arms. High, higher, far higher than seemed possible for a man to reach. Its arms grew out past his body, up to the ceiling where the candles still flickered. The hands were joined by others, a few at first, and then dozens.

The disembodied shadow hands.

Eva's breath caught in her throat. She tried to peer around the floor, but the darkness was so consuming, she could only see a few feet past herself. Quickly, she spun around and sprinted to the stairs, pushed by Sarracenia, who cried out in protest, but Eva kept climbing up until she was able to reach one of the soon-to-be-dead candles. Then, she ran back down. Sarracenia stood in silence, jaw slacked at her actions.

Eva continued to run down, in between the rows of shelves with empty wine bottles. She kept her gaze on the ground, yet despite this, she was moving so quickly she almost tripped. The candle practically fell from her grip, but she managed to hold it. Once her balance was regained, she stood and lifted her skirts to inspect the object which had nearly sent her plummeting.

At first, she thought it might have been a root, by the color and the way it stuck out of the ground. Yet as she continued to gaze upon it, she realized it was far too smooth to belong to a tree. She held the candle in front of her to light the way.

She kept seeing similar, root-like shapes in the near distance, but beyond that, the shapes took on a more familiar look. That was when she saw the skulls.

Eva turned, going along another aisle, once again finding more of the same discovery. Not all were down to bone quite yet. Some still had flesh and clothing. Others were corpses just setting to rot. What really caught her eye, however, were the items she saw alongside the fresher of the dead.

Paintbrushes.

Tears welled in her eyes. This is what became of the artists before her. The rumors were true — she was indeed killing them. That was not the worst of it, however. Eva had long since accepted that she worked under a monster who needed to hunt. No, the cruel, unnecessary part of it, was what she had been doing with them afterwards.

Their souls, having no opening to escape from, were trapped in this place forever to serve the same woman who had killed them.

Chapter 16

Eva

This will be the last time' is what her father said every time he took credit for her work. And every time, she would protest, but he would calm her down with his words, offering her comfort and affection in the moment. Empty promises of what she wanted to hear. She knew that each time he received praise, the way his face lit up, it would never end.

She had threatened not to paint anymore. If he wanted the credit so badly, he could take lessons from Jacques himself and be done with her. She always feared he might hit her during these outbursts. The redness in his face and tightness of his mouth suggested as much. But his hand never came down.

Instead, he would point out how miserable she would be if she never produced another painting. Eva argued that it could not be any more painful than spending days to weeks on a piece just for him to take the fame and glory. Then he would say that he was only trying to give her work to the world, that there were more walls to fill than their own — walls far more powerful.

Eva did not care about status. She only wanted her due.

Once, at an auction, her scenery pieces were being presented. Before the payment process proceeded, someone asked who the artist was. She had been standing there with her father, waiting for him to give his whole pitch, but to her surprise, he stood back.

Uncomfortable with the silence, Eva slowly turned to look at him. He did not move his head, only his eyes stared at her. Daring her to go on ahead and prove him wrong on his front. Prove that these clients, who were so eager to purchase this painting, would still want it in their parlor after discovering the true identity of the artist.

As much as Eva wanted to believe that they would indeed accept her as is, she could not bring herself to move forward and bring it into reality. Because the rejection, which was certainly a considerable risk, would have crushed her more than any time her father had stolen credit away. So, she lowered her head, until her father took over.

Back in those days, Jacques and Venus still lived with them. Eva could not believe that her father held no embarrassment over the arrangement. It was one thing to argue that his friend was visiting for the summer or whichever season, but for him to be the husband of his youngest and living full time in their manor... it presented the image that Jacques could not provide for his small family.

Venus had been quiet during those times. She would sip on her tea, eat little else, and try to take up as small of space as possible. She did not show much interest in playing cards anymore. When the sisters were alone at night in the parlor, they mostly sat in silence. Eva would bring a book, so she would be doing more than staring at her sister. She took many breaks, however, as an invitation for a conversation which Venus never took.

She also no longer visited the stables to see her beloved horses. Once, Eva had convinced her to take a seat outside, close to the manor, and brought her favorite one over to her. For a few minutes, the melancholy had left her sister, and she almost became herself once more as she petted the snout of her favored beast.

Then that night, Eva came in to find her sister crying. At first, she had mistaken her for being asleep, because she was lying so still with her face in the pillow. As she ventured closer, however, she could see the quick rise and fall of her shoulders and heard the faint sobs she was attempting to drown out.

"Venus," she gasped, sitting down on the bed. "What's wrong?"

Her sister did not answer immediately. She shook her head into the pillow, even when Eva pressed a hand on her back in comfort. Eva had learned that she needed to be patient these days when it came to her sister. Finally, Venus sat up, cheeks matching her red and tear-stained eyes. She sniffled, and Eva offered a handkerchief before she was finally able to speak.

"It is Jacques..." she answered, her words barely audible. Of course it was her husband.

"He isn't hurting you, is he?" Eva asked. She knew to veer on the edge of caution, yet the words were said before she had the sense to pace herself.

Venus shook her head, then frowned, and shrugged. "I don't know..."

Eva was confused — wouldn't she know if her husband was hurting her or not? She had been so naive in those days.

"Well..." Eva continued, speaking slower this time. "What has happened, then?"

Venus swallowed and wiped at her tears as a means to avoid the question, before she finally answered, "he wants children."

Eva's eyes went wide. "You are but a child yourself!"

Her sister had no response. She merely shook her head and allowed the tears to flow once more. Eva sat and waited for Venus to calm down again before saying her next words.

"He will not..." Venus perked up at her sister's statement. Eva placed a hand on hers and gave it a light pat. "I will take care of it."

The next day she was out in the fields. It was Sunday, so she was not expected to paint that afternoon. The rest of her family was at church. Eva had complained of stomach cramps, but she probably did not need to even give the excuse — she was allowed to miss church with the rest of her family whenever she wanted.

She never could decide if this fact hurt her feelings or not.

Today, it worked to her advantage as she headed out to the forest she had once run into in an attempt to escape this place. This was not her first time back into these woods since that night, however, now thoughts of her sister — her Rom sister — flooded her mind. The way she had accused and disowned Eva.

She had deserved it. This situation would not have come to fruition had it not been for her foolish choices. She had failed her Rom family, the people who had raised her and who in turn she had helped raise. She could still recall the feeling of her younger siblings and cousins' hands as they gripped against her skirts to drag her off to one of their games. She would not fail the only family member she still had.

She traveled through the trees until she found the particular bush she had been searching for. Summer was closing in, but the mugwort had grown tall and strong. She pulled out the small carving knife she had packed away in her apron's pocket and got to work cutting off as much as she could. She did not know when she would be back, or how much longer the plants would survive.

She stuffed handfuls into her pocket until the leaves began to fall out. As she left, she cradled the bundle in between her arms to prevent further spillage. It would be best to dry them out somewhere in the sun, but also in a spot where they would not be noticed.

Eva had just the place in mind. With her sister's lack of interest in the horses, the stables were only visited for food and weekly cleanings. There was a window close to the roof, above an indoor balcony. She would dry them out in batches, concealing the rest within various hidden places inside her room.

Upon her arrival home, Eva did as she planned. The last of the mugwort was stuffed at the bottom of an unused vase by the time her family returned. It would take a few days for the batch in the stables to dry up enough for a tea, but that should still give them plenty of time.

...

And so it carried on like that. Eva's paintings were sold under false pretenses, and Venus entered the marriage bed in much the same circumstances. The two sisters would now sit in the parlor after dark, Eva with her paint, and Venus with her tea.

"Do you remember..." Venus started one night. "When you asked me what I thought you deserved to accomplish as an artist?"

Eva paused her brushstrokes. "Vaguely..."

In truth, she *did* think about that conversation. She thought about it quite often, these days.

"Do you recall what I said? That this was just the way of the world for women?"

"Yes."

"Why did he do it, then?"

"Why did who do what?"

"God."

This made Eva put her brush down and face her sister. Over the years, she had been forced to read the Bible, so she was not wholly unfamiliar with

240

the Gadje God. But that was still how she saw him — this was the god of the Gadjes. As her gods were the ones for Roms.

They never seemed to understand that there was enough room in this world for all gods, despite their insistence that their god was somehow also three. If their god could not be the only god, then no one else was allowed to pray to theirs.

"What about God?"

"Why did he make us?" Venus took another sip. "I know his will is not mine to question... but, if this is truly all there is for women, then why did he make us? We exist so men can have a partner, but didn't God think about us? How we would feel about this?"

Eva shook her head. She did not like to discuss this subject. Gadje never seemed to appreciate her answers. "I wouldn't know the reasoning behind your god."

Venus stared at her hard, in the way that reminded Eva how different their childhoods had been. She took another sip of tea.

...

Years passed by. Eva found herself growing taller, fuller, coming into her womanhood. She found herself staring into mirrors more often than before. Her father would make comments regarding her vanity, sometimes in jest, but often in criticism. He did understand her reasoning, however.

The face which stared back at her was becoming more and more like her mother's. The only difference was the color of skin. Her mother always had a lovely tan, even in the winter when the nights were long. Eva's skin only grew dark in the summer, after days in the sun. However, the curve of her nose, the shape of her lips, even the glare in her eyes, had belonged to the woman who had brought her into this world.

She did not bother to explain any of this to her father.

It did, however, perk up her curiosity. She took out her sketchbook and took a seat in front of her vanity. She recalled that time so long ago, when she had painted the duke's daughter, how she had sneaked in the night to sketch the face of her mother before she had lost it to faded memories. Now that face was worn in her skin.

Furiously did she study. She drew her face at every angle she could manage. She drew her hair up and down, messy, and combed neat. She drew her hands in all sorts of positions. She even drew herself in a multitude of outfits.

This last one was what she criticized the most. She possessed nothing in her closet which was appropriate for her mother to have worn. But she was too nervous to ask her father for a tailor. Instead, she confided in Venus and the two conspired with old clothes. Together, they tore and sewed, creating skirts and blouses. Their color was never saturated enough to be a proper representation, but the reference would suffice. Eva stood in this hodgepodge of Gadje clothing, turning this way and that, until at last she had molded out the sketch she felt would work.

She took to her paints then. There were canvases of various sizes awaiting to be used. Her father preferred to keep the larger ones for museums and higher-profile clients, whereas smaller ones would be used for traveling portfolios. While he would rather she use a small one for her personal project — if he had known about it — Eva went on ahead and selected the largest canvas they owned.

She propped it up on the easel and went straight to work recreating the sketch with her charcoal. Once the subject was in place, she continued with the background. She improvised this part. She had never been very skilled with backgrounds, or at least they did not come to her as naturally as human anatomy did, but she did what she could with her memory. The banks of sand and the small stream in the campground. The singular tree in the distance. And the fire was burning hot.

Then suddenly, she was staring at her mother once more, dancing by the flames. Eva had to stop herself for a moment, to take it in. Even though she knew it was a sketch from her own hand, the image brought back so many memories. She could recall the smell of her mother's hair. The touch of her hand, both in harsh punishment but also in gentle comfort. The sound of her voice as she sang, laughed, scolded, consoled.

This woman, who she would never see again except in her memories, and now in her painting. This woman, who was now dead.

Eva found herself unable to hold back the tears. They came out all at once, forcefully, as though being ripped from her eyes. They came so quickly that she bent forward, letting out loud sobs in accompaniment. She tried to wipe them away, but it made little difference.

She thought of her old friend, the duke, and wondered what he would say.

"The memory is overwhelming," she could picture him saying. *"To be suddenly confronted with a ghost. But you must see your gift as a blessing. There are many who have to wait until the gates of heaven to see their beloved again. You, however... you can provide a window."*

The memory of his pipe was strangely calming to her. Eventually she stopped fighting it and let them flow until she had no more. Then she stood there, eyes sore and somewhat swollen, throat aching, and nose running. She clutched herself as a means to self-soothe.

She had come this far — she had to finish what she started. Taking a deep breath, she stood up and walked over to her canvas. She applied the primer, took out her first jar of oils, and began to paint.

...

Eva was aware that a project of this magnitude would take some time. This meant that, in order to preserve her secret, she could only work on it here and there, often late at night, with only her sister for company. It also meant that her father would insist on commissions in the meantime, which took time away from her as well.

Still, she found herself not too bothered by the distractions. It was not a project she wanted to complete any time soon. After all, once she was done, she did not exactly have the option to hang it up proudly in her room. These late hours of her working on it would be the only time she could see it properly.

Besides, she felt a strange level of catharsis every time she laid on a new color or layer. As if it drew her closer to her mother. She dreaded the emptiness she would feel once it was over. It made the wheels in her head turn. One night, as her sister sipped tea behind her, Eva had a thought.

"Venus," she began. The sudden speaking surprised her sister somewhat, and she coughed a little on her drink. "What if... we ran away?"

Venus cleared her throat once more. "I beg your pardon?"

"Just the two of us. We could find ways to survive. We could look for another wealthy family. I could teach painting lessons to daughters of noblemen, and you could... you could be a governess, we..."

"Eva." Here she expected to listen to Venus' protests. How she would tell her how unlikely it was that two women would be able to make it on their own in this world run by men. That they were better off here than on the streets. Streets which Eva had grown up on.

Instead, Venus replied with, "that sounds lovely."

She blinked at first, startled by her sister's words. "Really?"

Venus nodded. "Anything would be better than here. I cannot hope that the tea trick will work forever, Jacques is already becoming suspicious, he's talking about seeing a doctor, and you..."

She had no words. None were needed. Both of them turned to look at her unfinished painting. The pact was made between them. They would save up their weekly allowances, and Venus would pick little by little from their father and her husband, until they had enough for at least a week of inns and food. Eva would use the connections she had made through her father to ask around for any families with daughters hoping to learn how to paint. A family who lived far, far away.

And within a month's time, they would make their escape. The dream made Eva feel lighter than she had in years. Since before the duke's death, when she and him would sit and chat for hours. Since before she had known the Baron, and went home every night to her mother, aunts, siblings and cousins. She now had a second chance at life.

The girls went to bed with sweet dreams and smiles on their faces.

...

The next morning, Eva threw off the covers and jumped from bed. She put on her favorite dress — one which was meant to be worn about the house, and not suitable for company, which made it the most comfortable outfit she owned.

She ran down the corridors to where Venus slept. The sisters had much to talk about this morning. Later that day, her father was planning a trip to meet new potential clients, and Eva wanted to know what Venus' game plan would be while the two were out.

She reached the room and did not bother to knock before she threw the door open. She was greeted by an empty room. Her brow furrowed. Had Venus slept in Jacques' bed the night before? That would certainly put a damper oin their plans, yet she had thought it only a day or two after her sister's last bleeding. The girls had been tracking to see how well the tea was working. It did not make sense for Jacques to try again so soon.

Eva was about to turn around to go and check, when she saw something peeking out from Venus' pillow. It was barely noticeable, but out of place enough that it had caught Eva's eye. She stepped closer and realized it was the corner of a letter. The envelope was simply labeled *"Eva"*.

She ripped it open without hesitation. Her heart sank as she read its contents.

"My dear sister Eva,

I am sorry for my dishonesty last night. Please understand that I truly do wish to run away with you, the only family member I have felt close to since losing my mother. Jacques is taking me away tonight. We are traveling to see the doctor, as I mentioned. I should have told you the truth, but the fantasy we built together was so intoxicating, I could not help but want to dream just a little while longer.

I am sorry. I am sorry, too, for neglecting to mention this part last night. Jacques received a letter. I had been curious to know if it was from the doctor, so I opened it despite myself. However, it wasn't. It was a request for a commission, from a countess in Italy. He does not know of the letter, I have hidden it for your eyes only. Read its contents, read its directions, and then run. Run and get out, live your life for both of us.

There is not much I can do, but I can offer this — use my name. The countess may not be impressed with either of us, but if you tell her you are the wife of a respected artist, one who has received lessons from her husband, then you might get your foot through the door. Then once you are there, I know you will dazzle her beyond measurement.

You have all my blessings, and all my love. If God is truly on our side, then maybe one day our paths will cross again. Until then, know that we are sisters, no matter where in the world we are.

Love always,

Venus."

A droplet hit against the letter, smudging the ink, and Eva realized that she was crying again. While she felt the sting of betrayal, she cried more for the thought of the pain her sister had been in last night, so much so that she had to dream her way out of it, even for just a few precious minutes.

How had Eva been so blind? Had she been so caught up with her painting that she neglected to notice what was happening around her? She did not deserve her sister's graciousness. She had to take the offer, though. If only for Venus' sake. She had to see this through. However, there was one hesitation within her plan.

The painting. There was no way she could bring it with her, the size of it daunting her. Yet she could not leave it behind, not now when she was so close to finishing.

Her thoughts were racing so quickly she could barely keep up. Then suddenly, it dawned upon her. She would have to scrounge the money, and it would be risky, but she could have the canvas delivered to the countess. The address was in the letter.

She ran to the parlor then, feeling a sense of inspiration at the notion of completing her painting. She forgot to go downstairs and collect some breakfast. She neglected to notice the absence of her father.

...

"We have an appointment this afternoon, dear." Her father said the following morning.

He only ever called her 'dear' when they were about to meet with a highly important client. She nodded as she took another roll. She was starving after having eaten very little the day prior. Her sleep schedule was thrown off after she had passed out for half of the afternoon. It had been worth it to finally be done with her painting.

She thought of it, lying beneath her bed, waiting for her to take it down to the post office. She would leave the next day, knowing her father had other duties to attend to tomorrow. She had just enough saved up for a few days' journey. The post office payment would be another issue, but one she could figure out.

"I want you in your Sunday best." Her father went on.

Eva nodded, chewing slowly. It was going to be torture to get through this day, knowing what lay in wait for her tomorrow, but it would pass soon enough. She needed a little bit of patience.

Although, while she sipped on her tea, it occurred to her that she should get rid of the remaining mugwort in the stables. While Venus may be gone, it would not help her if their father found out and wrote an incriminating letter to Jacques in regard to it. She stood up from the table, fabricating an excuse her father barely listened to, before heading out the door.

Eva felt her heart sink once again as she looked inside to see that Venus' favorite horse had remained. She had rather hoped they would have hitched it to their carriage, if only to bring it along. But it remained on the property, not understanding why it had been so long since its mistress had come in for a groom or a ride.

She gave the poor thing a pat, reminding herself to come back with an apple and a good brushing. Venus had probably been unable to give this creature a proper final send off, so Eva would have to do it for her.

She climbed up the ladder to her hiding spot for the mugwort, scooping up the dried bits, and vaguely wondering if it was safe for a horse to eat. That would be the most efficient way of ridding herself of this plant, but she could not recall the effects this plant had on animals, and she did not want to take the risk. So instead, she stuffed the bundle into her pocket, intending to bring it out to the field to bury it.

She heard a voice. It started small but grew quickly. It shouted her name, and she recognized it immediately. Her father was calling her.

In a panic, she threw off her apron and flung it on the balcony, determined to come back for it later. She rushed from the barn, where she met up with her father. He took one look at her and sighed.

"Did I not tell you to look your best?" He gestured at her appearance, which had now become disheveled with straw and sweat. "It's a good thing I called you now before you could make an even bigger mess. Go and clean yourself up."

Eva nodded, not appreciating being spoken to like a young child still. But she made her way to wash up, and the next thing she knew, the two of them were in the carriage, on their way to their appointment. She could not deny her curiosity about the level of stature of the prospective nobleman which awaited them.

Once arrived, her father instructed her to wait inside the carriage while their footmen unloaded. Eva was rather put off by this notion. Was she to spend the afternoon in the carriage, as well? Why bring her then at all?

She only caught the footmen from the corner of her eye, but just as she was about to protest, her father held up a hand for her to take. She smiled then, happy that she would at least be able to get out from these confines — no matter how many times she rode in one, she never felt fully comfortable inside of a carriage.

As they walked towards the manor — which was, indeed, very large, her father boasted.

"I've scored the biggest catch yet!" he bragged under this breath. "A prince, from a faraway land!"

Eva herself felt flustered. A prince? Royalty would be looking at her work?

"He won't be there, himself." Her father explained, as though reading her thoughts. "He has an expert here to inspect before approval. You must be on your best behavior to impress the man, all the same."

She nodded, unsure as to why he was pressing the issue so diligently. She had gone along with the scheme for so long, why now was he so concerned?

The doors were answered by a maid, and the two stepped inside. They were seated in a parlor and given more tea to drink, as well as a baked dish neither of them recognized. Eva took a little to be polite, but her father declined, ready to get straight to business.

A man came in soon afterwards. By his aura and attire, Eva guessed him to be the expert her father had mentioned.

"You are the Baron?" He asked. Eva did not recognize his accent.

Her father stood up and shook his hand. "Yes, I am!"

He seemed unimpressed, as he looked up and down her father, then jotted down something on his parchment. Eva had to suppress a laugh as her father shrank back. It was not often that she got to see him acting so small.

"And what is it that you have to present to me?" The expert asked.

Her father stood a little straighter. "My masterpiece!"

Eva raised an eyebrow. She could not recall painting anything especially noteworthy of late. Her commissions had been given to the proper patrons. What was her father referring to?

"Nothing less would be suitable for his majesty!" he went on.

The expert seemed intrigued as he nodded and pursed his lips. Her father walked them both down to the other end of the room, where Eva took notice of the canvas underneath a sheet. She frowned at the sight. It was a far larger canvas than anything she had recently painted.

Except...

She stood up, her hands clenched into fists.

"Father!" She stated, but the men ignored her.

Her father took hold of the sheet and ripped it down. There stood her most prized possession. Her dancing mother.

The men continued to talk, but Eva heard nothing except for her own blood boiling as she stomped over to them. She took a grip on her father's shoulder and forced him to spin around. He stared at her incredulously, not believing she would have the gall to perform such an action.

"You cannot mean it!" She said through gritted teeth. Her eyes were already wet. She did not even understand how he had found the piece, but it mattered very little. This was not his to sell. "You cannot! Not this one!"

Her father gave the expert an apology and took hold of both Eva's arms, escorting her out of the room. Once out, she turned to make her demands once more, and he slapped her hard across the face. Her cheek burned with a thousand needles. Tears came out, not from the pain or sadness, but from pure, unbridled rage.

"How dare you!" her father growled in hushed words. "Did I not tell you to be on your best behavior? Are you so stupid that you cannot fathom the importance of this client?"

"I don't care!" Eva replied, not caring that her voice rose higher than his. "It is not yours to sell!"

"Not *mine?*" Her father repeated. He chuckled bitterly. "Who supplied you with the oils, then? Or this extra-large canvas? Was it your own money? Was it your mother's money?"

A shot of hatred jolted through her at the mention of her mother.

"Oh yes, child..." he went on. "I know that is no self-portrait. It has been decades, but you never forget the face of the mother of your child. I cannot imagine why you wasted our largest and most expensive canvas on such follies, but this is by far your greatest work yet. And here I have found a client worthy of homing it. Yet you defy me? How can you possibly be so ungrateful?"

She had been clothed, fed, and housed all this time. Allowed to paint for several wealthy clients. All it cost was her dignity, and her family.

Had selling her soul been worth it?

She said nothing, even when her father snapped his fingers, she made no remarks. Eventually, he huffed and left her standing there, returning to the expert inside. She could hear him making apologies.

She thought about the letter from the countess which she had still in her pocket, too scared that it would be discovered if not on her person directly. This was her chance of escape, and now there was no painting to hold her back or to take her money.

She would need to return home — grab her supplies, her apron. After that, she would be free. It could happen tonight. There was no reason to wait. She knew how to find the countess, her family had traveled back and forth between Italy and France before. It would be a long journey, but not an impossible one.

Tonight.

...

When the moon was full in the black sky, Eva got up from bed. She changed back into the outfit she had on before their afternoon appointment. She took the brushes and a knife — more paint could be made later. Although a canvas would be harder to come across. Best if she brought that as well.

She would need to grab her apron from the stables in order to carry them long term. She walked into the crisp, night air, breathing in the sweet rain of summer, and tiptoed over to the stable. As she opened the door, the horse inside startled, but she had come prepared. Eva held out the apple in offering, which made the horse calm immediately. She rubbed at its snout before climbing up to where her abandoned apron sat waiting.

As she fastened it on, she realized that she had forgotten about the mugwort. Part of her wondered if she should scatter it throughout the stable to save on time, but she still worried about its impact on the horse. She looked over at the poor creature, watching as it finished its treats. What would happen to it after she had left? Would her father even remember that the beast was in here, now that Venus was out of the picture?

Eva sighed. She flung the mugwort this way and that, not caring where it landed, knowing what she would do next. She opened the door, placed everything she could into her pocket, and mounted the horse.

The two were off into the night.

Chapter 17

Eva

Eva woke up that morning with a splitting headache. She hadn't even had that much to drink the night prior, but she could imagine the reason why. She pressed a hand to the bridge of her nose, pinching it as she sat up in bed.

She tried to blot out the memories of what she had seen. How the disembodied hands which she had feared and had repulsed this entire time were artists — *human* — exactly like her. So that is the fate which awaited her should she no longer please her mistress.

The thought made the bile in her stomach rise, until she could no longer hold it back. There was an empty vase in the corner, and she let out the contents of her body into it. She found a strange sort of comfort in the action, that something, even as useless as this, was happening as a result of what she had witnessed. As though she were letting out everything that made her evil inside out and down a dark hole.

She wiped her lips. Was that really how she saw herself? As evil?

What else could she be, at this point? It did not matter how much she had hated her father; he did not deserve to be eternally bound to the earth like this. None of them did. She could no longer play a part in it.

Could she still potentially run to the princess? She had seemed impressed with Eva last night, and had even discussed a potential commission. She might be safe from the countess' grasp there. Did she deserve such luxury? To live in a palace while her predecessors rotted in the ground beneath her very feet? If anyone deserved such torture, it was Eva herself.

No... no, nothing would be accomplished by her death. Sarracenia would simply go forth to her next victims. It was the countess who needed to be stopped.

Those were the two tasks Eva had to complete before she left — free the souls in the wine cellar. Put an end to her mistress.

It surprised Eva to realize that she had started to cry. At first, she thought these were the tears that had welled up from her vomiting, but they kept coming. Then she merely allowed her heart to weep for its breaking.

No matter how she looked at the situation, she was betraying the one person who had unquestioningly appreciated her art. Years of lies with her father, the ball last night when all the guests dismissed Eva still. The princess had looked her way solely because Sarracenia had pointed in her direction.

Was Eva so desperate for validation that she felt guilty enough to cry? Was that the only thing she was... a painter?

Eva realized she had been asking the wrong question. It did not matter what she wanted in life. What mattered was — who was she?

She was Eva, daughter of a Rom woman and a Gadje man. Sister of Baroness Venus Faucher. Sister, cousin, and niece to more. She was resourceful, never letting her guard down enough to forget how to survive. She knew about herbs and how to create medicine and oil with them. She had compassion in her heart for those in less fortunate positions than her own.

She was not evil. She was not a monster. She was human, and she was leaving this place.

Eva got dressed. It would be close to dawn soon, and the sun would brighten the day. It would be torture for her headache, but it was the one thing Sarracenia seemed to avoid above all else.

Which did give her an idea. If she managed to trick her mistress outside while the sun was still... oh, but how would she even accomplish that? The countess was not someone easily fooled. It was the only idea she had, however.

Eva headed out of her room and down the stairs. She would not be having breakfast in the greenhouse as she had so often. She needed to be around other humans, even if she felt she did not deserve their presence. She planned to go into town, walk around and clear her mind. A solution would come to her soon enough.

The bright sunlight did indeed sting her eyes and pierce her head, but it faded quickly as she continued to walk down the front yard to the gate. She went to the door to open it up, only to find that it would not budge. Eva frowned. That was odd.

When she and her mistress had gone into town before, the gates would open automatically... except, that was never the case, was it? Every door which opened by magic was being pulled by those disembodied hands. Perhaps even the carriage had been pulled by them as well, however far their reach expanded. Eva shuddered at the thought that the mistress had somehow concealed corpses within the carriage itself in order to gain this ability.

They worked on Sarracenia's command. She may suspect what Eva's next actions would be and attempt to lock her in. Eva grasped onto the iron. It was cold beneath her touch, so much so that it nearly burned her flesh. She pulled on the gate, she yanked at the lock, doing something, anything, she could to try and open them. Her efforts were in vain. The countess was not about to let her go.

Eva turned around, pressed her back against the gate, and slumped down to the ground. She folded herself up and rested her head against her knees.

"Hello?" came a little voice.

It surprised Eva so much that she nearly fell over trying to turn back around to see. Some time had passed since last she had heard this voice, but she would never forget it. Maria stood on the other side of the gate. She looked at Eva wearily, her lips unable to decide if they should smile or not. Eva did not have words for the situation.

Fortunately, it was Maria who spoke first. "I am glad that you are still alive..."

Eva did not know if she meant despite the countess or despite what her family had tried to do to her. She would not hold it against the child, however. She stood up and brushed off her skirts.

"It is nice to see you again," she replied, meaning it honestly. Her thoughts had been jumbled as of late, but they still returned to the little Romani girl at least once a day. "Do your parents know where you are?"

Maria shook her head. "No, they think I am out begging. But I've been wanting to stop by..."

Eva thought about the young girl coming to this place more than once, standing outside certain danger, and it made her shiver.

"Is this your first time here?"

Maria nodded. Eva sighed. At least there was that.

"You shouldn't stay," she warned the little girl. "There is evil here."

"I know."

Of course she did. It had been Eva who remained in the shadows about her own mistress. She thought about the first time she had read the letter, the sense of relief and exhilaration she had felt at the potential prospect. She remembered how, despite the long, grueling weeks of aggravation painting her first piece, she had felt so excited upon her mistress' approval. Naive, until that evening at dinner, when Sarracenia displayed her true nature.

What a fool she had been this entire time.

"You need to leave, too." Maria pleaded. "Please, the princess is back! You can paint for her, you can — "

"I don't want to paint for nobles anymore, Maria." It was the first time the thought had fully formulated into her mind. "The princess seems very nice, yes. But I'm done with living off of the charity of the rich."

"What will you do?"

Eva bit her lip as she mulled it over. She would not be welcomed by Maria's family anymore, but would there be another clan of Roms willing to take in a lost soul like hers? Could she perhaps start a clan of her own? She thought of those she had lost over the years, those who had died, and those who had left. And suddenly, it dawned on her.

"I'm going to find my sister."

Maria tilted her head. "You have a sister?"

Eva nodded. "A poor thing who's married to a horrid old man. I don't know where he's taken her, but I can figure it out."

"Where will you go?"

She didn't know. It didn't matter right now. The only thing that mattered was getting out of here and finding Venus.

Eva turned slowly to look back up at the manor. Her eyes fixed on the spot where her mistress' bedchamber lay. Where she slept. Suspicious or not, her body would force her to rest until the evening. If she already had her guard up about Eva, so much so as to lock her in, then every moment was precious time wasted.

It had to be now. Not tonight, when her mistress was at full power. *Now*.

"Listen, Maria..." she whispered. "I know that I am the last person your family would want to help. But... I am leaving. Today. If they can come and find a way to open these gates..."

"We can come back tonight!"

"No!" The word came out louder than she had intended, and Eva shuddered, as though at any moment her mistress would be right behind her, ready to pounce. She cleared her throat. "No, Maria. The countess will have regained her strength by then. It has to be now — she is weakest in the daytime. Your family has a chance to be rid of her, but they must come now. Do you understand?"

Maria nodded, yet she stood in place, her eyes wide with terror. She must have been imagining the feat yet to come.

"Go!" Eva hissed. Still, the little girl remained in place. Eva reached out past the gates as far as she could manage and snapped her fingers. *"Go!"*

Then Maria went off like a shot. Eva was left alone. She thought of everything she would need for the journey. Her supplies and paintings could remain here — she never wanted to touch them again, after what they had created. So, the only things which remained were food and her horse. Both would be easy enough to secure, she would go around back to the greenhouse and pick up as many fruits and vegetables as she could stand to carry.

She had to do that now, before anything else could happen. Everything to follow would be so great that it would require her undivided attention. So she filled her pocket with apples, peaches — bananas would be too soft for the journey — carrots and potatoes. She took as many as she could walk with.

Then, she went around to the stables for her horse. The poor thing, when had she last gone to properly inspect it? She expected it to startle in terror at the sight of her, but instead it approached her with almost gratitude. Despite herself, she went ahead and handed over one of the apples.

She could already imagine the look on Venus' face when not one but both of them strode up to save her. Eva told herself not to get ahead of things, that she could not be certain she would survive this day. That face, that elated face of her sister, was exactly the motivation she needed. No matter what today brought, she would survive — to see Venus once more.

She brought the horse out front. The creature would be safe up here. Even once Maria's family got here, they would not harm a helpless animal. She tied the food to its back, just out of reach of its mouth, and then headed around the corner.

Before she did anything else, she needed to free the souls in the wine cellar. As she ran back towards the building, she realized that she had no real plan to accomplish this. She did not think she could simply pull them out, despite the fact that they could grab things, she had a feeling that she could not grab them.

What then? The wine cellar itself. She had to destroy it.

How would she do that? She remembered where it was in relation to the outside, could she somehow dig a hole, open a barrier to allow them passage to the great beyond? No, if access was all they needed, then how were they opening the gates?

Their bodies. Their corpses had been left to litter the wine cellar. Which brought her back to needing to destroy the cellar itself, but how?

Eva found herself standing at the edge of the manor, and she pressed her hands to the wall as she circled around it. The stone tickled and pinched against her palm, until she passed a window. The carnivorous plants clung to the glass, covering all rays of the sun.

Two sets of them curled together, the ones her mistress had referred to as Sarracenia and Venus fly trap. How she had thought the two of them were so connected by their names. A name which had been a lie.

Yet Eva could not take her eyes off of them. She inspected the teeth of the fly trap, as she had done many times before. She looked in deeper, certain she saw something in its mouth, but it shut close, as though to keep the secrets of her mistress. She gasped at the sudden motion, but it did not deter her.

She peered at the plant, the sunlight betraying it as she saw a large mass being projected through its head. It had indeed swallowed something. She turned to the other one, the Sarracenia, and without a second thought, reached her arm down it. The acid stung on her arm, but not as much as she had anticipated. Most of it was probably due to her own discomfort at what she was doing.

She found another mass at the bottom and pulled it up. The mound was a mess of shreds within her wet hand, but she still recognized what it once had been.

It was a hand.

The fingers had been chopped off, save for the thumb, which remained outward in rigora mortis. Eva dropped it as soon as it dawned upon her what she was holding. She felt as though she was going to be sick. She had her answer. It was the plants. They were feeding on the flesh of the fallen artists, growing and multiplying off of their deaths. Their very existence was what held these souls in place.

To free them, she did not need to bring down the whole manor. Just the plants. And that was a far easier task to accomplish.

Eva ran around the premises, picking up every stick she could find. She piled them in front of this one window. It would not be enough, though. She would need to go bigger.

She had no choice but to return inside. Her stomach dropped at the thought. She tried to convince herself that her mistress would of course still be asleep, that she could not remain out here doing nothing — the morning would soon become day, and who could say how long she had after that?

She ran back inside, not stopping to turn around and watch within the corners. It took a while for her eyes to adjust to the darkness once more, and she nearly ran into the stairs, but managed to catch herself before falling. She darted up them, admittedly crawling a little to get up all the way.

She thought she heard a clatter, and that did cause her to pause, but it must have been her imagination, because she saw nothing. She carried on full force to the room with the fireplace. The one which held her painting supplies.

The fire was lit, despite the sunlight outside. It caused the door around it to glow. She remembered the first time she had ever walked down this hallway, down to this room. Eva could not help herself and paused directly outside of it. There, still hung in the corner, was the former Countess de Sarracenia.

Eva looked up at this woman who did indeed look so much like her mistress. What kind of a mother was she, that her daughter had turned out the way she did? Eva did not have time to wonder or pity. As she turned to face the door once more, she was met by a terrifying sight.

All around the door, as though sitting in waiting, were the hands of the fallen artists. Their fingers curled in almost unnatural angles, tips looking sharp. Eva had never felt one touch her skin directly, and she hoped she never would, despite her pity for them now. She stood frozen, waiting for them to make the first move, so she would have reason to run.

As time continued to pass, however, they ventured closer to the door, and pushed it open even further. Eva stood back, hesitant to trust this. Yet, what choice did she have?

She took a step closer. When nothing happened, she took another. Until at last, she was within the room itself. She turned back, for a moment, before stepping up to her canvases, where her oils were placed.

Before attending to them, however, Eva took one last look around the room. One last look at her paintings. The ones which had given her such high esteem. Higher than she could have ever dreamed of accomplishing, especially back when she was a poor girl on the streets with her sketchbook.

These paintings, her mistress, repulsed her.

She picked up one of her oils, about to place it in her pocket, until she recalled that she had left her apron out by her horse. She pursed her lips, uncertain how well she would be able to move with them in her arms. Then, one of the shadow hands approached her, crawling over the canvas. She watched it with curiosity, briefly wondering who they had been before. It reached out and picked up another one of her oil jars. She smiled at the gesture, and then began to wave her hand in encouragement, trying to get the others to join in.

Once each of the jars had been picked up, she whispered, "outside... throw them on every window that you can but throw them outside!"

They took off in every direction. Before Eva took off herself, she approached the fireplace. She stared up at the painting above it. The one she had originally created. She could no longer see a portrait of her mistress.

All she could see was the sweat and blood it had taken to create this painting.

She reached inside the fireplace, rather impulsively, burning her fingers once, before she managed to find a stick outward enough for her to pick up. The flame on it was low, but it would last until she returned outside once more.

With the new light, the hallway was lit in a way she had never seen before. The dust hung in the air, collecting in multitudes around her. Small shadows scurried in the corners — rats and spiders, fleeing from a light they were unused to. Her own shadow danced beneath her. It was an unusual sight in such a dark place. It stretched out before her, making her shape look peculiar and large. It reminded her of the shadow hands, and what might happen to her if she was caught, and she ran a little faster.

She heard a smashing sound, which then froze her in place. It was followed by another, and another. She realized it was the shadow hands doing as she had instructed, but the noise of it concerned her. Would it be enough to wake up the countess?

She could not worry about that. She had to get this fire outside.

Eva did not stop, not even when she ran underneath the countess' bedchamber, until she was through the doors and outside of the manor once more. The sun did indeed prick her eyes again, but she shut them and ran blindly.

Back at the window, where she had pulled the hand from the carnivorous plant, she wondered just who it had belonged to, and how many times it had painted for its owner before their demise.

Eva held up the jar of oil she had retained and threw it against the window. The fly traps shut in protest, now being the ones covered in a foul-smelling ooze. Then she raised up her torch and brought it down.

The fire was instant. The flames rose up, scorching the plants. Eva had expected them to scream, but they merely browned before curling up into black ash. It burned well, but it wasn't enough. She had to carry the torch around.

She ran to the other windows, looking for ones with broken bits of glass on them. She brought her torch to all of them, and it yielded the same result. She counted, making sure she had known how many jars she had possessed, so she would know once she had gotten them all.

Yet it still wasn't enough. Despite how strongly the flames burned, the fire seemed content in its lower corner. It was not spreading upward.

Eva heard another noise. It was the sound of shouting and anger. She looked up to the gates and saw the Romani. They had torches themselves and were attacking the gate.

Eva dropped hers — the flame had long since died out — and rushed over to her horse. She did not want to be caught up in what was about to transpire. She barely reached her animal before the iron gave way to the crowd and broke open. They rushed inside; torches held high.

Eva climbed up on her horse, directing it back in order to let them pass through. She tried to find Maria, but as far as she could see, there were no children within the mob. While a part of her was relieved, she was also disappointed. She had rather hoped to see the little girl one last time before never returning.

As soon as the last of the Romani broke through, Eva hitched her horse out of there. Even from behind, she could feel the heat of the fire rising, and as their shadows grew, she looked back, only once.

The entire manor had been set ablaze. The smoke coming from it was so thick and black that it covered the sun in a dark haze. She could not make out if any of the shadowed souls were indeed escaping. She did, however, spot one shape in the distance.

From atop the blazing manor, Eva spotted a large bat flying out into the distance.

Epilogue

Venus

Venus sat in her favorite chair, embroidery in her hands. She had always found the task rather tedious before, but Jacques had insisted that she take on more ladylike hobbies. She suspected that the thread and cloth for embroidery were merely cheaper than the paints and canvases she had preferred once.

No matter, her vision of a flower was slowly coming into focus as she wove her thread to and fro. Then, sharp pain as the needle sank into her ring finger. She gasped as she stood up and dropped the cloth. A loud hiss escaped past her teeth before she sucked on the wound. She kept a spare handkerchief in her drawer — she rushed over to it.

Then, she spotted something outside the window. At first, she thought it was merely the postman come to bring word. Then she recalled that he had already passed by earlier this morning. Who would call upon them at this time of day?

It certainly wasn't her father — he had stopped returning her letters, and at any rate, he would not be approaching himself on only a horse. Jacques had no other friends besides him, though. Neither did Venus, for that matter.

She gazed out and fixed upon the figure. It had been some time since their last encounter, so much so that she blinked to ensure that this was no mirage.

There, coming down their pathway, was her favorite horse.

With her sister.

Angela Flatt

About the Author

Angela was raised on a diet of gothic horror and fairytales. Her earliest memories are of putting together homemade picture books using copy paper and pencils. Now she moreorless does the same thing, but with technology. She lives with her cats, birds, and fish tanks.